NOBODY'S
FAULT

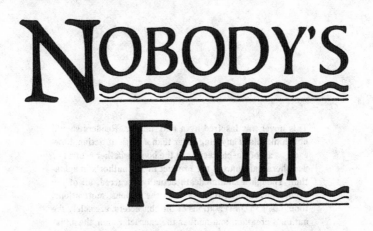

NOBODY'S FAULT

NANCY HOLMES

BANTAM BOOKS

NEW YORK • TORONTO • LONDON • SYDNEY • AUCKLAND

This novel was inspired by a real murder. Readers should not think this is anything other than a work of fiction, however, as all of the characters in the book, whether central or peripheral, are purely the product of the author's imagination. Though a similar death actually occurred, all of the events surrounding it, as well as the actions, motivations, thoughts, and conversations of the characters, are solely the author's creation, and neither the characters nor the situations which were invented are intended to depict real people or real events.

Bantam Books are published by Bantam Books, a division of Bantam Doubleday Dell Publishing Group, Inc. Its trademark, consisting of the words "Bantam Books" and the portrayal of a rooster, is Registered in U.S. Patent and Trademark Office and in other countries. Marca Registrada. Bantam Books, 666 Fifth Avenue, New York, New York 10103.

Quality Printing and Binding by:
Berryville Graphics
P.O. Box 272
Berryville, VA 22611 U.S.A.

This book was and is for Greg Bautzer

ACKNOWLEDGMENTS

With special thanks to
Jean Schwartz, Mary Carter, and David Stickelber

Such is youth;
Till from that summer's trance we wake, to find
Despair before us, vanity behind.
                            —GEORGE SANTAYANA

Nobody's Fault

CHAPTER

London, April 11, 1974

Silently, stealthily, he let himself into the darkened house. As he turned his key in the lock he thought only of what he had come to do. It was raw April, spring still buried in English cold. The neighbors would be tucked in their beds watching telly if they were not asleep already. The quiet street was deserted at this hour. It had not gone ten yet, and the regulars in the corner pub had another hour to drink before closing time. By then he would be gone. Long gone.

And everything would be all right again, with sunshine everywhere.

Amanda Warrington was sitting cross-legged on her big bed, mending socks, when she heard a gentle tap on the door, then Jenny's hoarse voice.

"Lady Warrington," Jenny said, "I'm just going down for some tea. Would you like me to fix your eggnog for you? I know you don't want to miss the news." Sweet Jenny. Amanda took a thick eggnog with a nerve-calming powder in it every night before bed. She hated the stuff, but it served the double purpose of soothing her, to help her sleep, while putting a little weight on her too-thin frame.

"Come in, Jenny," Amanda answered in her mellifluous voice. "I was just about to go down myself. Are you feeling any better?"

"A little bit, thank you, Lady Warrington," Jenny said, entering the room. Tonight was supposed to have been her night off but her cold was close to flu and Lady Warrington had kindly offered to let her change for the next night, if she was well enough then.

Patrick had dropped off to sleep on the chaise longue in his mother's room, which he often did when he had finished his homework and was not quite willing to go up to bed. The boy loved being with his mother; Jenny understood that easily.

Amanda Warrington was vaguely flattered by Jenny's fascination with her looks. She hoped the girl's interest would remain, as she was the best nanny to come to work in the house for months, and she was young and cheerful. Patrick liked her and that was what really mattered. She was certainly not a trained nanny but in the three weeks she'd been there, she had worked out very well.

"Jenny, thank you for going down," Amanda said, looking at her bedside clock. "The news is almost on and I would like to see it. Nothing for Patrick, though. He can snooze a few minutes more. Then I'll get him up so he can go back to sleep. It seems to me that nine-year-old boys spend their lives sleeping if one lets them—when they're not banging into things, that is."

"But he's such a really nice boy. The last family I worked for had a filthy little monster. Patrick is a super kid."

Amanda was delighted that Jenny liked her job. She'd obviously worked at some difficult ones before; she'd told Amanda how depressing it was to work for crabby old people who didn't know how to treat a person. Amanda knew she liked having her own room on the top floor of the house, next to Patrick and the nursery. Amanda had explained very little to her about Charles. "My husband and I are separated," she had told her. "He takes Patrick out after school and every other weekend." Charles had made no comment about Jenny and he had seen her enough times now to raise an objection if he was going to.

It was nice to have her there. She was younger than Amanda but they were practically the same size. Jenny had a little more weight on her, and, Amanda thought snobbishly, her bones were those of a lower-class girl. Amanda's own bone structure was delicate, almost too delicate, and although she knew she was no longer at her peak, she also knew her coloring was still subtly vibrant, and she took pride in the fact that her tawny skin had kept its flawless dewiness. She wore little makeup, only enough to accent the gray-blue of her eyes. She knew Jenny envied her head of hair the most. It was still a glowing mass of titian, still subtle rather than bright. She had tied it back tonight in a ponytail with a gray satin ribbon. Jenny had mentioned that when she let it flow loose, she looked like one of the American film stars of the war years, a Lana Turner or a Rita Hayworth.

Amanda sighed and brought her thoughts back to Jenny, who was still standing in the doorway, waiting.

"Anything else, Lady Warrington?"

"Do remember about the hall lights, Jenny. Don't forget to turn them off this time." It was nice to have someone ask if they could do anything for you, someone cheerful for a change.

"I'll remember, Lady Warrington, I won't forget this time."

It was almost time. The door to the basement kitchen would open and there she would be, her body outlined faintly in the dim light from the hallway on the floor above. Mean and frugal woman—there never had been any light anywhere when they lived together, not at the beginning and not at the end. The dark worked for him now, he thought, as the bitter remembrance of cold rooms, cheerless rooms with never any light or sunshine anywhere, flashed through his mind. And if she reached for the switch before he got to her, there would be no light; he had already taken the precaution of unscrewing the fuse. His palms were sweating, even though the gloves he wore were not thick or bulky. His hands were nevertheless steady, closed firmly around the heavy iron bar, and he was ready for her. His ears picked up her footfall on the hall stairs, the creak on the fourth step that he knew so well.

Come on, you little darling. Come on, you mad devil. I've got something here for you, something you'll never forget, but you won't have a chance in hell to remember either. Just come on. Open that door, my beloved—I'm ready for you.

A faint light from the street fell like a gray pool across the sink at the basement kitchen window, not enough to see anything by, but of some help to him as he waited in the darkness. Too bad the basement entrance had been boarded up and enclosed to make a wine cave, but it was one of the first things they had done when they moved into the house. As it was, it was better that way in the plan he had worked out in meticulous detail for months. There was nothing suspicious about his leaving by the front door at that time of night and it was safer. He could see a broad swatch of road from the narrow hall window that bordered the front door and make sure there was no one about on the street. Royal Hospital Road had always been a quiet street at night—not a traveled thoroughfare, as so many in Chelsea were now. At the Farrier's Forge at the end of the block the regulars would be having their pints of lager. *Never mind the Farrier's Forge,* he thought, as his ears picked up the telltale squeak on the step. She was coming.

The door opened and her figure was outlined in the dim light exactly as he had visualized. She was wearing flat shoes, bare-legged as usual, and although her body was no longer as willowy as it once had been, it was still small and somehow voluptuous. He was ice-cold now. As she came down the two steps from the landing and reached for the light pull, he raised his arms and, with the full force of his two hundred pounds behind it, swung the iron bar through the air wildly, yet with a deadly accuracy. Metal met her skull with a doom crack. An involuntary scream of terror was frozen stillborn in her throat as she started to sink to the floor of the kitchen.

He hit her again, full force, and then three times more. Each time he struck her he heard the crack of iron against her skull, a sound he had not anticipated and one that he would never forget. He had practiced the delivery of the blows against a wooden beam in the garage of the Ormonde Gate flat to make sure that the ski bandage wrapped around the end of the iron would keep his hands from slipping. It had.

He was aware of something warm hitting him in the face, spurting all over him, and realized it was her blood. It seemed to have begun with the second blow—something else he had not anticipated, such a vast amount of blood. It must be all over the place but he couldn't see it. He felt a sudden ebbing of his strength. Was she dead? He dropped the bloodied weapon on the floor beside him.

It was done. He knelt down beside her body, squinting in the absence of light, pulling the glove off his right hand to feel for a pulse in her blood-slippery throat and on her wrist. There was none. She was dead and there was no doubt about it. Her body was warm, her blood warm on both of them, but she'd soon enough be cold forever. He stood up and went over to the sink and turned on the tap, rinsing his hand off and drying it with the tea towel hanging in its usual place on the cabinet door beneath. Almost euphoric, he pulled the bloodied glove back on. It was done. He reached for the heavy canvas sail bag he had brought with him and started to shove her body into it, grunting and breathing heavily with the effort it took to get the dead weight into what would now be her shroud. He tied a cord around the open end of the sail bag. The contents were no more than a sackful of flour or potatoes to him. It was done, all over. It had happened so quickly—it almost seemed as if it should have taken longer. *May her soul rest in the same sort of hell she made for me,* he thought. He was right on target in his timing. All he had to do now was see that the coast was clear out front, then bring the sail bag out and put it in the boot of the car. Then the short drive to Ormonde Gate, where he'd clean up and change clothes. He would be at the club around eleven, as planned.

If by some fluke Patrick should happen to come downstairs later, looking for her, or if the nanny should stop in for a cup of tea when she got back from her evening out, they would see the blood. But if no one came to the kitchen, as he anticipated, it would be morning before they missed her. Patrick should be asleep in his room by now. Amanda always sent him to bed in the half hour preceding the ten o'clock news, before she came down for her bedtime drink. God knew his plan hinged on the regularity of her habits, but even if Patrick was still awake and she didn't come right back up, he would pay no attention. Sometimes Amanda slipped out to the Farrier's Forge for cigarettes. God help him if she had decided to go out tonight, he thought, but it was a useless thought. She would never have left Patrick alone in the house with the nanny out for the evening.

There was one last precaution to observe. He took the wool ski mask from his pocket and pulled it over his face. He would wear it until he was outside the front door. In the unlikely event of Patrick's appearing, he was dressed as a burglar and he would bolt as a burglar. But that would not happen. Now he was going to go up, check outside to make sure no one was around in the street, then return for the sack. He'd already seen to it that there was no light on at the front door.

He groped for the murder weapon in the dark and found it at the foot of the stairs. It wouldn't do to forget it. He listened at the landing for any noise in the hall but there was no sound. The coast was clear.

He opened the door and started up into the front hall. His eyes were used to the dark, and only a dim light came from the hallway a floor above.

He heard a voice.

"Jenny?" the voice said. "Jenny? What's taking you so long?"

Amanda's voice.

Blinding red fireworks exploded in his head. And a thousand shimmering fragments surfeited his brain, baffling him, stunning him, leaving him breathless. Something unreal was happening to him. He was hearing things. That sound—the recent crack of the iron bar on her skull—was affecting him, doing something strange to him. It was a trick, a ridiculous treachery. Amanda's voice had come back to haunt him, calling out to him from the depths of the sail bag in the dark kitchen, torturing him once more with her madness.

Amanda's voice.

"Jenny! What are you doing? Is there something wrong?" He heard a tiny edge of panic in her tone, a tone he had heard a thousand times before.

In the split second before his hands closed tightly once more on the weapon in his hands, this time in mad fury, he knew that the intense little figure rushing down the stairs toward him was Amanda, Amanda alive, Amanda wrecking his life again. His mind disintegrated into a kaleidoscope of ghastly visions, all merging into fear of her. His chest heaved in wild terror. She would stop him again. She would keep him from getting away, as she had in the past. His single blind thought was to get out of the house as quickly as he could, get away from the sound of her voice. He had to stop her this time, do away with her once and for all, never let her know that he had been there. Didn't she know she was dead, still bleeding, but dead, in a sail bag on the kitchen floor below them?

He swung the iron wildly as she got closer, missing her, then swung it again, this time finding a mark. The blow must have landed on her neck or shoulder—he heard no crack of metal against bone. He had to stop her now, before she realized that it was he. She had no way to know, he thought, no possible way to recognize him. He was only a burglar caught in the act, about to get away.

He heard her voice again.

"Oh, my God," the unmistakable voice said.

He flailed out and she screamed as the iron weapon found its mark, this time knocking her off her feet. God damn her, how had she gotten out of the sail bag and what was she doing, coming from upstairs? How could she have escaped the fate he had so long and so carefully planned for her? It was wrong, all wrong.

Battling to control his panic and to silence her forever, he felt her body falling against his legs. He hit her again and then again around her head and suddenly he felt himself falling. She had wrapped her arms around his legs and thrown him off balance. On the floor now, he felt her grappling with him; their bodies were almost locked together, rolling over and over in the dark hall. He could barely see the front door and he tried to roll toward it, half-dragging her with him, his eyes on the doorknob that was now above his head. If only he could turn it; if only he could shake off this screaming devil who had come back from iron death in the basement to torment and destroy him. He remembered well how totally devoid of fear she had always been, especially when defending herself. God knew they'd had more battles than he could ever count, her ferocity controlled only by the effect of his silence. His only weapon against her had been silence.

His mind quickened. Never truer than it was now, the power of his silence. He must not open his mouth; he must not let her hear his voice as he had heard hers. His safety lay in her not knowing who he was. He was nothing more than a common burglar. He must not speak. He would get away, and it didn't matter if she was dead or alive. He was safe as long as he could stay silent. He would make it out the door.

She was flailing at him now, her voice choking and breathless. That voice, that maddening voice.

"Oh, Christ," he heard her say. "What are you doing? Robbing my house? How did you get in here and where is Jenny? What have you done to her, you rotten bastard?"

In a crazed state, he fought for control of himself. Jenny? Who the hell was Jenny? If he could just get this hellcat off of him he would do away with her in one blow. The bitter realization that everything was going wrong was bile in his mouth. Why had she come down? What could she have heard? Why did he have this wild bitch on top of him keeping him from getting out the door? Suddenly he felt a sharp rivet of pain shoot through his shoulder. Her teeth had found their mark in the soft muscle of his shoulder. She bit him again. This time her teeth went deeper, and as he grappled with her, rolling her over and throwing himself on top of the now sobbing mass of her, to his utter despair he heard his own voice. He heard himself shout at her, at the foot of the stairs by the door that led to the life he wanted, a life without her. His own voice, betraying him.

"You fucking bitch, you fucking murderous bitch," he screamed, his shoulder throbbing. With lightning swiftness and precision she reached up and tore his mask off, the poor woolly ski mask that was as defenseless against her as he was. There was an incredulous, defeated expression in her eyes as they looked into his.

He felt her sag against him.

"You," she said, her voice deep, hoarse. "It's you. You came here to kill me. You've killed Jenny and you meant to kill me." Sensing that she was momentarily helpless, his courage came flowing back.

Now he had to kill her! At that very moment. The damage was done and it had to be done once more. He felt himself come together, fused with hatred for her and blind with rage and pain. He freed an arm and struck her across the side of her head, knocking her halfway across the hall floor. Her head struck the newel post. He lunged at her and, landing on top of her, reached for her throat. He strengthened his hold on her small neck. *Now we shall see. It won't take long now.* Her passionate defensive strength was no more; she was a lump of puttied flesh in his hands, her head bleeding from the blows he had struck her. She was panting for breath—gasping from his death hold on her neck. He was breaking her fragile hold on life easily now. All he had to do was finish her off and open the door not ten feet from him and get out and away and never think about her again and this time she would be dead and it would be done and over, all over.

He felt her teeth again. Enraged, he reached for her throat and through the silk of her blouse he felt the long string of opals she always wore break loose and scatter over the floor around them. Those goddamned Warrington opals, his mother's opals, the ones he had given her when they were married. They were creamy fire opals, fine ones though not the finest, but she had never taken them off since she'd read somewhere that opals were bad luck unless worn constantly. Now they were no longer against her skin, and the noise of them pit-patting on the oak floor of the hall was like the patter of raindrops on a roof, soft but insistent.

"Oh, no," he heard her whimper, and again her body went limp against him. "You've broken them, just as you have broken our lives, broken our love, broken everything you ever put your hands on—cards, dice, anything, everything. What difference does it make, any of it? None of it matters. It's all broken now, like the opals, all lost, and Jenny is dead, poor simple Jenny, dead instead of me. Is this what you really wanted to do?" She pulled herself away from him and tried to sit up, her body half-lying against his side. She started to cry, soft sobs of anguish and loss, like a small child put to bed alone in the dark. Her fingers reached idly out for a few of the opals on the floor around them and she picked up one of them and put it in her mouth, sucking it the way a child sucks a thumb. The only security she had, an opal in her mouth.

He felt her limp body against him and he knew there would be no resistance anymore, no attempt to fight him or to defend herself. The anger had gone out of him. He looked at her, and even in the dim light he could see the damage he had done. Already dark blotches and red swellings were beginning to show on her delicate face, and he could imagine what the marks on her throat would look like tomorrow. He saw the blood on her, too, on the side of her head and her hair where he had struck her, and more all over her clothes, and he realized that it had come from his own body and that it was Jenny's blood that had rubbed off onto her. Jenny. She must be the new nanny he had seen once or twice, the girl who had come to work for Amanda a few weeks before.

He felt the warmth of Amanda's body against him and he heard her sobbing and he felt her tears on his hand, the hand that was around her neck still. He was holding her poor little head against his chest, the opals strewn around them on the floor.

"Amanda," he said. "I have killed her. What am I going to do?"

She raised her head and looked at him, tears rolling down her face.

"I don't know, I don't know. I've got to help you, whatever you have done." She wiped at the tears on her face and saw blood on her hand. She shook her head, dizzy and weak. She sagged against him, almost fainting, too weak now to feel fear.

"Come on," he said. "We've got to get the blood off of you." He stood up, pulling her with him. She clung to him, his arms supporting her as they went up the stairway, the fourth step creaking as always, to her bedroom above. At the landing her knees buckled and her body sagged. She began to fall, her head rolling back on her shoulders, her arms clinging to him. He picked her up and kicked the bedroom door open. The only light in the room came from the television set. He reached for the switch by the door, and the reading lamp by her bed went on. He laid her down on the bed and, as he did so, heard Patrick stir in his sleep on the chaise longue. *Jesus Christ,* he thought, *Patrick.* The boy had slept through it all. How could he not have heard her scream, not heard them fighting in the hall below? Patrick opened his eyes and sat up, seeing his father standing beside the bed, his mother lying on the bed covered with blood.

"Patrick," Amanda said faintly, but with authority in her tone. "Turn off the television set and go to bed. Go to bed, right now."

Patrick stared at the two of them. Getting groggily to his feet, he went over to his mother and sat down on the edge of the bed beside her.

"Are you all right?" he asked, seeing the blood on her, and looked up at his father standing next to him.

"Yes, darling, I'm all right," she said. "We've had a fight but your father is here and he will take care of me. You go to bed. Everything will be fine."

"Patrick, go on. Do what your mother says," Charles said. "I'll come up and see to you later."

Patrick did as he was told. They had had these terrible fights before, as long as he could remember, in fact, and that's why his father had left them. Since then, his father would come to the house and take him somewhere for a meal or a film, or sometimes they'd go back to his father's flat in Ormonde Gate and just be together. Or they would go to his aunt Davina's big house in Hampshire for the weekend. He liked that—he loved his aunt Davina. Maybe his mother and father were getting back together again. Maybe that was good. Maybe this fight would be the last one. Sleepy and sad, he knew better than to say anything to either of them. He switched the telly off and left the room as he had been told, closing the door behind him.

"I'll be up to see to you in a minute," his father said. Maybe he would, maybe he wouldn't, Patrick thought. He forgot a lot of things he said he was going to do.

Charles Warrington looked at his wife lying on the bed, one arm dangling over the edge, her eyes open and watching him. He knelt down beside her, touching her brow, pushing the blood-matted hair away from her eyes. The larger wound on her head had stopped bleeding and was congealing into an ugly mess in her hairline. He touched it gingerly and saw that he still had one of the black gloves on. He pulled it off and touched her again with his clean hand. Her eyes were looking steadily into his and he saw the look in them that she had always given him when she wanted him. She brushed his tousled hair back off his forehead and pulled his face down next to hers.

"We'll make it all right," she said in a low, faint voice. "We'll tell them you came by to see Patrick and when you let yourself in you found a burglar in the house. He killed her—he killed Jenny. The burglar killed her. You could never do a thing like that." She reached for him, her hands feeling for his belt buckle, searching to find the opening to his trousers, but her hands were too weak to open the belt buckle. She rubbed her hand against him, stroking him up and down, feeling for him, still looking up at him with that look of hers.

"Shut up," he said. "Shut up."

He unbuckled his belt and unzipped his fly and rolled over her onto the bed, pulling her to him, reaching up her skirt for her, wanting her more than he ever had in his life. There never had been anyone like her. She was the only one he ever had wanted. The rest of them were nothing to him. *Amanda, oh, Christ, Amanda,* that bundle of heat in his arms again, the only woman that made sex of any importance. He tore open her blouse and buried his head between her soft small breasts, kissing them, passion for her obliterating everything from his mind. It was exciting—she was the same. They had always been the same together, wanting each other and taking more than there was to give but giving it all. It was the only reason they had stayed together for so long. Their lovemaking had always been too powerful for them; all there was between them had been dominated by the animal desire they felt for each other. Only when they made love was there any sense to them. The rest was all hatred and jealousy and despair.

When they finished with each other, he lay looking at her. He had felt real domination over her this time. She had cried out with pleasure, something she had done only in days long past. He knew how exhausted and wounded she was from the battle, but she still had plenty of strength left in her. Her eyes were closed now, her breathing even, and her hands still held him, her fingers curled around what was left of him, this time in tenderness, not trying to squeeze the manhood out of him. She opened her eyes.

He touched her face and he saw the blood all over her and all over him, the disheveled mess of both of them, their clothes and the bed linens, all in chaos. *Never better,* he thought. *Never better.*

Rising from her side, he got out of bed and looked down at her. Her gaze was still steadily on him.

"You bitch," he said. "There never was anyone like you." He touched her shoulder with a small proprietary gesture. "I'm going to clean us up."

He went into the bathroom and filled the basin with cool water and ducked his head into it, wishing that there was a shower, as he had always wished there was one in this house. He mopped his head with a towel. He ran the basin full of warm water and soaked a large towel in it and squeezed it out. He would clean off her face and hands and get what blood he could out of her hair. He was moving slowly and thinking slowly, but he felt euphoric. A small warning from his conscience told him that he was avoiding the inevitable, stifling the knowledge of what had happened downstairs. His reflection in the mirror confirmed that thought; he was deathly pale. He quickly picked up the still-warm towel and went back into the bedroom.

She was gone.

The bed was empty. The door to the bedroom was open. She had gone up to see about Patrick. Of course, she had gone up to see about Patrick.

He heard the front door of the house slam shut two flights below him and the noise of it cracked through his head like the whack of the iron bar against Jenny's skull. His vision filled suddenly with splintering reds, jolting him into full awareness of the horrific mess this night had become.

There was a difference. He was calm. He knew he still had a chance, regardless of everything that had gone wrong. Ah, Amanda. Fool that he was, he should have known what she would do. He moved swiftly across the room toward the door.

It would be his word against hers—and his would prevail. Everyone knew she was dangerous. They all detested her; all of them had heard her revile him in public and most of them had been witness to some of her violent little scenes. He started down the stairs, his thoughts racing. There was no evidence he'd been in this house tonight. With one shred of luck—and God knew he was due some—he could follow the original plan, get to the flat, change, and get to the Wyndham before anyone came looking for him. Any small discrepancy in his time of arrival there would be covered for him by Gavers, by Robin, by Neil. They would all lie for him. All he needed was twenty minutes.

Amanda would have gone screaming into the pub on the corner or the police station a block farther on. Inevitably, the police would come to the house to see if she was telling the truth, but they might jolly well take their time about getting there. It would not be the first time Amanda had fled to them with her own version of some happening, some fantasy of her own. The police knew that they had had domestic fights but they knew, too, just as all his friends did, that she was a bit off.

He had a chance. All the activity would first be centered around Royal Hospital Road. When they found the nanny's body the matter would turn serious. But not until then. He had time and he had a chance.

Then he remembered Patrick.

Patrick, his son. His son had seen him tonight and could never lie, wouldn't know how to. *Fuck it,* he thought. It was over and he might just as well walk down to the police station and tell them he had bludgeoned the nanny to death thinking it was his wife—the wife he had wished a thousand times to kill. The plan had gone wrong. No point in his bothering to go home to change, to incinerate the bloody clothes he was wearing.

Despair and fatigue assailed him in equal portions. *The hell with it,* he thought. He was going home to Ormonde Gate.

If they came for him, they would find him. If they didn't come, they would never find him. He would take his passport and what money there was in the safe and the keys to the car. By the odds alone, he decided, he should get one break tonight, the break of not being apprehended like this, covered with blood and with some remnant, some probable trace of his recent passion for his wife. He knew then where he was going to go and what he was going to do and how he was going to do it.

"Adieu, Patrick," he said softly. "I love you so."

Even as he was telling himself what he was going to do, he knew he was going to do no such thing. He would no sooner get into his flat than Amanda would have the police on him. He couldn't carry out his plan to get rid of the clothes he had on. He was not going to have a shower and change of clothes. He wouldn't be able to get money and his passport out of the desk drawer. In short, he had a borrowed car and the key to it, plus the single keys to his flat and the house. That was all. He had no money; he could not even make a phone call. He was beyond panic. As he started the car, he remembered the tire iron. It was in the hall where he had flung it down when he tried to choke her. The last straw! He had not only killed the wrong person and let his intended victim get away, he had failed to pick up the murder weapon. Any thought of going back now and finding it was out of the question. It was too late.

He knew now there was only one thing left for him to do. So be it.

2

The past rode with Charles Warrington; it was his only passenger on the lonely road that night. The chaos and tragedy of the recent hours were with him, but he had banished the emotions of rage and frustration that had accompanied his violence. He concentrated fiercely on his driving. It would be ludicrous to be caught speeding now, as he had been so many times before on this same road. Enveloped in the lulling security of the car and the benign darkness of the surrounding Kent countryside, he drove with his usual skill but with a wary eye on the speedometer.

A bottle of Bombay gin, unopened, lay on the seat beside him. Funny, he thought, as long as it was there, he didn't need it. If he wanted a drink and it wasn't there, he'd be cursing and fuming to have one. Spoiled, that's what he was. His Lordship must have what he wanted when he wanted it. He felt a smile of self-contempt rounding his lips. His Lordship had nothing, had never had anything, and certainly now would never have anything again. One thing only he had, a son who meant everything to him. The boy was the only force in his life that counted. He squirmed uncomfortably when the thought of Patrick came to him.

"Fucking hell," he said. Let his own life pass in front of his eyes, but not his life of the past four months. Before that. Where did good memories begin? What was the best thing that ever happened to him?

The win. The best day ever. Only once in his life had he felt that way, never before and never since. At the chemmy table in Biarritz. Ten, twelve years ago, 1962, just before Gavers had opened the Wyndham Club. They had been on holiday together for a week and luck was with him. He had won at everything he touched. There had been the horse, the filly called Moi Aussi, who had won him the equivalent of two thousand pounds. Then the dice at backgammon. He couldn't lose. Roulette. He had, in his accustomed way, put six chips straight up on six numbers. The 33 had turned up and repeated and he had eventually walked away from the table several thousand pounds more ahead. Then later, after dinner, the big game at the big table. He had gambled steadily for over an hour, winning some, losing some, but always staying ahead. He won an incredible fifty-three thousand pounds on the wheel, more than he had ever won at one crack before, and he had quit while he was ahead.

"Charles," Gavers had said, mock delight on his face, "I'm glad you won it here, not from me as of next week. I don't need you taking a fortune off me the minute my doors are open."

"I am going to walk out tomorrow and never again set foot in that boring office," Charles said. He had hated every minute of his job and had done it only because he had to do something. Not anymore. Not with Gavers opening the Wyndham, where he was a partner and could concentrate on gambling. That was all he wanted to do.

Driving back from France, Gavers had spoken to him.

"I do want you at the Club and I do want you as a partner. You will draw people there, and we may have many friends, but to run a successful gaming establishment we have to attract the big money. You can attract it. Your title certainly doesn't hurt in that regard. But we have to talk about something if you're serious about it."

"What?"

"You were lucky the other night. You're an excellent poker player and a good backgammon player and a fair bridge player. But basically, you're careless and undisciplined. You really must work at improving every game you play, Charles. I'm serious. Luck is not enough, and you've never been overly struck with it. The other night was a fluke. You're impatient at roulette and reckless at chemmy and I don't need for you to lose to me. Croupiers love impatient aristocrats."

Knowing Gavers was right, Charles had spent the next year diligently applying himself, improving himself at every game. It had worked, paid off. He seldom lost at poker. The dice counted at backgammon and he learned not to buck them, to walk away if they were not good to him. For a few years, life had been rosy . . . until luck deserted him.

He was almost at Faversham. No more time for the past, he thought, the good old days that weren't so good. And what was Amanda doing now? Probably telling the police her version of the story. He felt his stomach churn. Amanda, the source of all his troubles, his downfall. Damn her.

He pulled over on the lay-by after the roundabout and stopped the car. He opened the gin bottle and took a long swig. Despair hit him. He felt the blood on his pullover, stiff now that it was dry. The blood of an innocent girl he had killed. His mind revolted against the memory. It couldn't be true, this nightmare—even he couldn't be so unlucky. He took another swig and closed the bottle, started the car and drove the one mile more to the Riggses' house. Rosie would be there. They could call Neil. Rosie and Neil could help him out of this godawful mess. It would be his word against that mad bitch's, he thought.

For one second he remembered the look in Amanda's eyes as she lay on the bed, covered with blood and wanting him. He remembered how she felt when he was making love to her . . . and how he felt, lost in her. Whose fault was all this? Was it all on his head?

He turned into the driveway. The light was on at the front door and in Rosie and Neil's bedroom upstairs. It was after midnight, he imagined; he'd left his watch in the flat when he had gone out earlier.

There it was. Earlier. When he had gone out to kill his wife. Now he was a blood-soaked murderer who couldn't even succeed in killing the right person.

Jimbo, the Riggses' Irish wolfhound, began to bark as Charles parked the car.

"Shut up, Jimbo," he called as he got out of the car. He patted the dog on the head. Jimbo's hackles came up as he smelled the blood on Charles's clothes. "It's all right."

But it wasn't all right. Nothing would ever be all right again. How had it come to this? he wondered bitterly. How could it have come to this?

11:30 P.M.

When the dowager Countess of Warrington arrived at the house the police were already there. She was escorted into the dining room where a portly man seated at the table rose as she entered. The portraits of Warrender ancestors lining the walls seemed out of place to her but, oddly enough, not the stranger at the table.

"I am Chief Superintendent Manners, ma'am," he said politely. "King's Road Police Station."

"What has happened here, Superintendent?" the countess asked. "Where is my grandson? I have come to fetch him."

"He's safely asleep upstairs, ma'am. There has been an accident in the
house however."

Manners looked to be a right sort of person to her. "So I've been told.
For the moment however, I should like to see about my grandson."

"Of course. Go right upstairs, ma'am."

"I will be taking him home with me." She was a no-nonsense woman.

"When you have seen that he is safe, if you will come down before
waking him so we can fill you in as to what has happened, I'd appreciate
it. Then we will have a car escort you and your grandson home."

Penelope Warrington looked at him without answering. Charles had
meant what he'd said to her on the telephone a short time ago. She
could feel that something terrible had happened. She turned and went
up the stairs. The door to Charles and Amanda's bedroom was open.
Several policemen were in the room but she didn't pause, continuing
straight up to Patrick's room.

He wasn't there. Dear God, where was he? She took a deep breath
and tried to compose herself.

She switched on the light in the nursery and looked around, then
went on to the nanny's room. She turned on the lamp and saw Patrick
curled up in the nanny's bed, sound asleep.

Penelope looked down at the sleeping face of her grandson. Poor little
boy. She tucked the blankets in and turned off the light and went down
to the dining room. Patrick was safe, at least.

The BBC reported the murder on the 7:00 A.M. broadcast on Friday
morning.

"The body of Jenny Boyce, twenty-six, was found at about eleven P.M.
last night in a canvas sail bag in the kitchen at Number Twenty-two
Royal Hospital Road, Chelsea, a house belonging to the Earl and
Countess of Warrington. Lady Warrington apparently had been attacked
by the same person who killed Miss Boyce but she was able to escape to
the Farrier's Forge, a public house at the bottom of Royal Hospital
Road, to seek help from the police. Lady Warrington was bleeding profusely from head wounds apparently administered with the same
weapon used to murder Miss Boyce. Miss Boyce had recently been employed as a nanny in the house. Chief Superintendent Ronald Man ners
of the King's Road Police Station discovered the body in the kitchen.
Lady Warrington has been separated from Lord Warrington for over six
months. Lady Warrington is at present in Chelsea Hospital. The whereabouts of Lord Warrington is unknown."

★ ★ ★

April 12, 1974

Solidly built of pink Victorian brick, the King's Road Police Station resembled a charming bed-and-breakfast hotel rather than a police station. It had a brick entrance courtyard. In the summer, hanging brass pots filled with geraniums and purple and white petunias dangled on either side of the front door. A pair of ancient gaslight lampposts were still in use at the curb. Inside, it was all business.

The Chief Superintendent, Ronald Manners, had called his force of about forty men together for a briefing on the morning after the murder. This was one of the most serious cases to come across his desk in years. Murder and mayhem were practically unknown in the Royal Hospital Road area. It was a gentle part of London, the area where the red-coated Chelsea pensioners nodded good day to one and all, where Christopher Wren's magnificent Royal Hospital architecture dominated the landscape. Burglary and fights were the most serious crimes that Ronald Manners had to deal with.

Ronald "Buster" Manners was one of the best investigators on the London police force and he was somewhat wasted in this aristocratic stronghold, where hard-core crime was a rarity. There was an affability about him, a sort of hail-fellow-well-met quality that was not contrived, although it was misleading. Beneath his song-and-dance-man appearance was a shrewd, curious, and determined man with a keen intelligence.

Though he'd been born in the East End of London, the only thing lower-class about Manners was his faint cockney accent, some of which he had shed during his war years. Those years were terminated when the communications shack he was occupying near the Franco-German lines was destroyed, thanks to a near hit by a British bomber. Fascinated by code work, he had applied for police training as soon as he was mustered out. Dreaming of Scotland Yard, which had no room for him, he had worked his way quickly into the top ranks of the regular police force by the sheer power of his native intelligence. An insatiable curiosity about his fellow man made work a pleasure for him. Now, with the murder of Jenny Boyce, Buster Manners had something to work on.

He went over the report with his men, detailing the known events of the previous night. Today they would start on door-to-door investigation and questioning.

"It was a real brute of a murder," he told them, "the grisly kind that the press loves and exploits to the hilt. They will soon be descending on us to hinder the investigation as best they can, so let's get it clear.

"Here we have a peer, one of that privileged set," Manners said. "A handsome aristocrat, a swell with a name that stretches back through English history. He has apparently killed this poor girl Jenny Boyce, mistaking her for his wife, from whom he was separated. He keeps a flat around the corner in Ormonde Gate which he took when they reached a parting of the ways. He undoubtedly had a key of his own to his former residence and when he let himself in, he must have thought it was the girl's night out. Normally the nanny did go out on Thursdays. So he apparently lay in wait for his wife to come down to make the eggnog she had each night. There was no light on in the hallway or the basement kitchen and someone had fiddled the fuse box. He repeatedly struck at her with sixteen inches of tire iron. Then, after thinking he had done her in and trussing her up in a sail bag, he runs into his wife, alive as she could be, when he was attempting to depart the scene."

From what he had seen later at the house last night, Manners told his men, Warrington then tried to finish his wife off with the tire iron, but she got away from him somehow and turned in the alarm from the neighborhood pub.

"Charles Henry Edward Keating, Eleventh Earl of Warrington, is known to his friends as 'Winner,' an interesting nickname," Manners informed them. "He is a registered gambler with no profession beyond that. His chosen occupation has kept him most of the time at the Wyndham Club in Upper Brook Street, a private gaming club which belongs to a Mr. Gavin Driscoll. I am familiar with this scene only because I read the toff gossip columns."

Behind Manners's desk, a bookshelf held half a dozen reference books, newspaper-sized scrapbooks, and a dogeared copy of *Burke's Peerage,* which he reached for now. Manners had become a willing student of the peerage when he had moved as a professional into this neighborhood, a stronghold of the upper classes.

" 'The Eleventh Earl of Warrington,' " he read aloud. " 'Charles Henry Edward Keating, Baron Keating of Longholt, of Longholt on Wye, in the United Kingdom. Education: Harrow. Oxford. Lieutenant, Queen's Own Guards (Reserve). Born October 12, 1932. Succeeded his father 1965. Married 1964, Amanda Mary Gordon, daughter of Naval Lieutenant Richard Michael Gordon, killed July 1940. Has issue. Lord Patrick Anthony Henry Keating, born April 1965.'

"That's what we know about them," Manners said. "So far. But whoever did it was not the brightest, as you will see, and we do not know if
Lord Warrington did it at all. The forensic boys should be able to shed
more light on the murder. The man involved intended to kill, not rob.
He had carefully removed the fuse in the downstairs box, so the victim
could not see him. Nothing seems to be missing from the house, and
there is plenty of silver in the drawers and closets, and pictures on the
wall that were up for grabs. Now who did this man intend to kill? Lady
Warrington has not been able to make an official statement yet but she
has said, both when she reached the Farrier's Forge and in the ambulance on the way to the hospital, that she believes her husband intended
to kill her and that he mistook the nanny, Jenny Boyce, for her. Apparently they were close to the same size. When Lady Warrington met up
with her attacker, she heard and recognized her husband's voice in the
ensuing battle. They continued to battle after she succeeded in un-
masking him. She said that when he took her upstairs, ostensibly to help
her, she felt that he still intended to kill her and that's why she fled.
Lady Warrington may or may not be telling the truth. She and Lord
Warrington have been separated for some months, and we've been called
several times in regard to their problems.

"Now to Jenny Boyce. We know considerably less about her. It seems
that she had been having a little walk-out with Ron, the barkeep over at
the Farrier's Forge. So far it had been only a little slap and tickle that
had hardly got going, since she'd been working in the neighborhood for
no more than a few weeks. Ron said that she, too, was separated from
her husband, a merchant seaman with whom she had lived for less than
a year. We have his name and address. It seems he used to beat her.
According to Ron, her family lives in a trailer out near Blackheath.
They are being informed of her death now.

"So that's it for the moment. I will question the Boyce girl's parents
after Scotland Yard is through with them. You will question everyone in
every house and place of business within a twelve-block area about the
movements of the Warringtons or Jenny Boyce in the last few days.
Lady Warrington will be questioned officially later today. Her head is
full of stitches. I have turned over the murder weapon to the forensic
boys. They should have a lot to tell us in a few hours.

"By the way. Two more things. Look for blood everywhere—on the
sidewalks, walls, everywhere. There was a lot of blood in the house, so
there may be a trail outside. And remember that when you question the
aristos, they are going to close ranks on you. Most of those I've seen are
totally selfish, self-centered exhibitionists, accustomed to patronizing the

likes of you and me. They treat the law with a kind of amused contempt. Just be patient with them."

After much discussion the men left on their rounds. Brian Billings, who had long ago been tagged as Buster Manners's eventual successor, stayed behind for a few minutes after the others had left the room.

"What do you think, Buster? Any feeling?"

"What I think," Manners said, "is that I would like to know the exact whereabouts at this moment of Lord Charles Warrington."

11:00 A.M., April 12

The first thing she felt was a blinding pain in her head, a white tunnel of agony that forced a cry from her, making her beg for the dark nothingness again. There was something binding her head; she reached her hand up to her forehead to wipe it away and found neither skin nor hair, only a rough kind of cloth covering one side of her face. Her right eye was covered with a heavy substance that would not move. It wasn't a scarf or a hat, just something on one side of her head. She felt for the other side of her face, touching her left eyelid and feeling a small bit of skin above it. Then the rough cloth again. What was it? She was in a bed, a strange bed with binding covers. It was dark.

She heard a voice and felt a hand removing her own hand from her head. "There," a woman's voice said, "it's all right. You're all right. Don't be afraid. You're going to be fine." An Irish brogue tinged the voice. Amanda opened her left eye and saw gray walls and shadows, nothing else. Her mouth was numb, as if it were full of wool.

The voice spoke again. "Go back to sleep. I'm just going to wipe your face and give you some water."

Amanda turned her head and looked at the possessor of the sweet voice. A nurse, whose hand held hers, patted her arm. "A few more hours sleep and it will all seem better."

Suddenly the pain intensified and Amanda cried out, her arms flailing in the air. She sank back involuntarily into the aching void, not caring about this strange place or the nurse. Jumbled thoughts that wouldn't come together flashed quick messages in her head but nothing took form or shape. Hadn't Jenny tapped on the door and asked if she could make her an eggnog? Where was Jenny now? Had she taken Patrick up to bed? No, Patrick was still with her; they were watching telly. Why was Jenny telling her to go back to sleep?

She drifted, the pain diminishing. The bed reminded her of the bed in the Venice hotel when they had been on their honeymoon. The sheets were the same sort of rough linen and there was the same large pillow roll that had kept her propped up as she was now—like an old person who couldn't breathe without being propped up. But she wasn't an old person. Never mind. Charles had half torn up the bed getting the pillow unwound from the sheet, and then thrown it on the floor. He'd flung the ugly damask bedcover and heavy blankets away, too, leaving the big bed like a white slab with the two of them on it. "They call this a *matrimonio*," he had said. "A bed for married Catholics who sleep together propped up but haven't made love for years. At least it's big enough for us." He'd leaned over her then, his naked body looming.

Then he disappeared and she heard the woman's voice again. And a man's. They were whispering.

"You still have to wait," the woman's voice said. "She is beginning to come to, but she doesn't know where she is yet or what's happened to her. Poor little thing—so thin, and hurt."

Who had come to see her and why weren't they allowed to come in? She needed someone to talk to, someone who was not a nurse or a servant.

Where was Charles? She was hurt; someone had hurt her and he should be there to take care of her, to hold her. "There never was anyone like you," he'd always told her. Those words sent bells ringing in her head. He had said them to her again just a little while ago.

Suddenly, with a pain far worse than that in her head, it all came back to her. The dark hall, the blows, the fight to save herself, the wounds, the blood all over them, the bed. Then as he went into the bathroom, she knew that when he came back he was going to kill her. No mistake this time. And Patrick too. Charles had gone mad.

Patrick! What had happened to him? Where was he? She screamed, or tried to. The sound that came out was more of a chortle, which brought the nurse instantly to her side, trying to calm her.

Hysteria building, she clawed at the nurse with the little strength available to her.

"Where is my son? What have they done with him?"

Mary Reilly, the nurse, held her steadily. "Hold on," she said. "He is perfectly fine. He's with his grandmother. You have had a terrible accident. Don't worry now, your son is safe, and you're going to be fine. Try not to think about it. Try to sleep some more."

"Go away," Amanda said. "Leave me alone." As long as Patrick was safe she had nothing to worry about. With his grandmother or with her sister, it didn't matter. They both hated her, but they would take care of Patrick.

She was desperately tired; she ached all over. Why should she face

this? Where were the happy days? And where was Charles? As the
tension left her body it was replaced with a feeling of hopelessness. She
turned over onto her side in the fetal position, and tears came swiftly.
Weeping, she knew now that he would never make love to her again.
The one hold she'd had on him was gone, gone forever. As much as she
wanted her old power back, the power of knowing that he would always
want her, always be unable to resist her no matter how black his mood,
she knew it was gone. Perhaps if she went back to sleep, she would wake
up with the same confidence, the same knowledge that he would love
her again.

No, she thought, *not this time.* He had tried to kill her, had meant to
kill her.

No, she thought. He would never love her again.

How could they have come to this? How could they have come to
this?

• • •

Surrey, July 1940

The child was screaming for her life. The blood flowing down from
a deep gash in her head was in her eyes and beginning to mat in her
white-blond hair. It was all over her yellow pinafore. She swiped at her
eyes and cheeks, trying to rub the blood away, pulling at the harness
that kept her safely in her seat. She gulped her breath between screams,
completely terrified.

She reached frantically toward her father, not knowing that he was
already dead, any more than she knew what death was. The other car
had hit them head-on as they rounded a bend on the narrow country
road. Roads in Devon were fifteen to twenty feet deep in hedgerow in
August and the woman driving the other car was very old and had been
halfway across on the wrong side of the road. She was dead, too, im-
paled on the steering column. The terrible noise of the crash, only moments before, had brought some of the local people hurrying to the
scene. These accidents were not new to them; there were several each
summer.

"Jesus God," the Craig boy had said, running with his father toward
the car and the sound of the child's screams. Eddie Craig tore the car
door open, thanking God it hadn't been jammed, and yanked off the

harness that held the child in. He dragged her toward him, pulling her bloodied body out in his arms, then handing her over to his father.

"Quick, Dad!" he said, breathless and sick with fear. "Both cars will blow up and be on fire any second." They ran, the little girl sheltered in Mr. Craig's arms. They had gotten no more than twenty yards away when the gas tank of Lieutenant Gordon's car exploded. They felt the blast under their feet and turned in time to see the car burst into flames. Both Craigs knew that if there was even the remotest chance that the child's father had still been alive, he was gone now.

The wail of a siren from the nearby main road meant that Sandra Craig had gotten through to the police and the ambulance and had given the location of the accident. The now-exhausted sobs of the blood-covered child were devastating to them. Poor, poor little girl.

Amanda Mary Gordon was two and a half years old on that summer day when the father she adored was burned to death in the accident from which she escaped alive. In that summer of 1940 her father had been on his last leave before being shipped to Scotland for Arctic warfare training, and as they grew up, Amanda and her younger twin sisters, Davina and Pamela, would talk about their father, dreaming about what might have been. He might have been killed during the war. Sometimes, when asked, they would say that he had been. He might have lived and been with them to this day.

The twins had been less than a year old when the accident happened and didn't know their father. But little Amanda Mary knew and adored him and she never recovered from the horror of the accident or from his loss. She became a deeply disturbed child from that hot July day on, with recurring nightmares that plagued her formative years. She often came awake soaking wet, screaming and weeping.

The doctor in Reading had prescribed sedatives for her and explained patiently that Amanda was bound to have emotional problems after such a horrendous experience. But, he had said to her mother, there was a war on and the child was not the only person in trouble. She would get over it, with time, he had said; she would gradually forget.

Amanda Mary Gordon never got over the accident, and she never forgot her father.

Wiltshire, 1932

Charles Henry Edward Keating weighed nearly ten pounds at his birth on October 12, 1932, and no one, despite the ruffled fine linens of babyhood, ever took him for a girl. He grew into a stolid little boy, strong and awkward and passionate about sports. He was an only child but he was never fawned on by his parents; in fact, he was left almost entirely in the company of his Scottish nanny, Mary Eleanor Bruce, known as Brucie. All the warmth and affection he was given came from her. Brucie had a stern look about her that was a façade, meant to reassure his parents of her disciplinary expertise with "the boy," as she called Charles. In private, she adored him.

It was Brucie who taught him to play games, anything and everything they could bet a shilling or two on. He learned checkers and whist and cribbage, refused chess, and grew mad for all card games. She egged him on to finish his homework quickly so they could play. There were few boys of Charles's age nearby, so Brucie was his childhood companion.

His father, Richard, the 10th Earl, was not a particularly attractive man. His nature was cold, and for reasons that Charles never could understand, he spent his life battling the circumstances of his birth. He resented being a peer, and he admonished Charles throughout his childhood to beware the traps of aristocracy and devote himself to the condition of the common man and his problems. Richard Warrington's only interest was politics and his one desire was to further the cause of the Labour Party, a subject of eventual embarrassment to his son.

When Charles was thirteen he was sent to Harrow, as generations of Keatings and Warringtons had been before him. His father had advised him that there he would learn about the weakness and incipient treachery of the so-called privileged classes—regardless of the fact that all Keatings were privileged and had traditionally gone to Harrow. "The best way for you to learn is from the inside," his father told him. "Five years spent in a lukewarm bath of snobbery will teach you. You'll see that they are basically an irresponsible lot. The Labour boys will take over this country one day, you mark my words, and you'll be better off if you understand that, as I do. And your mother as well."

Charles's mother, the fifth daughter of a minor baron, had gone along placidly with her husband's wishes. She preferred life in the country. The Warrington home was a sprawling, gloomy Tudor house on the River Avon near Corsham, about eighty miles from London. The fields and meadows that surrounded it were open and sunny, making up to some extent for the somber house.

Charles grew to six feet by the time he was twelve and bore very little, if any, resemblance to either his mother or father. He looked like a real Keating, like generations of Keatings before him. He had inherited the appearance of the aristocrat, from the high forehead and strong eyebrows that defined his clear, dark-blue eyes, to the physical structure of his body. "Keating Dandies," they had once been called.

From the moment Charles arrived at Harrow he loved it. When he returned home for the Christmas holiday he found that his parents had pensioned Brucie without bothering to tell him, a fact that enraged him and caused a blazing row between them.

"Why?" Charles almost wailed. "She has no other home. She belongs here. How could you turn her out?"

"Don't be silly," his mother said. "The Scottish can always take care of themselves, and besides, you're a man now. You don't need a nanny."

In full rage, he stormed from the room and threw himself on his bed. Pummeling at his pillow, halfway to tears, he found a note that Brucie had left under the pillow, giving him her address near Folkestone. "Don't worry, boy. I've enough to retire but I'm not ready to take on another charge. You, my bonnie Charlie, are my favorite and you'll turn up in Folkestone for a card game soon enough I'll wager."

After that, he seldom went back home on breaks or holidays, preferring to stay at school or visit his schoolmates in their warmer and livelier houses. Harrow bred individualists. He had his own room and was allowed to furnish the closet-size space as he chose; it was his private domain. No one entered rooms at Harrow without the permission of the occupant; even the housemaster had to knock when doing his nightly rounds. Work was done in his own time, a hardship for Charles because he was lazy and not a particularly bright student, but he applied himself and managed to scrape through, mainly out of fear of being sent down. At Harrow he learned that being first in studies or best in sports was a minor accomplishment. Harrow's credo was that it was vital to be independent, and independent he became.

Charles was not entirely untutored in family history, but his parents' attitude toward the title led them to minimize anything to do with his ancestry, foolish or glorious. He was brought up as if the Keating and Warrington lines were of no importance. He had little knowledge of particular events of the past. But history caught up with him in a fight at a soccer game.

Bullying and homosexuality were a normal part of English schooling. Charles gave little thought to either; he was too big for the one and too masculine for the other. He was an aggressive player in any game and stronger than most of his contemporaries. One afternoon he kicked a goal that not only gave his side the winning score but looked as if he had deliberately attacked the goalie of the opposing team. The boy, a well-known homosexual, was hit hard in the face with the ball and he went after Charles later, half-crying and bleeding profusely from the nose.

"Bloody Keatings," he said. "Bad blood in every one of you. Bullies with no brains. One of your forebears, with typical Warrington idiocy, managed to blow up his allies instead of the enemy. Starting it all over again, Charlie?"

Charles walked off the field in a fury, barely controlling a desire to kill. He was stung by the personal viciousness of the goalie, who up to that time Charles had barely known, beyond his reputation as a homosexual. Antony Price, his best friend, tried to divert his anger with words.

"Let it rest, Charles. You know it happens to all of us. There's hardly ever been anyone here who doesn't have a black sheep ancestor. Or some religious fanatic. It's nothing. Let it be."

But the incident bothered Charles more than it should have, partly because it made him realize how little he actually knew or cared about his ancestry. He felt cheated. It sent him to the history books and the family archives and opened his eyes to his own bloodline. Some of the Warringtons before him had been distinguished men with distinguished careers. For the most part they had been in the military, and some of their campaigns had been inglorious. The more Charles delved, the more he discovered. How could he have been so unaware of his own family story? It angered him that his father had taken a cavalier attitude toward the importance of history. When he finally learned that the origin of the family fortune was as absentee landowners in Wales, he had to grant his father some justice. The Keatings, Charles learned, had indulged in some pretty high-handed treatment toward those less privileged than themselves. In fact, they had raped the lands, taken everything and given nothing in return. They were ruthless and hated, then as well as now. Richard Warrington had turned to Labour out of a bad conscience, trying to make up for past behavior. Charles still had no sympathy for his views. The common man made him uncomfortable. He'd rather smash in a fag goalie's face at Harrow than fool for one instant with any member of the lower classes.

His own bloodline intrigued him. He came upon descriptions of past Keatings and Warringtons and couldn't help but know that he was a carbon copy of former ones, even to the famous Keating streak in his hair—a white streak at his left forehead that all Keating males, without exception, inherited. He learned in one book that the Keatings were "proud, narrow, overbearing, and peremptory" men, and in another that they were "stern, fierce, and merciless." Merciless? One was "the very model of a Byronic hero, dark, passionate, and romantic." That was a bit of all right, but it made him slightly uneasy, knowing that he actually had begun to look somewhat like a Byronic hero himself. As he plowed on, he also discovered that his forebears were lazy, not particularly intelligent, and, more often than not, unlucky.

He had finally had enough of dwelling on the past. He was what he was, and he had no idea of what he wanted to be in the future. To hell with it all for the time being.

CHAPTER 3

Hampshire, June 1964

For a moment, coming awake in the sun-filled bedroom, Amanda had no idea where she was. An insistent shaft of piercing sunlight forced her to open her eyes and then quickly raise a hand to shield her face from the blinding early morning light. She turned over on her back, still half asleep and mumbling to herself, and then sat up almost involuntarily in the twin bed, her hair tumbling over her face. Where was she anyway?

The bedroom was pristine white, with oval moldings decorating the ceiling and bordering the fireplace; there were four large windows. A hand-painted mirror hung over the fireplace, with two armchairs upholstered in rose-printed chintz in front of it. The same rose-printed chintz had been used for curtains that hung from floor to ceiling, with sheer voiles under them, all very light and airy, and completely ineffective in blocking out the brilliant sunlight streaming through the windows. A bench at the foot of her bed was covered in a narrow pink-and-green stripe and the folded bedspread that lay on it was made of the same satiny stripe. Someone had carefully folded the bedspread, Amanda thought, some invisible servant who bloody well should have drawn the curtains the night before. She was in a foul mood.

What time was it? She looked for a clock on the bedside table. There was no clock, only a small white porcelain ashtray with a pink rose painted on it. There wasn't a book in the room either. She glanced toward the two windows where the offending sunlight had invaded her sleep, and looked out over wide green lawns to a horizon uninterrupted by trees. She pulled at the tangled straps of her short lavender satin nightgown, fully awake now and distinctly uneasy.

The sound of running water came to her from the closed door of the bathroom on the far side of the room, and Amanda saw that the bed next to hers was rumpled. Of course. Her mother was up already, having a bath. Oh, yes. They were at Richard Marston's house in Hampshire. They had arrived the night before and had a boring, though brief, dinner with Davina and Richard's mother. Pamela was arriving this morning. Richard was in London for his bachelor dinner. Richard and Davina were being married at four this afternoon. That's why she was here.

Not wanting to think yet, Amanda continued her critical scrutiny of the room. Roses, roses, roses, chintz, chintz, chintz. Amanda hated the whole look. England was riddled with the stuff. You'd think Richard's money was new.

The bathroom door opened and her mother tiptoed into the room and came across to her bed, squinting without her glasses to see if Amanda was awake. She was wrapped in a voluminous white terry-cloth robe with a small rose from the chintz appliquéd on the collar. How sweet, Amanda thought, how very sweet. What a wonderfully thought-out house code, so the idiot laundress can manage to get everything back to the right room. How very clever, the way these people run their country houses.

"You're awake, darling," her mother was saying. "It is the most beautiful day. More good luck for Richard and Davina." It annoyed Amanda that her mother always used Richard's name first when referring to her daughter and the man she was going to marry. Richard this, Richard that; poor Davina relegated to single file behind him. When Davina had almost married Timmy Bartlett, it was "Davina, my daughter Davina, and Tim." Never Timmy, even though no one else ever called him Tim. Tim. The Tim who had no money. And as for poor Pamela, she'd run off and gotten married at sixteen to a perfectly nice young man, quite rich, and gone to live in the North of Scotland on a large estate where no one was ever invited to visit. He'd kept Pamela isolated there for almost eight years now and refused to come to the wedding, although he had allowed Pamela to come just for that day.

"It's the longest day of the year, too," Amanda observed tartly as her mother leaned over to peck her on the forehead. Mrs. Gordon reeked of Floris Lily of the Valley bath oil, too sickly sweet for the early morning hour, or any hour. Like the damn roses, Amanda thought. She hated sweet scents. "The summer solstice, twenty-first of June," she said. "It's going to be light forever. What are we going to do from now until four this afternoon? What time is it now?"

"Seven," her mother said. "Just gone seven." She sat at the dressing table, peering at herself in the silver-framed mirror, carefully regarding her small, undistinguished face in the bright morning light. Amanda was always in a bad temper in the morning, especially this early. She'd be all right once she had a cup of tea. Tea and a good breakfast would fix her up. Mrs. Gordon wondered if there was anyone about in the kitchen by now, and what she and Amanda were supposed to do about their breakfast. It was Richard's house, but in his absence last night, his mother hadn't bothered to give them any instructions about the morning. Mrs. Gordon really wanted to go down by herself, so she could look around and see every room in what would become her daughter's country house soon after four this afternoon.

The house she was staying in, she had been informed by Richard's mother last night, was called Lea Place. When Richard's father had died a few years before, Richard had inherited the huge house a mile down the road, where Elizabeth Marston still lived. She did not have to move; it was not a matter of titles and primogeniture, but rather of Richard's preferring Lea Place. The Marstons had bought the larger place, Ransome House, from an aged bachelor Earl whose title would die with him. She loved her gardens and the responsibility that went with the huge old house, and she knew that when she died Richard would take it over. A girlfriend of Richard's who was a decorator had "done it up" for him, Elizabeth Marston explained.

That was before he'd met Davina, Mrs. Gordon exulted to herself. When Elizabeth died, Richard would have both houses. He and Davina. It was all so fortunate and this afternoon she would see the very grand Ransome House at the wedding reception.

Mrs. Gordon dressed quickly. "I'll just run down to the kitchen and see about some tea, Amanda. I'll bring some up for you."

"Mother," Amanda said irritably, then bit her tongue and changed her tone. "Thank you. I would love some." Her mother had no way to know about servants bringing tea or the ways of country houses, and she, Amanda, had not been very nice so far today.

Amanda went to the bathroom and ran cold water from the tap into her cupped hands and splashed it over her face. Taking one of the white linen hand towels, appliquéd with the ubiquitous rose, she patted her face dry and looked at herself in the mirror. In the morning light, with no makeup and her titian hair tumbling on her shoulders, she was all tawny-beige, not a whisper of pink on her. She took off her nightgown and held it up to her face, watching the blue-lavender tones of the satin change her eyes from blue-gray to blue. It was a trick she loved to do. Fringed with shining lashes, her eyes changed color dramatically depending on the color she wore. When she wore gray, her eyes went to gray flecked with black, and her skin turned ivory-beige. Amanda was not in the least unaware of her beauty. She loved the way she looked when her overall coloring was subtle, when she could walk down streets without anyone's noticing her unless she wanted to be noticed. She infinitely preferred the role of observer to that of participant and she liked being out of focus, camouflaged from the world. Davina and she had even argued furiously about Amanda's dress for the wedding. Davina wanted her to wear butter-yellow silk and carry yellow freesias. Amanda would have none of it; she hated yellow. Davina capitulated, knowing she would lose the battle one way or another anyhow. Pamela had agreed to the pretty yellow at least. Amanda's dress, hanging in the closet in the other room was the color of Devon cream. She had acquiesced on the freesias.

Amanda knew that she was jealous of Davina today and her jealousy was making her uneasy. Twenty-six years old to Davina's and Pamela's twenty-four, she felt wasted. She had never behaved like a young person. When she was a child her mother would occasionally tease her about being the "old lady" in the family, but Amanda didn't mind. She had kept to herself, a serious, solemn child who loved studying and did well in school; she would never have had any friends if it hadn't been for her sisters, who were exactly like their mother although they were fraternal twins and looked nothing alike. Both of them were just like their mother: naïve, trusting, and with sunny natures. Amanda missed her father. She had always missed him. She knew his face only from pictures but she remembered how he had felt and smelled. In her private heart she longed for her father, longed for him to kiss her and hold her again. The twins and her mother were nice, but they were silly.

With Davina's engagement all of Amanda's competitive instincts had come rushing to the fore, and she didn't know how to cope with such strong feelings. She loved her sisters. They had kept one another's secrets and fended for one another to keep their mother at bay. But Pamela had run off at sixteen, so she hadn't really been a part of their lives for many years now. Davina and Amanda had both had lovers, if they could be called that—minor sexual skirmishes were all that the few transitory escapades could be called. Davina got on easily with men. Amanda did not. They only wanted one thing. Davina coped sunnily, but Amanda knew that she herself possessed a powerful sexual allure that she was a total failure at using.

Sighing, she dropped the nightgown on the floor and turned on the taps in the tub. She began the ritual inspection of her supple body. Her grooming was flawless. Her hands were small and neat, her ankles were perfect, and her feet were narrow and pretty. Her nails were immaculately polished in clear lacquer and the skin around them was as soft as the skin on the rest of her body. An Italian who couldn't pronounce her name but who had been smitten by her had said to her: "Amanicara . . . even your cuticles are beautiful"—which pleased her momentarily, but then he became too insistent and she had stopped answering his phone calls. There was something rare about her skin and she was uneasily aware that she exuded an alluring fragrance, a subtle scent from deep within her that magnetized men. When they touched her, they touched her again, running searching hands along the smooth skin of her shoulders and arms. They would hold and kiss her hands, and they all tried to get her into bed.

She liked sex; she just didn't like the men she had it with. What was the point if you didn't want them and they just wanted to take you and leave? She had never in her life seen anyone she really wanted, really meant to have. After the inevitable struggle that most evenings ended with, she would say something biting or derogatory to get rid of the poor sod who had bought her dinner, and that would be that. She seemed to enjoy putting men down, and even the most ardent or drunken swordsman-on-the-prowl for a bit of crumpet quickly felt her sting and left her to herself.

Drying herself and looking at her naked body in the old-fashioned floor mirror, she was thinking about sex. She fancied Richard a little bit, but that was not why she was jealous of Davina. Richard had flirted with her first, but Davina had swooped in and gotten him before Amanda had even considered him. Feeling her bad temper building, she rubbed her favorite bath oil on her still partially wet body. It was Floris Ormonde, not the sickly Lily of the Valley her mother was saturated with.

She was jealous of Davina because everything had come easily to her. Pamela was buried away in Scotland and Amanda might as well be buried with her. It was Davina who was the golden girl of the three of them. Life was so light for Davina, and now she had Richard and was all set, while she, Amanda, was nowhere.

Any annoyance Amanda had felt about the rose-printed chintz in her bedroom at Lea Place vanished with her first sight of Ransome House. Lea Place was nothing more than a cottage compared to Ransome House, which was fit for a queen—and her baby sister Davina would be queen there one day. Instead of an uneasy jealousy, Amanda now found herself the victim of mixed emotions. It was not Davina's good fortune that Amanda had come to grips with; it was her own sense of failure. Pamela and Davina had both always looked ahead, always aspired to a class above them but not impossible to achieve. Davina was quite open about her desire to move up in position, but she had not seemed unduly ambitious about it. Although it was common knowledge that the Gordon girls' background was middle class, they were not the only ones—and besides, they were all stunning to look at.

With Pamela gone, Davina had become the more popular of the remaining two. She was uncomplicated and life-loving, and everything came easily to her. Amanda was complex and riddled with anxiety, quietly critical of everything and everyone; a judge without humor and a critic without cause. She knew that she was her own worst enemy, but rather than try to change that condition, she withdrew into herself and took pride in her lonely state. She was the one who should live in the isolation of the Scottish highlands.

To her astonishment, Amanda found herself completely unprepared for the impact that Ransome House made on her. She had visited practically every palace and castle and stately home that England was justly famous for, and to her way of thinking, there was something wrong with each of them. The fact that England was filled with incomparable private treasures that she probably would never see and certainly never own had not bothered her at all. She knew that behind all the magnificence and the grandeur, there was discomfort and misery for the lord as well as for the lowliest servant. Ransome House was the single, rare exception to what she had seen before.

Ransome House was one of the many great English houses built in the late eighteenth century, and unlike most of them, it had always been magnificently maintained. As succeeding Ransomes enlarged and embellished it, it became more splendid—never bastardized, as so many others had been. William Colt Ransome, the great benefactor of the line, brought it to full glory through personal tragedy. Widowed after a brief year of marriage—thanks to a massive rock fence, a bad horse, and a clever fox—he left Ransome House in deep depression and roamed the Continent for six years. When he finally returned he had developed into an ardent collector and a skilled architect. He added a library and a picture gallery as flanking wings, doubling the size of the house and quadrupling its quality. Thomas Chippendale made furniture for him, and Turner sketched the rooms. Five years after Colt Ransome's death, another tasteful Ransome added the conservatory, which was the only room Amanda had ever felt was perfection. In the showy houses the emphasis was on dignity and magnificence rather than ease and informality, and great luxury meant cold and chillblains for lord and lackey alike. What was so desirable about that? Ransome House throughout its history had been a bastion of comfort and hospitality, of true taste.

The house had lost nothing by Marston ownership—quite the opposite. In the postwar 1950's, all of England finally began to capitulate to comfort and warmth. Great houses that continued without those elements were regarded tolerantly, but they were no longer envied. The Marstons knew only one way. When Richard's father bought Ransome House lock, stock, and barrel from the bachelor Earl, he proceeded to bring it to full flower. Ransome House in the past had required and supported a staff of fifty. Richard Marston changed all that. He pensioned off family retainers generously without taking away their security or dignity. He housed those he could on the estate in small cottages of their own, establishing loyalties not felt toward the bachelor Earl. Ransome House ran more efficiently with a staff of fifteen, proving that it was possible to treasure the fine things of the present without fifty in staff. Now Davina was marrying into that privileged state. The door was open for Amanda too. She knew all she had to do was walk through it, if only she could.

The wedding ceremony in the tiny village church had been sentimental and charming, and by Amanda's amateur count, there were at least four to five hundred at the reception. They ebbed and flowed through every corner of Ransome House, wandering happily back and forth from garden to drawing room, conservatory to great hall. They all seemed to know their way around and some settled down in the massive white-and-gold drawing room while others chattered away over the buffet lavished across forty shining feet of polished walnut table in the Red Dining Room. White-gloved, white-coated waiters served a never-ending supply of icy champagne from silver trays in Val St. Lambert flutes.

Amanda caught the atmosphere of gaiety as she made her way from room to room, alone but chatting with everyone as she passed, taking glass after glass of champagne and downing them quickly. Smiling, she repeated, "Yes, yes, I am Davina's sister, and yes, it is divine, the whole wedding," a dozen times or more. And "Yes, I do work in London, and thanks so much for asking me to join you but I promised to meet some friends in the conservatory." She slipped from room to room like quicksilver. She felt secure and as if she belonged, although she knew it was part of a passing mood.

Pamela and her mother scarcely left Richard and Davina's side. When the couple danced, everyone applauded, and when they cut the cake Amanda was there to kiss Davina and take a first bite of the cake. She even danced briefly with an old uncle of Richard's who obviously fancied her. She excused herself and went to the powder room so she wouldn't get stuck with him, but she was not rude to him.

At nine it was still light, and the same sun that had bullied her awake fourteen hours before was now lingering, washing the house and gardens with such a display of color that Amanda knew it was reluctant to set, hating to leave the scene of nighttime frivolity and joy. As she watched the end of sunset color she realized that she was exhausted. The feeling was only momentary, due probably to her overenthusiastic appreciation of the house. The time had come for her to stop looking at inanimate objects and concentrate for a change on human beings rather than material possessions.

Looking around for someone to join, she saw Gavin Driscoll standing at the entrance to the conservatory, talking to a pretty girl in a remarkably short miniskirt with a young man who was dressed like a Beatle. On impulse she decided to join them. Gavers, as everyone called him, had been Richard's best man and his roommate at Oxford. Amanda had been seated next to him a few nights before at one of the many prenuptial dinner parties and he had been nice to her. He had also been slightly drunk and had left her to go off and play backgammon with someone he described to her as a "pigeon," whatever that meant.

Gavers saw her approach. "Amanda!" he said, taking in her cream-colored silk dress, ignoring her eyes for her body in one aggressive appreciative glance. "Dear sister-in-law of my best friend, come and talk to us. No, just come and join us. You don't have much to say, as I remember."

Amanda found herself about to respond with a stinging remark. There it was again. The arrogance of a no one, patronizing her. Gavin Driscoll had no title, no fortune—he was nothing more than a common gambler. No, she would not rise to the bait, not this time. Instead, in a soft tone she said the first thing that popped into her mind.

"Gavers, how can you say that I don't make conversation? The last time I saw you, you left me alone at the table to go off with someone you referred to as a pigeon. You seem to prefer the wrong birds." Laughing, but looking at him with serious eyes, she linked her arm through his and moved her breast against his dinner jacket.

There was a burst of genuine laughter, which pleased her. Perhaps it wasn't that difficult to put out all that ridiculous talk.

"Amanda!" Gavers said, folding her hand into his. "I feel a distinct need to be alone with you. Adieu, dear friends, whoever you are. We are away." He doffed an imaginary hat in the air and led her quickly through the crowded library, down the long gallery, then into the vast domed entrance hall and outside to the stone terrace. They were alone, the great entrance doors open behind them, twenty wide stone steps beneath them. Gavers sat her down, positioning her with her back against a gigantic bronze urn filled with white geraniums and trailing ivy.

"Stay," he commanded her, as if giving an order to a dog. "Mr. Brown," he said, catching sight of the butler, "Mr. Brown, do you think it would be possible for you to bring a bottle of that excellent champagne and two immaculate glasses to us, quickly? An emergency, you know."

"Of course, Mr. Driscoll. At once." Mr. Brown had known all of Richard's friends since their early childhood. Gavin Driscoll had grown up in this house.

Gavers sat beside Amanda and put an arm around her shoulders. A last line of deep reddish-purple edged the horizon. The rest of the sky was dark and the stars had begun to shine.

"Christ," he said, "isn't it beautiful? I would like to own all of Hampshire. Wouldn't you?"

"Yes," Amanda said. "I would." Mr. Brown appeared with the requested bottle of champagne in a silver bucket plus the two immaculate glasses. He set them down beside Gavers and poured them each a glass. "Will that be all, sir?" he asked, gliding smoothly back into the house without waiting for the answer.

"Amanda," Gavers said. He seemed to start every sentence by announcing her name. "Would you like to make love? There is a faded blue satin couch under the servants' stairway in the left wing, not more than thirty seconds from here, and I have slept drunk on it more times than I care to remember and I have always known that I wanted to make love there. Does that appeal to you? Can we do something about that?"

"No," Amanda said, without moving out of the circle of his arm, but without stiffening as she usually did. "But I would love to own Hampshire. Can we do something about that?"

Gavers kissed her on the lips. He didn't change his position; he simply turned his head and kissed her.

"I knew there was something to you," he said. "We are so much alike. Did you know that? We are both after the same thing. Not Hampshire. Are you sure about the lovemaking? I wish you would at least give me a try. I am very good at it, extremely good, I've been told, and you are like a beautiful animal. A clouded leopard, actually. Have you ever seen one?"

"No," Amanda said. She remembered that Gavers had been born and brought up in Africa and that his father had been an ambassador in several out-of-the-way posts. Gavers had been sent back to England to school and now he had two passions, one of them gambling. Earlier on, he had discovered he had a substantial talent for it. He would bet on anything in high style, with anyone, and he usually won. The other passion—a quieter and deeper one—was for rare animals and birds.

"The clouded leopard is the most beautiful of all the carnivores. You have the exact coloring but your teeth are not as good. The clouded leopard has the strongest teeth of all the cats. I'm only being rude because I want you."

"What do you mean, we are both after the same thing?" she asked, feeling sure that her refusal would result in his getting up and leaving her now. She was not carrying the conversation—she was being literal again instead of light.

"There aren't that many Richard Marstons. There are hundreds, nay thousands, of you's and me's. We have to trade up and we want to. Both of your sisters have married well. It's up to you now to marry better. My best friend has married someone he loves because he can afford to do exactly as he pleases. We can't do that, either of us. You and I have to marry titles. Don't you know that?"

He looked out across the horizon once again and she watched the expression on his face. He wasn't handsome, although he had a beautiful mouth. His arms were long and he had a barrel chest, but he wasn't tall and his blond hair was already beginning to thin on top. Even so, there was an intense physical presence about him. She did want him.

Her sense of loneliness—of inadequacy—came back. Suddenly there were no answers to his questions, not even brittle ones. She could think of nothing to say. She sensed he was right about their being alike but she didn't care. Whatever it was that had bolstered her up and enabled her to make superficial conversation for a small part of this one great party was deserting her now.

A midnight-blue Bentley drew up to the house on the gravel driveway beneath them. The man who got out of the car and came up the steps toward them was tall, a little over six feet. His hair was dark-brown and shining, parted sharply, and had a pronounced white streak on one side. He had a look of the past—not a century past, but of a time that was not quite today. The mark of the aristocrat was on his face, in his shoulders, in the way he walked. There was no lack of confidence about him, nor in the cut of his dark-blue pin-striped suit. Savile Row, of course. His shirt collar probably had been designed and made to measure to his neck, the style decided upon some years ago. Turnbull and Asser, of course. Amanda instinctively felt sure that all the clothes that hung in his closets were exactly alike, made as he wanted them made with little variation and worn as he chose to wear them. His body was large in frame, and although not graceful, it was the body of an athlete. He was a rugby type, she thought.

"Charles!" Gavers said, pulling Amanda to her feet and once again making his definitive announcement of a Christian name. There was an entire world of difference in the way Gavers pronounced "Mr. Brown" when he summoned the head butler and the way he said "Charles" to the man who had now come face to face with them.

"Where the hell have you been?" Gavers asked genially. "I couldn't believe that you would miss this wedding. This is Amanda Gordon, Davina's sister." Facing Charles, Amanda could see that his eyes were deep blue.

"Flight from bloody Geneva was canceled," Charles whatever-his-name-was said. "I had to charter, and halfway over France an engine went out. I've been on the ground all day in Rouen trying to get another plane." He and Gavers were slapping each other heartily on the shoulders. Charles did not even glance at Amanda and made no attempt to acknowledge the introduction.

"Come on then," Gavers said. "Let's go in. Toast the bride and all that." Charles walked through the door first, striding ahead of them down the hall.

"Who's Charles?" Amanda asked, irritated. "Doesn't he speak to a woman when he's introduced? Or look at her?"

"No," Gavers said, laughing. "As a matter of fact, he doesn't speak to women at all. Oh, to one or two occasionally. Your sister is one of them. Amanda, listen, this is going to be the longest night of the year. Stay near us if you can—come back to us. Don't go home, please. I'm going to gamble now. Charles is the pigeon I left you for last time." He gave her a wicked smile and took her hand and kissed it. There was an odd look in his eyes.

"Amanda, his name is Charles Keating. His father is old and when he dies, Charles will become the Eleventh Earl of Warrington. See if you can get him to speak to you. If all else fails, there's me and the blue couch. I'll find you later."

He was gone. He had somehow left her standing with a group of people she had never seen before. He had done it so smoothly. She was alone again, as before. She excused herself and went to the powder room. She looked at herself in the mirror. She didn't look tired at all, and she wasn't. It was going to be a long night, just as Gavers said, and she was not going to miss one moment of it.

Charles Keating. Lord Keating.

He doesn't speak to women. Think of that.

The future Earl of Warrington.

★ ★ ★

Amanda watched Charles Keating the rest of the long night. She hardly took her eyes off him and what finally began to fascinate her was that through the hours, until well after four in the morning, he was never once even slightly aware of her careful scrutiny. She didn't mean for him to be aware of her at all, didn't want him to be, but her observation was so intense that she fully expected that at some point he would catch her at it. He might sense he was being watched, or think she was flirting with him or trying to get his attention for some reason. But no, never for one moment was any notice taken. He was completely oblivious to her.

She learned a great deal about him, storing carefully away the most minute detail in what she made up her mind to call her Keating file. Charles Keating had everything she wanted, represented everything she aspired to, and with mounting excitement, she knew with certainty that she could and was going to have him.

She watched him at the backgammon table, gambling for five pounds a point with Gavers and some of the others. She watched him carefully with Davina, since Gavers had told her that her sister was one of the few women he spoke to. She watched him when he danced, which he did twice, the first time with Elizabeth Marston and then with Davina. He was slightly clumsy on the dance floor but not too bad a dancer and seemed to enjoy it. She watched him when he went to the buffet in the dining room and got a huge load of food on his plate. She watched him —much later, when breakfast was served and they all sat together in the conservatory—take an equally huge amount of scrambled eggs and sausages, which he bolted down quickly. She watched him drink and she counted his drinks, as he went from champagne to red wine to cognac and, finally, to straight gin, which he took with an inordinate amount of ice for an Englishman. She saw, standing behind him at the backgammon table, the white stripe of hair that was so definitive and observed a four-inch fine-line scar on the back of the left side of his head at the hairline. She took in his scent, and decided that it was a combination of his hair oil and Guerlain's Cuir Russe. He was apparently comfortable only in the company of men, and as she watched she decided that he didn't dislike the ladies, he simply didn't know what to do with them. His big body appealed to her, and she suspected, too, that if he kept eating and drinking the way he was now, he would go to fat in another ten years. She liked the deep tone of his voice and found that often when he spoke, there was a pomposity about him. The establishment Englishman. She felt he was deeply shy in some ways, and probably secretive. But she also saw the sweetness of him, a quality he tried to cover in his pompous way, and—as the time passed—she knew he was really quite naïve, like a schoolboy sportsman who wanted never to grow up.

She was perfectly sure he knew practically nothing about sex and nothing whatsoever about lovemaking. That was a plus for her.

Gavers had lived up to his word and returned to get her after the first gambling session, drawing her in with whoever was around them. By the time Richard and Davina left she knew several of the men and women by their Christian names, and she was known as Davina's sister, er, Amanda, was it?

She marveled at the party. The British upper classes had a seemingly endless capacity for enjoying themselves; they were noisily consuming vast quantities of drink, dancing wildly, and laughing even louder as night turned into day. They were never, never going to let this party come to an end. Elizabeth Marston left them at two, as did Amanda's mother, trailed by Pamela. Amanda danced a few times. She danced with Gavers, who was quite drunk by then and pressed his body close to hers and reminded her noisily about the blue couch, and with the Nigels and Roberts and Williams and Dereks and Peregrines. But all the time she kept her sights on Charles Keating, who never once noticed her, looked at her, spoke to her, or even considered asking her to dance. That was exactly the way Amanda wanted it.

At dawn Gavers brought her back to Lea Place. She felt the steady physical attraction that had grown between them, but she knew much better than to allow herself to be diverted for one instant with Gavers.

She did let him kiss her. He pulled her down on the flowery couch in the sitting room, his hands roaming her body, prepared to make love, but she pulled herself up and teased him out of it. He was not angry; she found to her relief Gavers could take it or leave it.

"But some day?" he asked, as she took his hands off her.

"Of course," Amanda said, knowing if she started with him it would be the end of them. Having him a little bit on the hook could only be helpful to her.

"It's meant to be," Gavers told her, holding her face in his hands. "I like girls who say no. Why are you saying no? How about having dinner with me tonight?"

"No," Amanda said. "I can't. I've got a new job as an assistant to a producer of a film company in Wardour Street. I have to go home with my mother and sister later today and move my things into town. I've found a flat in Lennox Gardens. Maybe next week."

"Ah," Gavers said. "Good. Then I don't have to commute to Hampshire to see you. Besides, I want you to see my house in town. The only thing I'm missing is a clouded leopard in my bed."

Amanda laughed. She knew he would keep pursuing her and he could be useful to her, very useful in her master plan.

"Gavers, you've got to go. I did have a wonderful time, all because of you."

"Amanda," Gavers said. "We are going to be together soon, for dinner at least. Do you have a phone number in town yet?"

"Yes," Amanda said, and gave it to him.

"Good night, good morning, my beautiful little cat. Don't forget me."

"I won't," Amanda said, giving him a warm kiss on the lips.

On her way upstairs to the rose-printed chintz room, she gave full thought once more to Charles Keating. It would happen. It was only a matter of time. What was it that Gavers had told her? Oh, yes.

She had *her* pigeon too.

London, July 1964

T wo weeks later the phone rang in her flat in Lennox Gardens. She was fairly well settled and enjoying her privacy more than she had anticipated.

"Amanda, come for the weekend. Please come!"

Davina's voice, warm and kind, was welcome to Amanda. She had been waiting for her call.

"Davina, why? You've just gotten back this minute from your honeymoon. How was Venice?"

"I'll tell you if you come. There's a golf tournament this weekend, naturally, and Richard will be gone all day so we can talk. Besides, I need some help with the house. Your sense of color—there are some things that need changing."

"Who else is coming?" Amanda asked, crossing her fingers. She couldn't believe she was crossing her fingers, that she already knew somehow what Davina was going to say.

"The usual golfers . . . Gavers . . . Jeremy Morton. Do you remember him?"

"Jeremy Morton? No. Should I? Who else?"

"Not really. And Charles, of course. Charles Keating."

The name she wanted to hear. Charles Keating.

"Richard will bring you—he'll call you before he leaves the office. Oh, darling, I forgot to ask you about the new flat. It must be marvelous to be away from Mum and in your own place. How is it?"

"Wonderful. Tiny. Three flights up. Minuscule sitting room, and a bedroom darker than a cave, now that I have to get up in the morning and get to Wardour Street before nine."

"I can't wait to see it. Bring me some smoked salmon from Harrods. Enough for ten for dinner on Friday. I'll pay you back. The weather's lovely."

"I know," Amanda said. "I can't wait to see you." She rang off. *Charles Keating,* she thought. *It's you I can't wait to see.*

CHAPTER 4

"I think Gavers is quite smitten with you," Davina said, watching as Amanda unpacked. Knowing she hated single beds and any shred of light in her room in the morning, Davina had put her sister in a seldom-used tiny spare bedroom that occasionally accommodated an overflow houseguest. The walls and the double bed were covered with dark-blue hessian cloth and there were only a few pieces of furniture: a chair and a chest of drawers with a mirror over it, all lacquered white. There wasn't a rose anywhere. Amanda loved it.

Davina went on: "Why didn't you drive down with him? He rang up Richard and told him that he'd fetch you, and then you called to say you were still coming with Richard. What's all this about?"

"I like Gavers," Amanda said. "But I have a distinct feeling that he looks upon me as his weekend bit of crumpet. I'm not going around paws-up for a womanizing gambler who has temporarily run out of titles to lay."

"Oh, la!" Davina said, laughing. "He's nicer than most of them, you know."

"I do know," Amanda said, "and even though I like him quite a lot, I am going to make it tough for him."

"Well, at least keep him on the hook, darling," Davina said. She did wish that things were easier for Amanda. Men were bowled over by her looks and her extraordinary sex appeal, and many of them seemed to treat her as if she were a whore—a fact Davina resented. Amanda dealt with men ruthlessly and Davina understood. It was all a façade that stemmed from hurt in her young years. Amanda had promiscuously taken one of the local boys into her bed. It was her first passionate sexual attachment and she had been devastated when he walked off and left her a few weeks later. He'd quickly had enough of her—perhaps too much. In retaliation, Amanda took on his best friend, who unceremoniously dumped her after a few nights, just as the first one had. She had been deeply hurt the first time and infuriated the second. If this was all men wanted of her, then she'd show them. Davina could sympathize when Amanda carried out undeclared warfare on the men who came later. She did go to bed with quite a few of them, but in trying to defend her own fragile sexuality, a slashing, ego-stinging criticism became part of her nature.

Gavers would be good for her. He was more sophisticated than even his closest friends, and he was nicer, as Davina had pointed out. There was a sweetness about him, along with a wild charm. An affair with Gavers would draw Amanda into a magical circle, Davina's own circle since she'd married Richard. Anyhow, Gavers was crazy for Amanda, and a summer romance might teach her that all men were not bastards.

"Richard says that Gavers really loves women and is sensitive to them and has never hurt anyone. He makes friends forever."

"Nice," Amanda said. "But Gavers and I already have an understanding. We're not for each other. Don't worry, Davina, I'm not going to be nasty to him."

"I didn't mean that, darling. I just want you to have a good time, and the rest of them are hopeless. Robin is desperately in love with the Westminster girl you just met. Jeremy Morton is nice but I have this odd feeling that he might go gay. You're the excitement of the weekend. Charles is hopeless too."

"Why hopeless?" Amanda asked, carefully arranging her hair ribbons and scarves in the top drawer of the painted chest. She glanced at herself in the mirror. Funny, even the mention of his name brought her into some kind of sexual focus. She felt alive.

"He truly is uncomfortable with women and I'm sure it's because he is desperately shy," Davina said. "I know he quite likes me—which astonishes Richard. He says I'm the rare bird that Charles can communicate with, maybe because I'm sort of colorless and safely married to his best friend. My God, you two would be a disaster together. I don't dare put you next to him at dinner, not tonight or tomorrow."

Amanda turned actress in an instant.

"Davina," she said, eyes serious, voice imploring. "Please do seat me by him. I'd like to try to draw him out if I can. Let me have him tonight. If it works, fine—if I can get him to speak to me at all. Put Gavers on my other side; then he and Charles can talk over me, or I can at least have Gavers if his lordship refuses to speak to me. He's probably quite nice, poor sod."

"Not a bad plan. We're ten tonight, and thirty for dinner and dancing tomorrow. You just might hit it off with Charles if you really try. I've got to go and see about the table and the flowers now. Drinks are at nine or a little after. Dinner's at ten. I'm so glad you're here." Davina kissed Amanda on both cheeks.

"So am I," Amanda said. "So am I."

Charles Keating was not as unaware of Amanda Gordon as Amanda thought he was. He had indeed noticed her when Gavers introduced them the night of the wedding. He had not broken his habit of pretending that women did not exist, therefore there was no obligation or necessity to speak to them. Why should he? But he felt her watching him, felt her hardly take her eyes off him, and as the night wore on he became increasingly aware of her. She had piqued his curiosity. She was good-looking. She had arrived with Gavers and she'd left with Gavers later.

On the golf course he spoke to Gavers about her.

"Are you having at Davina's sister, whatever her name is?" he asked, taking a sand wedge from his bag and assessing the distance to the hole. It was about forty yards and the wind was at his back. Easy shot.

Gavers looked at him and laughed.

"You sly old coot. Do you want her?"

"Good God, no. I was just wondering if you'd taken up with her, as I haven't seen you much since the wedding because of all this French business of mine. She's bloody good-looking."

"That she is," Gavers said. "She's got a peculiar sort of man-hating character, not at all like Davina. But, Christ, she has sex appeal and I am certainly planning to get to know her much better over this weekend. What?"

"Bit of erotica about her," Charles said. He made a perfect shot with the wedge and his ball dropped seven inches from the hole. He had Gavers on this one.

"Yes. Nice for a change. What?"

Charles sighed. "Boff away, old boy. You can handle her."

Amanda came down for drinks as late as she possibly could. She had already decided her plan of action. Gavers was the first person who had to be taken care of; she had to get him out of her way and she knew how to do it.

Drinks were being served on the flagstone terrace that surrounded the swimming pool. In the late dusk the fat candles in hurricane globes were beginning to show their light. The men all stood gathered together, talking over the afternoon's golf, and tomorrow's. Davina and the women guests were sitting on blue-cushioned wicker couches beneath a wide deep-turquoise awning. What a pretty scene, Amanda thought, and what a serene life Davina had managed for herself.

The ubiquitous Mr. Brown was buttling tonight, on loan from Elizabeth Marston. When he appeared to announce dinner, Davina called over to Richard.

"Enough golf talk for the moment, darling." She took her husband's arm and led them into the dining room. Amanda immediately noticed, to her annoyance, a last-minute change in the seating. She had Charles on her left, which was fine, and Robin was on her right. Robin would spend his entire time mooning over the Westminster girl on his other side and she would have to talk to Charles or to no one. That was not according to her plan. She looked at Davina crossly, and saw from her expression that Robin had changed the seating. *Blast him,* Amanda thought.

The smoked salmon was served with an excellent chablis and, to her delight, Amanda found Gavers solving her problem for her. He had engaged Mary Westminster in conversation and seen to it that Robin was left out. Amanda and Robin chatted all through dinner, while Charles occupied himself with Davina. It was going to work out all right.

After dessert she turned to Charles, mouthing platitudes.

"I'm so sorry not to have had a chance to pay some attention to you," she said, in a patronizing tone. She was wearing a quiet blue-gray short chiffon dress, nothing spectacular, but she knew how well she looked. She was shaking slightly in anticipation. When she reached for a cigarette, he lit it with a gold Dunhill lighter and she concentrated on not letting her hand shake. God, he was the most marvelous-looking man she had ever seen. And a title went with the looks.

"You're Davina's sister, I know," he said. "And I understand you have a flat in town." He can't help himself, she thought. He just does sound stuffy and pompous. His next question was the one she was waiting for. "And what do you do?" he asked, lighting his own cigarette.

"I fuck," she said, looking straight into his eyes.

Charles nearly choked on the drag from his cigarette. His recovery was swift, however.

"Gavers?" he said, inclining his head in Gavers's direction.

"No," Amanda said. "You. Tonight." She rose from the table and went to Gavers, who had already risen and was ready to leave the dining room. Charles was left sitting alone, nonplussed, stunned.

"Gavers," he heard her say, "I thought we were going to be seated together. Never mind, we can be now. Shall we go back out on the terrace? I need a drink."

She never said another word to him for the rest of the evening, and Charles nearly went crazy trying to decide whether to go right up to bed or to get dead drunk . . . or what. He settled for a waiting game, and for conversation with Richard, who was talking about the best hotels in Venice.

Richard droned on, and this time it was Charles who played a better cat-and-mouse game than Amanda had with him. She could not possibly have been aware of his close attention as he talked quietly with Richard. There were none of the usual card games tonight. Davina had banned gambling for the evening—they gambled enough on the golf course all day. Charles was just as glad; he doubted if he could have concentrated on anything but Amanda. What the hell had she meant and what was she planning to do and how was she going to do it? Had she meant what she had said or was she just being a bitch? Gavers said she had a peculiar character. She had a peculiar tongue too.

He watched her with Gavers as they sat and talked. There was nothing between them, no flirtation. Gavers looked faintly bored. She had done something to turn him off. Christ, did she really mean what she had said? He'd soon know.

Tonight would be an early night, as they were teeing off at nine in the morning. What the hell was he to do now? He didn't know where her room was and he wasn't sure anymore where his own room was. Maybe she meant to stay down when all the others had gone to bed and have at it on one of the couches. Whatever she meant would soon be apparent.

Everyone was kissing everyone good night when he saw her coming toward him.

"Charles," she said. "Good luck tomorrow." That did it. She had been teasing him, slut that she was. Even so, he leaned down when she reached to give him a kiss on the cheek. He felt her breath on him as she whispered in his ear: "If you turn left when you come out of your room and come down the hall to the back steps, you will find a door slightly open to a sort of servant's room back there. If you don't, I'll understand." She was gone before he exhaled. He did not know he had been holding his breath.

★   ★   ★

Charles took off his clothes in his room, thanking God he had a room to himself. He didn't want Gavers to know about this right now. He didn't know about it right now himself. He put on the terry-cloth robe in the bathroom and his flat leather slippers. He opened the door and looked down the hall to see if the coast was clear. It was, so he followed her instructions until he found the slightly open door, just as she had said he would. He entered, closing the door softly behind him. The room was pitch-dark, and suddenly his back was against the wall. He felt a pair of soft hands reach for the belt on the robe and untie it. The same hands wound around his waist, and a body moved into his, breasts pushing against his chest, legs finding their way flat against his, hair, masses of hair and a small face against his chest and the hands again, this time taking him into them, rubbing him, stroking him, pulling at him. She was breathing heavily—no, not heavily, sharply, no, not sharply; she was breathing the way he was breathing, the sweet breath of pure desire. He reached for her head and the silky hair tumbling about it, and drew her face up to his and kissed her. He wished that he could see her, naked as he knew she was. There was some wonderful scent about her, not flowery, and her skin was like no skin he had ever touched. He couldn't tell who was touching the most but they were entwined now, still standing, still kissing, and he knew he was about to mate with someone in a way he had never mated before. Then her little hands and small arms came around his waist halfway and she was drawing him to the bed, wherever it was. She moved against him and somehow they were in the bed and she was on top of him, reaching for him and putting him in her, smoothly, smoothly, and with a movement he had never known before. Then she stopped moving, but she was on him, all over him, her hair in his mouth, her face on his, her breath on him. She was moaning softly into his ear. He could hardly contain himself and he knew he wasn't going to for long but he also knew that they were coming together, right now, and he came into her as if he had been waiting for her all his life. It wasn't over, not as long as they were sealed together and she was still moving, still moaning and still coming, as he was. Then the muscles inside her began to relax and she twined her arms around his neck and curled her body around him even more than it had been before and he felt the peace of aftermath and he searched for and found her lips again. She stopped him then, shushing him as if he were a baby. He heard her voice in his ear, softly. "I lied to you," she said, their two bodies closer than ever. "I don't fuck," she said. "With you, I make love."

It was a beginning. Even the night was just beginning.

Sex, until he met Amanda, had not been a motivating force in Charles Keating's life. He could take it or leave it, and he had taken it when the occasion presented itself under the proper circumstances. Those circumstances had most often been on trips to the Swiss mountains or the French Alpes-Maritimes with Gavers. It wasn't that he didn't love beautiful women—he did, but English girls had always made him nervous. They were too aggressively aware of his looks and his title and he had the uncomfortable feeling that the latter was of inordinate importance to them. He never allowed a girl to attach herself to him. He loved to dance and he enjoyed parties and social life as well as gambling, but he preferred sports, which he excelled in.

His seeming indifference drew women to him, bringing out their competitive instincts and making him wish they would simply go away. It never occurred to him that the day would not come when he would get married and have children, but that day seemed in a far and hazy future. Along with this sexual vagueness, he knew nothing of the ecstasy that could exist between a man and a woman. He had never been in love.

Amanda burst upon him like a rocket. She combined elements that threw him completely. Her frankness was startling at the least. She had the subtle looks and delicate coloring that appealed to him—the whiff of erotica he'd mentioned to Gavers—and she was quiet, not blatant, like most English women.

What Charles had not expected when he closed the bedroom door behind him and felt her hands upon him was the torrent of passion that came from him and found its repository in her. He never once thought of her as an experienced woman who could twist any man around her fingers sexually. It never occurred to him that she was a calculating schemer who was more interested in his title than any other girl had ever been. All he knew was that he had never felt nor tasted, seen nor smelled, heard nor wanted anyone the way he wanted her and had her. He knew beyond a doubt that they felt the same about each other. In that, he was right. He wanted her for once and for always. He would never let her go.

★ ★ ★

Amanda knew she had done her work well, but she was totally unprepared for the result. When Charles left her near dawn, "corridor creeping" back to his room—which was part and parcel of the fun of English country weekends—she fell asleep knowing he could easily betray her. Just another bit of crumpet she well might be, and it frightened her. Considering the insatiable passion they had shared, truly shared, through the whole long night, she doubted it, but men were men, as she had learned before, and Charles was a man.

She slept until noon, fighting off thoughts of him, hoping against hope that this time it would be different, that he would be different and that he did care for her and meant all the things he had said. He had held her before he left, stroking her hair, looking at her and running his hands along the length and width of her. "You are the most beautiful thing I have ever seen or known and I adore you. There's never been anyone like you. I'll see you this evening." With that he was gone.

He was besotted with her and it was this that unnerved her. When he came in from playing golf, he had come directly to her room and literally swept her into his arms, kissing her hungrily, and looking at her with adoration. This was not the man she had been intending to trap.

He pulled her down onto his lap on the one straight chair, eye to eye.

"Tell me you love me," he said. "Tell me now. Don't let me make a fool of myself if you don't. I don't want anyone to know about us because I want to keep you all to myself, but I can't play that game. They'll know the minute they see us together. Tell me that you love me."

"No," Amanda said, warm all over and disbelieving, "I don't love you. I loved you last night but that was then and now is now. Why should I love you?" She was teasing him and she knew he knew it, but she was more frightened than she had ever been. He was here with her, saying what she wanted him to say, holding her as if she belonged to him and as if he meant to hold her forever, but how long would that last? She thought she was so smart, but she wasn't. The same thing would happen all over again. He'd stay with her for a while, as long as it amused him, and then he, too, would leave her, just as the others had. She had to control him, and she had to control him by controlling herself.

"All right," he said. "I don't care if you make a fool of me then. I love you and I have never loved anyone before and that is never going to change. I'll prove it to you."

And he did. He'd left her then without another word and gone to his room to change. Fifteen minutes later he was back, resplendent in his dinner jacket, opening the door without knocking and taking her in his arms again. She was bare to the waist, her white chiffon dress still hanging on the closet door. "Jesus," he said, his hands on her breasts. "Put it on quickly or we'll never get out of here." He grabbed the dress and helped her step into it, hooking up the back for her, kissing her bare back and shoulders.

"Come on," he said. "We've got to go down there and face them. I am never going to leave you alone again."

And he didn't. They walked out onto the terrace together and he stayed beside her until dinner was announced. Davina took notice of their arrival together, and Gavers too. When they went in to dinner, they were seated together and Charles talked only to her, holding her hand under the table, going on about the things he loved to do. Had she been to Monte Carlo? They would go to Monte Carlo; there was a ball there in two weeks' time, and she would go with him. Would she? Could she? If not, she'd have to quit her job, which he had asked her all about. Then, in August, they'd be in Sardinia. It was the Aga Khan's racing week, all the finest sailing yachts would be there then, and they would stay with Karim in his house. No, they would stay in the hotel in Porto Cervo, the beautiful hotel where they could be more alone together than they would be if they were houseguests.

He was a changed man, putting Amanda in a state of consternation. Everything he said, he meant, and everything he said was spontaneous and full of fun. There wasn't a shred of his former arrogance or pomposity. He was joyous. When Gavers came to ask her to dance, Charles looked up at him, grinning.

"For a little while you may, old man, but not for long." Then he had cut in on them barely five minutes later, but not before Gavers had a chance to compliment her, in his way.

"Sorceress," Gavers had said. "What have you done to him? As if I didn't know. You're on your way, Amanda." It was odd, his using her Christian name last. His tone held a modicum of respect that Amanda heard clearly.

For the first and only time in her young life, Amanda was happy. She decided not to think anymore. It could all change tomorrow. She would be back in her flat in Lennox Gardens, going to work for an already declared lascivious producer in Wardour Street again on Monday. All this was almost too good to be true.

Charles Keating was not the only one who was hopelessly in love.

★ ★ ★

In the following weeks, they became inseparable. Charles had a small flat near Regent's Park, filled with books and family memorabilia and an astonishing wardrobe. There were clothes for skiing, bobsledding, tennis, and golfing. He must have had fifty sweaters. There were morning coats, dinner jackets, smoking jackets, robes, ties and socks, cummerbunds and vests, perfectly polished shoes, boots, and slippers. His suits almost without exception were either dark blue or gray with a narrow pin stripe.

He had hats for shooting everything from elephant to Oriental partridge, and he had guns, everything from small pistols to powerful rifles with telescopic sights to a matched pair of Purdey shotguns.

"My God," Amanda said. "I've never known a *woman* with a wardrobe like this. Where are you going to house it when you're fifty?"

"We'll have houses for it all," he said, drawing her down beside him. "These are mere necessities." He looked slightly ashamed. "I do love clothes, good clothes. I have a valet who comes in and takes care of things for me. Do you mind about all of them?"

Amanda melted. "Not the way you look in them. I just didn't realize how much it took to put you together." She loved the way he dressed. He was a gentleman and an aristocrat and it stuck out all over him.

"I have something here that I can't wear but I think you can," he said, getting up and rummaging around in a drawer, finally pulling out a leather Garrard box. Amanda opened it and found a diamond dragonfly pin on a black velvet pad. It was about three inches long, obviously the exquisite workmanship of the Victorians. It was a lovely piece.

"Do you like it?" he asked. "I could tell you it was my grandmother's but it wasn't. I love jewelry and I bought this for you at auction the other day."

Amanda started to cry. He had caught her unaware again. He had treated her like a queen ever since the first night. He treated her like a lady; he treated her like a goddess; he treated her like a little girl. He was unfailingly courteous to her.

"Darling," he said, pleased with himself, "come to bed."

Late summer 1964

They spent most of their time in her small flat. Amanda talked the lascivious producer into letting her work solely in the afternoons, not wanting to give up everything to live only for Charles. She was secure now in their love, but a tiny doubt would creep in occasionally and she decided that working while Charles was gambling in the afternoons was the wise thing to do. He would come back to her around eight, bringing wonderful foods for them to eat and marvelous wines to drink. Every weekend they were with Davina and Richard in the country. Gavers had disappeared to India for a few months and Amanda was glad. She didn't want him around watching her, as he did.

One night in Lennox Gardens, she had one of her nightmares. The car was burning and Charles was in it and she was going to lose him. She came awake with Charles's arms around her, soaking wet and weeping, terrified. She told him then about her father and she was struck with the thought that Charles was like a father to her: He was taking care of her the way her own poor father had not had the chance to. He was man; he was father; he was friend.

He was lover. They were lovers. Deep inside she understood that there was something unusually strong in the sexual partnership between them, and that here she had the edge. Wild as she was about him, she still held the upper hand. All she had to do was look at him a certain way—and she did, often—and he was hers.

"You're a devil," he said one morning when they were in the country. "Richard's waiting downstairs now. We're late already."

"Go," she said, looking steadily at him. She was propped up in the bed, wearing the short lavender satin nightgown. She parted her legs, ever so slightly, not taking her eyes off him, and putting her foot softly up under his tennis shorts.

"Go?" he said. "I don't do anything but come when you look at me like that."

"Then come," she said, opening her legs a little farther. "Come here, darling."

CHAPTER 5

Charles and Amanda were married in the chapel of Saint Margaret's Westminster, on September 26. Her wedding dress was made of shining ivory-cream satin, simple to the point of perfection, with a round neck and long sleeves that came to handkerchief points on her wrists. She carried a single calla lily, and wore a strand of forty-three flawless and rare Australian opals given to her that morning by Charles just after he and Lady Warrington had taken them from the family bank vault. The Warrington opals. Her hair was in a soft bun on the nape of her neck. Her illusion tulle veil was attached to a crown of pearl-encrusted leaves, and it flowed out over the long train of her dress. She had never looked more beautiful. Or as regal.

Charles was handsome in his morning coat with a gray vest and a fawn-gray satin tie, striped trousers, and a white carnation in his buttonhole. Amanda could hardly look at him, he was so stunning to her. They were both living in a romantic ecstasy they thought would never end.

Her sisters were her only attendants, and they were both elated by Amanda's beauty and the coup of the wedding. Gavers was best man, and Charles had asked Richard, Robin, Jeremy, and Neil to be his ushers.

Shafts of late September sunshine dappled the bride and groom and members of the wedding as they piled into chauffeur-driven Rolls-Royces and Bentleys after the ceremony and made their way to the Hyde Park Hotel, where five hundred friends had been invited to the reception. Charles's parents had arranged for everything and paid for it all. Champagne flowed, music played, and hundreds of calla lilies in tall crystal vases vied for attention with the masses of white camellias that were piled into silver bowls on every table. It was the most glorious occasion, the happiest and best party ever. Everyone toasted the bride and groom with magnum after magnum of champagne, enjoying themselves enormously. When Amanda and Charles left the reception, off on their honeymoon to Venice, everyone laughed and cried as they bid goodbye to the superbly handsome and fortunate young couple.

Amanda was two months, seventeen days, twenty hours, and seventeen minutes pregnant.

The Wyndham Club was situated in one of the finest eighteenth-century houses still standing in London. The Upper Brook Street mansion had been derelict and about to be torn down when Gavin Driscoll had succeeded in saving it. In return for a long lease that cost practically nothing, he promised to restore the house to its former glory. It had suffered considerable war damage, then neglect in the years afterward. Gavers knew there were very few people who wanted to battle the problems of restoring and staffing such a grandiose mansion, even if they could afford it. But he wanted to. The house was the perfect setting for his gambling club and putting it back together became a passion with him. The roof was gone, the wiring was a hodgepodge of potential fire, and there was no heating. The kitchens would have been inadequate in the most unenlightened decades of the eighteenth century, but the rooms all had superb proportions and the double Venetian stairway between the first and second floors, with its domed ceiling, was of such classic beauty that from the beginning Gavers never failed to marvel at it.

The restoration took more than two years and was both painstaking and frustrating, but when the Wyndham Club finally opened, Gavers realized that it had been worth every moment of sacrifice and every trip to his bankers to beg for additional funds in order to complete it. Liveried attendants greeted members when they arrived, and a major domo and head barman saw to every need. On the ground floor, the sound of backgammon dice could be heard. The ballroom above was used as the main gaming room, and the atmosphere was far less casual there. The familiar click of the roulette ball as it fell into the wheel and the subtle noise of cards being drawn from the *chemin de fer* shoe were the main sounds. There was always a faint scent of liquor and cigar smoke, enough to know that it was a club rather than a home, but it quickly became a home to Gavers and the members he drew into the magic postwar circle he surrounded himself with.

The inner circle of the Wyndham, as it was soon referred to, consisted of five men aside from Gavers, each of whom contributed in his own way to the cachet and structure of the club. Charles Keating was a permanent fixture from the day the doors opened, and as a passionate gambling aristocrat, it was he who set the tone. Richard Marston and Jeremy Morton had both put in some money, and although neither of them was a serious gambler, their social connections were invaluable. Robin Bryce lent little more than his immense charm, but it, too, was an important element. The fifth man was Neil Riggs, and he was the solid business backbone of the Wyndham. Gavers needed a man he could trust.

Neil was a small man with dark hair and a ferret's eyes and the capacity to fade into the woodwork while he oversaw everything that was happening. His skin was pallid white and the dark beard that shadowed his pale face was constant, regardless of how long it had been since he shaved. There was a neat rapier quality about him. Once, he had driven racing cars nervelessly, then gotten bored with it and left the circuit. He knew the gambling world and it was Neil who decided which croupiers worked for Gavers and which did not. He had no pretensions about cutting a social figure. That sort of snobbery had no appeal for him; it was the intrigue of gambling that fascinated him. His wife had more than enough social background for both of them. Her father had once been the Lord Chief Justice, and she had taken a degree in architecture at Bristol University and worked for three years in London before marrying Neil. She had given up her career with the birth of their first child and infinitely preferred life in the country to London. The Riggses had a roaming Victorian house in Kent, an hour or so south of London. As a country-bred girl, Rosie Riggs was not bothered by Neil's spending most of his time at the club. She came, as Davina Marston did, when they were bid to parties, but it was not the centering factor in their lives and it was obvious that Gavers wanted wives on the scene only occasionally. Jeremy and Robin were bachelors who constantly brought beautiful women to the club—which suited Gavers fine.

Gambling alone was not all that Gavers was interested in, but it was his primary source of income. He knew how much money could be made and he meant to make every pound he could, in order to support his consuming passion for beautiful animals and birds. He was gradually acquiring a small but magnificent collection, including a pair of clouded leopards, which he prized. Clouded leopards were almost extinct in the world, a fact that caused Gavers real pain. Obviously, such wild creatures could not be kept in London, so he set about looking for a place in the country. He finally found the hundred or so acres he needed, south of London by little more than an hour. There was a practically derelict house on the property but it was Georgian and could be fixed up. The place was called Melbridge, and, in addition to land, it had several large ponds for his birds. He had managed to bring back a few pairs of Japanese cranes from a trip to East Africa and some equally rare Seychelles doves. He commissioned Lord Snowdon to design an aviary for them, where they would seem as free as they were in Snowdon's Regent's Park aviary.

Gavers knew that keeping exquisite birds and animals in captivity was a particular pleasure of the privileged rich, as well as a source of income. At Woburn Abbey and Longleat, both the Duke of Bedford and the Marquess of Bath collected less discriminatingly, but with an eye to luring tourists in order to defray the enormous costs of supporting their stately homes. Gavers, however, had no intention of letting his collection be seen by anyone except himself and his friends. He wanted no money-draining palace or castle. For his purposes, Melbridge was perfect.

Robin teased him. "We should address you as 'Sir Noah,' " he said. "Melbridge is your ark."

"I like to spend money on my friends," Gavers replied, not displeased with Robin's quip. "I have only a dozen close friends, as you know, and more than half of them are either four-footed or winged."

"And some of them are members of the Club," Robin teased on, knowing that Gavers's misanthropic feelings were real.

Pretty girls were more welcome than wives at the Wyndham. Amanda soon learned that the club was a masculine domain and she was proud that Charles took her there as often as he did. The long hours of gambling were of no interest to her and she often dined with him and then left on her own and came home. Her pregnancy had made her lazy. She liked lolling around in bed, not doing much of anything, and she was delighted that Charles had the Wyndham. If he wasn't going to work at a regular job, he had to have something to do and the Wyndham filled time nicely.

January 1965

"I've found a house I think will do," Charles said, pulling off his overcoat. He threw a wad of fifty-pound notes on top of the chest of drawers and tucked a number of neatly folded ones into the neckline of Amanda's blouse, winking at her as he did so. She fixed him a gin on the rocks in a heavy crystal double old-fashioned glass.

"Where?" she asked, handing him the drink and settling down in his lap in the big leather wing chair. He patted her now abundant tummy and nuzzled her neck, taking in the scent of her that stirred him always. It was a routine they had gotten into, one they both looked forward to. Right after the wedding they had decided to keep his flat and give up hers while they looked for a new place to live. Amanda had practically nothing to move into Regent's Park—which was just as well, as it could not accommodate much more than Charles's copious wardrobe. She was out and about on everyday errands, but she was always at home before he arrived from his regular afternoon gambling session. He played bridge one or two afternoons a week and backgammon the others. If he won, he always gave her a little to spend on nothing and if he'd lost and was depressed about it, she would persuade him into thinking about something else. He had been winning quite a lot lately.

"Chelsea," he said, "near Royal Hospital. It's a nice house. Nothing grand about it, but the price was good and the lease is a long one."

"Ooooh," Amanda said. "Chelsea. How marvelous! What's it like and how did you find it?"

She had been looking, too, only to discover that the available houses were all either too large or needed so much done to them that it would cost a fortune and take forever. Charles wanted a house, not a flat. "So we can have a dog. And a garden. And a baby," he'd said.

"In that order?" Amanda teased him. Chelsea! One of the best parts of London.

"It's actually on Royal Hospital Road. It's brick, rather plain-looking Georgian on the outside, but five stories and it has a nice garden. David Bartle's been in it for a few years now but he's being transferred to America. I've pretty much told him that we will take over the lease from him, but I want you to see it. We can go at noon tomorrow."

"Marvelous, darling. Have you seen the inside?"

"Not really—just the garden and the ground floor with David for a quick run-through. It has five bedrooms and I think it will do fine."

Amanda loved the house. So much space! Charles was right about its being nice without being grand, but it thrilled her to be going to live in Chelsea, near the great Christopher Wren Royal Hospital and the beloved Chelsea pensioners.

Charles knew well that the house he'd taken was nothing special but he had gotten a long lease and it was a perfectly fine house. They would no doubt move to a larger one in a few years' time.

There was an ample dining room on the ground floor at the front and a small study plus an entrance to a walled garden in the back. The kitchen was in the basement. The entire garden area was paved in flagstone, so no struggling grass had to fight for existence in the shade thrown by two large elm trees. Amanda decided that as soon as spring came she would fill huge terra cotta pots and long wooden planter boxes with masses of white azaleas. They could easily entertain a hundred friends for cocktails on the ground floor and in the garden, without ever having to spill over into the first-floor drawing room, which ran the entire length of the house. It had once been two rooms, but now it had become one, paneled in a mellow pine. There was a fireplace on one wall and lovely views of the garden at the back. Amanda began making mental lists of those who would be sent engraved cards for her first "at home." "Lady Keating. At Home. Wednesday, May the fourth." She knew how life would be in her house on the Royal Hospital Road, how grand it was going to be.

Moving in was a happy time for them. Charles's not having to go to work meant that he could devote himself to the house. It was his first real home, aside from his bachelor digs in Regent's Park. Now, with his luck riding high, he could be more than generous about having the house done up properly, and he was. They rarely disagreed about anything. Amanda's sense of color was superb and her choice of beautiful fabrics for the couches and chairs and curtains pleased Charles enormously.

Most exciting to both of them was an unexpected windfall from Charles's parents. Longholt, the family seat of the Warringtons in Derbyshire, had been sold even before Charles was born. Growing up in the gloom of the dreary Tudor house that his family preferred, Charles had occasionally dreamed about Longholt. It must have been quite something. His mother had once shown him pictures taken of it. "You cannot possibly imagine," his mother told him, making a gesture of despair with her hands, "how dreadful it was to live there. The rooms were all huge and the corridors were hideously cold always. We clung to the fireplaces for dear life most of the year. I couldn't wait to get away from the unending bills and the problems of Longholt. The dry rot."

Charles had seen by then how some of his friends—most of his friends—lived. He only wished he could have seen Longholt, where generations of his family had lived.

His mood sweetened with the arrival of the first van from storage. "Charles, dear," his mother had said, "there are things from Longholt that have been stored away for years. I'm sure you might be able to use some of what's there and you're welcome to any and all of it." The Warrington heritage, lying fallow in storage through all the years, was a treasure trove. Amanda was in a state of near ecstasy as carton after carton was opened to reveal the trappings of her husband's family.

"Your parents must be daft," Amanda said, watching as two men carefully hung a particularly fine Georgian mirror in the entrance hall. "How could anyone not want to make use of at least some of that exquisite crested porcelain and this divine monogrammed silver? It weighs a ton. How could they possibly not have wanted to live with—to look at some of these pictures? I don't understand them at all."

"I never have," Charles said.

They saw the senior Warringtons rarely. Richard Warrington was not in the best of health; in fact he suffered from chronic heart trouble and serious circulatory problems. Lady Warrington—Amanda still could not cope with thinking of her as Penelope—watched over him carefully. They now lived quietly in a large flat in Wandsworth, still fairly active with Labour matters but hampered by the Earl's declining health. Amanda did not dare even dream about the day when Charles's father would be gone. When that time came, she would be the Countess of Warrington. Lady Keating was one thing—it was fine for the moment—but to be the Countess of Warrington was something else altogether.

"Charles, look at all this linen," she said, pawing through a large carton. Six dozen damask napkins, yellowed with age, were embroidered with a small crown over the Warrington family crest. "And on the list it says there are one hundred and forty-four crystal water goblets and seven dozen finger bowls."

"We should sell them to Gavers," Charles said, grinning at her, pleased to be the possessor of Longholt's treasures. "Never mind that stuff. Look at this." He held up a faience figure of a parrot, about fifteen inches high. "It's Höchst, couldn't be anything else with that perfect coloring. Worth thousands."

Amanda loved it when Charles was excited about something. He dropped pronouns and prepositions, and got stuffy and pompous to cover his delight. She took the brilliantly painted bird in her hands and gasped at its beauty.

"Who's Mr. Höchst?" she asked, impressed as always by Charles's considerable knowledge of antique porcelains and objets d'art. He really knew so much.

"Not a him—it's a place. Where porcelain was made. Faience. It was probably painted by Zeschinger. German, eighteenth century. Good stuff."

"Well, it's going by the window in your study where it can look out into the trees. I wish there was another one—we could put a pair of them on the mantel."

Charles laughed. "You little fool. Half the world would give an arm and a leg to have one Höchst and you want a pair of them. Greedy girl. Girl after my own heart."

In a month's time they had moved in and the house was almost complete. Charles's favorite room was his red-walled, plaid-carpeted study on the ground floor, where the Höchst bird did indeed look out of the window into the trees. Amanda's was their pale-beige and green bedroom two stories above it. Among other things in the treasure trove of Warrington possessions, she had found half a dozen opaline plates and bottles, which she had put on her dressing table, the glowing sharp blues and greens sparkling within the serenity of the room. She still couldn't believe her good fortune.

Once they were settled, Charles's habits proved to be quite regular. His life was gambling. He was registered as a gambler for tax purposes in the United Kingdom, and as the first member and founding partner with Gavers at the Wyndham, he had discovered the perfect setting for the life he wanted to lead. He explained it to Amanda.

"Nothing interests me as much as gambling—even at sports, not just the wheel or the tables or the board. I gamble on every golf shot. I bet when I ski down a mountain. I take a chance that the horse is going to win. It's a deal I make with time and the odds, and it excites me when nothing else does. Except you. I even bet myself that you would come along. I didn't have time to go out and look for you and then all of a sudden, there you were. I won you."

Amanda was more than content with Charles's chosen profession. It meant they would go to glamorous places like Biarritz or Monte Carlo or Saint-Moritz, so he could gamble and she could be the beautiful young Lady Keating. The setting of the Wyndham Club pleased her as well. Perhaps she and Charles would have a house like that some day. Meanwhile, she was content with the one they had. On top of it all she was going to give birth to a child who would be titled. Amanda had long ago decided that she was going to have a boy. Lord Patrick Anthony Henry Keating, future Earl. That name had a ring to it.

Each day, Charles would leave the house about noon and go to one of his clubs—St. James's or White's—to meet friends and indulge himself in the first Bombay gin martini of the day. Then it was on to the Wyndham. On Thursdays, like clockwork, he played bridge with a regular group after lunching at the Wyndham. He was at the club for his usual drink and the same lunch the other four days of the week. Amanda made fun of the predictable nature of his habits. "A private detective could make quick mincemeat of you," she told him. "You must have had the same thing for lunch for the last ten years. 'A Bombay martini, barman,' " she mimicked. " 'And, captain, in half an hour his lordship

will have some potted shrimp as a starter and then the cold roast beef.
But if it happens to be winter, he'll have the roast beef hot. And pink.' "

"I'll give you something hot and pink," he said, reaching for her.
Pregnant, she was warmer and more exciting to him than ever. When
she had first told him about the baby, he had been amazed at his own
reaction. Instead of cursing the fates and wanting to get away from
being trapped into marriage, he felt wanted, needed for the first time in
his life, and he liked the feeling. Maybe it was the way she had told him
about the baby that had made him want to marry her at once. He'd
awakened about noon in the same bed where they had first made love in
the country. Lying on his side, he had opened his eyes and found himself
looking at right angles at her naked body outlined against the white-
painted door, her back against it. It was the only place in the small room
where a full-length view was possible. He had discovered that she loved
posing naked for him, desiring him, making him desire her. Dressed, she
was subdued, camouflaged like a sparrow. Nude, as she was now, she
was shining, or so it seemed to him. Her skin was lustrous, her hair wild
gold, and her lips were moist. Her body was perfect and she was point-
ing everything at him, her nose, her nipples. She was even tilting her
pelvis at him, the slight movement he now knew so well, bringing him to
the same state of insatiable desire that he always felt for her.

"Come here," he muttered, voice still thick with sleep and tinged with
an about-to-be-satisfied lust. "Come back to bed. I want to make love to
you."

"Oh, no," she said, "you come here. There are three of us in this
room now and we have a decision to make. If you don't want there to be
three of us, then you can get up and leave and I won't care. I'll still be
the two of us. You can't ever take you away from me now—I'll have you
forever. But if you would like to be alone, I'll open this door for you."

He was on his feet in an instant, picking her up and holding her like a
small dog, her legs dangling, but eye to eye and nose to nose with him.

"Like to be alone?" he said. "Never! I love all of you. The three of us
are going to get married."

London, 1965

Patrick Anthony Henry Keating was born at nine o'clock in the evening on April 1, 1965, but not without some dramatics. Amanda had gone into hard labor at two in the afternoon and Charles had been informed at the club just as he was sitting down to his lunch. The housekeeper, an edge of panic in her voice, told Charles that Amanda's pains were coming so quickly that she couldn't speak. He sped home and bundled her into the car, trying to calm her as they drove the few blocks to the Chelsea Hospital. The pains racked her, one every minute, and she could hardly catch her breath between them. By the time they got to the hospital, she had begun to scream involuntarily and her agony unnerved Charles completely. The doctor was waiting in her room, delighted with her progress. He took Charles out into the hall, leaving the nurse to undress Amanda.

"We'll have her in the delivery room soon now," he said cheerfully. "This one shouldn't take long."

Charles, his nerves raw, tried to light a cigarette. A guttural scream came from the room. Desperately wanting to flee the hospital, Charles made a mental note never to have another child.

"Can't you give her something? She shouldn't be having that much pain. It's unbearable." Bloody barbarians.

"Absolutely not. It would only slow down her progress. This is perfectly normal, you know. When the pains are twenty seconds apart, we'll get her into the delivery room. Then I can give her a little anesthetic, but not now."

Charles plunged back into the room and sat on the bed beside her, letting her dig her fingers into his arm, wiping the sweat from her face and wishing that he was anywhere but there. By God, men shouldn't have to go through this.

Just as suddenly as the pains had started, they stopped. Amanda lay back, waiting for the next wave to hit her, holding Charles's hand in a steely grip. Nothing happened. The nurse took the respite in stride, straightening the bed linens and mopping Amanda's face. She lay face up, bracing herself for the next assault. Ten minutes went by. Amanda's grip on Charles's hand relaxed. The nurse felt her pulse and left the room, returning almost immediately with the doctor. He put his stethoscope on Amanda's distended stomach, the cheery expression of a few minutes before no longer on his face. Before Charles took in what was happening, Amanda had been wheeled into an operating room and a Caesarean section performed. It saved Patrick's life. The umbilical cord had wrapped around his neck, almost strangling him, and had they not been in the hospital, he would have choked before birth.

He was a beautiful little boy. In a week they were home and the routine of a house with a new baby in it was set into motion. Patrick's nursery and the nanny's room were on the top floor above Charles and Amanda's bedroom. Charles spent hours watching him, looking at him awake or asleep. He loved holding him and he watched avidly when Amanda breast-fed him. It was impossible to believe they had almost lost him.

Charles continued his afternoon routine at the club, returning home in time for Patrick's feeding. They still spent the weekends with Davina and Richard. Davina was pregnant, due in July, so life at Lea Place was somewhat domesticated. It had been an unusually cold spring, too wet to play golf, and by the middle of May, Charles was restless and irritable.

"Boring," he said one evening in London after Patrick had been fed and tucked into his crib. "Bored out of my mind. Let's go somewhere. It's too late for Switzerland and too early for France. Let's go to Nassau —we can stay with the Peeks."

"What about Patrick?" Amanda asked.

"Patrick and nanny go with us wherever we go." Charles might be bored with his everyday routine but he adored his son and wanted to be with him.

"Super!" Amanda said. "Pretty clothes again, and I can stop nursing. Seven weeks is enough." She, too, looked forward to getting away from the terrible weather. She had been having headaches again in the past few weeks and some strange depressions, for no reason at all. She put it down to lying about Patrick's being premature, knowing no one believed her, and to the fact that she had no girlfriend to talk to except for Davina on the weekends. She didn't like most of the wives or girlfriends of the Wyndham members, and so far they were the only ones she had met. Rosie Riggs was a close friend of Charles's but she had never been nice to Amanda. Amanda put it down to jealousy. Rosie already had two children and a large house in Kent, but as they never invited Charles and Amanda for the weekend, it was obvious that Rosie didn't like her.

Nassau would change all that. The Peeks apparently had a beautiful house—Charles had been there many times before—and Amanda looked forward to her first visit.

Charles set about making the arrangements. Amanda decided to valet for him. Charles was a dragon about his clothes but she made a point of learning from Mr. Roger, Charles's valet, while they were still in Regent's Park, how to fold his jackets and trousers properly. Charles liked being pampered.

"You're as good as Mr. Roger," he told her. "And you come at a better price."

"Slave labor," Amanda said, glad to please him. She needed every hold she could get on him, no matter how small. Falling in love with him had not been part of her plan and she knew she was vulnerable because of it.

The evening before they were to fly to Nassau, a fierce spring rain beat on the windows of Charles's study and the wind was lashing the trees outside. Charles was going back to the club later for a party at the end of a backgammon tournament. Amanda had no desire to go with him— there were last-minute things to do and she knew it would be all hours before he got home.

At nine o'clock the phone rang and Charles answered it. She could hear the agitation in the voice on the other end, the urgency. "What happened?" Charles said into the phone. "Right away," he said, and hung up.

"Father's dead," he said. "Heart attack half an hour ago. Get hold of Neil and tell him I'm not coming tonight and ask him to cancel our flight. You call the Peeks. I'm going over to Mother's."

"Do you want me to come?" She had always felt inadequate about Charles's parents.

"No, I'll call you from there if there is something you can do. Why does everything have to happen at night? Why couldn't this have happened three hours ago when we could have gotten hold of someone? Bloody fate. I'll call you from Wandsworth."

She watched as he got into the car and drove off in the teeming rain.

Closing the front door behind her, she went back to the study and put another log on the grate, then went to the small fridge next to the drinks cabinet. She opened a bottle of champagne and carefully wrapped a white towel around its neck, then filled one of the flutes from Longholt with the crystalline wine.

She took her glass and stood in front of the fireplace, looking at herself in the ivory prisoner's mirror that hung above it.

"Good evening, Countess," she said to her reflection. Her imagination took her into another realm. She saw a room, a room like the white-and-gold drawing room at Ransome House. She was moving from one of her guests to another. It was after dinner, and coffee was being served. Soon, she and Charles would have a huge house, grander even than Ransome House, and she could play the role of Countess to a fare-thee-well. It would be marvelous. This small house was fine, but Charles was an Earl now and she was a Countess. There would be invitations everywhere, and everyone would remark on her beauty and her adroitness as a hostess.

"Good evening, Countess," she said again, raising her glass to her reflection in the mirror.

The estate of the 10th Earl of Warrington was settled without complications but with an eventual surprise for Penelope Warrington, now the Dowager Countess, and Charles, now the 11th Earl. Although Charles was to share equally in the estate with his mother, and a trust fund had been arranged to provide for Patrick, Richard Warrington had seen to it that a small yearly income was all there was for Charles.

"He has certainly hamstrung me," Charles said furiously to his mother after the will had been read. "There is not one cent for me. He's fixed it so you can draw on the principal but I cannot, nor can I borrow on the trusts or sell them. He's bypassed me."

"You still have an income of eleven thousand—that's increased by two thousand a year. Surely you can live on that, and you cannot spend the rest of your life gambling. Somewhere, sometime, you are going to have to do something more productive. When you left your job in the City after winning all that money, your father became concerned about your habits. He was only trying to protect you, Charles."

"He left a mighty large sum for the Labour Party, however," Charles said, stubbing out his cigarette angrily. "And you can do what you want to. How could I possibly go into any business when I have no principal to invest?"

"You can always borrow from me," his mother said. "Your father and

I discussed it thoroughly. At this stage in your life, if you could get at the principal it would go right onto the gaming tables. You are a registered gambler, a fact that was far more painful to your father than his involvement with Labour has been to you. Your father was trying to protect his grandson from the poorhouse. If you convince me that you are serious about a valid business, I will always lend you money. And remember, there is some money coming to us from the bank accounts. Not much, I'm sure, but better than a poke in the eye."

She was referring to the last paragraph in Richard Warrington's will, which directed that whatever amount there was in two offshore bank accounts was to be divided between Penelope and Charles. One of the accounts was in Jersey, the other in the Bahamas, but all of them subject to British taxes. Penelope Warrington had not known they existed.

Richard Warrington had left a note for his wife and son regarding the secret accounts. "As rigid as my rules may have seemed to both of you, whatever has accrued in these accounts is for you to use as you see fit. This small cash residue is given to you with love and no rules imposed."

The letter was so unlike his father that Charles was baffled.

"Mad money," he said to his mother. "Not like him at all. What will you do with yours, go to the theater?"

"Charles, don't be so bitter. If there's enough, I might take a cruise. You know your father would never travel. I would like to go some place warm, some place like the Caribbean or South Africa. What about you? Please, please get something substantial. Don't try to double it at the tables."

"A new Mercedes. There will never be enough for that but I saw a blue saloon the other day. Finest car ever made."

Two weeks later they were called back to the solicitor's office and informed that the amount of accrued funds in the two bank accounts was more than a million and a half pounds. The Dowager fainted dead away. When she came to, she informed the solicitor that there was of course a mistake. Her husband would never have taken that amount of money out of the country and on top of that he would never allow that large an amount to come under the control of either herself or her son. Charles was nonplussed. His first reaction was that indeed the old boy had made a mistake. He was also amused. The old boy wasn't all Labour after all.

There had been no mistake. Charles was euphoric. Almost three quarters of a million pounds for him, even with taxes! What could his father have been thinking of? Whatever it was, he approved. He bought the Mercedes that afternoon. Now he had substantial money, he thought. It only remained for him to see what he could do with it.

★ ★ ★

Charles was generous by nature and the windfall inheritance from his father made him even more so. As well as the big blue Mercedes for himself, he bought Amanda a sporty little silver Triumph and took her to Asprey's and had a diamond necklace made for her which he designed himself. It was a simple row of round diamonds, with a baroque pearl clasp, that sat perfectly on her neck. The diamonds were two to three carats each, so it was not a major piece of jewelry, although Amanda considered it one.

"Everything you have once belonged to someone else," Charles said when the necklace arrived. "That doesn't seem fair. Now you have something designed for you that belongs to you alone. It's a start." He looked quite pleased with himself.

"It will always be my favorite," Amanda said, touched by his generosity. "But, Charles, I adore the opals and the dragonfly you bought me before we were married and the diamond earrings you gave me when Patrick was born. All in all, I have quite a lot."

A few weeks later he came home with a small leather box for her. In it lay a large emerald surrounded by round diamonds only slightly smaller than those in the necklace. The emerald was an excellent color and there was a small attachment that made it possible to link it onto the necklace, which Charles did, looking over her shoulder at her in the mirror.

"Now that makes it an important piece of jewelry," he said, looking even more pleased with himself.

"Charles, I adore it," Amanda said, flattered, but wondering where she was ever going to wear such an imposing piece. "Should you be spending so much on jewels and cars and me? What about a place of our own in the country? There must be something near the golf club and Richard and Davina's. Wouldn't you like that? Land is a much better investment."

"Not on your life," Charles said. "I hated living in that Tudor monster in the country as a child. I only go to Richard's because of the golf, or the shooting. The sports. Let Richard spend his money in the country —that's his life. When we find a larger house here in London that suits us, then I'll think about that. I want a much bigger house soon. And don't think jewelry isn't a good investment. I bought this stone at auction for a very good price. It's going to double in value in ten years' time."

"I hope your winnings keep doubling too," Amanda said. He had been on a roll. They had been at the Club every night for the past few weeks and Amanda knew he was playing for much higher stakes than he had before the windfall from his father, but she knew, too, that he had been winning consistently. Everyone at the Club was remarking on his long run of luck. All she could hope was that it would last.

Suddenly, his luck changed and his mood with it. There were no more fifty-pound notes folded under her coffee cup, left as a little extra for her. He was at home in time to change in the evenings, but not long enough to stay for dinner, and several times he didn't come home to change at all. He withdrew into himself, hardly speaking to her. The weather was filthy, so they skipped going to the country for the weekends. Patrick picked up a bad cold and fever and Amanda was up with him to relieve the nanny during the night for the better part of two weeks. It would all change, she thought. Soon it would be summer and Patrick would be well and Charles would have gotten through this bad patch. She hoped against hope that he had invested some of his recent winnings where he couldn't get at them but she knew better than that. Finally she went to see Gavers, dropping by one afternoon at teatime.

"Where have you been?" Gavers asked her. "You were here every night for a month and now I haven't seen you for weeks."

"Charles hasn't invited me to come lately. He's here, isn't he?" She knew he was; she had seen him at the backgammon table as she came in.

"Yes. He's got a new pigeon, but things aren't going the way he expected."

"Who is it?" she asked.

"A Lebanese. New member. Charles is determined to show him who the better backgammon player is."

"And who is?"

"Charles. But the dice aren't cooperating. The fellow won't be here much longer—he goes back to Beirut next week. Charles will be all right."

Amanda decided to go with Charles that evening, even if it meant sitting at the widow's table waiting for him. She wanted to see the Lebanese. Didn't they ever have names? Sharif or Mohammed, or something? A new member. Lebanese, you know, doesn't have a name. It was typical British snobbery not to know either the first name or the surname of those who were considered socially inferior.

When Charles came home, she was dressed and ready to go. He bathed and changed, made no comment, and took her with him. Gavers joined them for dinner but Charles hardly spoke to either of them. He had bolted down two double martinis before dinner and left the table before coffee, his face expressionless.

Gavers went off about his business and Amanda sat alone. What was she doing here? she wondered. Why in the world was she sitting there alone? She had come to see the Lebanese fleece her husband, so she ought to go and watch it while it was happening, she thought. She went into the room where Charles and his opponent were seated at one of the backgammon tables. He did have a name, Amanda had discovered by going to the front desk and asking George to look him up in the roster of members. It was Raschid. His surname was unpronounceable.

As she watched the play, she saw immediately that Charles was having bad dice and he was obviously still in a nasty mood. It was a disastrous combination. They were playing for fifty pounds a point, forty-five more than he usually played for. She was about to leave— there seemed to be no point in continuing to watch—when they finished a game and Raschid turned to her.

"A man with such a beautiful wife should spend more time with her," he said. "Enough for tonight, Charles?"

"As you like," Charles said. "How much do I owe you? About six thousand, I believe."

"Yes. Exactly."

Charles took out his checkbook and started to write a check. Gavers hove into view. Charles signaled for a drink and Amanda heaved a sigh of relief. At least he couldn't lose any more tonight.

"Charles," Raschid said softly. "I've been winning for some time now. Would you like to cut a card? Double or nothing?"

Amanda looked frantically at Gavers, who ignored her.

"You cut first," Charles said.

Raschid cut the six of spades.

"Not very good," he said. Charles cut the five of clubs.

"Once more?" Raschid asked.

"Leave it alone, Charles," Gavers said.

"As you like," Raschid said.

"Cut," Charles said.

"You go this time."

Charles cut the king of hearts.

Raschid cut the ace of spades.

"Enough for tonight," he said. "I'm sorry, Charles." He wasn't. Charles wrote out a check and handed it to him without a word.

Enough for a house in the country, Amanda thought as Raschid said good night.

"Well, Winner," Gavers said. "Let's have a drink."

Winner, Amanda thought. Winner Warrington. The name was bound to stick. She hated it.

Charles was furious. He leaned across the bar to Gavers, a glazed look in his eyes. He had not stopped drinking all evening.

"I don't mind the loss," he said, "I mind the man. I mind that you ever let him in as a member. I blackballed him in the first place, as you remember. He's the wrong element here."

Gavers was not about to argue with Charles under the circumstances. He rose from his seat.

"He's also lost close to half a million pounds here in the last two weeks. Cheer up, Winner. Tomorrow is another day. If he can lose to me, he can lose to you."

Amanda prayed they would stop calling Charles "Winner." They drove home in silence. Charles drank a tumbler of straight gin before coming to bed.

The name did stick. Robin heard about it the next day. Winner Warrington. The alliteration was too good. Charles and Raschid had one more session before he left for the Middle East. Amanda didn't care to know how much Charles lost that time. She was just grateful Raschid was gone.

CHAPTER 7

July 1965

A manda finally decided to have it out with Charles about the Wynd-ham, the Wyndham group, the Wyndham Club, the Wyndham world. She planned her little speech carefully.

"You're so intelligent, you have such an educated mind, and your knowledge and taste in everything is superb," she told him. "You could do anything. You know food and wine, antiques, silver, paintings. You are a sportsman. You're a champion sailor, you're good at golf, shooting —everything. Can't you translate any of this into doing something be-sides gambling and life at the Wyndham Club, forevermore?"

"Darling," he said, flattered, "you must remember that you are one of the few wives who come here, one of the only ones allowed. I allow you. Gavers has a girlfriend here now and then; so does Robin, but they're single. You know that Neil rarely brings Rosie, and if you think about it, most of my friends never bring their wives. You are privileged to come."

Amanda knew it was true. Rosie's absence from the Club was a boon, of course. Amanda had talked to some of the wives who appeared when there was a big tournament or a special party. "Do you really come often?" she was asked. "Why on earth do you bother? All these men talk about is gambling."

"You have houses in the country," Amanda answered. "I live in Lon-don and if I stay at home alone, I never see Charles. As we never go anywhere else, I come to the Club to be with him."

"But you're not *with* him. He's always at the tables. What do you do?"

"I wait for him. We go home together, breathing the same air at least."

★ ★ ★

Her pretty speech to Charles had gotten her nowhere. When she tried again, his expression changed to the closed-out-loner look she was beginning to know so well. His answer to her was abrupt.

"We all pay sometimes, Amanda. Maybe this is the price you pay for the privilege of being a Countess."

August 1965

In mid-August, Charles and Amanda were invited on a holiday in the South of France. Gavers had been given a yacht, or rather he had accepted the use of one in payment: A disastrous evening of *chemin de fer* had inspired the Italian owner of the yacht to offer it to Gavers for two weeks in high season rather than come up with the thousands of pounds he had lost, a truly embarrassing situation for him. He could well afford to pay, but somehow there was a certain cachet to paying off the debt with his yacht.

When Amanda was bidden to the Club for lunch, she knew something was in the offing.

"Only the five of us," Gavers said. "We can ask anyone we run into there to join us for a day or two if we want to, but that's all. Too many bloody cooks can spoil any cruise—somehow everyone gets to arguing. We can get out of port every day, to the Isles of Cannes or Saint-Tropez, and still be back in the evening so we're not too far away from the big table. Monte Carlo! I'm sick of not being able to play in my very own place just because I own it. Owners miss all the fun. We might make a nice little win on this trip, eh, Charles? What?"

"Who are the five of us?" Amanda asked Gavers, wondering who the other couple would be. "Are Rosie and Neil coming?" She prayed not.

"No," Gavers said. "Neil has to be here. Robin is coming. And a beautiful girl, who is mine." He seemed to leer slightly as he said it. "No one you know, Amanda, but someone you may even like, someone from off the beaten path."

"In other words, not titled?" Amanda shot back. She was irritated with Gavers for making a mystery of the girl. Why not say who she was? Gavers always had a girl. The fact that he was still a bachelor was obviously because he preferred it that way.

Gavers laughed. "How could she outrank you, dear Countess?" To her annoyance, Amanda had risen to the bait instead of playing the game she knew how to play. Somehow she was jealous. Why should she be jealous of any girl of Gavers's? She had everything she wanted. She sat quietly for the rest of the time while the men made all the plans. She thought about Robin. He had more charm than even Gavers, and she was glad he was going. She knew him slightly and now would have a chance to really get to know him.

The yacht Gavers had fallen heir to was called *Cattivo II*—"Mischievous," the owner explained. "That's what it means in Italian. A little wicked. It's my second mischief, and so beautiful." Her playboy owner was a bad gambler but he was a knowing yachtsman and *Cattivo II* was perfection, something Gavers had known well before he accepted the offer of her as payment for the gaming debt. She was 125 feet long, with a clipper bow and a crew of eight, including an excellent chef. There were twin identical master cabins and two smaller cabins that were more than adequate. *Cattivo II* was moored beside Sam Spiegel's *Malahne* on the far side of the harbor, the place to be. Onassis's *Christina* took up a berth alongside Rainier's *Deo Juvante*.

Deo Juvante was smallish and ugly. Amanda wondered how a Prince, ruler of this silly principality, could have a ratty little yacht like that, especially with a wife as exquisite as Princess Grace.

Gavers and Robin and Charles were used to the sort of luxury that *Cattivo* provided, but it was Amanda's first experience, and she promptly fell in love with the world of yachting. Everything seemed to go right, from the day they arrived. Even the weather was perfect.

Gavers's girl, who shared the adjoining master cabin with him, was French. Chantal de Briand was a Duchess, born into one of the oldest and most esteemed French families. In fact, her father was the first Duke of France. There was not a trace of snobbism to her. Her English was perfect, as well as her Italian and German, and she quickly discovered that Amanda could speak a small amount of French, which she encouraged her to do.

"*Les hommes, jamais,*" she said. "Not a word does an Englishman speak of another language, ever. But your accent is perfect. It doesn't matter what you say—the French never listen. They will simply think you are French."

My cup runneth over, Amanda thought. Charles was losing thousands or more every night and she actually liked the girl that Gavers was sleeping with. She missed Patrick, but Charles had rightly decided that this was to be their trip, a sort of second honeymoon.

"Cap Ferrat," Gavers said to the captain the afternoon they came aboard. "I want to wake up there tomorrow, not before noon, and jump into the sea. We are invited to lunch with Mary Lasker at La Fiorentina, the most beautiful villa in the world. And the next morning, I want to be tucked into the port at Saint-Tropez. The next day, captain, you may choose the place." The captain, used to an owner who rarely moved out of the harbor and who used *Cattivo II* as a floating hotel rather than as the seaworthy yacht she was, was euphoric.

"With pleasure, sir."

"But back in Monte Carlo each evening. We have to make the running costs of the yacht every night. That's not peanuts, you know."

They were invited everywhere and they went everywhere, their one cardinal rule that they would be at the casino at about midnight.

Amanda was in love with the days. The first morning, when they had dropped anchor near the little port of Saint-Jean, David Niven had come aboard and taken them back to his villa, where they lunched in bathing suits on the sunny terrace. "Knew you were here instantly," he said to Charles and Gavers. "It's the girls I came for, not you buggers. I watched them on deck in their bikinis through my telescope and decided to pay you a visit."

One evening they dined at La Leopolda, the magnificent villa built by Leopold, King of the Belgians, which now belonged to Gianni Agnelli, the suavest of the Italian tycoons. He found Amanda very attractive and sent a bottle of champagne to their table along with an invitation to dine, annoying Charles, delighting Amanda.

Cocooned in the luxury of *Cattivo II,* the five of them lived sybaritically. Amanda and Chantal sunned together, swam together, or read and watched the men playing backgammon. In the evenings at the casino they wandered about, taking in everything that went on, with Robin as their escort. The three of them had staked out a small table in a corner of the bar that was reserved for them every night. Amanda had no desire to know how much Charles was losing, or winning.

"Why does champagne only taste perfect here?" Robin asked. "It's never quite the right temperature anywhere else. Incidentally, I've been watching all the hard-eyed old crows around here glaring at both of you. Young, beautiful, both of you passionate, and mine, all mine."

Amanda had a question. "Chantal, did you say that the woman we just saw was with Charles once? I'm not jealous—I just can't imagine Charles being anything but terrified of her."

"Never mind her," Chantal said. "You mean the dangerous Donina. The only thing they had in common was gambling."

Amanda shivered. Gambling. Was there nothing else?

"Let's go back to *Cattivo*," Chantal said. "It's long past three. The nights are beautiful but I love the days. These glittering creatures with their ugly little men and their millions are insane."

"Oh, no, not yet," Robin said. "Aimé Barelli is playing at the Sea Club, just next door. We're going there, I've already told Gavers and Charles. I'm going to dance with both of you at the same time and ten men will come to cut in instantly. Let's have some fun. I'm fed up with all this expensive, serious indulgence."

The next morning Amanda came on deck to find an enormous man taking up almost the entire length of one of the yellow linen couches. He had pushed aside the pink and blue canvas cushions in order to make himself more comfortable and stretched his arms out along the banquette, giving himself the look of a pasha. He was smoking a huge cigar and wearing the classic white slacks of a Riviera summer with a perfectly cut blue silk shirt the color of a tropical sea which exactly matched his eyes. Charles and Gavers and Robin were gathered around him in a semicircle of deck chairs and Amanda noticed at once that it was they who seemed out of proportion, not the gigantic man they were quite obviously paying court to.

It was the giant, as Amanda dubbed him for herself, who looked right and made Lilliputian figures of the others. He fixed his eyes on Amanda the moment she appeared and, without interrupting his own conversation, assessed her as carefully as a slave trader about to spend good money and wanting good value for it. Flicking the ash from his cigar vaguely in the direction of the sea, he indicated with his other hand the small space left beside him where she was to sit—which she did as if it were where she belonged. There had been no break in his heavily accented, booming voice as he continued with his conversation.

"He wants Onassis out," the giant was saying, pronouncing the word *vants*. "And as it is his principality, he can get him out. In order to do so, he has approached me to take over the gambling, which obviously I know a great deal more about than does Onassis. Or Rainier himself, for that matter. I am thinking about it."

Putting the cigar in an ashtray in front of him, he turned his attention to Amanda, taking her hand in one of his huge ones.

"And which one of these boys do you belong to, my dear?" he asked, turning the blue of his eyes on her with an intensity she had not felt before, seeing into her and through her with kindness and complete interest.

Charles leaped to his feet. "John, it's Amanda, my wife. John Latimer, darling."

"Ah, the new Countess of Warrington. Good for you, my dear. The title is always important." He turned to Charles. "Why haven't you brought her to Les Amis before this to meet me?"

"I must, John. I shall," Charles said with unusual enthusiasm. Amanda decided that the giant must be in his mid-fifties and that, regardless of his enormous size, he was in fine shape. Certainly he was perfectly groomed. His hands, his hair, his feet were obviously cared for by experts, and this was a man who never shaved himself. He also had a tremendous sex appeal, which he was directing at her right now. Even so, for some reason, she was at ease with him.

Amanda loved the way he patronized the men. He was almost condescending in his manner. She had never seen Charles or Gavers even somewhat in awe of anyone as they were now. She had an odd feeling that they were all a little afraid of him and that their fear had nothing to do with his size. It was something beyond that. Now she realized who the giant was. She had heard Charles and the rest of them speak of him often. John Latimer the gambler, John Latimer the legendary figure who owned Les Amis, the only other private gambling club in London of any consequence. The rich, the famous, and the beautiful frequented Les Amis; even a few of the royals had become members. Prince Philip's membership had been a source of immense pride and delight to Latimer. Titles were important, as he had pointed out to Amanda.

The two clubs had many things in common. The majority of Gavers's members belonged to the closed, private world of the aristocracy, and the Wyndham had a social cachet that was enviable. Their scandals and secrets were well known among themselves but never revealed to outsiders. You were "one of them" or you were not. Les Amis was less snobbish and much more fun. The two clubs occupied two of the great houses in London; Les Amis in a grandiose mansion just off Piccadilly, a former Rothschild domain which included a ballroom and, more recently, a sauna and a private film theater added by John Latimer. The house was superbly proportioned for the size of its present occupant. There were certain similarities between Gavers and John Latimer, as there were in their clubs, and they were friends on the surface. But, above all, they were competitors and each took the other's measure daily.

"What about the casino offer—are you going to do it?" Gavers was asking, somewhat impatiently. When he was with John Latimer, infor-

mation was important. "You could, you know. You're the one person
who could best Onassis in this situation and get along with Rainier.
Rainier wants you to take it over, I should think, because the Greek is
getting too greedy."

"And too famous," John said. "You would think, in some circles, that
he owned Monte Carlo. Rainier does not like that. But no one bests
Onassis, not yet. Nor do I want to. He's a devious little Greek with an
exaggerated sense of self-importance, but I also happen to like him. He
has balls and an ugly yacht." He paused. "This is no longer the time to
discuss it. You will be my guests tonight on *L'Amie*, which you will find
moored beside you when we return to Monte Carlo." Amanda felt
somehow that he was speaking only to her. "Come at ten. Then I will
take you to the Hôtel de Paris for dinner on the terrace. We will all go to
the casino later." He was speaking only to Amanda now, ignoring the
others. He took her hand and kissed it, eyes invading hers once more.
Then he turned it over and licked her palm, his tongue hot and expert,
his eyes still linked with hers. Amanda felt the goose flesh crawl along
her arm and settle deep in her body. She was mesmerized. Here it was
broad daylight, and three men, one of them her husband, were watching
while this behemoth of a man was making himself quite clear to her.
Couldn't they see what he was doing?

"I will see you this evening, little Countess, and we will have some
time alone together," his deep voice boomed. He rose from the banquette with the grace sometimes given to very large men. Standing, he
was more gigantic than ever. With a wave of a new and unlit cigar, he
was gone. There seemed to be a large amount of empty space on the
deck of *Cattivo* now, useless space.

"Big John," Gavers said, watching as the huge figure stepped lightly
aboard his launch. "That's an extraordinary proposal of Rainier's. It's
worth another fortune. I wonder if he will take it. I wonder if I would
take it."

"**H**e is an extraordinary character, everything about him," Robin
said later as they walked along the *quai* looking at the yachts, en route
to the Hôtel de Paris to meet their host. He had called, asking them to
meet him there and suggesting that they have a nightcap aboard *L'Amie*
when they came back to the port later. Charles and Gavers had gone
ahead to the Winter Casino, to play roulette for an hour before dining.

"How much does he weigh?" Amanda asked, emphasizing each of her
words. "I have never seen such an enormous man, ever, anywhere."

"He is six foot five and he weighs twenty-one stone which translates into close to three hundred pounds. Don't you know anything about him? He is somewhat of a legend."

"No," Amanda said. "Not really. Oh, of course, I've heard all of you talk about him—big John this, John Latimer that—but how was I to know he was a giant? How long has he been here? We certainly couldn't have missed him."

"He must have just arrived," Robin said. "He never lets anyone know much about his movements. I think he enjoys being something of a mystery character."

"My father knew him years ago as 'Polish Pete,'" Chantal said. "He was born in Warsaw and at one time was the heavyweight champion of both Belgium and Poland. I've seen newspaper clippings about that part of his life. Otherwise, everything about him seems to be so much hearsay, and as no story can be checked, he is a mystery figure. Some say he creates the legends to suit himself. However, my father is truly fond of him."

"How did he get to England?"

"Aha," Robin said. "He stole a train car full of cigarettes somewhere in eastern Europe and with the profits he bought his way out of Europe and arrived in London in the middle of the blitz."

"*Stole* a train car?" Amanda said. "What did he do, strap it on his back and walk into England with it?"

"Whatever he did, it worked. He claims that his family had a tobacco factory in Belgium," Robin continued. "At any rate, he was with the Polish Army in France. That's when Chantal's father came across him. He was in Spain for a while, no one knows where or why, and from there he got to England and joined the Royal Army Service Corps. You know how we felt about the Poles and what happened to Poland. John Latimer became the clearinghouse for them. The first Les Amis was a small place in Stratton Street, a club for Polish officers, run by John. They were an incredible lot, those men whose country had been wiped out from under them. I was in knee pants. You know that's what's wrong with our generation—Charles's and Gavers's and mine."

"What is?"

"We missed the war. Our fathers were killed or wounded, as our older brothers were, and we were too young to be a part of it. I have a guilty conscience about it, even though I know I shouldn't. But there is no substitute for that war we were not in. Gambling certainly isn't."

Amanda looked at Robin's grave face. She sensed a sadness about him. She still didn't know him well enough to know why he was sad, or if he knew himself.

"You mean you felt cheated, felt that you'd missed all the excitement?" She had heard that sentiment expressed before.

"Yes, and that we didn't get maimed or blown to pieces. We weren't men; we were little boys growing up, defended rather than defending. I was sent off to America to be safe and I was ashamed of that. We're sort of a useless generation, still searching for something to do, something to make up for having done nothing."

Amanda's father came to her mind. She had often pretended that he had been killed in the war instead of in that senseless automobile accident. She shuddered slightly, not wanting to remember again what she knew of what had happened on that quiet country lane: the burning car, the screaming child that she had been.

John Latimer was seated, pashalike as before, at the corner table on the terrace, waiting for them. He rose and seated Amanda and Chantal on either side of him. Robin was put next to Chantal.

"I am isolating Gavers and Charles on the far side of the table tonight," he said. "These silly men who gamble all the time when they have beautiful women to amuse them bore me. What fools they are." He sat down and spoke to the captain hovering expectantly nearby, waiting for his orders.

"Bring caviar and Polish vodka, frozen beyond ice, André," he commanded. "Now we enjoy ourselves."

They spent an hour at the casino after dinner and Amanda had watched, fascinated, at John Latimer's march through the ornate gambling rooms to his favorite seat at his favorite table, which was always kept open and ready for him. Everyone knew him or wanted to. He let some approach him as if granting an audience, and he paused once to tease a beautiful woman affectionately, making extravagant promises for the near future with her. He became hard-eyed and unapproachable to others who tried to join him. He had risen from the table long before his party had had time to become bored, and his hulking blue convertible Bentley had been waiting at the door to take them back to the yacht.

Now the port was magically still. Charles and Gavers were still at the gaming tables but Robin and Chantal and Amanda had settled down in chairs that swallowed them in perfect comfort on the L'Amie's afterdeck.

It was very late. Amanda had been so engrossed in John Latimer's conversation that she hoped they would still be there on the L'Amie at dawn, talking, as they had talked this night away. One of the most fascinating things about the man was that he did not indulge in monologue, as most self-centered entrepreneurs did. He conversed and he made sure you did as well. Amanda had learned more about Robin and Chantal tonight than during the entire previous week on the yacht. She was surprised at how easily forthcoming she had been about her own background. She had not tried to embroider it; she simply said that her father had been in the British Navy, that he had been killed, that one of her sisters had introduced her to Charles, and that yes, she did very much like being a Countess. She hoped that she would be a good mother and she adored Patrick, and no, she was not at all fond of gambling. And that Chantal was one of the first women she had liked who didn't intimidate or bore her and that was probably because she was French rather than English. Yet Amanda kept the headaches and her loneliness to herself.

Amanda had learned that this huge, larger-than-life character with the deep voice had never married because he had a stronger preference. "Mistresses," he said. "Always mistresses. I am between them now. I prefer six to seven years with each one—in that time one can really savor a woman and help her, then send her happily on her way and never become bored with her. Occasionally I make an exception with a married lady, but husbands get in the way. My mistress must be young, of course—I do not make love to older women." This was stated as if by a papal nuncio, and his eyes were once again boring into Amanda's.

Robin and he returned to the subject of the Rainier proposition. "I will not do it, of course," Latimer said. "And he knows it. There is room for only one man here: Rainier. He and Grace are the principality. Onassis will learn. I am being used to threaten Onassis, but they will come to terms. Les Amis is exactly as I like it and I have it on the best possible terms. Mine. I have only to settle on a new mistress, and I am enjoying the looking around." He did not look at Amanda.

"It's a fortune, John," Robin said, "and you have never been averse to money. You aren't throwing up a smoke screen, are you? You know I'll repeat everything to Gavers. What's to stop Rainier, if he actually does want to take Onassis out, from asking Gavers to do the same if you decline?"

"Gavers can't handle it. He's too English and too involved with his friends. He may understand gamblers, which indeed he does, but the games of the Mediterranean world are not the same. The Monegasque are tougher than the Maltese, and the Maltese are tougher than the Egyptians, and the Egyptians are tougher than the lot of them put together. I know—I had occasion once to be beaten up by them."

"You?" Amanda said. "Beaten up?"

"Ah, my dear little Countess, I have been felled more than once. We learn from such experiences to stay in our own waters. Robin, I suggest you take Chantal, who is almost asleep from this boring conversation, back to your own yacht. We will wait for Charles and Gavers. Amanda and I. I am leaving for London in a few hours so it makes no sense to go to bed. I may never see Amanda again, since her husband has not seen fit yet to bring her to Les Amis." He rose as he spoke and Robin and Chantal rose with him. He saw them to the gangway and returned to where Amanda was curled up in the big chair, the skirt of her short chiffon dress billowing around her knees, a printed stole on her shoulders against the cool of predawn. Looming over her, he searched her face for a moment.

"I want to talk to you," he said, *vant* coming through as the constant accent. Amanda had almost said "vant" and "vill" a few times. His personality was so strong that one tended to copy his accent involuntarily.

"You're leaving for London?" she said. "So soon? You've hardly been here."

He sat down, a balloon of brandy in his hands. She was silent as he lit the last cigar, waiting for him.

"You don't belong with them," he said, ignoring her question. "You know that, don't you? You made an endearing little story tonight about your simple background—pretty girl from nowhere marries Earl—but I determine an intelligence in you that is not comfortable in this shallow atmosphere. I know them. You are alone in a sea of wastrels—handsome worthless wastrels. Except for Gavers—he is a gentleman and courageous. I imagine he's the only one of them who has been even half decent to you."

"Robin," she said, in a small voice. He was insulting everyone she knew.

"Of course, I keep forgetting about Robin. He drinks too much. But none of the women interest you, frozen bitches that they are, eh? Gavers would be decent—he admires you because you caught the Earl and took him by surprise. Gavers wants to be titled, preferably a Royal Duke, more than anything else, but he's had to settle for being the ringleader of the pack. He aspires to you for some good sex. He probably makes silly passes at you. The thought of being Charles's good old school-tie friend on the one hand and your good friend in bed on the other appeals to Gavers. In the morning he would always side with Charles. Most of his attention to you is because of Chantal. You know about his love affair with Chantal?"

"Only because we're aboard the yacht together."

"No, the real story. Gavers, his masculine ego at stake, makes it look as if Chantal is a girl he sleeps with when it amuses him. Ten years ago he was so desperately in love with her that he was suicidal. Her father absolutely refused even to discuss her marrying him and she, of course, adhered to her family's wishes. Gavers had never lost before and he had no chance of marrying her. As a gambler, he understood that the odds were against him. He's been trying to get even ever since. His one security is that she has not married anyone else. He brings her off like this, once or twice a year on trips, and he loves her but can't forgive her for being who she is. Now he seems to prefer not being married; he is an enemy of women, and you are included in that sphere. He is as ruthless as any Siberian tiger. So be careful. You are not one of them. You don't, by any chance, want to be 'one of them,' do you?" There was a sneer in his tone when he flipped off "one of them."

She was silent. This trip had been like a dream come true for her until John Latimer had come upon the scene. It was the first time since she and Charles had been married that she had felt that perhaps she did belong, would belong forever to the privileged class she had married into. Did that mean she wanted to be "one of them"? Was it so wrong to want to be one of them?

"I don't know," she answered quietly. "It has to start somewhere, doesn't it? I'm not the first girl from nowhere to catch a title. I'm one of hundreds. Maybe I do want to be one of them. Should I not want to?"

Her feelings for John Latimer were ambivalent. His conversation was disturbing to her. She knew that what he was saying was true, but why did he have to single her out just when she was beginning to feel secure? If she *had* been one of them, she would have ticked him off quickly. On the other hand, he seemed to feel strongly about her, as if he knew something about her that she didn't understand herself. But whoever she was, here she was at four o'clock in the morning, listening to a man tell her things she didn't want to hear, a man who was not impressed by everything that she, Amanda, aspired to. A man she hardly knew, a man she did not want to know.

"No, you should not," he said, putting his big hand over her small one. She felt an infusion of his strength. "You probably know that you are wasted, not appreciated for what you really are. You think it's because you have no background and no money, only beauty, and that alone does not give you carte blanche into the aristocratic atmosphere. That's the flaw in you. Most of the girls who married titles before you are as tough as boots and understand the rules. Then they start making them. You have no capacity for that. The English, more than any other people, love ignoring or freezing out those they consider pretenders, anyone they can possibly get away with thinking of as beneath them.

You could get away with beauty or intelligence, but not both, and they can and will do you in. You're vulnerable, to Charles, to Gavers, to all of them. And you have a son now who already belongs to them by birth. I may sound like the voice of doom, but you have to fight these people—this so-called society—with anything, everything you have got to fight with. I did, and had no trouble because, from the beginning, I have treated them the way they should be treated—as if they are slightly inferior to me."

"You certainly have," Amanda said, a smile on her face, remembering Charles and Gavers and Robin gathered around him like schoolboys, deferring to him in every way.

"You're not impressed with them either, beyond wanting to be a Countess, which is a commendable ambition on your part. Too bad Charles doesn't have some real money; then you could take it away from him, rather than letting him lose it all to his good friend Gavers."

"The only thing that worries me is what you said about Patrick." Patrick was hers, not just one of them. Or is that what he would become? Would he, too, try to close her out in years to come?

"Such a sad face. Don't worry about Patrick now. When you come back to London, come and see me. You are too beautiful to be unhappy. Now let's talk about better things, more pleasing things. Do you know how Gavers got his house in the country? Melbridge?"

"No. I've been there, of course, and it is something to see, the exotic deer, all of his animals, running around as if they were free. I admire what he has done."

"He had needed a place in the country for a long time, a house with enough land for his darlings. The small estate he found was a little over a hundred acres and a house that was derelict. No one had lived in it since long before the war. Gavers does fancy himself the great white god of any rare creature, as you know. That may account for his fondness for Charles. Anyhow, the price on the property was eight thousand pounds. Mind you, it may sound cheap now, but this was 1958 and things were very different then.

"Gavers didn't have eight thousand pounds. He probably didn't have five hundred, so he did what he knew best how to do. He won eight thousand pounds on a racehorse and bought the place. He set about restoring the house—a lot of hard work and no money. One day, rummaging around in the basement, he came across a coin collection left by God knows who, God knows when. He took it up to London and, as it turned out, sold it for eight thousand pounds. So he got Melbridge for nothing. That's what I like about the man."

"Is that how you got Les Amis?" Amanda asked. "Was it your train full of cigarettes that got you a Rothschild mansion?"

Taken off guard, he roared with laughter.

"Sly puss you are. Yes, of course that's how I got it. Gavers and I have that in common: the love of winning something, not losing everything. We enjoy life too much to lose. I am going to win you. You are aware of that by now?"

Amanda knew the conversation had reached the point he had been leading up to. She said nothing.

"I want you and I'm going to have you. If I read you right, and I'm sure I do, no one has ever gotten *you* before. You've been the seductress choosing your prey. Now I am going to seduce you. Don't sit back alarmed and prissy all of a sudden. I'm not talking about tonight, I am not even interested in trying for you yet. You'll know when I am. Now it's time for you to go to bed. That silly ass you are married to will be back any minute now."

He pulled her up from the chair.

"Dear little Countess. I will be waiting for you in London. You are going to belong to me. I may be your salvation."

The days slipped by, filled with blue sky and bluer sea and the mingled fragrance of carnations and roses, the definitive scent of the Côte d'Azur. Amanda's sense of belonging, of being one of them, solidified in this irresistible atmosphere. She put John Latimer and his conversation out of her mind. She didn't quite want to dwell on the fact that she had allowed him to criticize her husband and his friends as strongly as he had.

Part of her growing confidence was thanks to Chantal. Chantal was smart and her disposition was a delight, her merriment infectious. She was simple, truly chic, and easy to be with. She invited Amanda to come and stay with her in France.

"When you want a few days away from London," Chantal said, "come over. I have excellent relations with all the couturiers and even better arrangements with the boutiques on the Left Bank. You have an open invitation. I don't expect you to get Charles away from his regular routine, but he can do without you for a day or so."

The invitation pleased Amanda. She told Gavers about it.

"Chantal likes everyone," Gavers said.

A small alarm went off in Amanda's mind.

"That's the one thing that's wrong with her," Gavers continued. "She's always liked all of us, loves being with us, telephones us wherever we are. She'll ask why we aren't with her at Quatre Mai, her great château in the Loire, or at her hunting lodge in Austria or her chalet in Zurs. Or in her Hôtel du Vallieres in Paris where only she has a view of Notre Dame at dawn."

"What's wrong with that?" Amanda asked. Gavers was doing exactly what John Latimer had told her he would do.

"Nothing," Gavers said. "She has a perfect life. She is rich and free, beautifully mannered, intelligent and clever, and she has superb ankles."

"Then what? You make it sound as if you are criticizing her. Or are you in love with her?"

"In love with her? Hardly. Never." Gavers sighed. "She has an old soul. Used up. She watches everything and everyone; she understands everything and everyone. But her father and her brother control her. She doesn't care about anyone, but then she's never been in love. She has no passion, no real passion. It's all surface with her."

"How is she in bed? Or do you just sleep together?" Amanda meant it as a sophisticated bit of small talk, the kind she had become more adept at than ever on this trip. But underneath, she wanted to know.

"She is fabulous. A rocket. She is the best. But when I'm making love to her I am always lonely. And when I finish making love to her, I'm lonelier." He was looking at Amanda, searching out her eyes. "How is it with Charles?" he asked softly, holding her hands in his.

"Stop it, Gavers," she said, looking away and taking her hands back, flustered.

"You asked," he said, eyes hardening slightly in the fading light. "I answered. You haven't." He got up, pulling her up with him, laughing now. "Come on, it's getting dark. We need a glass of champagne."

"Yes," Amanda said. "I do."

"Robin!" Gavers roared at the top of his lungs. "You silly ass, put down your silly ass drawing pad and if you haven't drunk up all the champagne already, bring a cold bottle and fill our glasses. This trip isn't going to last forever, you know, any more than the drinks are." He was Gavers again, in control again.

Robin came gleefully from the forward deck, where he had been sketching. He was so talented that with a few quick strokes of his pencils and crayons he had captured their daytime pleasures: Amanda and Chantal playing cards on the afterdeck; Amanda curled asleep on the sundeck, Chantal reading beside her; Amanda on Charles's lap. Robin recorded everything they did in his big sketch book, making a record of the life they were leading and always with a bottle of champagne beside him.

"Time for another glass," Robin said, pouring.

Amanda drank hers quickly and escaped to their cabin, where Charles was sleeping. It was her favorite time for them, these late afternoons when the light was all purples and blues and pinks, and tiny electric eyes had begun to twinkle along the shore. She loved making love to Charles as they made their way back into port through the calm sea. She took off her bikini and showered, thinking about the way Charles looked, his face beautiful in repose as he slept. She slipped into bed beside him, stroking his back, entreating him to come awake. He stirred and turned over, pulling her to him without opening his eyes. In the ritual of their lovemaking, Amanda thought about Gavers. "How is it with Charles?" Gavers had asked. *It's wonderful, Gavers, wonderful,* she thought as Charles's passion grew to match hers, although he was still more asleep than awake. She was glad that John Latimer was gone. Charles was not a silly ass at all. He was her husband and a peer of the realm. John Latimer was a Polish wrestler.

On their last morning aboard, Amanda came up the ladder, hair dripping wet, toweling robe drawn loosely about her, returning from her early swim.

"Good morning," Robin said, taking in her sleek tan skin, wet hair. "Coffee?"

"Mmmmm. What are you doing up this early?" she asked, combing her hair back from her face. The smell of that coffee, the delectable French *café filtre,* was one of the great pleasures of the morning.

"I've been watching you," he announced, again as if reading her mind. "Today has been the best."

"Today? Why today? I didn't know you were even awake."

"I've watched you every morning," he said, handing her a cup of steaming coffee. "Since this is our last day, I decided to disclose myself. The entire American Sixth Fleet has watched you too. I sent binoculars over for all five thousand of them aboard that aircraft carrier. They deserve to drink in your beauty. So do I."

Amanda laughed.

"I hate leaving," she said gently.

"You should. You're a summer girl—you belong to summer. You need sunshine and blue sky. England has never suited you. You are pinch-faced there, and serious. You never laugh or even really smile. You should have been born here and brought up here and still live here. Your French is even good."

"I do worry about Charles gambling so much."

"You should. There's nothing you can ever do about it. But you don't have to worry about it tonight. This is our last night and we aren't going to gamble. We're staying here in the harbor all day and going ashore in Villefranche to one of the crazy little restaurants on the port. We haven't had a chance to do anything like that yet. Tonight's the night."

"Good. I'm out of evening clothes."

"Don't wear anything. You're beautiful naked."

They sat drinking coffee, watching the little boats pulling water skiers behind them flash about in the bay. Two weeks, two beautiful weeks were coming to an end.

At least they had Robin's drawings for remembrance.

Charles and Gavers had played roulette the night before and won. Gavers insisted on a partnership agreement and insisted, too, that they stay away from the *chemin de fer* table.

"I've paid my dues there already," he said. "I didn't come here to end up another sucker for the Société des Bains de Mer. I have contributed all I intend to, to the shoe at the chemmy table, and I've gotten the boot. Now let's use our heads and take a little money away from these boys."

Charles agreed. He had lost heavily, more than anyone knew in the past weeks. *Chemin de fer* was the true gambler's nemesis. It was Charles's mortal enemy at Wyndham but he couldn't seem to stay away from it. No matter how much he won at bridge or poker, backgammon or roulette, it was *chemin de fer* that swallowed him as a shark swallows the smaller fish. It was the most alluring game of them all; the rest were all little games. A man who won consistently at chemmy, if such a creature existed, had the respect of everyone. In the eyes of a casino owner, the croupiers, shills, and fellow players, winning at the big game was the top thrill in gambling. There was no game as disastrous.

Gavers and Charles opened up a roulette table and stood across it from each other, the equivalent of ten thousand dollars in chips in front of them. Each time the wheel was spun they played five numbers straight up. No halves or corners, or red or black. Five chips went on a number and they had also agreed not to play favorites. The roulette wheel was an impersonal taskmaster and playing a favorite number could break you. So they scattered their chips from one end of the board to the other. From the first spin of the wheel it seemed as if they couldn't lose. Covering ten numbers out of the thirty-six and the zero gave them an almost one-to-three chance to win, but there were still twenty-six chances to lose each time. It didn't seem to matter. One of their numbers came up every time, putting the croupier into disarray and unnerving the next croupier who quickly followed him. In the beginning, having opened up the table, they were the only ones playing but word got around quickly that they were winning and other players were drawn to the action. Before they were through, every seat was filled. They played for almost an hour, placques stacking up in front of them, until at a certain point Charles broke the rules and doubled his bet on the zero. Gavers immediately gave him a warning look. They had an agreement. Locking eyes, they heard the appreciative gasps when the zero came up. Then it repeated. Gavers roared with laughter.

"That's our signal," he said. "We're through for the night. We can't beat our own luck." He tossed the croupier a five-hundred-dollar placque, and before Charles realized what was happening, Gavers had him out of the Sporting Club and into a car that took them the few blocks to their agreed rendezvous point. Gavers had arranged for someone to cash in for them and bring the money to Rampoldi's, where the others were waiting for them. They devoured a huge platter of spaghetti al vongole, full of high spirits and the euphoria that goes with winning.

"I'm taking no chances with you, Charles," he said. "For once, you're going away a winner."

The next morning he was jubilant.

"That's the way to do it," he said. "We are much more than even after that little win. Remember the gambler's credo? 'We broke even and how we needed the money'? Do you realize that we took away over forty thousand dollars? What we won will pay off everything to do with *Cattivo*, every last luxury that we have indulged ourselves in, and we will both be taking home a nice little sum. And leaving lavish tips for the captain and the crew. There's a little champagne and caviar to leave aboard for them too. They have been wonderful, yes? What?"

"As they should be," Charles conceded.

"You pompous ass," Gavers said, grinning at him. "You're right, of course: as they should be. But the point is they were, and that is rare among yacht crews. Do I detect a faintly sour note because I got you away before you had a chance to lose what we worked so hard to win? Is that what is wrong with your normally sunny disposition this morning? Winning makes you nervous, does it? Well, you can lose it all in my place when you get home, so cheer up. And don't start thinking about getting back into Monte Carlo tonight. We're going ashore in Villefranche to one of those marvelous little bistros and have a simple supper and a massive amount of wine and that's it. The cars will fetch us at ten; the flight to London is at noon. Don't sulk on our last day, you poor devil, just because you're going home ahead of the game."

"All right, all right," Charles said grumpily. Amanda marveled at

how Gavers handled him. Why couldn't she do that? Or did she have to
be an inveterate gambler herself to know how to deal with him?

Charles admitted to himself that he did begrudge Gavers's having
successfully denied him the chance to have one more crack at the big
table last night. Of course they had done well, very well, but it made him
uneasy to quit now. One more night. If he had one more night, he could
take away a real fortune, not just enough to cover the expenses of the
boat and crew plus a little pocket money. That was mundane. Gavers
was a peasant in his thinking. Now was the time to triple their winnings.
In the back of his mind, he began to scheme. He could go to the little
casino in Beaulieu right after dinner—that would be easy; it was not
even a five-minute walk from the port. But there was no real challenge
there. The big table at Monte Carlo was where he wanted to be, just one
more time. How could he arrange to get there?

At eight they gathered for farewell drinks on the afterdeck, watching the sunset and faintly nostalgic about leaving the yacht. Their last
night together, the end of a perfect holiday. Robin made a final sketch of
Amanda and Chantal, both wearing gauzy white cotton dresses that
emphasized their golden, sun-tanned skin. Amanda found herself holding back tears. Why did it have to end? She had never been this happy
before, never had Charles so much to herself.

CHAPTER 8

October 1965

Amanda had prayed that when she and Charles returned to London their lives would take on a new pattern. It was not to be. He resumed the exact schedule he had had before. Amanda longed for Friday afternoons when they would drive to the country to spend the weekend with Richard and Davina, taking Patrick with them. She dreaded their return to London on Sunday night, knowing full well that she would see little or nothing of Charles during the week except for the very few hours they spent in bed. Amanda was usually asleep by the time he returned from the Club, and Charles by then was exhausted and sometimes quite drunk. At least Raschid had not returned. They did make love in the early mornings but it was an animal-like ritual with no conversation or tenderness, and that sort of impersonal sex left Amanda frustrated and depressed.

Perhaps it was because they had lived in such a paradise on *Cattivo II* that the contrast of their normal lives seemed so stark now. Amanda knew that wasn't all there was to it, and she had sense enough to realize that things were somehow worse now than before they had gone on holiday. Why? It must be money. Charles must have lost more money in Monte Carlo than he was willing to admit, even to himself. She could ask John Latimer, who might tell her. Gavers wouldn't. Since their return Charles had been so remote and dour that Amanda felt sure things were still running against him. Funny, in those days before they married, she was so naïve that she thought gamblers always won. Charles had been in such good humor then. No more.

As her tan faded, so did her hopes. Looking in the mirror, she remembered Robin's remark about her being a summer girl. He had described

her as "pinch-faced" when she was in London. He was right. She was
pinch-faced again.

There was a particularly ugly scene one day when Charles came down
for breakfast. She was at her desk. Box after box of crested notepaper
and *pour mémoire* cards and engraved invitation cards had arrived from
Smythson's. The bill was enormous. Charles exploded.

"What did you order all this for?" he demanded angrily. "What in the
world are you planning to do with it? You don't write to anyone ever
that I know of, and when, pray, are you planning to send out these
invitations? 'The Countess of Warrington. At Home.' What's all that
about?"

His anger stripped her of even a fragile confidence. "I thought now
that we're settled into the house, it might be nice to have some friends
come in," she said meekly. "We've never had anyone here. We could
have a big drinks party or some small dinners. Then we might be invited
to a few more parties. I could wear my emerald—I've never even put it
on since you brought it home." Her voice was flat.

"I see everyone I want to see at the Club. We don't have to fill the
house with acquaintances. Leave it alone, Amanda."

Knowing she was on dangerous ground, Amanda still persisted. Now
she was angry herself. Why did they have to live like this? "There are at
least two super parties this fall, one of them Daisy and Jake Chesney's
big ball at Claridge's for their anniversary, and you've refused both
without even asking me if I'd like to go. Surely our entire social life is
not going to revolve forever around the glorious Wyndham Club? Is it?
That's the only place you ever take me. We never go to Les Amis, where
there are people who do something besides gamble. It's not as fascinating as you may think, your allowing me to sit silently watching as you
gamble, approving as you lose thousands with your stoic calm."

She had never attacked him before and never used the sarcastic tone
she was using now. The ferocity of her reaction surprised and frightened
her. She could have said the same thing in a different tone, demurely or
sadly, and it might have been effective. Instead, she heard herself revert
to the old Amanda, the sharp-tongued shrew of the past. Was she once
more alone, without love, adrift?

Charles stared at her coldly.

"You don't understand and it's obvious that you never will. We have a
perfectly nice house, a son and a nanny and a daily. We go to the
country every weekend. We each have a car. You buy clothes constantly.
That's more than most women have, ever. I like a private life. I won't
have this house filled with effete poofs or boring old people with titles
who impress you. I have a handful of friends and that's exactly as I want

it. And that is the way it is going to be. We're not going to the Chesneys' ball because there is a backgammon tournament at the Club that night. I'll pay this ridiculous bill, but don't order anything more like it, ever again. You'll be eighty before you have occasion to use it up."

"I'll be eighty and dead before I will be allowed even to pretend to be the Countess of Warrington," she slashed back at him. "I thought it would all be so different. Is there something awful about privilege? About title and rank? You hated your parents' Labour connections— they were an embarrassment to you. But you're no better than they were; you're ten times worse. You have the looks and the title and the connections. You have plenty of money and friends and yet all you do is stand at gambling tables losing." Her tone had changed to a lament. Why couldn't she get through to him, or at least learn how to lure him away from his incessant gambling? He was so much more intelligent and knowledgeable than Robin or Neil or even Gavers. He was a peer. They weren't.

What sort of life were they leading and what was it leading to? She was left alone all the time except for a baby and a lower-class servant girl and a second-rate nanny. Her head began to ache with the sure signs of the oncoming, blinding migraine that she thought she had finished with. She picked up some of the Smythson boxes and opened the doors of a cabinet they used for storing some of the silver they had so much of. Slamming them into the cabinet, her eye was caught by the Warrington crest on a dozen tankards that seemed to taunt her from their hidden place of repose. Never used, never even displayed, all these beautiful things. Like herself.

"I do keep forgetting how much your 'elevation' to Countess means to you," Charles said stiffly. "I must try to remember once in a while. Perhaps you could drop me a little line on some of this overabundance of notepaper to remind me occasionally? Pay the Smythson bill and let's hear no more about it."

He threw some notes down on the desk and turned and left the room.

November 1965

For a week after that bitter scene Amanda was never free from headaches that came and rarely went, torturing her. Arriving at Richard and Davina's for the weekend, she went to bed. It was the worst migraine she had ever had. She lay in their darkened room in agony, not able to eat or drink and not knowing or caring if it was night or day.

Finally, on Sunday afternoon, Charles took pity on her. He sat down on the bed beside her and took her hand.

"We are looking for a good doctor for you," he said. "Davina says you have had these headaches for years but never this bad. She's been told about a doctor in Pont Street who apparently knows more about migraine than anyone else. I'm going to make an appointment with him and take you tomorrow. If he's no good we'll find someone else."

Amanda nodded, too miserable to care. When they left Lea Place, Charles put the nanny and Patrick in the front seat of the car and made a bed for Amanda in the back for the drive into London. She was completely helpless. An overwhelming sense of failure engulfed her but she was too ill to think about it. All she knew was that it was her fault, her fault and her failure alone.

On Monday morning the headache was still there. She got up shakily, hoping tea or something would help her. She had lost five pounds and her face was the color of cement. Charles took her to the doctor promptly at one and stayed with her. Amanda was oblivious to both Charles and the doctor.

Dr. Archibald Stirling prescribed Valium, and Amanda got the distinct impression that he thought her a neurotic creature with nothing better to do than lie around all day, waited on hand and foot. However, he wanted to see her next Tuesday, alone, when the headache had gone. Fine, Amanda thought. Anything. Nothing will work anyhow.

She took the Valium, which made her somnambulant. For the greater part of the week she slept. She spent her waking hours with Patrick, feeding him, cuddling him and kissing him, playing with him. Charles was a shadowy figure who came and went, not speaking to her beyond a perfunctory goodbye before he left around noon. After the second day, she stopped answering, pretending she hadn't heard him. They acknowledged each other's presence as little as possible and when Friday came he went to Lea Place alone for the weekend, with no explanation. She was too lassitudinous to fight with him. Resentment built in her. She was not the failure—he was.

On the following Tuesday she kept her appointment with Dr. Stirling. The headache had retreated, leaving her weak and shaky. Seeing Dr. Stirling again gave her a glimmer of hope. Could he help her? Would he?

"Are you feeling any better?" he asked, and once again Amanda felt that he was patronizing her, as he had the week before.

There were blue circles under her eyes. She was very pale and quiet. "Yes," she said. "I've had these headaches since I was a child. Did I tell you that last week? I felt so frightful, I can't remember." Might as well try to disarm the old bastard and get him on her side. Charles had probably filled him up with a lot of rubbish about her.

"No, but your husband did."

"I'm surprised he bothered." Her tone was faintly sarcastic.

Dr. Stirling looked at her. Was this a simple case of trouble in a marriage? One never knew at first, but he had not gotten that impression from Lord Warrington, who seemed quite genuinely concerned. "My wife has a history of headaches since childhood but, according to her sister, never as severe as this. She is quite an intense person," Warrington had told him. Tension was the major cause of migraine, hidden tensions that were always difficult to deal with, but there was more to Amanda Warrington's problem than that. Archibald Stirling had researched migraine for many years. It was a fascinating disorder to him and a deeply serious one. It was not to be dealt with lightly. Scores of unexplained suicides were caused by it. The pain alone made death desirable to some. This young woman had obviously had a bad time with migraine for a very long time.

"Why do you say that?" he asked gently. Along with his expertise, Dr. Stirling had a sincere sympathy for anyone who had been felled by more than a week of migraine.

"I don't know," Amanda said, unwanted tears streaming down her face. The innate kindness in the doctor's tone had undone her. "This one was the worst. When we got married, they went away for almost a year. Now they're starting again." The tears flowed. To Dr. Stirling's practiced eye there was something unusually vulnerable about her. Taking a handkerchief from her bag, she blew her nose.

He let her take the time to calm herself.

"I can't stop crying," she said. "Sometimes I don't even know that I am crying. I didn't mean that about Charles. I'm just so depressed."

"We'll see what we can do about that. It will take time and tests and questions, but we will do what we can. How long did you nurse your baby?"

"Only for seven weeks. I'm afraid I wasn't very successful at it. My milk was no good and he needed more." Again the sense of failure.

"Tell me about your eating habits." Along with the pathetic quality there was something more about her, the something that long ago had brought migraine into her life. It would come out eventually if she kept coming to him. It might not be curable, but the source of the trouble would be revealed.

Suddenly impatient, Amanda looked at Dr. Stirling as if he were a moron. *What do I eat?* she thought. *What's that got to do with it?* She forced herself to use a sweet tone to answer him, the saccharine tones of the phony befriending her. What was Oscar Wilde's line? "No gentleman is ever rude unintentionally"? Well, no lady is saccharine without reason either.

"Very little. I've never thought much about food. Tea and toast for breakfast. Soup for lunch. I eat alone most of the time. In the evenings, I pick at whatever's in the fridge. I don't care much about food." The tears had stopped.

"Then I don't need to ask if you consume large amounts of chocolate or cheese. Or drink a lot of red wine. Those three things, especially in combination, have been established as contributory to migraine, although they are certainly not the cause of it. From the look of you, and from your apparent lack of discipline when it comes to food, a decent diet alone may alleviate some of your headaches. How old is your child now?"

"Almost eight months."

"It is possible that you could be suffering from postnatal depression. How have you felt generally, since he was born?"

"Wonderful." Her face lit up for the first time and her eyes brightened. "He's such a good boy and I do have a good nanny. My husband and I went on holiday in late August and I felt wonderful then, and I did eat much more." The tears started again. Of course she had eaten more then. Charles had made love to her all the time and she was a summer girl. She wasn't left alone in a dark house in filthy weather with a husband who didn't speak to her. Patrick was the only light in her life and he couldn't make conversation.

"With a nanny in the house, couldn't you get out and have a good lunch with a girlfriend occasionally?"

Amanda remained silent, not answering Dr. Stirling. If only she had a girlfriend, she thought; if only she had anyone of her own. Maybe she could go to Paris and visit Chantal. Then she could eat like a horse. And have someone to talk to. The tears stopped and Amanda felt a beginning of hope, of excitement. It was immediately replaced by fury. What was she doing here talking about herself to this idiotic doctor?

"Oh, do stop preaching to me," she said. "Having lunch with a girlfriend is hardly going to cure what's wrong with me, and postnatal depression certainly doesn't start eight months after a child is born. Just give me some more of that stupid Valium that you doctors depend on to earn your fees and perhaps I can sleep the rest of my life away and not bother you—or anyone else—anymore. No one would miss me." She stood up abruptly and pulled on her raincoat. Stupid doctor, treating her this way.

"Sit down, Lady Warrington," the doctor said in a clear tone of undisputable authority. "I am not your enemy. I can help you."

As quickly as it had come, the unreasonable mood left her. Amanda was appalled at the way she had behaved. What in the world had possessed her? She had lost control of herself and been insulting to the kindly doctor. "Dr. Stirling, forgive me. I don't know what happened. I've never done anything like that before."

"My dear, migraine is not just a headache that is worse than other headaches. It is a serious disorder with serious consequences. Two weeks of pain have left you weak and very much off balance. I would like to see you every Tuesday for the next few months, and I want you to stay on the Valium as prescribed. My nurse will give you a diet that I also want you to promise me you will follow as closely as possible. Next week, we'll complete your physical examination. So far all your tests are fine—blood, heart, and so on. Now we must try to establish a pattern from which we can draw some conclusions." He led her to the door of his office.

Amanda apologized once more, shaken by her outburst, paler than ever.

Dr. Stirling sat alone in his office when she was gone, his next appointment not for half an hour. Complex woman, he thought. What she was going to need was not just a GP like himself but some first-rate psychiatric care. Next week he would feel that out with her and if she resisted he would discuss it with her husband. Her migraines were a manifestation of some deeply rooted emotional problems. They were a dramatic cry for help, but he wasn't sure what anyone could do for her.

Amanda went to Paris.

"*Mais bien sûr,* come at once!" Chantal had said over the phone, a lilting excitement in her voice. "My chauffeur will be at Orly to meet you—his name is Roland. Which flight will you be on and how long can you stay? We will go to the country for the weekend—you must see Quatre Mai as well as the house here in Paris."

Amanda laughed, reassured by everything Chantal was saying. Her call had been tentative; she had changed her mind several times before she finally summoned the courage to pick up the phone. It was Tuesday afternoon; she had just gotten back from Dr. Stirling's office. Charles was at the Wyndham and would not be back until seven at least and then only to bathe and change for the evening session. If Chantal would have her, she could spend two nights or maybe even three and still be back on Friday in time to go to Davina's. Chantal seemed thrilled she could come. It was all arranged and she must hurry—there was a small dinner tonight at New Jimmy's. Régine was the rage of Paris and Amanda would love New Jimmy's.

It was all so easy. She put a few things in the small Gucci suitcase, a Christmas gift from Charles. The only other time it had been used was on the Monte Carlo trip. What did one wear in Paris in November? The same as in London, no doubt. The weather might be the same but the look certainly wasn't. English bodies and French bodies tended to be unattractive, but the way the French adorned themselves made the English look as dowdy as they generally were. Chantal would help her buy a dress or suit that would look right in Paris. *Chic* was a word that belonged exclusively to the French. Impulsive or no, she was going.

She found her passport and begged Nanny Blake successfully to take two days off next week instead of this Thursday. She hugged and kissed Patrick, and left a note for Charles on the Smythson notepaper to tell him she would be at Chantal's and giving him the telephone number, nothing more. She cabbed to Heathrow and took the five-thirty Air France flight to Paris.

Roland was waiting for her outside of customs at Orly, wearing a midnight-blue uniform, cap in hand. He retrieved her suitcase and put her smoothly into the back seat of a sleek navy-blue Citroën. It was already dark, so Amanda saw nothing much but traffic until they crossed the Seine and Roland slowed to maneuver skillfully through a web of narrow gaslit streets. Amanda felt transported back into another century. Gaslights! They hadn't been used in England for fifty years at least.

The wide double entrance doors to the Hôtel du Vallieres—the De Briands' *hôtel particulier*—were at least fifteen feet high and so thick that an army couldn't have broken them down. As Roland helped her from the car, a liveried footman greeted her. He was uniformed in the same midnight-blue—obviously the De Briand color—but with white ruffled linen at his throat, and lapels and cuffs of palest robin's-egg-blue velvet on his jacket. Amanda could imagine him wearing a powdered wig and opening doors at Versailles a century or so before.

The entrance hall was candlelit by an elaborate chandelier, and eight-branch sconces ten feet over Amanda's head. With one look at the sweeping curve of the great stairway, Amanda realized that she had walked into a world of power and luxury she had never seen before.

★   ★   ★

Amanda's visit to Paris stretched into a full week, and then another. She called each day about Patrick but she did not speak to Charles, nor did he call her.

Chantal's world was four centuries old and the De Briand fortune was indestructible. In its present manifestation, two men controlled it: Chantal's father, Philippe, and her brother, François. Amanda was not privy to family confidences, obviously, but she was fascinated by the Hôtel du Vallieres and Quatre Mai, the great château in the Loire Valley. François had observed her interest and opened the De Briand history to her. François was not as vibrant, as vital as either Chantal or Philippe de Briand, but he was beautifully mannered and attentive to Amanda in his quiet way. Amanda asked Chantal about him. Was he married? Did he live with them? What did he do?

"He's a treasure," Chantal said. "I adore him, as I am sure you have observed, perhaps because he is so different from my father and myself. We are so opinionated, so forceful. François is the philosopher, the one who understands time, understands the long view of things. He's not particularly happy at this stage of his life—an aborted romance—but that will pass. Sometimes I think François should have been born in a gentler century. He's reflective and calm. Then he turns up with some new technique or product and I realize that he is more sophisticated and up-to-date than my father or I could ever be. We were all born in the wrong century."

"Which would you have preferred?"

"The sixteenth," Chantal said pensively. "That was the most exciting time for the De Briands, and the century in which I would like to have lived. Then we were still adventurous and free. Now we have obligations and power, but nothing to match the excitement of the beginning, the first sense of achievement."

"You have so little of the snob to you," Amanda said. "In the two weeks I've been here I've seen you with everyone from Malraux to the lowest *plongeur* in a bistro. You are the same with all of them. You and François and your father seem to take it all so lightly."

"Ah, *mon amie adorable,* I may not seem to, but actually I do take being who I am very seriously. *'Duchesse'* is not of vast importance, all in all, since I am the fourteenth De Briand Duchess and the fifth Chantal, but who I am and what I represent means a great deal to me."

"Being the Countess of Warrington means a great deal to me, too, but I am not allowed to care, since I only married into the aristocracy. Charles must care, but he won't let me." Why not say it? Chantal could give the best advice.

"Of course he cares. The English love not to show it. Cold—most of them are so cold. Gavers with a title would be the worst. But after this visit, you may be able to take on some vestige of being a Countess. Charles needs to be called on the mat, as you say. By the way, your French is getting to be quite marvelous."

Amanda was pleased with the compliment. Thanks to Chantal's thoughtfulness she was having lessons every morning.

"In two months," Chantal said, "you could be fluent. Why don't you stay for another week?"

"Chantal, Charles is going to murder me or divorce me as it is now. Not hearing from him is getting on my nerves. I have to go home."

"Wait a little longer," Chantal said. "He will call."

C harles's voice on the telephone was gruff and uncommunicative.

"When are you planning to come home?" he asked. "Nanny Blake has been on duty for two weeks without a day off now, and you've missed two appointments with Stirling."

"I don't know," Amanda said, eyes on Chantal, who was making a gesture that distinctly translated: *Cool, be very cool.*

"What do you mean you don't know?" he asked coldly. Amanda heard the anger in his voice and yet another tone, patronizing her, treating her as if she were beneath him.

Her tone was honey. "Oh, Charles, I am having such a good time and I miss you and Patrick madly, but I need a few more days. I'll try to get there before the weekend. Are you going to Richard and Davina's?" As if she didn't know; he never went anywhere else.

His anger surfaced full tilt. "What do you mean, you'll try to get here before the weekend? That's enough, Amanda. You are to come home tomorrow. Do you understand?"

Oh, yes, Charles, I understand, she thought. Looking at Chantal, pretending to be Chantal, she said nothing, holding the phone in one hand and running the other through her hair.

"Goddammit, Amanda!" Charles's voice exploded on the phone. "Are you still there? I want to know which plane you will be on. I'll meet you at the airport."

Surely Chantal couldn't be this right; it couldn't be this easy. Chantal had told her how to handle him but she hadn't believed her. And yet it was true. Enrage him, Chantal had said. Don't be afraid to enrage him, and make him come to you.

"Charles," she said, her voice very in-the-middle, not warm and not cool, the tone one used to speak to a servant, "I'll try to get home soon. Just give Nanny Blake a little bonus. I do speak to her every day and she tells me Patrick is fine. Darling, I'm late, Chantal is having a dinner tonight and I must run. Big kiss to you, darling, and good luck." She hung up and turned to Chantal, triumphant.

"He'll be here before teatime tomorrow, if not before lunch," Chantal said, winking at Amanda.

"Oh, I hope so," Amanda said. "I could no more get on an airplane and go home to London and walk into that house to face him than fly to the moon. I would be undone."

"That's the last thing you should do. He has to come to you. This house has been soundproof for centuries. You need a big battle with him, a noisy one, and you must cry a lot and tell him that you're not good enough for him. Make him have to drag you home forcibly and let him think that if he leaves you alone for so much as half a day in the future, you'll be gone and he'll return to an empty house. This time, gone with Patrick. Come, we must dress, my *amie adorable.*"

Charles was escorted up the curving stairway to the rooms in which his wife was staying as if he had been expected. Cheeky bastards, the French. Madame la Duchesse and Madame la Comtesse were out but were expected back around six, he was told. His suitcase was put on a carved ivory luggage rack and a manservant immediately unpacked it and went off with two suits to press and a pair of shoes to be shined. A *femme de chambre* arrived, smiling sweetly, her arms piled with white Porthault towels.

"Pour vous, monsieur," she said, taking them into the bathroom, still smiling sweetly.

Charles grunted affirmation. It annoyed him—not that he didn't speak French, but that they did.

Charles looked around carefully at the rooms that Amanda had lived in for two weeks now. Normally his quick eye took in the contents of a room, recorded in his mind what was interesting, and then forgot it. Most rooms had nothing of real value in them and weren't worthy of close attention. This was entirely different. The Hôtel du Vallieres was one of the finest houses built in Paris in the seventeenth century and it had been maintained magnificently. All of its contents were beyond museum quality, right down to the andirons he recognized as having been made by Gouthière, the master bronzer of the eighteenth century.

Charles had not expected to be overwhelmed. In fact, he had not expected to be in Paris, but in the morning, when he was wakened by Patrick's crying, he had made a quick decision to go to Paris and bring Amanda home. It was past time for her return. Last night, after speaking to her on the telephone, he realized that he had best go and get her. Granted he left her alone too often in London. On the other hand, it had been only a few months since they had been in the South of France with Gavers. That should keep her. And Chantal actually seemed to like Amanda, but now it was time for Amanda to come home. She had enough delusions of grandeur already without being exposed to Chantal's world, the atmosphere and trappings of De Briand wealth, for too long.

Charles wasn't fooling himself one bit with these thoughts. He was furious with Amanda and he meant to have it out with her. She had gone off without so much as a by-your-leave. She had missed appointments with Dr. Stirling. Her behavior was not normal. She was not taking care of Patrick properly. Two weeks in Paris, for example. She should be home taking care of him herself, not leaving him entirely in the hands of the nanny.

His eye was caught by the beauty of the flowers in both the sitting room and the bedroom. Heavy silver bowls, rather than vases, were massed with white sweet peas. Sweet peas were not in bloom in November in London. Apparently they were in Paris. Where the hell did the Frogs get them? He went into the sitting room and poured some gin into a heavy crystal glass—both gin and glass to his liking—from the bar. He looked at the Savonnerie carpet beneath his feet, observing how it fit the room exactly. Obviously it had been woven for the house, at least a hundred years before. The *bureau plat* where he seated himself was worth more than the house in Royal Hospital Road.

He picked up a newspaper, one of five laid neatly in a row on the desk, but it was *France Soir* and he couldn't read it. He rifled through the rest and found the *International Herald Tribune*.

The door opened and a man entered the room.

"I beg your pardon, sir," the man said. "I had no idea you were here. I have come to comb Madame la Comtesse's hair. I am Alexandre." He was dark and quite good-looking. Charles had heard ladies nattering on about Alexandre this and Alexandre that, how expensive he was and how brilliant. Now he was here waiting to arrange Amanda's hair. Past time to get her back to London.

The butler entered the room to ask if M'sieu would care to have tea in

the library with M'sieu le Duc? M'sieu would. With barely a glance at
the waiting Alexandre, Charles left the room. Perhaps M'sieu le Duc
would give him a drink rather than tea.

Both Philippe and François de Briand were waiting for him in the
library and he was immediately offered tea or a drink, whichever he
preferred.

"We have enjoyed your wife's visit, Lord Warrington," Philippe de
Briand was saying. "And now yours. We have a small dinner here at
home tonight but unfortunately, my son and I are leaving for Cairo
tomorrow morning. I believe Chantal is planning to spend the weekend
in the country at Quatre Mai and I hope you and Lady Warrington will
be joining her."

"I think not," Charles said. "I'm afraid my wife has overstayed her
welcome. I'm planning to return to London with her in the morning."

"What a shame. No, we have enjoyed having Amanda with us immensely, she is a charming young woman."

For the next half hour the conversation was forced and lifeless. When
Charles had downed his second drink, he could stand it no longer.
Where the hell was Amanda? He excused himself somewhat abruptly,
saying he might have a nap. When he left, François looked at his father
and started to laugh.

"I've seen some angry husbands before, but his lordship seems to be
in a rage, wouldn't you say?"

"Did we know he was coming?" Philippe asked.

"Chantal seemed to think he might turn up. I know she left instructions to take care of him if he did."

"He needs a nap. I hope his behavior at dinner is a little lighter. She is
by far the more attractive of the two of them. Thank God we don't have
to spend a weekend with him."

"I'm sure he feels the same about us."

"I don't like him," Philippe de Briand said. "I find him somewhat
reprehensible."

François laughed. "He'll be more attractive this evening. You never
have been much on the English, you know."

Roland was driving them back into Paris after a meeting with André Malraux, the Minister of Cultural Affairs. Chantal had invited
Amanda to come along. Malraux had expounded on the availabilities of
De Briand funds used to support the restoration of châteaux that had
suffered both war damage and an absence of money and desire on the
part of the owners to keep them from irreparable disintegration.

Amanda sat quietly, taking in as much as she could of the language she loved. Malraux deplored the attitude of his countrymen toward the preservation of their heritage. He could provide government funds, and if the De Briands would add to them, he could force matching funds from the owners whose fortunes were rarely as intact as the De Briands'.

"Why does your family have to support them at all?" Amanda asked.

"It's a traditional responsibility. Some of the families resent my father's position as first Duke and our wealth, but some are truly without funds. Malraux and I play games together. He knows that we will aid them. He holds that as a weapon over them. We have been extremely lucky, blessed, in that no war has ever damaged De Briand lands. The Germans left us alone when we were occupied in Paris, beyond their enormous appetite for our wines. They called politely at Quatre Mai, clicking their heels, but made it clear that we would be safe." She sighed.

"Some form of *noblesse oblige?*"

"Very clever, Amanda. In the long history of my family, we have covered the map of Europe in one way or another. My grandfather and great-grandfather never ravaged the Germans or anyone else. We have even kept wars from happening. The Germans respected us; orders were from the top, so the occupying troops chose to leave us alone. There is resentment of our special position and we were treated as collaborators, although everyone knows better than that. Malraux and I negotiate for the sake of France. We will do our part."

"The French spend a lot of time detesting each other," Amanda said.

"Yes, and you talk of French manners! When De Gaulle was in England during the war, one of your papers did a story on him, describing him as 'Our Once and Sometimes Friend.' It was correct. He took your hospitality and reviled you for it. He was behaving in a manner protective and productive for the French, and the French hated him for leaving France to do it. That's French manners for you."

"I wish I could get Charles to behave in a way that was protective and productive for me," Amanda said.

Chantal laughed at Amanda's pulling global politics into her personal life. "Everything is relative."

Amanda laughed too. "I wish that my Charles would be my once and sometimes friend."

Chantal turned serious. "You must make that so. You have to establish your position, make him respect it and you. He doesn't know you have it in you to change his life for the better. Fight with him, Amanda. Fight with him—tell him who you are. Then woo him again. I can't wait for the *feu d'artifice,* the fireworks between you. Amanda, you must be strong. There are times between a man and a woman that are proving times. From those confrontations comes strength or weakness. Someone wins; the other loses. You've got him right where he should be now, off balance and angry. He wants you and he is furious with himself. I think you really do love him and I know that he loves you. I have seen Charles for years, in Biarritz, in St. Moritz or Monte Carlo, with Gavers. Charles was always drawn to beautiful women, rarely English. He would hit and run; he would 'boff' a girl, as he put it, and dance and drink and gamble and play games, but then he'd leave alone, without remembering her name. Until you. You have to find a way to make yourself all-important to him. It's the only way to replace his gambling, which is at a danger point now. We've had this conversation before."

They were at the house. The footman opened the door. The Earl of Warrington had arrived, he informed Madame la Duchesse.

Chantal kissed Amanda. "You see," she said. "He's here. Remember, keep him off balance. Raise hell with him."

Coming awake, Charles was furious. There was an ugly taste in his mouth from too many cigarettes and too much gin.

When he returned after tea, he had taken off his shoes and stretched out on the satin-covered bed, plumping up the pillows beneath his head. He had fallen asleep almost instantly.

The next thing he knew, Amanda was there on him, crawling on him, God damn her. He lifted his head, cursing, and tried to rise from the bed but she was all over him. He turned his head away as her lips searched for his, realizing that his breath was awful, but her sweet breath and lips came down on his anyway, and he had her naked body to contend with. God damn her, he thought, and he pushed at her, hard, trying to shake her off. Then he found he was no longer angry; he was awake and strong and aroused and he wanted her more than he had wanted her in months.

It was like the first time they had been together but more exciting to Charles this time, Amanda naked as before, as she loved to be, and he fully dressed. They were in a bed that kings and queens had made love in. French love, whatever the difference was. Instead of the all-too-familiar pattern of their chilly and desultory life together in London, this was Paris. Amanda, Amanda, Charles thought, as the scent of her assailed him.

Amanda was playing a game of sexual strip poker with him, hot to his touch. The fire in the bedroom burned cheerfully against the November cold, but it was nowhere near as warm as her skin. Sitting on top of him, she undid his tie.

"Stop it, you bitch," he muttered, teeth clenched, grabbing at her with his strong hands. When she was like this he was sometimes afraid of her, afraid that he might not be a match for her. Never mind, he'd give her more than she was asking for, and she was asking for it this time. She had to learn who made the rules. Her skin was setting him on fire.

"Don't you dare speak to me that way," she said, breaking loose from his grip and stuffing his tie into his mouth, trying to choke him, making him fight her.

Now she was unbuttoning his shirt, rubbing herself against him, her breasts against his skin and breathing that hot breath all over him as she moved down on him. She undid his belt and struggled with the opening of his trousers until she could get her mouth on him, take all of him into her mouth. He almost choked spitting his tie out and he grabbed her by the hair, removing her delicious mouth from where he most wanted it to be. Damn her again, she was going too fast for him on purpose—she knew he was entirely too aroused to let her stay there. What the hell did she mean telling him not to speak to her that way? He'd show her who had the upper hand. He grabbed at her again and the two of them wrestled until he rolled over hard on top of her and pinned her beneath him. His trousers were still crippling him, halfway down his legs, and his shirt was unbuttoned and hanging loose. God knows what had happened to his jacket, or had he taken it off before he lay down? Amanda's little face beneath him was impertinent, her body was wriggling, and she was making fun of him. Suddenly she gave a fierce little shove and they both rolled off the bed, falling onto the platform and the rug in a tangle of arms and legs. Amanda was laughing and Charles now saw the humor in it, a grown man struggling, in a half-dressed state, struggling against this tiny, naked sex goddess, fighting her but wanting her more. Christ, how he did want her. He shook off his trousers, finally free to get on top of her and force himself into her with such a strong thrust that she screamed and beat at his face; the combination of pain and enormous pleasure making her come. She was so hot inside that he was lost himself and came seconds after her, cursing her again. This was how she got control, when he should have it.

He hadn't meant to let go; he'd meant to dominate her until he was ready, regardless of what she wanted. Even now she was moving with him still in her, locking muscles around him, and he gritted his teeth and bit into her neck, both of them rapturously continuing as if it were the first and last and only time they would have each other and as if they had forgotten that this was the way it was between them whenever they made love. Everything else was a battlefield; so was this, but they were right for each other. It was only when they made love that they were right together.

Gasping and wet all over, Amanda curled herself into his arms and started to cry. Charles knew who held control now—she was always vulnerable after they had made love.

"I love you so. I'm so glad you're here." As she said the words, Chantal's face appeared in her mind. Fight with him, demand his respect, Chantal said. How could she? She didn't want to fight with him. He was her husband and she wanted him to be nice to her, speak to her, make love to her.

"Fine way to show it," he said, his normally slicked-back hair curly all over his forehead. "Your fancy hairdresser is probably out there listening in on us, or maybe he's been watching."

"No, he isn't and hasn't," she said, humorlessly. "I sent him to Chantal when I came in."

"Good. Time for a bath. Pretty bathroom." He picked her up and carried her into the bathroom and put her down in the empty tub in the center of the room. He turned both taps on full, and as the water rose to cover her body, he slipped in beside her.

"There never was anyone like you," he said, holding her in his arms. "Now I suppose we have to dress for dinner. I don't want dinner. I want you again."

Amanda looked at him, patting his face, nuzzling him. Maybe they could be happy. Maybe something would work out and she would never have one of those headaches again. He did love her—he had come to Paris, hadn't he? This time when they got back to London, it would all be different. How could she fight him? He wouldn't put up with it. Why must she fight him?

"The fancy Alexandre had best not come back before we finish this bath," Charles said. Stupid of her to have gone off and left him; she would have to learn that she was not to do things like that. He'd let it alone for the moment, until they got back to London.

They stayed in Paris for four more days. Chantal was delighted. Philippe de Briand and François had left for Egypt.

Charles took to stopping by the Traveler's Club for the afternoon backgammon sessions and he won for a change. He was in a fine mood —also for a change. It was like the old days. He bought Amanda a Ceylon sapphire set in rose diamonds and hung on a slender platinum chain. The stone was of the best quality. Chantal approved, but when

Charles left them in the Espadon at the Ritz to go to the Traveler's Club after lunch, she cautioned Amanda.

"You haven't won anything yet. You'll be back in London next week and it'll be exactly as it was when you left if you're not smart. You shouldn't let him go to the Traveler's and you should pretend the sapphire is not really much. Nice, but not much."

"Let im go to the Traveler's!" Amanda said. "How could I stop him? Chantal you think the sapphire is lovely—you said so."

"Of course it is, but you've got to get what you want. Don't soothe him. Raise hell whether he wins or loses, throw the money in the street if he wins and swear that he cares more for everything else in the world than he does for you. Throw the sapphire in the street, tonight!"

"Chantal, I can't, I can't."

"All right, keep looking at him with that adoring expression as you did all through luncheon today and you'll be home in London with less than you have now. You've almost lost, but not quite. Stay here. Don't go home with him. Keep up your French lessons—it's a language you do well in. And you know François is mad for you, and you treat him like a dog. Why, why can't you be that way to Charles?"

"Chantal, I know you're right, you know I do. It's just that when he's sweet like this, I like to please him, and he is being sweet."

Chantal's hand made an impatient little gesture in the air. "Amanda, but do not lose the moment. You must establish yourself as an object of respect and affection. He's selfish and self-destructive and only you can help him. Gavers knows that, I know that. Why can't you see it?"

Amanda was suddenly impatient with Chantal. Charles loved her. Things had changed since he had come to Paris. He made love to her every waking hour; he couldn't get enough of her. And the headaches would never come back now. She had a plan that would make things even better. Nanny Blake was fine, but the daily was not. She would find a first-rate cook-housekeeper. Then Charles would gamble three nights a week and she would make him stay at home two, and they would have dinner parties on those nights, using all the divine things from Longholt that hadn't been used for years. She wanted to discuss with him again a house in the country of their own. Why not? Did they have to spend every weekend with Davina and Richard? A house nearby would be nice, near the golf course, naturally. She would bring it up tonight.

But when she did, Charles brushed her off, shushed her. She decided not to push it.

"We'll talk about all that when we get home," Charles said. And that was that.

★ ★ ★

London, December 1965

Amanda, through simple lust, lost rather than won the battle that she herself had initiated. The most important agreement that could have been made between them never came to fruition.

Charles took full advantage of her weakness. He had expected trouble in Paris, anticipated it. She had been clever to leave him, especially to go to Chantal and her sophisticated world. Obviously she had meant her departure as a message. She wanted some changes, and for the sake of peace he was willing to give a little. He was beginning to be bored with the Club all the time. He wondered how she and Chantal had spent their nights in Paris, where they went and what they did. Whom had she met? Men were drawn to her like flies. Chantal's brother, François, was obviously attracted to her. A prototypical Frenchman to Charles, François was attractive, but nothing to worry about.

Not long after their return Charles decided that the daily was not really necessary more than three times a week. It would be better if Amanda had more to do with the house herself, since she had little else to do. She was also instructed to let Nanny Blake go. It was time that she, Amanda, spent more time with Patrick, caring for him herself rather than leaving him in the hands of a nanny. Amanda bowed her head and took it.

Chantal called. Amanda was afraid to tell her what had happened, but Chantal sensed it. Amanda had not had the courage to take the reins into her own hands when she had the perfect opportunity. Understanding power, Chantal knew that Amanda had made an irreparable mistake. Her affection for Amanda would continue unchanged—she was such a pretty little thing—but her respect for her dissolved.

Amanda woke up one morning soon after with the familiar signals of recurring migraine. Desperate, she telephoned Dr. Stirling's office, only to be told that he was on holiday in Scotland until after Christmas. When Charles came down for his morning tea and breakfast, which she served him now in his study, he found her in tears.

"Migraine again?" he asked. He knew the signs. The blue circles were under her eyes and her face was pinched with pain. She didn't answer him.

"Call Dr. Stirling," he said. "Perhaps he can help you."

"He's gone, through Christmas."

"Too bad. Try to get through it."

She screamed at him, lashing out at him, hurling abuse at him. She was practically incoherent, going on about a cook and money and his hours and all the same old rubbish she always brought up. His face closed down. He left his tea still hot in the cup and without saying a word he went out the front door.

The battle was over without ever being fought, but it was the beginning of a long war between Amanda and Charles Warrington that was not to be won by either of them.

CHAPTER 9

In the following years Charles and Amanda continued living together in the atmosphere of an armed camp. On the surface their habits were unchanged. Gambling was the core of Charles's life. Amanda had no life beyond Patrick. She knew no one beyond the confines of the Wyndham Club members and she developed a resentment of those she knew there, even Gavers. She had nothing in common with them . . . nothing in common with anyone.

They continued going to Lea Place for the weekends and Amanda realized that even Davina preferred Charles's company to her own. Richard always had. Amanda knew that she made little attempt at the social niceties. She was quiet and she was no good at the small talk that made up the bulk of the conversation. How many hours could they talk about golf? Then it was shooting, how many poor birds they had downed, or racing, which horse had been bred to which mare, which filly had won the Oaks in 1932. Charles was good at this sort of talk and Davina adored him.

Charles was away on gambling trips, sometimes with Gavers, but often on his own to Nassau or Mexico or Gstaad, depending on the season. Charles stopped asking her if she wanted to go. Patrick was her life. At least he was growing into a nice little boy.

Amanda knew that Charles was lost. They were both lost. There was no money and Charles's debts, which he never discussed with her, mounted steadily. The windfall from his father was long gone. Amanda had no idea how deeply in debt he was. No one actually knew.

Amanda wondered if this was all her life was to be. As Charles drank more, she drank less. As he thickened, taking on a stone or more of bloat, she became bone-thin and pale. It was not an unbecoming look. In fact, she was startlingly beautiful except for the hopeless expression in her eyes.

The headaches continued to plague her and she retreated more and more into herself, reading and studying books from the library down the street, ignoring the pain that became almost normal in her head.

Her sense of failure grew and she began actively to blame Charles for the circumstances of their life. There was no one else to blame and it unnerved her when she became verbally violent, screaming and lashing out at him at home. They fought in front of Patrick and the nanny, causing more than one nanny to leave, and behind closed doors when they were at Davina's. Amanda could not resist baiting Charles. If he wasn't going to speak to her, she could at least enrage him into fighting with her.

Time passed. She thought occasionally of calling Chantal and going to visit again, but she didn't. She passed Les Amis one afternoon and thought of going in and asking for Mr. Latimer, but she didn't. He wouldn't even remember her now. Several invitations had come for them from Les Amis but Charles had refused to go.

London, April 1970

"**W**hat's the famous line, Winner?" Robin asked jovially, cleaning his paintbrushes on a piece of cloth. " 'Gentlemen never welsh on debts and friends never discuss them.' Is that it?"

"What the devil's that got to do with anything, Robin?" Charles asked, irritated. He was hot. All of the windows in Robin's Victorian studio were wide open but the April day was unusually humid and the heavy coronation robes seemed to have doubled in weight since he'd put them on over an hour ago. Scarlet and ermine in April—why was he wasting his time doing this? Another portrait of himself. Why? Amanda had painted one of him, having taken up art with a vengeance the year before, and it had been bloody awful, filled with slashing reds and royal-blues and purples. He had indulged her by posing in exchange for a few moments' family peace. Now Robin had prevailed upon him to pose again. His father had worn these robes for the coronation of the Queen in 1953; God knew he himself would never wear them more than once a year for the opening of Parliament. Elizabeth II, like Victoria, looked as if she might be around forever. Where was he going to hang another portrait, and this one full-length at that? The dining room was filled

with family portraits. Amanda was thrilled with them; the pictures became her ancestors. For more than a hundred and fifty years there had
been Earls of Warrington, and with the exception of his father, who had
declined to be painted, they had all been proud of their heritage. Once
again, Charles came face to face with bloodline, the startling resemblance from Keating to Keating, Warrington to Warrington, that had
carried down through the years, each with the white streak of hair at the
temple, handsome to a fault. They were tall and strong. They were dark,
passionate, and romantic-looking—Byronic in appearance.

Why was he sitting here like this? he asked himself, coming back to
reality. Another portrait being painted of a man who had done nothing
so far to distinguish himself beyond serve for a few insignificant years in
the regiment of his ancestors? It made no difference; the new picture
would probably never be hung. There had been no dinners lately in the
red-lacquered dining room. In Amanda's present condition, no one
would accept an invitation from them, certainly none of his friends, and
she had none. What was Robin saying? Something about gentlemen
never welshing on their debts?

"I'm being cheeky," Robin said, turquoise eyes crinkling in perpetual
good humor. "If that line is correct, then you may be no gentleman and
I am no friend. Even so, how the hell are you going to get out from
under? Is there anyone you don't owe except me? If I had any money I
would have given it to you long ago. But, Winner, I am serious. How
long can you go on this way?"

"None of your bloody business, Robin," Charles said, lines tightening
around his mouth. "I've had enough for today."

"All right, we'll give it up," Robin said, washing his brushes and
returning them to the antique Chinese paintbrush pot on the table beside
his easel. "Come and look. It is going to be a staggeringly good portrait
if I do say so. And what have you had enough of, posing or worrying?
The banks are after you, your friends are becoming increasingly less
tolerant, and the moneylenders are moving in for the kill. Is it true that
you are borrowing at forty-eight percent now?"

Without answering, Charles studied the portrait. The inherited looks
jumped out at him. Dark. Passionate. Romantic. Not showing, he
thought, were the inner qualities of self-destruction. Weakness. Arrogance. Vanity. But still, there were divine rights, were there not? A peer
was above the laws that applied to common men, was he not? No one
could arrest him for his debts, could they? No ordinary court could try
him—was that no longer true? He sighed. That was no longer true.
None of those privileges of the past were true any longer. That was then,

old boy. What are you going to do about now? He turned to Robin, cool blue eyes meeting Robin's warm ones.

"Don't you worry, old boy, I'll take care of it," he said softly.

"How?" Robin persisted. He was like a dog with a bone. "You're up to your ears. You're drinking more than I am. Your shirt collars are too tight. Oh, to hell with all of those things, Winner—they're temporal. But you're losing, every day and every night now, and that's not. It's constant. You haven't held a winning hand in bridge or a winning card at poker for so long I can't remember, and the dice are against you at backgammon. It's all taking its toll. Don't you think it's time we borrowed a little more money and went off on a trip somewhere? Got away from it all?"

Charles grinned, his introspective mood broken. No one could be angry with Robin. He was a sympathetic and generous friend, and everything that he said was true. There were other problems concerning money that even Robin did not know, fortunately.

"Gavers won't lend us any," Charles said wryly. "I have no credit at the Club any longer and two checks have bounced."

"Four. This week," Robin said. "Two to Gavers. He doesn't like that at all. And two to Coutt's. Bankers won't put up with it."

"Fuck all," Charles said. "We need a drink. We can solve it over lunch." He knotted his tie neatly at the neck of his blue-and-white striped shirt. Robin was right. His collar was too tight. His belt was, too.

"Where have we got some credit left?"

"Nowhere. We'll go to Mirabelle. They wouldn't dare refuse us."

The Wyndham Club, April 1970

Amanda remained silent through dinner, eating listlessly. She had little idea whether it was fish or fowl. She felt no desire to speak to the men seated at the gleaming fruitwood table with her. Such a cozy system Gavers had devised, she thought, this communal table which seated twelve and provided delicious meals for those on the free list between sessions of backgammon or any other way they chose to lose money. It was also known as the "widow's table," a place where wives gathered to while away the time while the men gambled. Boardinghouse style, Amanda thought bitterly, everyone sitting together, not by choice. But the rent was expensive in this boardinghouse. The men nodded politely to her when they sat down, but the two chairs on either side of her remained empty. "That's Warrington's wife," she once heard one of them say, sotto voce, to a guest who asked about her sitting there alone.

"Odd girl. Don't know why she comes here. Don't feel obligated." She might as well be dead, she thought, or perhaps she was dead and just didn't know it. She was a ghost, sitting at that table.

She had come this evening because she couldn't bear one more night in the house alone. Amanda didn't at all like the new nanny, whom Charles had hired over objections. When she'd told Charles she planned to come tonight, he'd half-grunted in response. Why did she come? she wondered, looking down the length of the table to where Charles had seated himself away from her. Why did she ever come? He wouldn't even sit next to her.

Over coffee, Tally Stuart joined her. Tally was an effetely handsome American with a substantial private income from citrus groves in Florida. He spent half the year in London in a suite at Claridge's, and had it been possible, he would have lived at the Club. He was obsessed with backgammon. Backgammon was at its zenith. Everyone played. People spent their lives learning and playing. They planned their parties, their travel arrangements, and their lives with one eye on the tournament schedules. They played in California, in Palm Beach, in Gstaad and the Bahamas, as well as in London. There was talk of a new tournament starting in Marrakesh in the spring and Tally was of course planning to go. He played the game well, having learned from top players like Joe Dwek, Ted Bassett, Tim Holland, and Philip Martyn, the experts at it. He would never play any better than he did already, but to his immense satisfaction, he won an occasional tournament and that was enough for him.

Tally treated Amanda as if she was an attractive human being, as he treated almost everyone.

"How are you, pretty lady?" he asked, a soft accent of the South in his voice. He wasn't waiting for an answer; Amanda frequently only smiled at him in reply. Tally turned his attention to the other end of the table.

"Winner," he called down to Charles. "Have you gotten your reservations for San Diego yet? Vietor is expecting us in La Jolla next Thursday and I'd like to fly out with you." Jack Vietor was a member of the Wyndham, another American who shared the current passion for backgammon. He held a tournament house party every year in his white mansion by the sea in California, and his close friends all looked forward to it. Charles was going. Amanda was not, nor did she care to. She had been to one or two of the tournaments and she hated the faraway ones even more than those at the Wyndham. The women, especially the American women, were brassy and loud and dressed in colors garish enough to give Amanda a headache. And their voices—dear heaven,

where did they get those voices? In her reverie she heard Tally's voice
once again.

"Winner," Tally said. "Ted Bassett called me from New York. He
wants to go with us."

Something in Amanda snapped. She rose to her feet and screamed at
Tally.

"Don't call him that, you bloody idiot. His name is Charles. Charles
Henry Edward Keating, Baron of Keating, Earl of Warrington. His
name is not 'Winner.' How dare you call him by that despicable name?
He's the biggest loser this club will ever know, so why insult him by
calling him what he is not . . . " Her voice trailed off and she stood
there shaking. The expressions of the men around her at the table were
stiff and unsympathetic. She saw Charles rise to his feet and come toward her.

"Amanda, I'm taking you home," he said. His expression was ugly,
the hatred in his eyes more than familiar to her. He gathered her things
from the table, took her arm, half-dragging her away, but not before she
had time to pick up her untouched glass of red wine and hurl it in Tally
Stuart's face.

Tally was as vain about his clothes and grooming as Charles was. His
shirt and tie were ruined, his face was dripping red wine, and his dark-
gray suit jacket was soaked. His amiability vanished.

"Get her out of here, Winner. Why the devil do you bring her anyway?" He was brushing himself off with his napkin, avoiding Amanda's
eyes. He had gone out of his way to be nice to her, more than anyone
else ever did, and now this.

"There you go again," Amanda said. " 'Winner.' You can't resist it,
can you? Like 'Tally.' You all have such endearing nicknames. I suppose
yours has to do with your tallywhacker but I wasn't aware that you used
it that much. You seem to spend all of your time with men. Obviously
you have about as much luck as Charles does."

Her face was contorted and her hair had come out of the ribbon that
held it back on her neck, letting it fall loose on her shoulders. She looked
beautiful but unkempt, and quite mad.

Muttering something under his breath, Tally headed for the men's
room as Charles escorted Amanda to the door. She was subdued now,
walking with her head down, tears running down her cheeks.

"I'm sorry, Charles, I'm so sorry. It's just that I do hate that name—
that's the name that came between us. The minute Gavers gave it to
you, our lives changed. Why do they have to call you that?" She was
weeping forlornly as he put her in the car.

They drove down Brook Street in silence, Amanda crying, Charles cold and remote at the wheel. As they neared Royal Hospital Road, Amanda remembered the new nanny.

"I hate that woman," she said. "You've hired her to spy on me. For a year you left me with no one; now you have a guardian for me. Patrick hates her. She's an old prune and she's ugly. You know I can't stand having ugly people around Patrick. Or me." She blew her nose.

Charles kept his silence.

Amanda snapped again. "Charles, at least speak to me. You sit apart from me at the Club, you leave me alone for days, and now you'll be gone for weeks. I can't stand it much longer. Why don't you leave me? You never speak to me, you haven't made love to me for six months, you don't give me any money, and the bill collectors are at the door twice a day now. Why don't you just walk away from me the way you walk away from everything except another place to lose?"

He parked the car on the street in front of the house and came around and opened the door for her, helping her out as if she were the most beautiful woman in the world. He had cursed her ten minutes ago, but essentially his manners never changed; they were innate. He was riddled with them, manners he couldn't help. He hated her, he wanted to be free of her, he longed for the day he would never set eyes on her again, but he took her out of the car as gently as if she might break. He escorted her up the few front steps and opened the door with his key. He helped her off with her coat, which he hung up in the hall closet. He looked at her as if she were not there, not real, as if she were an angel or a ghost. How could she be so beautiful and so mad? The older she got, the more beautiful she became and the more insane. She was right about one thing —he had hired the nanny to watch her and to see to it that she did Patrick no harm. She was getting worse all the time. Scenes like the one with Tally tonight were nothing unusual. She indulged herself in them often. Now she was throwing wineglasses.

Without a word he went back out the front door, got into the car, and headed back to the Club.

A few months before, Charles had had the opportunity to buy one of the houses in the mews behind them. It was a terrible little house, two houses away from theirs but partially connected to their garden. When it was offered to Charles for a ridiculous price with a long lease, he snapped it up.

"For Patrick," he told Amanda. "When he goes to Harrow, whether we still live in Royal Hospital Road or not, he'll have a place of his own. The maintenance is practically nothing and it is a good investment.

Besides, it gives us a place to park a car in the mews." Their own house had no garage, so Charles paid to park the Mercedes in a nearby rental garage, and Amanda's Triumph stayed in a resident parking place on the street.

"It's got no heat and we've got to put a water heater in, but you're right. Charles, we can fix it up and rent it out for a few years."

"I don't want to rent it out. Go ahead and put some furniture in it, whatever leftovers we have, and get some heaters. We'll find some use for it."

Amanda was so grateful that he had invested in something tangible, anything that didn't end up on a gambling table, that she paid no attention to the almost derelict shape of the little house. She had it cleaned up, painted, and made use of every piece of unused furniture she could get her hands on. When she finished, it was still a sow's ear but at least it was clean and comfortable.

One morning soon after, she woke up to find Charles's side of the bed empty. She had leapt up, frantic. Charles had never stayed out all night before. Had he been in an accident? Or worse, was he still locked into some endless game at the Club, losing, losing, losing? She went to the phone and called. No, Lord Warrington was not there, he'd left about three.

Instinct sent her to the mews house, where she found him. He was sleeping there. So that's why he had bought the house. Now he had a place to sleep, a place of his own where he could stay away from her, where he could spend even less time with her.

She flew into a rage and went into such a bout of hysteria that Charles was afraid she was going to choke to death. He gave in to her pleas and promised not to sleep there again. Amanda immediately set about searching for a tenant, whether he liked it or not, but no one materialized and the little house stayed empty and unused.

He was now sleeping like a baby, in his own bed, their bed, and she was battling migraine again. The memory of the night before at the Club was painful. She had to see Dr. Stirling. Looking at her watch, she saw that it was only eight o'clock. His office opened at nine.

Her nerves shattered and her head splitting, she slipped into a sweater and skirt, pulled on her raincoat, and let herself out of the house. She walked to Pont Street, to Dr. Stirling's office. He might come in early.

She sat down on the stoop and leaned against the railing. She was very tired. The next thing she knew, she heard Dr. Stirling's voice speaking gently to her, and he was helping her to her feet.

"You poor child," he said. "What in the world are you doing asleep on my doorstep? Come in. Come in." He took her arm, and led her into the office with him. He could tell from looking at her that one of the worst of the migraines was upon her. He took her coat and sat her down in a chair next to his desk. She yawned and put her head down on her arms on his desk.

"Dr. Stirling, I don't know how much more I can stand. I can't sleep, even with the pills, and now I can't stay awake, and the pain in my head is driving me insane. What am I going to do?"

"Which pills?" Stirling asked. He hadn't seen her for months. He had prescribed Cafergot for her, a strong anti-migraine pill, but she would be out of them by now.

"Sleeping pills. Seconal," she said.

"How many? Who prescribed them for you?"

"Two, at about two this morning. No one prescribed them. My sister takes them and I got some from her."

"You've broken your appointments with me over and over again in the past few months and now you're taking drugs prescribed by yourself. My dear, how can you expect me to help you?"

"I'm not sure anyone can. These headaches must be coming from the problems in my personal life. I can't sort any of them out—how can I expect you to?"

"I have seen your husband only once, the first day he brought you here, and he seemed quite concerned about you then. Could you get him to come with you to your next appointment?"

"No," Amanda said. "He's leaving for a month this afternoon."

"I think it might be helpful if you had some psychiatric help. We have not been able to establish any distinct pattern to your migraines, which leads me to believe their origins are not inherited and not physical. I know a number of good men in the psychiatric area and I would be glad to work with one. That way we might be of some substantial help."

"Oh, God," Amanda said. "Years of a shrink to find out something I already know. My problem is that my husband is a compulsive gambler. He is losing all of his money. He's drinking heavily and he's beginning to hate me. I am beginning to lose control of myself. Often. Last night I threw a glass of wine in a man's face, screaming insults at him—one of the few of my husband's friends who has been halfway decent to me. Give me the name of the man you want me to see, but I doubt if I can pay the bills." She put her head down on his desk again and wept. Suddenly her head felt better, as if a pressure band had been lifted. Maybe if she had told the doctor everything, she wouldn't need the psychiatrist. Maybe if she had someone—anyone—to talk to, she wouldn't have the headaches.

"The National Health, my dear, is not to be forgotten. The doctor I am referring to is at Hatfield. There is no charge there, as you know."

"It's a loony bin, Hatfield," Amanda said. "Am I that badly off?"

"I am going to call, with your permission, Dr. Roger Pennell there. Promise me that you will see him, and when your husband returns, take him with you. He is just as involved as you and he must share in it. I will call your home later today and confirm when Pennell can see you."

Amanda smiled, a tiny smile, but she undeniably felt better. Maybe Dr. Pennell could help her. Meanwhile, maybe a new dress would help. Harrods would be open in another half hour.

"Call him, Dr. Stirling. I promise you I'll see him, and again, I'm sorry. This is the second time I've broken down on you."

Amanda bought a wheat-colored suit with a cat's-eye-green silk blouse. She had exactly the right shoes and bag to wear with it. The day was crisp and sunny. Spring was coming. On the way home she stopped in a phone box and called a number she remembered from out of nowhere.

A proper voice answered: "Les Amis, good morning."

"May I speak to Mr. John Latimer, please. This is Lady Warrington calling."

CHAPTER 10

London, April 1970

Les Amis was the most glamorous place Amanda had ever been to and she was treated like a queen from the moment she set foot in the door. That first day, even before Charles left, she'd put on her new suit and gone out to have her hair done, then taken herself off to lunch with John Latimer and friends. Her entire mood had changed. If she could have lunch there once a week, she would never have another migraine and never have to apologize for breaking down in doctors' offices. It would be a different world.

She had been slightly afraid that Latimer would give her lunch alone, especially since she had called him, and then he would make a pass at her. She didn't want that. When she rang him, the delight in his deep voice was evident. "You have called at the perfect time. I will welcome you at one o'clock. There will be friends with me, some you might know." That had bothered her too. Who that she knew might be there? Hardly any of the lot from the Wyndham. Latimer's friends were well-known celebrities. John quickly put her at ease.

"May I introduce the Countess of Warrington?" John had said, seating her beside him, as he had when she first met him. She was glad to see him again. Why hadn't she called sooner? She was quiet through lunch, but gradually she relaxed.

Afterward, John turned to her. "Stay and have a coffee with me and tell me what you have been doing. My car will take you home when you like," he said. So she stayed, glad to bask in the warmth of his obvious approval. She couldn't have had a migraine just this morning.

"So Charles will be gone for a month," he said. "Good. You will come to me any day or night, as you like, day *and* night if you want to,

whether he is here or not. I see you need some fun. You look lovelier
than ever, but too subdued. Perhaps we'll go to the boat this weekend. It
is in Palma. The weather is perfect there now—I spoke to the captain
this morning."

"You know I can't go to Palma with you," she said, laughing and
wishing she could.

"We shall see," John said. "I wondered how long it would be before
you called. Don't you think five years was too long? You are hard on
yourself." He lit another cigar. Somehow, his cigars smelled wonderful
and the smoke never blew in her face. He was wearing a gray suit and a
gray silk shirt with a pale-pink tie. Amanda had never paid attention to
how men dressed, aside from Charles, who was perfection. They both
had great style. She had forgotten how huge John was, but here in the
ample, luxurious rooms of Les Amis, the giant was once again in perfect
proportion.

The month Charles was away flew by. The house was filled with
John's flowers. One day there were pale creamy roses with even paler
lilies. A few days later, a low crystal bowl filled with lilies of the valley
arrived. And the orchids. Amanda had never seen such orchids. She
bought a book to learn about them. There were oncidiums from Borneo,
tiny curly white ones with brown and yellow spots. Very rare. Blue-
flowered vandas, also rare, from Burma. She memorized the names as
she matched the live flower to the photograph in the book. He called
every morning, just after the nanny took Patrick for his morning walk.
They talked on the phone for twenty minutes to half an hour. He told
her who had been in the night before and amused her with gossip,
interesting gossip. He gave a big dinner party one night for Prince
Philip, something to do with the World Wildlife Fund, and he wanted
her to come. He would arrange for someone to bring her. She refused.
He called her the night of the dinner and suggested that she come in
later—he would send the car for her. She refused again. The next time
she went for lunch, he seated her beside Sean Connery. John was showing his latest James Bond film that night in his screening room. She
went. Sitting in the dark, she felt John's bulk beside her, inhaled his
scent, some light cologne that was made exclusively for him. He never
pressured her about anything. Her life was full, and for the month that
Charles was gone, not once was she lonely.

John Latimer understood Amanda. She was the seductress. A ma-
ture young person whose childhood has been scarred by profound emotional deprivation, as Amanda's was by her father's death, can crave

affection with an intensity that is overpowering. She was an emotionally disturbed child who grew into a strongly sexed young woman. There was no one to help her, to guide her, or to love her.

John Latimer was drawn to her not only because of her beauty but because of the complexities he saw in her. A lover of women and a past master in every art of pleasing them, he had long ago learned that beautiful women were too often satisfied with the trappings of wealth alone. Expensive presents and expensive trips were all they aspired to, and women who cared only for what they could get in the way of material possessions soon bored him. Amanda, with her childlike beauty, her waiflike quality, and her emotional problems, interested him. He wanted her and he intended to have her. He was willing to go through the hell he was sure would come with her, without abandoning her. He could teach her how to be a real woman, rather than a silly girl who used sex only to get what she wanted and who was, so far, bewildered where she should be sure of herself and without the faintest glimmer of understanding about the terms that bound a man to a woman forever. He could perfect her. She had all the necessary ingredients. Her beauty was wonderfully unusual; it was subtle and yet you could not ignore her. She had a faintly erotic power, yet she had not one shred of confidence or real knowledge of how to use it. The fact that she was involved in what John saw as a disastrous marriage was of little concern to him, and in the long run he might serve Amanda well. John cared nothing about Charles Warrington. He looked upon him as nothing more than another aristocratic gambling wastrel, a weak man of no substance and one he had no respect for.

When Amanda had finally called him, he was ready for her. It was easy to draw her into the affluent and glamorous world of Les Amis. He had the perfect setting and required nothing of her beyond her presence. The last thing he would ever have done would be to make any physical move toward her. He knew that she expected it and he saw her begin to wonder why he remained passive. He knew the time would come when curiosity alone would get the better of her. Was she not attractive? Was she not attractive to him? Did he not want her? He had told her, in precise words, that he did, and now he was doing nothing about it. The seductress was there, lurking, waiting, expectant, just below the surface. He knew it wouldn't be too long now before she showed her hand. Then, and not until then, their true relationship would begin.

Les Amis, April 1970

W hen lunch was over one day, the talk turned to the history of the house. The girl across the luncheon table from Amanda was Jean

Shrimpton, known as "the Shrimp," the most famous model in London. The Shrimp had expressed interest in seeing the house. Amanda's thoughts had drifted for a moment but she came back to reality, hearing John's voice.

"Everyone here has seen the rest of the house except you and Amanda. I would like the pleasure of showing it to you myself."

Amanda didn't care if it was the greatest house ever built; it was the atmosphere that she loved. She never felt, as she did at the Wyndham, that she was in a place where gambling was all, where fortunes were lost, where men were broken by their own stupidity or bad luck, where everything was dedicated to gambling and only gambling. Even in the great ballroom upstairs, now the principal gambling room, Les Amis never seemed as serious a gambling place as the Wyndham. Les Amis had a seductive and romantic atmosphere. In the evenings the music was wonderful. John had found the best trio in London. There was no music at the Wyndham.

She had been curious to see how John lived in his private world. Aside from the rooms she had seen, she knew he must live in a grand manner somewhere in the vast regions on the floors above the ballroom. Now she would have a chance to see for herself where he slept, where he dressed, how he lived. She knew the public man, but she had not yet gotten to know the private one.

"The stairway," John was saying, as he led Amanda and the Shrimp up the first flight to the ballroom floor, "is the finest stairway in England. I would have bought the house for it alone. Look." His huge hand gave a sweeping gesture and as they looked up, the grandeur of the stairway was fully revealed to them. He was right: It was magnificent. The heels of Amanda's shoes sank into the blue-bordered red carpeting beneath her feet as John explained the history of the Flemish tapestries that lined the walls.

"Now we take the lift," his deep voice boomed as he opened a heavily carved oak door, into a lift that barely contained his own gigantic proportions plus the two of them.

"The stairway continues to my private quarters but you have had enough of a walk as it is." The lift deposited them at a landing where the last curved balustrade of the great stairway came to an end on the top floor.

At the center of the landing John opened the double doors into his private apartments. There was a large drawing room with a small dining room off of it; a bedroom thirty feet long with a fourteen-foot ceiling; and his bath and dressing rooms, which were combined into one, mirrored everywhere, painted white and gold with pristine white marble floors. Everything of John's seemed to carry weight, Amanda thought; everything else seemed flimsy. In his private world she saw the Pole, the real man. In his private quarters, as in the club below, the furniture was ample and comfortable. All the chairs and sofas were covered with woven fabrics in deep blues, shades ranging from navy to midnight to royal. There were dozens of large down-filled cushions on the couches and chairs, covered in silk and satin, in tones from the palest of pink to rose and deep red. The room gave off a feeling of privacy and substance. A painting, a landscape by a Polish painter named Stalewski, hung on one wall of the room, and Jean Shrimpton and Amanda both exclaimed at its beauty. It was of an orchard, flowering plum trees in a profusion of white blossoms on spring-green earth. The genius of the painter had given it a breathtaking quality that both women felt on sight.

"My land that is no more, that no longer belongs to us," John said, knowing their response to the painting was genuine. He opened the French doors that led out onto a terrace overlooking Hyde Park and Apsley House, the Duke of Wellington's ocher-colored mansion just across the road.

"The park is in bloom now but not so lovely as my Stalewski." He was right. The park, in full glory, paled by comparison.

Something else had caught Amanda's attention. There were two windows still farther along the terrace, beyond John's bedroom. What was there? He had not shown them that part of his private domain. "Mistresses," she remembered his saying on their first meeting. "I prefer six to seven years with each one—in that time one can really savor a woman and help her, then send her happily on her way and never become bored with her." It occurred to Amanda that he might have a new one by now. The windows to the unshown rooms were open. No, there couldn't be anyone else. She would have known. John's attention to her was not casual. He called every day, and when she came to Les Amis she was invariably seated on his right. "I seat her by me not because she is so beautiful but because she is so small," he had said one day. "She makes me look larger than I really am." He couldn't have anyone else without Amanda's having known about her. He would be proud of a new woman and would have had her beside him at lunch. Or would he? Perhaps the new mistress appeared only at night, and she, Amanda, had come only that one night for the screening of the Bond film. No, there could be no one. Why was she uneasy? John Latimer was not her lover; she was not his mistress.

As they were leaving, Jean Shrimpton got into the car first. John took Amanda's hand and kissed it.

"The rooms you observed from the terrace are unoccupied at the moment," he said as he put her into the car. "But not for much longer." On her way home she thought about what he had said. What did he mean? Was he telling her there was someone new? He certainly was not making her feel that she was the object of his desire, regardless of what he had said on *Cattivo*. She was slightly miffed, but why should she care if another woman occupied those rooms with him? John Latimer didn't belong to her. He wasn't interested in her, if ever he had been. What in the world was the matter with her?

London, May 1970

"Have you been seeing John Latimer?" Charles asked as he knotted his dark-red striped tie. He was tan and relaxed after two weeks in California and another two in the Bahamas. The golf had been excellent in both places, he had won a packet at bridge and poker for once, and he hadn't lost too much at either of the backgammon tournaments. All in all, it had been a windfall trip.

"Have I been seeing John Latimer?" Amanda repeated after him, biding her time. Why in the world would Charles ask that? He'd hardly been back twenty-four hours.

"He invited me to lunch at Les Amis," she said, "before you went away—a weekly group that he gathers. I enjoyed it. Is that what you mean about seeing John Latimer?" She did not mention that Michael Caine had been at lunch. Ava Gardner had been at lunch. Sean Connery had been at lunch. Lord Snowdon had been at lunch, and asked immediately if he could photograph her for British *Vogue*. She'd said she would ask her husband.

"I just wondered. Someone mentioned it to me."

Who, Amanda thought. Who? She would wonder about that later. "As a matter of fact, I am going again today. Would you like to come? I know John would love to have you."

"No, I don't think so. I'm off to the Club. I'll see you this evening."

Gavers held two checks in his hands.

"I can't protect you anymore, Charles," he said. "You know that. When the gaming law was changed, it made it impossible for me to hold your checks, as I used to. If your checks are no good and I continue to let them stack up unpaid, Inland Revenue is going to come in and take my gaming license away. No one knows this better than you. You have been losing steadily for too long now and something has to be done about it. Why are you doing this to me? Why are you putting me in this position? It's not as if you didn't know the rules."

"Come on, Gavers," Charles said. "It's only for a few days. You know I've always made the checks good." He was slightly on edge. There had been another scene with Amanda this morning about her having fired the new nanny, a woman it had taken months to find and who had been in the house for less than a month. He had chosen her to be sure Patrick was safe and to keep a watchful eye on Amanda.

Gavers looked at him impatiently.

"I told you when I opened the Club and you came on board that if you were going to do nothing besides gamble that you had some homework to do. You did it, and very well, and you did all right. You're not all right now and it's embarrassing. You've tapped everyone you know and it's reached a point where your friends are not just avoiding you, they want their money back. A loan is one thing; a grant is another. You're breaking every rule and you're drunk half the time you're breaking them. For Christ's sake, Winner, at least stop drinking."

Charles felt like a child being chastised. He also felt a flash of anger. Who the hell did Gavers think he was, speaking to him this way? He had lost hundreds of thousands of Warrington pounds here. Why couldn't Gavers hold his checks for an unlimited time if necessary? He, Charles Warrington, had been highly responsible for the success of the Club from the start. He was the peer whose presence had drawn members. What the hell was the matter with Gavers? He was no fool when it came to the law, and he could bend it in this instance. The place was changing, Gavers was changing, and some of the new members he was letting in certainly lacked the style of the past. Charles badly wanted a drink.

"Stop drinking? I was just going to suggest that we have a drink in the bar. I am not comfortable in offices."

"All right," Gavers said curtly. "We'll have one last drink in the bar. Then you clear out. There is no credit for you here until these checks are paid up. Take them with you and I'll give you three days to find the money. If you can't, bring them back and I'll pay them off. The price for my doing that will be your membership. Something has got to stop you. Maybe this will."

"Fuck you and your drink and your Club!" Charles stood up so quickly that the checks fluttered to the floor. He looked at them and then at Gavers. The expression on Gavers's face was ugly, unforgiving.

"Pick them up, Winner. Pick them up and go find the money for them. The party's over."

Charles turned and walked out, slamming the door behind him. Coming down the great Venetian stairway, he was in a towering rage. He stopped in the bar and signaled for George, the barman.

"A triple," he said.

"Yes, milord," George responded, pouring Bombay gin into Lord Warrington's heavy crystal glass.

He brought it around on a small silver tray with a folded white cocktail napkin beneath it.

"Nice day, sir."

"Indeed," Charles said shortly.

Upstairs, Gavers stared at the door. Compulsive drinking and compulsive gambling were a lethal combination. The handwriting about Winner had been on the wall for some time and the scene of a few minutes ago depressed Gavers. He picked up the checks. One was for four thousand pounds, the other for twenty-five hundred. He went to the phone, looking at a picture on his desk of him and Winner in St. Moritz the day they made their first Cresta run. The good old days.

"Lillian," he said to his secretary, "I want you to get seven thousand pounds in cash out of the Westminster Bank account and bring it back before the bank closes today."

"Of course, Mr. Driscoll."

"Give it to the accountant on behalf of Lord Warrington."

"Yes, sir," Lillian said.

That's that, Gavers thought. That's the end of it. He's a goner.

For a few weeks Amanda was unaware of the rift between Gavers and Charles. Charles kept to his regular habits, leaving the house around one to make his rounds. There was nothing unusual about his movements. The first notice she had was one evening when he came home to change for the evening session.

"I'd like to come with you tonight," she said. She felt like getting out, going somewhere, anywhere. John Latimer had left for Cannes, so there had been no luncheon this week.

"I'm afraid not," Charles said stiffly. "I'm not going to the Club tonight." His back was to her.

Amanda tried to think what night it was. Charles played bridge once a week in some house or other, rather than at the Club. Maybe that was it.

"A bridge game?" Amanda really didn't care. She would stay home.

"No," Charles said, the stiffness still in his voice. "I'm not going to the Club anymore."

"You're not going to the Club anymore?" There was astonishment in her tone and, for a brief second, hope. Maybe it was over; maybe he'd had enough, she thought. The notion was stillborn. She knew he couldn't stop gambling—but what was wrong? She knew better than to question him. He would tell her what he wanted her to know—that was all.

"What about Les Amis?" he asked. "You've been there often enough over the past few months. Is your friend John Latimer about? Would you like to go there for dinner?"

Amanda was nonplussed.

If only John were in London. He would have arranged a table for them, or more likely he would have asked them to join him. Why did he have to be away now? She could of course phone herself. John had told her that she could come whenever she liked and bring whomever she liked.

"I haven't been there lately and I think John is away but I'll call and find out. Of course we can go for dinner. What time?"

"Nine-ish." That was all. There was no more information forthcoming. She would have to wait.

"So his lordship has seen fit to honor my humble place with his presence," the deep voice said on the telephone.

"John!" Amanda said, delight in her voice. "Yes, he's been there every night and a few afternoons. He seems to like it quite a lot. But it's not the same to me when you're not there."

"And to what do I owe the honor of his presence?" Was there an edge of sarcasm in his voice?

"He and Gavers apparently have had a blazing row. You know Charles doesn't discuss such things with me. I'd be the last one he would tell."

"Is he there?"

"Yes, he's still asleep."

"Why don't you come for lunch, the two of you?"

"I'll ask him, but he doesn't often take me to lunch. He might prefer to come alone."

"Unless you are with him, his membership might be a little difficult."

Amanda laughed. She knew he was teasing. She said nothing.

John's laugh boomed.

"Clever girl. Unless I hear otherwise from you, I'll expect you and Charles around one-thirty."

★ ★ ★

John knew exactly what had happened between Gavers and Charles before he had left Cannes. His secretary had called to tell him that Lord Warrington had been in for dinner one evening with Lady Warrington and that he had requested a line of credit. As he was not a member, she needed John's instructions. He had given a check for his losses, which were minimal, about a thousand pounds, the first evening.

"Inform Lord Warrington that we would be honored to have him as a member. Give him the form to fill out, and tell him that I will be back on Thursday and we can then discuss his line of credit."

It was obvious to John that Gavers had cut Charles off. Good. That would make it easier to see Amanda. A few more phone calls established just how deeply in debt Charles Warrington was, and the total figure surprised even John. Three banks were carrying substantial overdrafts, personal checks had begun to bounce with regularity, and some of his friends were beginning to avoid him. Now John had him to deal with.

At lunch, John was direct.

"I assume there is some momentary problem between you and Gavers," he said. "And I also assume that it will be temporary. It's too bad it took a row between friends to bring you here, but I am delighted to have you as a member. After lunch, my car can take Amanda wherever she would like to go and I will show you the place. We can discuss our business then."

Amanda was quiet during lunch, as she normally was, but it was a different kind of quiet. It was as if she were not there. John drew her into the conversation when possible but by and large the talk was about gambling.

"Whatever happened about Monte Carlo?" Charles asked. "When we last saw you there, when Rainier wanted you to take over?"

"I decided against it. There are too few places in the civilized world for pure pleasure. The South of France has always been one for me. Why should I work there?"

"Why should one work anywhere? Let the lower classes do the work. Jolly good chef you have, John. The food is delicious." Charles was obviously enjoying his cold beef. John had chosen an excellent bottle of claret.

"You must come for dinner more often, and bring Amanda with you. Les Amis is not the same as the Wyndham, in that we have more members from the entertainment world. Sometimes they are more amusing, a little livelier . . . " He let the sentence remain unfinished.

"Harrumph," Charles said. John knew he was registering disapproval, pompous ass that he was.

Charles's real concern was neither film stars nor roast beef; he was interested only in how far John was prepared to extend his credit. He hoped that John had not checked on him too carefully, although he was sure he would have. He was no fool. Luckily, he had invited Amanda to lunch there a few times. That might be helpful, but he had probably invited her because of the title. Latimer liked to surround himself with that sort of thing.

When Amanda left them, John took Charles to his office on the first floor. He told Charles that his credit was unlimited as long as he paid up once a month. He knew Charles understood that any returned checks would mean a limit on his line of credit, but he was sure that would never come up. He hoped Charles would be happy as a member of Les Amis.

Charles was more than pleased to be a member with an unrestricted line of credit. In one month's time he could win back all his recent losses and pay everyone off. He would soon be able to make it up with Gavers. A few wins would take care of everything.

At the end of the month Charles was invited to Acapulco to play in another of the endless backgammon tournaments. Their popularity had peaked, and although Amanda found it hard to believe that people built their lives around playing a game day and night, night and day, they still did, moving from one resort to another, immersing themselves in a shallow social world of their own making. When Charles told her he was going, she refused his halfhearted invitation to go with him, shrugging her shoulders.

"Don't any of your friends have anything else to do?" she asked. "At least before backgammon I'd see you occasionally." She hated her shrewish tone but it had become a habit for them to snipe at each other. "Besides, I don't want to leave Patrick."

"You might have a good time in Acapulco if you could just work up some enthusiasm for it. And by the way, Mother wants Patrick and Davina's girls for a week or two. I think it's a good idea for her to have them in the country with her."

"Of course it is. He's old enough now to enjoy being in the country with his grandmother. I'll find something to do."

With Charles and Patrick both out of the house, she was alone and felt a growing depression assail her. She had to find something to do. She called Davina.

"Could I come down for the weekend? Charles and Patrick are both gone and I'm rattling 'round here, feeling sorry for myself."

"Oh, darling, would you mind awfully if I said no?" Davina asked, her voice not apologetic. "It's the first time Richard and I will have been alone for almost a year. Do you mind terribly?"

"Of course not," Amanda said, and she meant it. "I envy you. Charles and I never have an evening by ourselves, much less a whole weekend."

Amanda still longed for a place of their own but Charles would not hear of it. She envied Davina's life. Richard was always at home with his family now. He had put a manager in his office in London and he had his own hands full running the farms and overseeing Ransome House. He was first of all a family man and Davina was the happiest person Amanda knew.

Amanda hung up the phone and looked for the morning newspaper. She could go to a film tonight, or possibly get a single seat for the theater. There must be something she wanted to see.

The phone rang.

It was John. Amanda had never appreciated the sound of his deep voice more.

"My little Countess. About my party tonight."

"Oh, John, forgive me," Amanda said, remembering that she had not responded to his invitation. "I didn't realize it was tonight. I can't come. Charles left this morning."

"I know," John said. "And I have arranged for Robin to bring you. He is depending on you even more than I am, since the lady he is currently in love with is also coming, but not with him. We decided that by bringing you he would make her extremely jealous."

"Robin will bring me?" Amanda asked. That might be all right. And she could go to a wonderful party rather than going to the films alone.

"John, I feel so awful about not answering your invitation." The heavily engraved card had arrived two weeks before and Amanda had put it in the desk drawer and out of her mind.

"Never mind that. I know you won't let Robin down—he is your friend. You will have a marvelous time. I have the gypsies to play, not like any you have heard before, and dancers and singers and wonderful food. It is a Polish extravaganza and I will not take no for an answer, nor will Robin. He is coming for you at nine-thirty."

"Of course I'll come, John. I can't wait." She meant it.

She rang off. *Of course I will.* What could she wear? She did have a very old Zandra Rhodes ball gown in her closet. It would have to do and it would. It was feather-printed taffeta, elaborate. She sighed. As they never went anywhere to dress up, she really had nothing to dress up in. Never mind. She would love watching this party. She was not a star. There would be plenty of stars there.

Some time later, the doorbell rang. John's chauffeur stood on the doorstep holding a large box for her. Amanda took it and, with a sense of excitement, went upstairs to her bedroom to open it. Underneath the mounds and mounds of tissue paper she found an apple-green silk dress with three starched voile petticoats. In one corner of the box she found a pair of dark-green silk pumps with little curved heels, some white lace stockings, and a small pouch bag hand-embroidered with tiny birds and miniature flowers. There were long strands of satin ribbon with faggoted edges and flowers appliquéed on them as fripperies for her hair. The dress was beautifully preserved, a traditional Polish costume, and from the look of it at least one hundred years old. Amanda knew before trying it on that it would fit her perfectly, and she knew also that John had planned all of this meticulously, as only he would. To hell with Charles and his silly tournaments, where he did nothing but drink and throw dice, wasting his life away. Tonight she was going to forget all that.

Robin appeared on the dot of nine, stunning in his dinner jacket, and half an hour early, but Amanda was dressed and ready.

"By God," he said, his smile lighting up when he saw how she was dressed. "You have never looked so delicious in all your life. That dress is a museum piece, but you certainly aren't. I didn't know you were a Polish Princess back then. I thought you were no more than a silly English Countess."

"Only for tonight," Amanda said. "Princess, that is. Countess doesn't count for much."

Robin was complimenting her and he meant it. He knew of the snide attacks on her behind her back. As court jester of the "Wyndham Group," as he called them, he had tired quickly of the viciousness and inaccuracy of the gossip surrounding Amanda. Granted, she had taken the business of being a Countess too seriously at first, not being sophisticated enough to know that within the group you could *be* a Countess but you were not to *want* to be a Countess. He also knew, if only with his eyes, that Amanda was their target first because she was stunningly beautiful and next because her natural intelligence made them uneasy. Her values were different, and that was not allowed. Rosie Riggs was eaten alive with jealousy of her, and even Davina indulged in criticism of her own sister. She resented both Amanda's beauty and the title, neither of which she would ever have. She was not unhappy with Amanda's unpopularity. Davina always ran with the pack, Robin thought.

"Well," he said, looking at her impudently, "that dress is a treasure. It was worn by a Princess a century or so ago, you can bet. They used to dress up like their servant girls on midsummer nights. They'd lark about in the summer moonlight, blind drunk, and then maybe a little roll in the royal hay?"

His laughing mood was perfect for the party.

"That reminds me," Amanda said. "Who is this bird you're leaving me for?"

"Aha!" Robin said. "You're so frigging gorgeous, I almost forgot. You've got to flirt madly with me tonight. This stupid girl Claire is giving me a packet of trouble. If I get her, she might last a month and that's a lifetime for me, you know."

"I'll flirt you silly, I promise. I'm not in practice, but I'll try. I haven't been to a party forever."

"If Charles could see you now, he'd take you out more often. You're a right raver. The only thing that worries me is leaving you. If I can persuade Claire to run off with me, John promised that he'd have his car bring you home. You won't mind, will you?"

"Of course I won't mind. It would be awful if you had to bring me home, wouldn't it, Robin?"

Amanda caused something of a sensation and Robin was the perfect escort for her. He knew everyone, and everyone wanted to know who Amanda was.

Robin noticed the keen appreciation of Amanda's beauty in John Latimer's eyes when he greeted them. She was by far the most alluring woman at the party, and the fact that she was a new face increased her allure. To Robin's delight, Claire had arrived before them and was no end annoyed to find Robin escorting the somewhat mysterious young Countess of Warrington, the unknown beauty whom everyone wanted to meet.

As they walked through the grand rooms together, Robin was surprised to feel Amanda shaking. She clung to him, and he didn't mind in the least feeling protective about her. When dinner was announced, Robin found that they were seated at John Latimer's table. Amanda was beside Robin, with the very shy Duke of Chichester on her right.

"Talk to him about dogs," Robin whispered in her ear, understanding her lack of confidence. "He's very large with the RSPCA and if you tell

him about your Labrador puppy, the one you're having so much trouble
with, he'll talk your ear off."

"What in the world are you talking about, Robin?" Amanda said,
looking at him as if he'd taken leave of his senses. "I don't have a
Labrador puppy. You know very well we don't have a dog at all."

"Darling girl," Robin said, taking her hand and kissing it, "a little
levity. This party is going to be great fun when everyone loosens up a
bit."

"Robin, I am a nit," Amanda said. "I told you I was out of practice."
She kissed him on the forehead, looking across the table at John Latimer
as she did so. In the quick second when their eyes met, she felt John's
explicit approval of her.

"I adore John Latimer," Robin was saying. "Do you realize that he
has seated Claire at the table behind us so that she sees nothing but the
back of my head and your beautiful profile. She didn't miss your kissing
me."

"Good," Amanda said. "And did you say my new dog is a golden
Labrador?" Without waiting for his answer, she turned to the Duke of
Chichester, who she knew was called Bunny.

"**B**y God," Robin said as they got up from the dinner table, "he *is*
the perfect host. He's had to be ruthless to put this group in the same
rooms without a dud in the lot. He has the cream of the crop tonight.
I've never seen the old Duke of Beaufort this far from Badminton before. And having a good time. John is a genius."

"He does have a way of taking people out of themselves," Amanda
said. "I've been here for lunch a few times with some really high-pow-
ered celebrities, and he's always made me feel like a queen. I go home
walking on air, and you know how difficult I am."

"I know how difficult you are supposed to be," Robin said. "I don't
know you as difficult at all, not in the South of France when I first knew
you, or now. Why do you suppose you have that reputation?"

"It's my fault, Robin, all of it. I hate the life we are leading. I've hated
it for years. When Charles and I were first married I was so naïve I
thought it would all be a series of glittering parties and fascinating
people with titles. I'd been 'elevated' and I wanted so much to be a
Countess, it was like a little girl's dream."

She looked down and hesitated. If she went on, whatever she said was
going to sound critical of Charles.

"And?"

Oh, to hell with it, she thought. For once she might as well tell the truth. It was that kind of night.

"Robin, we lead a miserable life. You know Charles's routine better than anyone. Unless he's on a trip, it's up at noon, one of his clubs for the first martini of the day, then gambling until six. Bath at home, kiss child, ignore wife, change, and back to gambling. Do you remember how much money he had when we were on *Cattivo*?"

Robin nodded. He knew what she was going to say.

"It's all gone, every penny of it. He's in debt to all the banks and not paying the bills. He usually gives me forty pounds a week for the household, but he hasn't given me anything for over a month now. I don't know what is going to happen to us. And I don't know what has happened to me. I must have been to ten doctors to find out about my depressions, my awful moods. You've seen me at the Club—you know no one wants to speak to me for fear of what I might say back. I do hate them all, except for you and Gavers, and I'm not sure about Gavers anymore because he's got most of Charles's money. I am beginning to blame him for that."

They were sitting at a small table watching the dancing. John had the best music. John had the best of everything.

"Even that shy Duke," she continued, "Bunny. He said, 'Call me Bunny.' How can anyone call a grown Duke 'Bunny'? But he's very nice and he owns a large part of Argentina, which he is trying to drag into the twentieth century with some rather advanced ranching methods. He is immensely rich but he still works and he's a responsible human being. He's never heard of the Wyndham Club."

Robin laughed. "The unkindest cut of all," he said, leading her to the dance floor. "Come on, this conversation is not for tonight. I'll come around one afternoon and we'll go back to it. Did you notice Claire sitting next to us? I've ignored her long enough, don't you think?"

"Just. Now what are you going to do?"

"I am going to let Bunny cut in. Here he comes."

Amanda danced with Bunny and then with Douglas Fairbanks, Jr., and then with Paul Getty. John Latimer cut in on Getty, and Robin, still not quite ready to reconcile with Claire, stood in the doorway smoking a cigarette and watching Amanda as she danced. That minuscule whiff of erotica fascinated him, and now he liked the way she had expressed herself, clearly not blaming Charles.

Robin put out his cigarette and went to ask Claire to dance. It was better not to get too close to anyone for too long. Two weeks with Claire would be about enough. Intimacy only made for unhappiness.

★   ★   ★

Two hours later, Claire, still filled with jealousy of Amanda, suggested to Robin that they clear out of the party and go to her place and let Lady Warrington fend for herself. Robin said good night to Amanda, giving her a kiss on the cheek and a wink toward Claire. Amanda felt lost, but John took over at once. The gypsies had been playing all evening, strolling from one room to another, but now they were getting into high form.

"Come," John said, leading her to his favorite banquette and seating her beside him. "This is the best part of the evening. You have worked hard tonight for Robin. Now you enjoy yourself with me."

"I want Robin to be happy," Amanda said. "He has a sad quality in his eyes."

"Do I see happiness in yours? Am I right?"

The time had come to thank him for the dress.

"John," she said, "I almost had to wear an old Zandra Rhodes dress."

"You would have been equally beautiful."

"I've never been to such a perfect party. I haven't had such fun, ever." It was true.

"This is the reason for parties," he said. "For friends to enjoy themselves."

The violinists came to them. The candles were flickering down to nub ends. It was close to four in the morning, and the few friends who were left gathered together to listen to the music, arranging themselves on the banquettes or on the floor at John's feet, mesmerized by the nostalgic beauty of the gypsy music. Amanda saw John begin to relax, his big frame settle comfortably, his friends around him. Nothing meant as much to him as to be the giver of pleasure.

She knew she should go soon. If she didn't she would be the last.

"My car will take you when you are ready," John said, reading her mind again.

"Not yet, not just yet. Not if they really are going to play some more."

"They will play until the year 2000 if you want them to. Or you can take them home with you."

Amanda touched his face with her hands. "Giver of pleasure," she said.

"Do you want me?" he asked softly.

There it was. Finally.

"Yes," she said, "I want you."

"Close your eyes and listen to the music."

She closed her eyes and listened to a single violin. She felt John rise from the banquette and when she opened her eyes, he was saying good night to the last of his guests at the door. Guido, John's major domo, was beside her.

"Contessa," he said quietly, "*venga qui.* I show you." She got up and followed him to the hidden landing behind the massive stairway, where he pushed the button for the tiny lift. The door opened immediately and closed behind her. When it opened, three stories up, John was waiting for her.

With the tenderest look, he took her hand, helping her out of the lift.

"No one saw you," he said. "Those who did see you belong to me."

CHAPTER 11

June 1970

The rooms that Amanda had seen once before in the daytime seemed subtler now, subdued, richer in the lamplight. The vivid tones of reds and blues that she remembered in the big drawing room were mellow in the soft night lighting. It had taken the hand of a genius to light the painting of the flowering plum trees. The room faded into shadowy opulence in the presence of the painting.

John sat down in the center of the big couch and rested his hands on his knees, the pasha again, searching her face.

"You are exquisite," he said. "Did the shoe fit?"

"Shoe fit?" she asked. "Sorry?"

"The ones you have on."

"Perfectly, of course. Everything fits perfectly. You knew it all would."

"Then the shoe will fit when you go home. Do not worry about that."

"John, I don't understand."

"Never mind. Come here."

She walked obediently across the room, aware of an excitement building in her. As she faced him, he turned her around and, reaching up, began to unfasten the hooks at the back of her dress. His fingers were sure and quick. The last one undone, he pulled the dress gently from her shoulders and let it drop to the floor. He put his lips against the small of her back and wrapped his arms around her from behind, hands holding her breasts. His breath was warm and the skin of his face was smooth and soft against her back.

"You like to be naked," he said. It was a statement, not a question.

"Yes," she said. It was true, but how did he know? It was as true as the desire warming her. She wanted to touch him.

Turning her around once again, he kissed her bare waist and then brought his lips up to her breasts. He took her onto his lap, cradling her in his arms, and with one hand unfastened her petticoats and pushed them aside, letting them slip to the floor. She had nothing left on now but the white lace dancer's tights and her shoes. He buried his face in her belly, breathing on her through the lace, reaching to take off one of her shoes and then the other.

"The stockings . . . stand up now." His big hands guided her to her feet.

"Let me," Amanda said.

"Good, my love," he said. He sat back, leaning against the deep-pink and red silks of the cushions while he watched her slip the lace stockings down over her hips. Amanda felt the sexual tension building in her, an excitement stronger, to her surprise, than anything she felt for Charles, and she realized that part of what she felt was fright. She had never had the slightest fear where Charles was concerned; she had always been the instigator of their lovemaking. With John, her desire was mixed with an infinitesimal fear. He was the seducer and she didn't know what he wanted, how he wanted her, or what he wanted her to do. She wondered if she was up to him, enough for him, or would she fail in her allure and bore him when he made love to her? With John, there were things he knew that she had never even dreamt of, and she wanted to know everything he knew, she wanted to feel everything that he could make her feel, and she wanted, most of all, to be better than any of the others, better than every woman he had ever known.

Her stockings were off, a pool of lace at her feet. She stood completely nude before him in front of the couch, looking gravely into his eyes, waiting for his lead. Suddenly there was something she wanted to do and she did it without thinking, raising her arms slowly above her head, reveling in her nakedness, pulling the ribbons with the tiny flowers from her hair. She would not be completely nude until they, too, were gone. She shook her hair free, and heard his throaty laugh.

"Look at you," he said, gesturing toward the huge Regency mirror at the far end of the room. Amanda turned and looked. The tableau presented was an unforgettable sight. Her naked body, pristine in the warm light, and the imposing figure of the big man centered regally on the couch were surrounded with priceless possessions that he adored. In the split second it took for her to take it all in, she knew that her memory would forever hold the lushness, the private lavishness of the scene. She belonged there. She was in place.

"Come back," he said. "Come back to me."

She walked slowly toward him, enjoying the bright look in his eyes as much as he was enjoying what he saw with them. She sat down on the coffee table across from him, perching on the huge art books that covered it, her legs on one side and her body leaning toward him on the other. John reached for her hands and pulled her across the table to him, turning her over so that she lay on her back, stretched out full-length on the books.

"Am I an offering?" she ventured, a tentative little smile on her face. She wanted him so now. When would he take her in his arms? When would he share his warmth with her?

"A feast, my baby, and more beautiful than anything in the books beneath you. Besides, I don't want to kiss anything in those books." The throaty laugh came from deep inside him again. He touched the tip of her nose with his finger, and then, with ardor, he began to stroke and caress her, at first with his hands and then he leaned down and put his lips on her, breathing his warm breath on her. His tongue found her nipples, then her navel, and then curled into her underarms. He put his face into her silky pubic hair, his tongue going no farther than the boundary of her thighs, not invading her. She shivered and laughed, then rolled over into his lap, pulling his face down to hers, reaching at the same time for his still impeccable tie.

"I want to be inside your shirt," she said. "I need your body. I want your skin." She found the buttons on his shirt and started to unbutton them. She wanted to please him. Timidity and fear were no longer with her.

"My darling," he said, holding her quietly, his face close to hers, "we have an arrangement to be made. I am a man who weighs at least two hundred pounds more than you, and I have no intention of crushing you to death." He maneuvered her into a corner of the couch, wrapping one of the paisley cashmere throws around her, and stood up.

"You have to arrange us," she said, watching as he undressed. His chest was still deeply tanned from the last weekend on *L'Amie* and his body, as she had known it would be, was in superb condition. His clothes vanished onto the floor, and before she had a chance to look at all of him, he picked her up in his arms, holding her, face to face, against him. She wrapped her arms around his neck and her legs twined themselves around his waist like a monkey's, and in this position he carried her down the length of the room and stopped in front of the big mirror.

"Look again," he said, and once more she found herself gazing into a scene of almost pagan beauty. She put her head down on his shoulder, wild with desire for him, and felt his fingers inside her, finding her wet.

"Good," he said. Holding her, he lowered her onto him, pushing himself into her smoothly, without pain.

"Oh," she said, throbbing around him in near ecstasy.

"Oh, yes," he said. "Now we begin to find each other." His hands held her buttocks and he began to slide her up and down his great body, up and down in perfect rhythm, moving as he did so in slow circles, almost as if he were doing a cadenced waltz, holding her against him and moving her up and down on him. His lips found hers, as searching and exciting as the rest of him. Amanda was lost in his arms and she moved with him now, taking all of him into her and then letting almost all of him go. She felt the strength of his hands as they held her and she felt herself begin to come, knowing that he was, too, and knowing that this time she would never stop coming nor would he. Oh, he was good, and the little thought that flickered through her head vanished as swiftly as it had come. With Charles, they were always in bed, always lying down. The sex between them was good but it wasn't anything like this.

"Oh," she said again, exhaling the breath left in her, burying her face in his neck, arms and legs still twined around him.

"Oh?" he said, making her look at him, teasing her. "Is that all you can say? That's not all, little darling. Soon now we will begin to really make love." He carried her back across the room and put her down on the big couch, wrapping one of the cashmere throws around her again. He stretched out beside her and shifted her body over on top of his. She lay on top of him like a feather, a whisper, weightless and dreaming.

"You see," he said. "It's so easy." He moved her onto him once again as if he were fitting a key into a lock, turning smoothly in her as he did so. It was as if they had never stopped, but this time she was on top of him and after the first onslaught of physical pleasure, she came alive as a willing partner, not just a receiver. John's deep voice was caressing her, an octave lower than usual. He made love to her with his voice as well as his body.

"My baby, my child, you are supreme," he was saying. "I love women —you know how I love them—the long ones with their elegance and their fine bones, and the ones with huge bosoms that drive men wild and cost them fortunes, but most of all I love your delicacy and the taste of you and the smallness of you and your ferocious courage.

"No woman has ever had skin like yours, the best, here and here and here." He touched the inside of her thigh, the back of her arms at the shoulder, and just beneath her bosom. As he spoke, they moved together again and Amanda knew that she would not be able to hold on to herself for any longer than she had the first time, nor did she have to. There was no reason to hurry. They had just begun to make love—John had told her so.

At some time in the long limbo of hours that followed, she woke from a deep sleep to find herself alone in the bed with the silky white linen. John was gone. She heard his voice on the telephone in the drawing room. She got up and went to the half-open door. As soon as he saw her he rang off, coming to hold her. Amanda had no idea what time it was— if it was night or day.

"You must have something to put on," he said. He picked her up and carried her through the bedroom and dressing room and bath, and at the end of the room he pushed a concealed mirrored door and carried her through to the bedroom beyond and put her down on her feet in front of a closet. He opened the closet doors and she saw that it was filled with clothes. There were shoes on racks, underwear and scarves folded neatly in drawers with glass fronts, silken things hanging on padded hangers. Were these the leftover possessions of the last mistress, abandoned when she left? Amanda was still sleepily thinking about this mysterious person, whoever she might have been.

"These are yours," John said. "You have to have something to wear."

In wonder, she took a shoe from one of the racks and put it on. It fit perfectly, just as the green ones for the Polish dress had. So that's what he meant—then the shoe will fit when you go home—knowing this moment would come.

"Choose something," he said, an expression of satisfaction on his face.

"You choose," she said.

He reached for a white knitted cashmere robe lined with gray satin. There were initials embroidered on the lapel, and before she looked, she knew they would be hers. They were, with a tiny crest embroidered above them.

"Do you think of everything?"

"Everything," he said. "The simple things are not the most important but they are the best. I wait for you, little Countess. Come back when you are ready." He disappeared through the mirrored door into his dressing room.

Amanda bathed and found in her closet a gray satin gown to go under the white robe. When she was ready she went back and found him seated in front of the fireplace in the small dining room. The newspapers were spread around him, there were two telephones beside him, and suddenly Amanda wondered what day it was. The wood fire warmed her back as she sat across from him and she realized that she was ravenous. Once more, he had provided everything. The simple things. Perfectly scrambled eggs with thin toast, pale slices of smoked salmon, silver pots filled with steaming coffee and hot milk, and on John's side of the table, brown bread and a small Polish salami he was slicing, holding a piece out to her.

"We talk now, little Countess."

Amanda sat down beside him, feeling wanted and still loved. As she looked at him sitting beside her, slicing thin slices of the Polish salami and handing them to her on a pronged silver fork, she knew that she had never known a man so at ease with himself before, a man with no self-doubts. His skin was glowing and she was proud that she had been part of it—they had made that together.

"Little Countess," she said. "I am no Countess at all. It's always been in name only. The closest I seem to have come to the real thing is this monogram you have put on my robe." She fingered the tiny embroidered crest.

"Why do you stay with him?"

"Because he loves me. I know he does. He can't help being what he is. Someday, I know he will come to the end of the gambling. He'll get sick to death of it and will stop."

"Little Countess. You are wrong on all four counts. I am not baiting you or putting you in a defenseless position, nor am I trying to hurt or anger you. This is not exactly a shipboard romance that we have embarked on. Do you know what I mean?"

"If it is, I'd like to have some more of them." She leaned across and kissed him on the cheek. "John, he can't go on much longer. He's lost everything. He has no more credit and no more trusts to lean on. He does love Patrick, and in his way he loves me. He puts up such a bluff. Why do you say I'm wrong?"

"You do not understand the passion that goes with gambling. Charles would never make love to you if it was going to interfere with a game. If he's good in bed it's because you make him so, because you are so foolishly in love with him. . . ." He paused. "Listen to me. You finally came to me of your own free will. I told you I was going to have you, but I let you come to me. I have waited for you longer than I have waited for any woman. You are worth it. You are valuable. Does that tell you something about yourself?"

"John, what woman could resist you when you want her?"

"Can you love two men at the same time?" he was asking.

"Can I? I seem to." The fear was there. "I don't know how it is going to work."

"Let me take care of that. The giant step has been getting you in my body, in my skin. You belong with me. I am going to persuade you to leave Charles and come to me. When you want to."

"John, how can I? I'll lose Patrick. I can't lose Patrick."

"You are not going to lose him. Never forget that any judge in England, regardless of what you do, would think twice before giving Patrick to his gambler father. He'll have you in the poorhouse or living on what charity his mother still feels for him in her soul. I will find a house for you and Patrick—the boy should not grow up in a gambling atmosphere. He needs a better life and so do you. We will always have this, our secret place."

"But when I leave, when I don't have your strength to lean on, I'll fall apart and have migraines again and feel like the adulteress I am. I've been told by more than one doctor that I am unstable, not responsible. No one likes me very much."

"You have been in the wrong rooms ever since you seduced Charles Warrington, married him, and became a Countess. Do you really think you are unstable?"

"Yes. I do. I do terrible things."

"I can change all that. I am going to change it. You run from doctor to doctor and there are no good ones here in England for your so-called emotional instability. I can and will find the right man for you. You are a fragile and courageous fool and I am going to protect you. Come here."

Amanda's desire for him was stronger than ever. It was a new feeling, the passion she felt for him. She watched him rise from the table and his hugeness was overwhelming. As he leaned over her, the sheer force of him excited her. She was in his arms and he carried her back into the bedroom. The bed had been made up by some unseen, silent servant; the white linen was fresh and the curtains had been drawn. Amanda still didn't know if it was day or night. John took her face in his hands and kissed her, then put her into the bed. He got in beside her and turned on his side, facing her, stroking her and holding her in his arms. They began to make love, this time as if they had always been together, had always wanted each other as they did now.

Hours later, she woke still in his arms. He was awake.

"John," she said, pulling herself up so that her face was above his, her hair tumbling over his face.

"Little Countess?"

"I thought I knew something about sex. I don't know anything about sex."

"Sssh," he said. "You know everything about sex. You just don't know anything about love."

★ ★ ★

June 1970

Charles Warrington was a lost lord in his own time and John Latimer had no intention of allowing Amanda to be destroyed in the wake of such misfortune and stupidity.

He understood the intricacies of her mind and the potential of her brain, knew well her weaknesses and her potential madness. Her reactions were erratic and her moods reasonably dangerous. She needed proper diagnosis and medication and John knew who could help her. She was scarred but not flawed; she was a jewel uncut. Aside from her dogged devotion to Charles Warrington, no man had really touched her. She was incomplete. John was in love with her. He would complete her.

Warrington was incomplete, too, but all gamblers were incomplete. Their obsession made anything else, everything else, no more than a substitute for gambling. John understood the tragedy of Charles Warrington. With no fortune and very little in the way of brain power, he was lost. The very existence of the Wyndham Club exposed his weakness and exploited it. No one was more aware of that than Gavin Driscoll and John Latimer, casino owners who could not be fairly criticized for providing the background for a man to lose a fortune. A century ago Warrington would have gambled as gentlemen gambled, in the private world of great houses and greater privilege. Estates might have been lost, possessions would have gone, but privately. A gentleman's business.

It was understandable for Charles Warrington to deplore the actions and attitudes his parents had taken in their associations with a Labour government. In his arrogant mind, postwar England was going to hell fast, to socialism and fascism. It was now filled with the wogs and the niggers and the kikes, all dreadful people. Inferior breeds swarming all over England now, admitted by the thousands, could never have gotten even the lowliest job on any of the great estates of England past.

John Latimer knew that nothing could be done about Charles except eventually to cut off his credit.

He had waited five years for Amanda to walk back into his life. He was going to have to wait even longer for her to leave Charles of her own free will. He was prepared to be patient. She was worth waiting for.

★ ★ ★

Some weeks later, Charles went off unexpectedly to Saint-Moritz on a last-minute invitation to a hastily arranged backgammon tournament. Amanda felt as if she were walking on air with a whole weekend to herself. Patrick was spending the weekend at Lea Place with his nanny. Davina had taken to inviting him alone, particularly without Amanda. There were no rows, but it was clear to Amanda that her sister did not long for her company.

Leading a double life had not bothered Amanda and she often wondered at her duplicity. Why was she happier—and Charles, too— when she was deceiving him? Why did she feel no pangs of a guilty conscience? What little life she shared with John satisfied and fulfilled her, although she was still unwilling to face the thought of leaving Charles. Somehow, in a part of her mind, she felt that marriage was forever and that children belonged with their mother and father. Divorce was unreal to Amanda; it was something other people did.

Her love affair with John stabilized her. Charles, if he paid any attention at all, noticed only that she was less of a nag. He accepted her behavior as a remission from her normal depressions and headaches. She was of little concern to him as long as she behaved herself.

As soon as Charles left for the airport, she flew over to Les Amis and slipped upstairs, hoping to surprise John. The ever-present Guido always told him the minute she arrived and nothing escaped his scrutiny. That didn't matter. She was reveling in the unexpected time they could have together.

She went to her closet and took out a pair of silvery satin pajamas with a tiny close-fitting jacket embroidered with seed pearls. They were new, and she put them on hoping it wouldn't be too long before he came upstairs. She waited, listening for the lift, and when she heard it she opened the door and rushed into his arms, seeing his face light up with the pleasure of having her there. They never had enough time together.

"I don't know which is which anymore," she said.

"Little Countess? The salmon or the caviar?"

She was sitting cross-legged and barefoot at the end of the big bed, watching John. He was propped against the pillows, tortoise-shell glasses on his brow, going over the nightly reports which were sent up to him at the end of every evening. It was a complete record of who had won what and lost what, paid what or borrowed. He went over the figures meticulously.

Amanda laughed and tucked her satin pajamas around her.

"Neither, you fool. Something else. When we were first together, I thought being with you was something apart, a secret that gave me a world away from the realities. Now the reality is only you, and the rest, apart from Patrick, is a nightmare. How long can it go on?"

"Until you come to me. All you have to do is come to me. I wait for you."

"Can I? Tell me the practicalities. I pack my bags and leave a note for Charles. 'I'm gone. You're rid of me. I am taking Patrick and you may see him whenever you like. I have gone to live with John Latimer.' Is that how I do it?"

"Why not?"

"Is that what you want me to do?"

"No. I want you to live with me in this world—which you thought of as a dream world, an escape, at first—until you can no longer bear to be anywhere else. When that time has come, when you come to me willingly, I have another house, beautiful, but small compared to this, in Down Street, two blocks from here. It is ready for you. You can move into it with Patrick; the staff are already there. No one will know where you have found the money to live in such grand style and you will immediately become a woman of great mystery. The lawyers will come and Charles will come, your sister and Richard will come, all attempting to find out how you have managed this. Where is the money coming from? It will drive them wild. You will tell no one. That little cat smile of yours that I have observed when you are dreaming fairy tales in my arms will be on your face and you will continue to tell them nothing. Charles will then rant and rave and threaten, you will cry and tell me you have to go back to him, and I will say go back to him if you want to. But you won't want to. You will want only me and I will keep you safe forever."

"Forever? What about the five or six years you say is the time you allot to your mistresses?" she teased.

"I will make an exception in your case—maybe six and a half, but I will never leave you. I will take care of you."

"You see? That's what I mean. I don't know which is which anymore. You never make me do anything. You let me do things on my own."

"My darling, you are not ready yet. You are getting warm. You are beginning to believe me. You are still thinking: Can I? Do I want to? How can I leave Charles? You deserve to make your own decision. Until then, I wait for you. Meanwhile, give me some salmon, a little piece with the lemon, as you do it so well. You may even light my cigar tonight."

She laughed again. Cigars were a part of him; he adored them and the ritual of lighting one was an art. She had tried to light one for him once and he had taken it from her.

"No," he'd said. "Not until you learn how." He'd taught her how to cut it, the silver cutter held correctly in her hand, then nipping it properly and holding the match until the flame caught, slowly, sensuously, and burned perfectly, the warm smell of the tobacco pleasing her as much as it did him. Since then he had teased her; if she was good, she was allowed to light them for him.

"And what would I do, a rich woman with no money, alone in a perfect house with a perfect staff in Down Street?"

"You would remain that most ineluctable of all figures, a woman of mystery. You would learn about being secure by keeping your own counsel. Then, slowly, in the normal course of events, I would invite you to lunch, even to dinner, and it would be remembered that we were friends. You would be seen with me from time to time, and everyone would speculate about us but no one would know. Then, when you were divorced, it wouldn't matter. You could do whatever you chose to do. That's what money is for."

"Is that how you want it to be?"

"That's one way. There are others."

"Do you think I will ever do it, that I will ever be able to do it?"

"I do. Until then, my darling, I wait for you."

Charles's routine had shifted to Les Amis, although he lunched elsewhere, usually with Robin or Jeremy. The routine of the house in Royal Hospital Road remained the same and a truce of sorts existed between Amanda and Charles. Amanda was up early to dress Patrick while the nanny fixed their breakfast. As Charles rarely rose before eleven and Amanda was always asleep hours before he got home, they neither went to bed together nor got up together. Their only conversation was in the evenings when he came home to change and occasionally to share an early evening meal with them for the sake of being with Patrick. She had no desire to go to Les Amis with him—quite the opposite—nor was she asked. She tried not to antagonize him but clashes occurred when she had to ask him for money, which annoyed him.

"Why do you constantly bother me about a few hundred pounds?" he asked when she presented him with a sheaf of overdue bills.

"Why? Do you think I enjoy asking you? How can I pay Nanny and the greengrocer and the milkman when there is no money?" It was a repetitive conversation and one she dreaded. "Can't you just deposit enough to cover the bills in the bank every month and then I wouldn't bother you?"

Charles looked at her coldly. "I would, my dear, if I could." The monthly harangues would end with his leaving some cash on the desk with a note instructing her whom to pay, avoiding the fact that there was never enough to cover what was due.

Amanda made the best of it. She knew John would give her anything she needed but she was loath to ask him. An intrinsic pride made her refuse to let him know how frugally they lived. She kept her problems to herself and lived for the pleasure of him and in fear of Charles's finding out about them.

After the conversation with John about the house in Down Street, she daydreamed about leaving Charles, but she knew she was indulging in fantasy, not reality. It was Patrick who stopped her; he was the bedrock reason why she could not make the decision John wanted her to make. She spent hours playing with him, teaching him games, and watching him grow. She watched Charles with him and she knew he loved Patrick as dearly as she did. The only time Charles ever lightened up and laughed was when he was with his son. Patrick adored both his father and his mother and Amanda couldn't bear even to think of separating them.

Patrick loved frogs. When Nanny took him to the Serpentine Pond in Hyde Park, he loved playing along the edges of the water. "A frog, Nanny—it's a big frog. Look, isn't he pretty?"

"He's a bullfrog," Nanny said. "They are sweet fellows. They hop around in the sun and swim a lot. They don't do much else but eat flies, if they can catch them."

"I like frogs and I'd like to be one."

He transmitted this important information to his father when they had their next evening romp together. They always had a romp when his father was at home in the evenings, before he was taken to bed.

"Do you like frogs?" he asked.

"I love them," Charles said. "They're good fellows and smarter than one thinks. They're very good at catching flies. I'll make up a frog-and-fly game for us."

Patrick was ecstatic. "You be the fly."

"And you're the bullfrog," his father said. "We'll call you Bufo and we'll call me Fly. You have to see if you can catch me. Snap at me."

It became their favorite game. Patrick would wait every evening until he heard his father's key in the door; then he'd run and hide. Charles would come looking for him.

"Bufo, where are you? This is the Fly and I'm bigger than you are and this time I'm going to catch you and eat you." Patrick would leap out from his hiding place and attack Charles from behind.

"You old Fly, I've got you and I'm going to eat you." They would roll around together on the nursery floor or in the kitchen. Patrick would finally give out and crawl into Charles's arms.

"I won't eat you this time, Fly. I'm too tired."

"You promise, Bufo? If you won't eat me, I'll take you up to bed and tell you a story." It was their game, no one else's. Patrick drew pictures of Fly and Bufo in nursery school, over and over.

Amanda loved watching them romp. They seemed like a normal family when they were together like this. One evening she called Patrick in from the garden where he was playing when she heard Charles at the front door.

"Bufo," she called, "you'd better hide. I think I hear your father."

Patrick came flying into the house, his face furious. "Don't call me that! I'm not your Bufo. I'm my father's Bufo and he's my Fly. You're not allowed to call me that. Only my father calls me that."

"Of course I won't. How stupid of me," Amanda said. She knew she had invaded something precious between father and son. "I promise I'll never call you that again."

CHAPTER 12

April 1971

"**L**ittle Countess, bring me your passport."

"My passport? Why?"

"I want to make sure it's up-to-date. We might be going somewhere."

"How can we go somewhere? Where?" She knew as she asked that he had something planned, worked out as only he could work it out. If she hadn't been caught off guard, she would never have questioned him. His big hand came down over hers and the look he gave her was one she knew well, his blue eyes giving away nothing and everything.

"Where?" she asked again. She sensed a new excitement in him.

"I believe Charles will be in California for a few weeks soon, and Patrick goes with his grandmother. Am I right?"

"Yes. Right." Then they would have some time alone together. John must want to go to *L'Amie*. He had mentioned recently how much he'd like to spend a few days aboard when she moved from her winter berth in Palma to Monte Carlo.

"Little Countess," he said again, kissing her fingertips. "Bring me your passport."

John did want to spend a few days on *L'Amie* but that was not his plan. What life he and Amanda had together was always in the cocoon of Les Amis, most of that hidden away. He wanted more than that: He wanted to be somewhere in the outside world with her, free to roam where they pleased. He wanted to watch her face as she was exposed to some of the places he truly loved.

★ ★ ★

Guido took her through immigration and led the way to the first-class lounge. The BOAC attendant asked her to sign in, and as she took the pen in her hand she wondered what name to sign. Guido had brought her passport, and he had her ticket and boarding pass, which she had not seen yet. She decided to sign her name Amanda Warrington, and as she started to write, she felt John's presence looming beside her.

"Ah," he said, "Lady Warrington. How nice to see you. Where are you off to?"

Suddenly she was up to the game, lightheaded with the pleasure of seeing him, dazzled by the thought of going with him, of being with him anywhere.

She turned to Guido. "Thank you, Guido, for taking such good care of me. May I have my ticket and passport, please?" Guido handed them to her without even a glance at John.

"Arrivederci, Contessa," he said. *"Buon viaggio."* He bowed slightly.

Amanda looked at her boarding pass. Seat 7A. London-Heathrow to New Delhi. Flight 764.

"India," she said. "Isn't it exciting? I've never been there before. And where are you going, Mr. Latimer?"

"What a coincidence," John said. "We're on the same flight. I'm on my way to Nepal."

Thanks to John's usual extravagant touch, the upstairs cabin of the plane had been reserved for the two of them, a private world with a steward to see to their every need. They had a light meal, also provided by John, who had no intention of trusting anything but delicacies from Les Amis, and watched the sun fire the Alps at dusk. The steward made up beds for them. When the plane landed in New Delhi at dawn, he helped them disembark ahead of the other passengers. When the aircraft door was opened, a white-coated Indian was waiting to greet John respectfully. A station wagon was at the foot of the steps, and a few minutes later Amanda was sipping iced tea in a small cottage adjoining the main airport, a ceiling fan circling lazily in the air above her. John and the white-coated Mr. Motawata quickly finished with the customs officials, and in less than an hour they were airborne again, this time in a private plane and accompanied by Mr. Motawata.

John seated himself on the couch beside her. "We'll be in Chitwan in an hour. You're not tired, I see."

"Chitwan," Amanda said. "Wherever that is. Nepal. How could I be tired?" She had noticed a royal crest painted near the entrance door of the plane and a replica of it in the main cabin by the altimeter. "John, don't keep me in suspense. Whose plane is this?"

"My darling, it belongs to the Maharajah of Kashmir, a longtime friend. He sent it to take us to Chitwan as efficiently as possible."

Amanda noticed a difference in John, a boyishness about him she had never seen. His guard was down; the constant wariness that was part of his nature had vanished. She put her arms around his neck and kissed him.

"I'm not going to ask you where Chitwan is."

"Don't," he said. "Go and change before you disturb my timing." He was holding her lightly to keep her from obeying him.

"Change?" Amanda said, like a robot. Into what? She'd brought nothing besides her makeup and a toothbrush, as instructed.

John waved her toward the rear compartment, where she found a small suitcase on a rack, opened already. There was nothing he didn't think of. She changed into a cotton blouse and slacks and walking shoes. When she returned John was immaculate in khakis, sporting a pink shirt under his safari jacket. Her excitement heightened.

The plane descended, and landed on a grass strip, rumbling up to a thatch-roofed enclosure. Half a dozen Nepalese transferred the luggage and supplies from the plane into a Jeep. They stood waiting on a wide plain. It was hotter than any heat Amanda had ever felt.

"Look," John said, turning her body to face north.

The Himalayas lay stretched in front of her, as far as her eyes could see. The snowy peaks shimmered in the late afternoon sun, hundreds of miles of them stretching across the horizon, more than twenty-five thousand feet up. Beneath their crests she could make out valleys of dark sapphire blue, deeper than the bright blue of the sky. Amanda was stunned as she stood on the hot plain, her breath taken away.

"The top of the world," John said.

"Why didn't I see them from the plane?"

"You were changing," he teased. "I wanted you to see them from the ground. This is the way they should be seen first. They will be invisible in half an hour. The Himalayas saved themselves for you. Sometimes they aren't seen for months."

"They wouldn't dare do that to you," she said, climbing into the Jeep. "They aren't mountains. I don't know what they are, but I never want to leave them."

They drove along the banks of a small meandering river, bumping along until they came to a primitive wooden dock, a few slats of wood hammered together, where they transferred into a pirogue and were poled across by the Nepalese boatman. Amanda never let her eyes leave the mountain peaks, and even as she watched, wisps of cloud were gathering quickly into larger ones on the crests, making them invisible, just as John had said they would be. The broad plain had given way to high elephant grass and there was jungle ahead. A herd of delicate spotted chital deer suddenly scattered in front of the Jeep, alarmed by the engine. It was getting dark.

"Now look," John said.

Three elephants were waiting at the end of the path, their dark hulks clustered together, tails flicking back and forth, ears flapping off flies. At a signal from the mahout, one of them lumbered gracefully, stoically, into a kneeling position.

"We're almost there," John said, his face filled with delight.

Amanda threw her arms around him. "I don't want to be there. I want to stay here where we are forever, soaked with sweat, alive, and with you."

"Still, darling, he is your transportation to the lodge."

"Whose lodge?" Amanda asked, wondering how she was supposed to mount the majestic creature kneeling placidly before her.

"The King of Nepal. He is our host. He will be waiting to dine with us."

Amanda started to laugh. A certain fatigue assailed her and all she wanted to do was to lie in John's arms.

"From a Maharajah's plane to dinner with the King of Nepal," she said. "Any more surprises?"

"A small one."

The mahout helped Amanda onto the elephant, showing her how to mount by using his curled tail to clamber up onto the howdah. John followed her lead, and the elephants moved with infinite grace, in a slow rolling motion, through thirty-foot-high grass along a narrow sand path. It had gotten dark. Amanda saw ahead of her the dim outlines of a dark wood lodge, supported by huge timbers, with a steep roof. Kerosene lamps were glowing along the broad first-story verandah. Her elephant moved straight toward the lodge and, at the last moment, gently bowed his great head under the pilings. Amanda found herself stepping from the howdah onto the verandah, aided by the mahout. She leaned on the balustrade, watching as John did the same.

The elephants moved off, disappearing into the dark.

"Oh," Amanda said. John laughed and pulled her to him, kissing her cheek.

"That's what you say when I have loved you particularly well."

"You've loved me particularly well today."

"More than ever."

"Do we have to have dinner with the King of Nepal tonight?" she asked. As tired as she now was, she wanted him.

"Did I say tonight?" John asked, enfolding her in his arms. "I made a mistake. I meant tomorrow night."

"Oh, John," she said. "Thank heavens. You and the top of the world are more than enough for me in one day."

They lived in a paradise for the next few days. True to what he had told her, the Himalayas never appeared again. Clouds covered the peaks, but Amanda knew they were there.

CHAPTER 13

London, September 1972

When John left his apartment he found Charles outside his door, about to knock.

"What the devil are you doing up here?"

"I have to see you."

"That is beside the point. What I want to know is how you got up here. My staff have explicit instructions that everyone who comes to my private quarters is to be announced to me."

Latimer was a man who did not like surprises. He was distinctly annoyed to find Charles on the landing; in fact he was furious. His anger had nothing to do with Amanda—she had been safe with him for almost two years now. It had to do with a break in the internal security of the club.

"Damn your staff," Charles said. "Let's just say I managed to slip past them. I've asked to see you since last week but you have not made yourself available. Why have you cut me off?"

"Charles, my office is the place for such discussions. I have never made a practice of talking business in hallways." He moved toward the stairway, assuming that Charles knew nothing about the lift. The day would soon come when Charles would be out of his life, out of their lives. It couldn't come a moment too soon.

"I don't give a damn where you discuss business."

"All right, Charles. I've stopped your credit because the time is long past for you to pay up. Last Thursday you went down almost ten thousand pounds. That's got to stop."

"Just a bad run. You know I have always settled my debts. I've brought people here you'd like to have as members. I won't be embarrassed like this."

"Money means nothing to you, Charles—yours or anyone else's. You have lost all sense of reality. How long do you expect me to go along with you?"

"As long as necessary," Charles said stiffly. "I'll walk out of here, John, and never return, if you don't reestablish my credit."

"As you like. I seem to remember your doing that with your good friend Gavers. He hasn't missed you, apparently. Why don't you go back to him? No more credit until you're paid up, Charles."

A guttural noise came from Charles's throat. As John started down the stairs from the landing where they stood, Charles grabbed him by the shoulder. John's response was quick as he turned and deflected Charles's arm. Charles struck out at him again, flailing at him but missing his great bulk. John cursed and lost his footing. He missed the step and began to fall. He reached desperately for the banister but it was too late. He hurtled forward down the stairs, thirty-six steps down to the landing on the floor below. Charles watched in horror, John rolling over as he fell. The fall was bound to kill him. There was nothing Charles could do except watch. John landed on his side at the bottom of the stairs, completely still, not a sound coming from him.

"Jesus Christ," Charles said, shaking his head to clear it. He ran down the stairs double-time and leaned over John's inert body.

"John!" he said, suddenly feeling faint. "Are you all right?" What an idiot question. A 295-pound man had fallen down three dozen steps and was lying at his feet, his huge body deathly still, his eyes closed. And Charles was asking if he was all right? There was not the slightest movement or sound from John. He must be dead.

Charles panicked. He had to get out. No one had seen him as he made his way to John's private quarters—he was sure of that—but it was known that he was deeply in debt at Les Amis and probably known by now that John had cut off his credit. They might think he had pushed John deliberately, even think he had tried to kill him. Charles tried to reason with himself. What had happened had not been his fault. Or had it? There could be an ugly charge against him. He must get away, down the back stairway—which he had observed by watching the movements of the staff. That was how he had found his way up.

How much time had passed now? And why had no one come up? Had no one heard the fall? Charles glanced around furtively, knowing he had to get downstairs quickly. He had signed in when he arrived, as each member did. It was known he was there.

He took the back stairway, fleeing down to the basement floor to the men's room, seeing no one on the way. He was sweating. He washed his face in cold water and tried to breathe evenly, willing his hands to stop shaking. Then he went up to the bar. Don, the barman, gave him a questioning look.

"Drink, sir?"

"No thanks, Don. I have an appointment in the City." Above all, he wanted to be away from Les Amis before John's body was discovered. He retrieved his hat and umbrella at the door and walked out calmly into Hamilton Place. He flagged down a cab and got in without telling the driver his destination. How long would John lie there before someone found him? A passing thought regarding his IOUs crossed his mind. With John dead, he would still have to pay up.

He felt no twinge of conscience about leaving without calling for help. John was beyond help. Charles was not responsible for the accident— John had lost his balance and slipped, hadn't he? Charles didn't know quite where to go now. There was no appointment in the City.

He decided to stop by Mirabelle in nearby Curzon Street to see if anyone was there. He would go home about six. Amanda would undoubtedly have heard about Latimer. It would be on the radio and the telly; John Latimer was a very well-known man.

Charles arrived home as usual, around six-thirty, to be greeted by a frantic Amanda at the door.

"Have you heard about John? Weren't you there?"

"I was, until about two-thirty. Then I had an appointment. What's happened?"

"He's in the London Clinic. He's had a terrible fall down that huge staircase. No one knows why it didn't kill him. His pelvis is broken and he's in intensive care, but he's alive. They won't let anyone see him. Not yet, but I must go as soon as possible."

Charles stared at her, unable to believe what she was saying. John Latimer couldn't be alive.

"Why are you looking at me like that?" Amanda asked. "Did you hear me?"

"Of course I heard you. I guess we have to be glad the fall didn't kill him. As to your going to see him, why would you do that? You don't know him that well."

"I don't believe you, Charles. John has been a good friend to you, and if it weren't for him, I don't know where you would have gone since you fell out with Gavers. How can you be so cold?" Amanda was pale and shaking.

Charles ignored her and went back to his study to fix a drink, his mind in turmoil. How could the bastard possibly have lived through that fall? And now what would happen? Now he, Charles, was really in it. *Start by defining yourself as a shit*, he thought. *John Latimer certainly will*. He sat brooding, tapping his fingers on the arm of the wing chair, reluctant to allow the thought in his mind to surface. Suddenly it was there, striking him with almost bodily force, a large element of fear accompanying it. Latimer could hold him responsible, could state categorically that he had been pushed. Charles went over the scene when John had come out on the landing. He had been angry; he had admonished Charles for the unexpected invasion of his privacy. Why should it annoy him so—Charles's having found his way to John's private domain —and why the devil should he merit such security? Who did the man think he was?

Charles's memory was fuzzy. He remembered having two drinks at the bar earlier. He'd told Don, the barman, that he was going to make several long-distance calls. Don had seen him afterward when he returned to the bar. Charles had said he did not want another drink—he had to leave for an appointment in the City. He was all right there.

Unless Latimer decided to do something about it, to say something. Charles was still in panic. How the hell *could* John Latimer possibly have lived through that fall? And now how long was he going to have to wait to find out what would happen?

He got up and fixed himself another drink.

Ten days later, when visitors were allowed to see John, Amanda went to the London Clinic. She had never felt as helpless before. All she had been able to do was call each day and ask how he was. Charles had been in a particularly testy frame of mind lately, hanging about the house more than ever. Amanda would have sworn that the day would never come when she'd wish that Charles was at the Wyndham and out of her hair, but she did now.

Charles was half out of his mind waiting to find out what Latimer was going to say. Or not say. Staying in the house bored him but he stayed. He did not want to go back to Les Amis. He knew his credit was stopped and he felt that the less seen of him there at this time, the better.

When Amanda got home she was very withdrawn, very subdued. She went to check on Patrick in the nursery and then came to talk to Charles in his study.

"How was he?" Charles asked.

"Terribly weak and in awful pain still," she said. "A broken pelvis for a man of his weight is unbelievably painful. I feel so sorry for him."

Charles noticed something odd about her look. She was pale, too pale.
Her beauty was wraithlike.

"Was he glad to see you?" Stupid question.

"Glad to see me?" she asked vaguely. "Yes, I suppose so, but he is still
very weak."

"Did he say anything?"

"Say anything? About what?" Amanda asked. Charles seemed inordi-
nately interested in her visit.

"About how it happened, Amanda. That's about what." He snapped
out the words.

"How it happened? He came out of his apartments and tripped on the
landing. That's all he said. A stupid fall. A stupid fall that would have
killed anyone else. No one knows how he could have survived that fall. I
just hope he will be all right."

"So do I," Charles said.

Good old Latimer, he thought. *I knew he wouldn't say anything.* There
was nothing to say, really.

Amanda was in complete disarray. With all her heart she wanted to
be with John every moment. To add to her distress, Charles was around
the house, night and day. Why the devil was he no longer going to Les
Amis? Everyone else was, according to Guido and the secretary Sally,
and there were daily reports on John's progress. She found herself wishing that Charles could go back to the Wyndham—anything to get him
out of the house. He complained constantly about the smallest detail, he
was drinking copiously, and he was not all that patient with Patrick now
that he had plenty of time to spend with him. Patrick whimpered when
Charles sent him away. Amanda found herself studying Patrick and
wondering for the first time if both of them wouldn't be better off living
with John.

September 1972

Ten days after his fall John was moved from intensive care into a
private room. It seemed as if the worst was over. He was in agony from
the broken pelvis. It was almost unbearable for a man of his size to have
to lie quietly in one position until someone turned him onto one side or
the other, bringing even more pain. His body was covered with bruises,
but the main concern of his doctors was the possibility of internal injuries. He was monitored constantly and sedated to kill the pain. By the

time he could be moved to a private room his doctors relaxed somewhat, as there were apparently no signs of internal injuries. Now, it was a matter of time. He would have to remain in the clinic for another three to six weeks at least and it would be a good six months before he could walk again.

John established residence in his private room and the trouble began for the clinic.

"You are starving me," he said to the nurse.

"You can have anything you want, Mr. Latimer."

"Not from this kitchen. From my club. My chef will prepare lobster and steak for me, every day."

"Mr. Latimer," the nurse said, "lobster and steak are entirely too rich for you. We have to keep your weight down."

"Then bring me my cigars."

"Mr. Latimer, cigar smoking is the last thing allowed. Absolutely no."

John looked at her with affectionate disdain.

"Absolutely?"

"Absolutely."

It made no difference. John's cigars invaded the clinic. To search his visitors for contraband was simply not possible—and they were not the only culprits. The hospital staff was equally guilty. Mr. Latimer had a way of getting what he wanted.

Amanda had arrived as soon as visitors were allowed, giving her name as Mrs. Gordon. She didn't want any particular notice taken of her presence because she was Lady Warrington.

John's accident had brought forth some inner strength in her. *Just don't let him die,* she thought over and over again. *Just don't let him die. We can work anything out. I can take care of him no matter what shape he is in. Just don't let him die.* John was her only security, the only person who had ever loved her and the only man she liked, much less loved. They had a life before them, together. He would be all right—he had to be all right. Her life depended on it. *Just don't let him die.*

"Little Countess," John said to her on her first visit, one of his big hands covering hers. "I am alive. You must be patient and put the terrors out of your mind. It's only time we have to deal with." He knew how fragile her confidence was.

"But six months?" Amanda said, tears rolling down her cheeks. "Before you can walk again. I can wait six centuries for you, but for you to have to lie here in this awful pain—I can't bear it."

"You can. And I can, as long as you show me your beautiful, worried face every day. Can you manage that?"

"Of course I can. Nothing could stop me."

To Amanda's immense relief, Charles was no longer underfoot. She told John that Charles had gone back to the Wyndham.

"Has he?" John said. "That's good."

"Yes, thank God. I never thought I'd say that, but about a week or two after your accident, he got very drunk one night and somehow made it up with Gavers. Gavers isn't giving him any credit, but he has some little money he finds somewhere and he's only playing bridge. He seems to be taking it pretty well. He must owe you a packet."

"We won't even think about that. It doesn't matter."

Each day, Amanda would leave for the clinic as soon as Charles left the house. At first she was allowed to stay only for an hour. She brought the papers and read them to John, and sometimes, if he was in too much pain to talk, she would sit and hold his hand. As Mrs. Gordon, she attracted no particular notice at the clinic. Gradually, since her presence seemed to have a calming effect on the patient, there was no objection to her staying far beyond established visiting hours.

One afternoon John woke to find her asleep in the chair beside his bed, her face serene and childlike in repose. He stirred, massively uncomfortable, an unreasonable impatience accompanying the constant pain he lived with. He knew for certain that as soon as it was humanly possible, he was going to bring Amanda and Patrick to live in the house on Down Street. No more waiting for her to decide; the decision was now on his terms. Nothing before had ever frightened John Latimer, but he knew that this fall could have—should have—caused his death. He was looking at the rest of his life with new eyes.

He also knew without a shadow of a doubt that Charles Warrington had had no intention of trying to harm him. No such thought had entered his mind. For sure, Charles vanished afterward and made no attempt to help, leaving him for dead. It was ironic to John, and in a way it amused him, to consider the agony Charles must have gone through when he learned that John was alive. Charles had long ago slipped into the vortex of irresponsibility, and John knew that by now he would have exonerated himself from any guilt for his actions at the time of the accident.

Watching Amanda's sleeping face, John determined to take action as soon as he was physically able to do so, to engulf Amanda in the safety that his love could give her.

★ ★ ★

Six weeks to the day of the accident, at ten o'clock in the morning, John Latimer died of a massive embolism. There had been no warning; the nurse arrived in his room to bathe him and found him dead. Embolism was the swift killer that all doctors feared but had no way of anticipating. Embolisms came with little, if any, warning, and there had been no signs of trouble for John Latimer. When Amanda got to the clinic, the nurse was waiting for her anxiously.

"Mrs. Gordon, we had no telephone number for you. Mr. Latimer passed away this morning quite unexpectedly. When his nurse went in, he was gone. It was a massive embolism." She saw the terror in Amanda's eyes and the drastic paling of her face. She reached out for her.

Amanda felt herself losing consciousness. As she slipped to the floor, the nurse reaching to catch her, her last thought was of her father.

October 1972

John Latimer was buried in the small Polish cemetery near Thornton Heath. His compatriots from the war days and after were all at the service, aware of the passing of a legendary figure. Some of them were in the ragtag uniforms they had worn when they arrived in England in the desperate days when the Polish Squadron had been formed. It was John Latimer who had provided them with a place where they could sleep, eat, and drink and, most of all, where they could gather and reassemble. Many had even more to thank him for—those whose lives had not taken as fortunate a turn as his had. It was a highly emotional service. Full military honors had been accorded him. One of the large wreaths was from Buckingham Palace and a representative of the Queen was present. Philippe and François de Briand came; Chantal was in Egypt and could not be reached in time. Afterward, the group of several hundred mourners went back to Les Amis to feast and drink, as stipulated in John's will. He had no known relatives. A letter in his secretary's possession gave instructions as to what was to be done in the event of his death, right down to the smallest detail.

On the night of the funeral, which Amanda had not been able to face, she took thirteen sleeping pills with a glass of warm milk and lay down in her bed to die. As luck would have it, she could not keep the lethal dose down and became so violently ill that she would have choked to death on her own vomit if the nanny had not heard her from two floors above. Charles was called at the Club, and by the time he got there, Amanda's stomach had been pumped out by a neighborhood doctor the nanny had called.

Charles rang his mother.

"Can you keep Patrick for a few days?" he asked. "Amanda's tried to do herself in."

"Charles!" Penelope Warrington exclaimed. "How? Why? I had no idea she was that disturbed. What has she said? Has she given any explanation?"

"No," Charles said. "Nothing but an empty bottle of pills. She's still half-delirious and keeps calling for her clothes. She holds on to me, begging me not to leave her, since I am all she has left."

"You don't sound terribly sympathetic."

"I'm not. I'm concerned about Patrick. What do I tell him?"

"It might be best if I speak to him first. He's used to Amanda's not being quite right, but he needs comforting now. I'll be right there. I'll take Patrick and Nanny home with me. She can get him back and forth to school. Then Davina can keep him in the country for a while, or he can go to Pamela in Scotland. A few days out of school at his age don't matter a whit. Amanda needs professional help. Charles, she needs it badly. It's not going to get better, you know."

Charles was impatient, being told what to do about Amanda. There had been plenty of bills from Dr. Pennell for her professional care.

"Hatfield is what she needs. She should be hospitalized. I don't know what brought this on, but it doesn't surprise me."

When Amanda came to, her head was splitting and her mouth was parched. Penelope Warrington was sitting by the bed reading.

"Where is Charles?" Amanda asked. She looked like a derelict child. She was afraid to see Charles.

"He knows I am here with you. He's at the Club. I'm truly sorry about this, Amanda. I had no idea you were so unhappy."

For the first time Amanda thought she heard some warmth in Penelope's voice, some concern.

"You must have the proper care now, real care. You must realize yourself that you are a very sick girl. You are young and beautiful and you have a lifetime ahead of you. Perhaps if you and Charles spent some time apart? I know you have had your problems, but to try to take your own life . . . . Why, Amanda, can you tell me?"

"I didn't know what I was doing," Amanda said, her voice a raspy whisper. It was true: She had no memory of taking the pills. "I didn't mean to do it. I forgot about Patrick—I forgot about everything. I don't know why I did it."

She turned her face to the wall and wept after Penelope left. So Penelope thought she had a lifetime ahead of her. How little she knew. Now there was no John, no life ahead of her at all. There was nothing.

Amanda was desperately worried about what she might have said and to whom, what she might have given away when she was unconscious. She withdrew into herself, refusing to speak, and she stopped eating. Charles wasted no time. He called Dr. Pennell in Hatfield, told him what had happened, and arranged to have her admitted for treatment. He expected resistance from Amanda, but when he told her, she agreed it might be the best thing for her. She turned her face away from him and closed her eyes.

The doctor advised Charles to leave it alone. Passive resistance was part of the aftermath of a suicide attempt. They would take care of her at Hatfield and when she wanted to talk, when she could, it would all come out. She was a deeply disturbed young woman and she needed hospitalization. Now that she was willing, perhaps they could finally get at the root of her anguish.

Amanda stayed at Hatfield for six weeks. She was an ideal patient. She slept well, ate whatever was put in front of her, and she began to paint again. She went each morning to her regular session with Dr. Pennell but she had nothing to say to him. Her answers to his gently prodding questions were always the same.

"I don't know. I don't remember," she would respond repeatedly to most of his questions.

Her paintings were repetitious, always of white-flowering trees in a soft green landscape. When Pennell probed as to why she painted the same scene over and over, she answered that spring was her favorite season, when everything was new, everything was reborn.

Charles was advised to telephone once a week at a specified time, which he did. Their conversations were always the same, about Patrick. How was he? Was he happy? Was he with Davina or Penelope? "Tell Patrick I will be home soon," she would say at the end of each conversation. "I will be home very soon."

A letter came to the house for her from John Latimer's secretary. Charles opened it. John Latimer had left a painting to Amanda in his will, one she had once admired at Les Amis. Charles rang up to say that

Lady Warrington was staying with friends in the country at present but as soon as she returned, he would have her get in touch with the office.

The newspapers were filled with a rash of articles concerning John Latimer's will. Having no family, no direct heirs, he had bequeathed his favorite possessions to his friends and employees, things that they and he had loved. *The Daily Telegraph* ran a lengthy article, almost gossipy in content, painting a somewhat intimate portrait of John Latimer.

"The Marchioness of Evenden and Claire was left a pair of priceless Persian silk rugs," the *Telegraph* exulted:

> The Marchioness, a close friend since Mr. Latimer's arrival in England during the war, was one of the original members of Les Amis and advised him on the purchase of the rare rugs and wall hangings in the great Rothschild mansion. She took delight in all forms of gambling and was proud that Mr. Latimer taught her the fine points of a number of games, at which she frequently won large sums.

The Marchioness was quoted as saying "John Latimer was one of the finest men I have known and my life will be considerably less lively with him gone." The article continued:

> One of the windfalls goes to Guido Gigli, longtime maître d'hotel at Les Amis. Mr. Latimer's wine cellar, one of the finest in England, and numbering over 30,000 bottles, was left outright to Mr. Gigli, whose intention is to open a restaurant in Mayfair. It will be known as Latimer's. Mr. Sean Connery, the actor, is a beneficiary also, of the one-of-a-kind cream-colored convertible Bentley which was especially made for Mr. Latimer. Mr. Connery had always admired it.
>
> There are more than two hundred bequests. The Duc de Briand, who helped Mr. Latimer get out of France during the last war, has been bequeathed a pair of gold Renaissance boxes that are the work of Benvenuto Cellini. Personal friends have been left Mr. Latimer's personal jewelry, including watches, cufflinks and rings, of which he had a large collection. Employees are to receive various sums of money depending on years of service.
>
> Other sums, from several thousand to several hundred thousand pounds, are directed to charities and several companions of Polish

origin from the war days. Sally Humphries, Mr. Latimer's long-time assistant and executive secretary, has been left a freehold house in Devon that even she was unaware that Mr. Latimer had purchased.

As Charles read on, he wondered at the value of the painting John had left to Amanda. Considering that the man had arrived in England during the war with nothing, he had certainly managed to accumulate a considerable estate. He owned property all over London; flats and houses were listed as substantially as if they were the Grosvenor Estate. Miss Humphries was again quoted:

"Mr. Latimer's yacht, the L'Amie, will be sold. The lease on Les Amis in Hamilton Place will be maintained until a new tenant takes over. Mr. Latimer was always meticulous about the details of his business affairs. Each year on his birthday, January 10, he brought his will up-to-date."

Charles chose not to think about the scene on the stairway. No one had seen him. John Latimer had not blamed him, and he'd had plenty of time to make an issue of it if he thought Charles had deliberately pushed him. Charles's only concern was wondering when he would hear from Les Amis about his chits—the outstanding IOUs. If Latimer was so meticulous, someone would surely get in touch with him soon. He had no desire to return to Les Amis, especially since he was back on the old footing with Gavers. The Wyndham was his club, always had been. Still, he knew the amount he owed to Les Amis was in the thousands, and it bothered him. How long would they give him to pay up? He decided to call the ever-efficient Sally.

"Lord Warrington," she said. "Are you calling about the painting? I can have it sent 'round whenever you like."

"No," Charles said. "My wife is still away and I was just wondering . . . I would like to inquire about my account. My bill has not come this month. Perhaps you could look it up for me?"

"Indeed I can. May I ring you back shortly?"

True to her word, she rang back in a quarter of an hour.

"Lord Warrington, your account seems to be current. Guido tells me you haven't been in, to his knowledge, since Mr. Latimer's death, as few of our members have. I spoke to the casino accountant, and aside from monthly dues, you are quite in the clear."

"Just send the dues bill around and I'll take care of it at once. Thank you, Sally."

He rang off, not believing his good fortune. There was no mistake. Casino accountants did not make mistakes.

So be it, he thought. It was thoughtful of John to have remembered Amanda in his will. And whether John had known it or not, he had been generous to him as well. Charles must remember to mention the letter and the painting to Amanda when she got home.

December 1972

Dr. Pennell's voice on the phone was calm but Charles detected a note of annoyance.

"She simply vanished," he said to Charles. "She was in the dining room for breakfast and returned to her room afterward. Her first appointment is with me, at nine. When it got to be nine-twenty, I asked about her. She was gone—no sign of her. She was wearing a sweater with a tweed jacket and flannel trousers. Her purse is gone but that is all. She has no more money than the weekly allowance patients are given for cigarettes and small personal needs. I can't imagine that she would try to go anywhere but home. Let us know immediately if she turns up, and of course we'll do the same."

"Of course I will," Charles replied, and rang off. He was in his dressing gown. It was just after eleven and he had an appointment at noon with the headmaster of Patrick's school, to discuss Patrick's changing schools for a while. Davina wanted to put him in the country day school the twins went to. Charles could come for weekends, and Patrick would have a healthier and more normal family life. When Amanda was finished at Hatfield, she would have to go along with what was best for the boy. Davina had checked Amanda out of her life as if she were no more than a casual friend, no longer desirable as a guest. Patrick stayed with Davina for the fall break and when he had come home with Charles, he obviously missed Davina and the twins. It broke Charles's heart to see the sad expression on his son's face. Patrick told his nanny that he missed Amanda and asked her every night when his mummy would be home, but never mentioned her name when he was with Charles.

Charles postponed the appointment with the headmaster and stayed at home to watch for Amanda. He was sure she would walk in any minute.

At four-thirty he called Dr. Pennell.

"No sign of her there?" Charles asked, knowing what the answer would be.

"No, and I had hoped your call was to say she had turned up. We have alerted everyone, including the local constable. You know how small Hatfield is. It's about a mile from here into town. She could have gotten a bus—flagged one down, I suppose. I'm quite sure she'll turn up there any time now."

At 6:00 P.M. Amanda walked into the house and went down to the kitchen, where Patrick was having his supper. He threw himself into her arms, and Amanda held him tightly, wiping away tears. Charles, who had heard the commotion, came into the kitchen.

"I told your father to tell you I'd be home soon, darling," she was saying.

"Amanda," Charles said.

"Charles!" she said, turning to him with a sweet smile on her face. "How nice that you're home. I didn't expect you would be here this time of day." There was not a shred of rancor or sarcasm in her tone. She reached up on her tiptoes and kissed him on the cheek. Charles felt a flash of annoyance. Why the devil couldn't she at least have telephoned? He heard himself saying something inane about how nice it was that she was home safely. Why would he even give voice to the thought? It was less than two hours from Hatfield to here. Where had she been all day? He still wouldn't ask in front of Patrick.

He waited to call Dr. Pennell until Amanda went to the nursery to put Patrick to bed.

"Now what do I do with her?"

"Don't question her. Let her tell you what happened, why she left and how she got there. I'll come in first thing in the morning and we'll decide then how to handle the situation."

When Dr. Pennell arrived the next morning, they sat in the lacquered red dining room. Amanda was both rational and reasonable. She had just wanted to come home. She felt that she was well enough and missed Patrick and Charles. Yes, she was sorry she had not mentioned she was leaving to Dr. Pennell, but it had never occurred to her that she should. She thought she was free to come and go as she pleased—there hadn't seemed to be any restrictions on her. Was it not all right for her to have left? If she had caused any trouble, she was truly sorry.

She began to cry when Dr. Pennell told her that she would have to return to Hatfield with him.

"Please let me stay at home for a few days," she begged, reaching for Charles's hand, her expression pleading with him to help her. "I will come back on Monday. I just want to be with my child and my husband. Please, Dr. Pennell, I'm much better."

"Do you know now why you tried to take your own life, where you got the pills to do it?" Dr. Pennell asked.

"Yes, I do. I had been having terrible dreams again, nightmares like the ones I used to have. Charles will tell you that I always had these awful dreams—you know it too. I dream that my father is being killed and leaving me again. I can hear him scream; I get muddled always when it's about my father. I've always kept some pills hidden so if those dreams come I can knock myself out. I don't remember wanting to kill myself. I just wanted to sleep. I didn't want to dream about my father anymore."

"Why couldn't you tell us that, Amanda?" Dr. Pennell persisted, quiet authority in his tone. "I have seen you every day for six weeks and this is the first time you have been able to tell anyone why you tried to kill yourself."

"I guess I am getting well. I didn't really try to kill myself," she said, reaching again for Charles's hand. Her face was unclouded, her tone beseeching. She was a little girl who had done something without meaning to, without realizing the trouble she had caused them. Now she expected to be forgiven.

"Very well," Pennell said. "I'm going to let you stay at home, but starting Monday you are to come to Hatfield every day for your regular session with me. If you miss one appointment, you will be brought back to stay. Do you understand?"

"Oh, yes, dear Dr. Pennell, I do and I promise you I will be there every day."

Charles saw Dr. Pennell to his car.

"She may be on the road to recovery. We'll see. I was thinking of trying her out at home in a few weeks anyhow, so let's see how the next few days work. Stay close to her but don't question her—let her talk, and tell me what she says. She is still keeping things to herself. She's evasive, but she's ashamed too. She may be through the worst."

Charles had a bout with guilt in the next few days, an emotion unknown to him. Amanda had never been sweeter or more feminine and pliable. How could he have been so insensitive, so uncaring about her unhappiness? She hung on his every word; she even cajoled him to play the piano, which he had not touched for months. They sang and Patrick sang with them, his little face aglow. Charles stayed away from the Club. It was an interlude of unusual tenderness.

There was one problem. On her first night at home, Charles had made no attempt to touch her when they went to bed. They had been apart for so long, it might be better to wait. Might be better to wait! He hadn't wanted to touch her for months. But now the thin-lipped harridan of the recent past had reverted to the desirable bundle of warmth that he remembered from what now seemed a very long time ago. The Amanda he only vaguely remembered seemed to be back.

The next night Charles awoke about four. He reached for her sleepily and moved over on top of her, pulling up her nightgown and parting her legs. There was no resistance from her but there was none of her normal passionate response. *God,* he thought, *she's gone cold on me again.* He had never forgotten two years, or two and a half years, ago when he had come home from one of the backgammon tournaments and she had been like a dead body beneath him. He knew she had been angry with him for having stayed away for more than a month and she was punishing him by denying him the one thing that bound them together. Gradually, she had warmed up to him again, but it had taken a terrible fight before she had. He remembered saying to her: If we don't have this, we have nothing and I will leave you.

Now she began to move a little. That was better. He felt her arms go around his back. Good. There was something different—she was letting him take the initiative, where usually it was she who led the way. Tonight, she was warm and bloody marvelous. Hatfield apparently had done some good. If only it would last. Charles felt himself coming, long before he wanted to. He was out of practice. They would have to change that. He kissed her and turned over on his side, pulling the blankets up around his chin. He was asleep in no time.

Amanda lay on her back, in the same position she had been in when Charles withdrew from her.

She had lied yesterday and today, and she would lie tomorrow. She had spent six weeks at Hatfield protecting herself from what only she could say, what only she could give away. She and John had succeeded in keeping a secret that belonged only to them and now she was capable of keeping that knowledge to herself. What she had with John could never be taken away from her. But he was dead. He would not want her to leave Charles now, she knew. She had no choice if she wanted to keep her home and Patrick. And Charles. There was no money but there was always hope. Hope that he would stop gambling.

Dr. Pennell would not make her go back to Hatfield. He knew she was not deranged, as they'd thought—only grief-stricken and with a secret to keep. She would go to her appointments with him every day and she would turn a sweet face to Charles, no matter how he behaved. He was all she had.

She couldn't remember what she had left at Hatfield, but nothing much. A few clothes and some books and pictures of Patrick. There was only one thing there that she wanted and that was one of the pictures she had painted of the flowering trees. She thought about the great Stalewski painting, hanging alone in the dark in the place where she had spent the happiest and most alive hours of her life. Those were the only rooms in which she had really been loved. What would happen to the painting—who would get it now?

Those beautiful white flowers blowing in a fresh green land. She fell asleep thinking about the painting, feeling her pillow soaked with silent tears.

"**B**y the way," Charles said one morning before he left the house. "You'd better ring up Sally at Les Amis. A letter came for you—I left it in the drawer of my desk. John Latimer apparently left you something in his will."

Amanda turned away from him, fighting to control herself.

"Left me something?" she said in a small voice, her back still turned.

"Yes," Charles said. "While you were away, there was a lot in the papers about what he left and to whom. I forgot to tell you about the letter. Sorry. Apparently it's a painting, one that you admired. He was certainly generous with his friends. I'll see you later."

"Fine," Amanda said.

Amanda knew the time had come when she was going either to sink or to swim. John had left her the Stalewski for a clear purpose. It was probably the only thing he could leave her that would not jeopardize her if something happened to him—as something had. She wondered when he had put it in his will for her, sure that it had been before his accident rather than after. An afternoon when she had been in his room at the clinic came back to her, shortly before he died. She had fallen asleep, and when she woke up he was watching her.

"When I get out of here we are going to have a different life together," he'd said. She had heard that tone before. It was indisputable. He obviously had made some decision that day and had every intention of getting well, healing, walking again, and living, not dying. If he'd had any indication that he was going to die, he would have handled things differently. No, the Stalewski was a message of love and protection, not death.

She went to Charles's desk and found the letter from Sally. After reading it, she picked up the phone and called her.

"Sally, it's Lady Warrington. I've just seen your letter."

"Oh, Lady Warrington, I'm so glad to hear from you. Since Mr. Latimer died . . . " Her voice broke and Amanda knew she was crying.

"Sally, don't," Amanda said. "He was such a wonderful man. We know, don't we?"

Taking Amanda's lead, Sally got hold of herself immediately. "I hope you are well. I wonder what you would like me to do about the Stalewski?"

"Send it over, Sally, whenever it's convenient. I am so flattered that he left it to me, and touched." She held on to her emotions. It could be done.

"I'll send it 'round tomorrow. There is a provenance on it that I'll send as well. It is nice to talk to you, Lady Warrington."

"Sally, I'll call you in a few weeks. Perhaps we could lunch together."

"With pleasure, Lady Warrington."

"Goodbye, Sally."

"Thank you, Lady Warrington. Goodbye."

Amanda found a change in Patrick when she got home that distressed her deeply. He had spent time with his grandmother, and every weekend at Lea Place, while she had been at Hatfield. He talked about the twins and Auntie Davina all the time now and his face lit up when Davina called him on the phone. Davina expected him to be there every weekend and Amanda's return home would not affect his presence at Lea Place. Davina made it clear that she preferred having Patrick alone, implying that Amanda was not particularly welcome. Perhaps she and Charles should spend some time alone together? At any rate, Richard would pick up Patrick on Friday and bring him back on Monday morning.

Amanda knew how much Patrick loved being there. She let him go.

CHAPTER 14

August 1973

In mid-August, Chantal came to London unexpectedly. She called Amanda from her suite in Claridge's.

"Can you and Charles dine with me here tomorrow night? Gavers is coming, and I thought I'd ask Robin, for old times' sake."

The remembered lilt in Chantal's voice gave Amanda a momentary lift, and memories of the trip on *Cattivo II* and staying with Chantal in Paris came rushing back to her.

"Chantal, how wonderful that you are here! I'm sure we can. I'll just ask Charles when he comes home. Where have you been? The last time I would expect you to be in England would be in August."

"I've been shooting grouse in Scotland. It's been filthy cold and I suddenly thought how foolish it would be to go back without trying to see you. It has been too long a time, don't you think? Unless I hear from you, I'll expect you at eight-thirty. Are you well? I have spoken to Gavers and he said you'd had a bad patch with your nerves. I hope you're all right."

"I had a bit of a rough go, Chantal, but it's all behind me now." Amanda was sure that Gavers would have told Chantal about her suicide attempt and her stay at Hatfield. "I wish we could see each other without the men while you're here. Could you find a moment for lunch or tea?" She could still talk to Chantal.

"Of course. We can lunch tomorrow." What Chantal did not say was that when Gavers had suggested they have dinner without Amanda, she had refused.

"Gavers, I want to see her, and it might be fun for the five of us to be together again."

"All right," Gavers had said. "But she's a pain. She's practically certifiable."

Chantal laughed. "I'll decide that for myself. It never occurs to you that Charles is difficult enough to drive her 'round the bend. There are two sides, my darling. You can tell me yours when we're by ourselves tonight."

The first thing Chantal noticed when Charles and Amanda arrived in Claridge's foyer for drinks was how tiny Amanda seemed, smaller than she had been; Charles's height sharpened the contrast even more. She was wearing a neat little black silk dress and the sapphire Charles had bought for her in Paris, and even though she looked as if she would blow away in a breeze, her beauty had intensified. She was like a Tanagra figurine, Chantal thought, delicate and breakable.

Thanks to Chantal's charm and effort, plus generous lashings of champagne, the five of them had a marvelous time together, almost recapturing the past.

Gavers was his old complimentary self to both Chantal and Amanda. He was surprised to find Amanda looking as well put together as she did. Chantal teased Robin about the drawings he had done of them.

"Where are they, Robin? You've sold us—you've sold our bodies and souls. I want a drawing for the memory, and so does Amanda."

"Of course you do, and you both shall have them. I'll go through the thousands of folders of my unsold talent and see to it that you both have one."

"The sad thing," Chantal said over coffee, changing both the subject and the mood of the conversation, "was John Latimer's death. My father went to his funeral but I was in Egypt and didn't know he had died until it was all over. It all sounded very peculiar to me, for John to fall like that. He was so light on his feet, and graceful. Father was one of his greatest admirers, and terribly upset by his death."

Gavers shifted in his chair, his expression changing from warm to cold. The old rejection died hard. If Chantal's father had been an admirer of his, he thought, he would have a wife beside him. What was the great difference between a Polish gambler and an English gambler? Would it have been the same if Latimer had wanted to marry Chantal? Chantal continued.

"Do you remember my telling you about John coming to Paris during the war and my father helping him to get to England? When he arrived, the one possession that he had gotten out of Poland was a glorious painting by Stalewski. He had managed to keep it hidden in his overcoat, and he left it with my father for safekeeping. When he was established in England, my father sent it to him, somewhat regretfully, because he loved it so himself. If I could find out where it is I would try to buy it from John's estate and give it to my father."

"A Stalewski?" Robin said. "My God, it's worth a fortune. Where was it? I never saw it at Les Amis. There are so few of them anywhere, except for the ones the good old Nazis confiscated and have hanging on their walls somewhere. What's it of?"

"Unforgettable," Chantal said. "White flowering trees in a strong, beautiful green land. Very Polish somehow. John adored it. Once when I was here, he showed me where he had it hung in his apartments. It was magnificently lit, in the drawing room, but he could see it from the bedroom too. I know it was probably his most treasured possession. He might have left it to someone. He did leave two superb gold Renaissance boxes to my father. He would only have left that painting to someone he loved very much. If it's possible, I'm going to try to track it down for Father."

Amanda was frozen in her chair. She saw Charles stiffen slightly. She said nothing.

"Ring up Sally in the morning," Robin said. "She's still at Les Amis and she knows where everything is. John left all instructions for her."

They finished their drinks. Gavers stayed behind and Charles and Amanda dropped Robin at his flat in Walton Street. After leaving him, Charles sped out King's Road at almost ninety miles an hour. Amanda saw his fingers, rigid on the steering wheel. Neither of them spoke until they were in the house.

"We'll have a nightcap," Charles said.

"You know I don't want a drink." Amanda didn't know what she was going to say.

"Drink it," Charles said, handing her a large vodka in the usual crystal glass. "Drink it and tell me about John Latimer and his favorite possession." He quoted Chantal: " 'He would only leave it to someone he loved very much.' Did he love you very much, Amanda? Did you love him very much as well? Apparently I haven't been paying enough attention to you. It is odd, isn't it, that you tried to kill yourself, as I remember, on the very night of his funeral? And during your stay at Hatfield, you repeatedly painted white trees in a green orchard—in fact, that is all you painted, I was told by Pennell, and you didn't know at that time that you had been left this magnificent painting. Odd, isn't it?"

Amanda said nothing. She had never seen Charles this furious.

"Of course, you are not as good a painter as that Stalewski, we know that, so we are lucky to have not just your efforts from Hatfield but also this extraordinary painting which is extraordinarily valuable and the favorite possession of John Latimer. Funny, I never saw it in Les Amis —in any of the rooms I frequented, that is. Could John Latimer, by any chance, have been your lover, Amanda?"

"Don't be ridiculous. You're drunk. You know he left things that he loved to people who appreciated them. I don't know why you're going on like this. I did admire the painting and John was a generous man. The only time I ever saw it was when he showed Jean Shrimpton and me around his apartments one day." Her hands were freezing cold and she knew that her lies had to be convincing. He would never get anything out of her about John. Never.

"Then I have a suggestion for you. Since you don't seem to love it as he did, why don't you give it to Chantal? Think what it would mean to her. She loves it and so does her father. I suggest that you tell Chantal tomorrow what you declined to mention earlier this evening—which I did find odd. That you have the painting, that John left it to you because you so casually admired it one day. Of course you want Chantal to have it for her father."

Charles's sarcasm gave Amanda a chance. He knew nothing; he was making a scene because he had not realized how valuable the painting was and because he was drunk. She was not afraid, she just wanted to lie her way through and not lose the painting.

"No," she said, "I will not. That painting is the only valuable thing anyone has ever left to me, the only thing that is mine, and I love it. I'm sorry about Chantal but her father means nothing to me. I will tell her and explain how I feel about it, if you insist, but I won't give it to her or to anyone else. It's mine." She was deadly calm.

"Then why don't you sell it to her? That bequest from your good friend can get me out of debt, if it's worth what Robin seems to think it is. You should want to help me, shouldn't you, Amanda?" His face was flushed, the fine lines larded over with bloat. He poured himself another drink.

"Sell it to her to get you out of debt? I'll sell anything before I'd sell that picture. I'd sell my jewelry for you—or do I still have any besides my opals and this sapphire? You keep the rest of it locked up in the vault, and I can't even get it out without your signature. Nothing belongs to me but that painting, nothing." She knew if she gave in, weakened for an instant, he would be sure about John. Only if she took a strong stand would he believe her innocent. Keeping the painting would deny that there had been anything between them.

"Righteous indignation, from you," Charles said. "Go on—go to bed. I don't give a damn what you do. Or what you've done. The truth comes out, Amanda. It always comes out. Remember that." He put a bottle of gin on the side table by his leather wing chair, then sat down heavily and loosened his tie. "Leave me alone. I don't believe you, and may I remind you that with all our problems, there has never been another woman in my life? If John Latimer had you, I'll find out. One thing more. Get that painting off the wall of our drawing room tomorrow or I will. I never want to see it again. You may keep it but you may not keep it here. Get out."

Amanda knew she had won this round. He was very drunk. She went over to him and put her hand on the top of his head.

"Charles, don't. Come to bed." He pulled his arm back and struck her across the side of her face, knocking her off balance. She fell to the floor, her cheek stinging, her head reeling.

"What in the world is wrong with you?" she said, eyes filled with tears. "He was the only friend I had. Why do you hate the fact that someone liked me? You bastard, you're drunk." She got to her feet and started across the study.

"Go to bed. I'm sleeping in the mews house."

"As you like," Amanda said.

In the morning, Sally called Amanda.

"Lady Warrington, I hope I'm not bothering you, but the Duchesse de Briand called me about the Stalewski. She had no idea where it is but she wants to buy it for her father. I'm sure you don't want to sell it, but you do know the Duchesse, don't you?"

"Yes, I do, Sally. In fact we dined together last night. You didn't tell her I had the painting did you?"

"Of course not."

"I should probably tell her myself, but then I would feel obligated somehow to let her have it and I don't want to give it up. Tell her whatever you think best—just let me know."

"Of course, Lady Warrington. Incidentally, I'll be leaving here at the end of the month and I'd like to give you my address and telephone number in the country in case you need me for anything."

Amanda suddenly thought of something.

"Sally, I'd forgotten about your house. Could I ask you a favor? Would you consider keeping the Stalewski for me for a few months? We have so many pictures here and I have no proper place to hang it. It's been in the drawing room, but it is quite overpowering, and my husband doesn't like it there. I'd hate to send it to storage and it occurred to me

that you might enjoy having it and that you wouldn't mind keeping it
safely for me for a while."

"I'd be delighted to keep it for you, Lady Warrington. When would
you like me to fetch it? I can send Guido for it at your convenience."

"Tomorrow if possible."

"Guido will be there at three-thirty. I'll send a note with him saying
it's your picture, in my possession, and to be returned to you on call."

"Thank you so much, Sally."

Charles hadn't slept in the mews house after all. He made no apol-
ogy the next morning but there was no further reference to their fight, so
Amanda let well enough alone. The less said, the better.

Chantal was leaving for Paris in the afternoon, so Amanda met her
for lunch at a small restaurant off Grosvenor Square that was quiet and
not at all fashionable. Chantal opened the woman-to-woman conversation between them, the things they had not been able to say the night
before.

"I wanted to see you more than I wanted to see the others," she said.
"I have thought of you so often and wished that you would come back
to Paris. How can you stay in England all the time?"

Amanda knew that Chantal had more or less given up on her when
she was unable to establish her position with Charles, and her own
inadequacy still rankled her. Why was she still incapable of taking good
advice, given for her own good?

"Chantal, I have to tell you something." Chantal was still the only
woman she had ever felt was a friend to her.

"*Dites moi,*" Chantal said.

"Charles and I had a terrible row last night and there's something I
want you to know."

"What?"

"I have the Stalewski. John left it to me."

Chantal was stunned. She started to respond and then remained quiet,
taking in what Amanda had said. Her mind flashed back to the yacht, to
John's fascination with Amanda. So, she thought, something did happen
between them.

"Then he must have loved you very much," Chantal said, softly. "As
I said last night, he would leave it only to someone he loved very much.
Amanda, I hope I didn't cause you any trouble, but I had no way of
knowing—"

"Chantal, John Latimer was the best friend I have ever had. He tried
to help me rise above the circumstances of my life, and I adored him. If

he were still alive, my life might have taken a very different course, but he is gone and I have the painting. I can't part with it. That's what Charles and I fought about. It's the only thing that has ever belonged to me and I can't let it go. Are you going to be angry with me?"

"Quite the opposite. The painting is yours. John wanted you to have it. And you stood up to Charles. Good for you."

"Chantal, you are going to think I am a real idiot now but I have decided something and I want to tell you. In ten million centuries I would never sell it, but I have to make some arrangement about it, because Charles won't let me keep it in the house. I will keep it safely somewhere where I can see it whenever I want, but I'm going to make a will and leave it to you. Which one of us do you suppose will die first?"

Chantal, caught off guard, started to laugh.

"You take my breath away. I never expected you to . . . . Well, you have this sense of humor. You're telling me that you have the Stalewski, you have not disclosed whether you actually had an affair with John, and you've stood up to Charles. And now you want to know which one of us is going to die first!" Chantal was still laughing. It was contagious.

"So it's not all that bad, my not giving it to you? You do understand?"

"Of course. I can't wait to tell Father where it is. He always thought highly of you, and so did François. Why don't you come back to Paris, to us?"

"Money. There isn't any. What does Gavers say about Charles?" Amanda did not want to criticize Charles openly, but she did wonder how Gavers felt about his constantly mounting debts.

"Gavers speaks in one-line paragraphs. Robin drinks too much and will never have any money. Charles drinks too much and will never have any money. Gavers isn't really interested in anything anymore. Amanda, a ticket to Paris would be part of our invitation to you—"

"I can't, Chantal. Please understand."

"Why do you stay with him? I used to think Charles would grow out of this ridiculous gambling-his-life-away. Gavers is right: It's a road to oblivion. You deserve something better. You are still young and you have never been more beautiful. *Why* don't you leave him?"

"People who have always had money don't know what no money is. Things are terrible between us. But I love him—I can't help it. Don't you think I'd like to get out, walk away and find another life? You sound just like John: Everything would be solved if I would leave Charles. If I do, he will go to any lengths to take Patrick away from me. You know I have had nerves and headaches and breakdowns, and I'm not getting any better either, no more than Charles is. Everyone in England thinks I am crazy and sometimes *I* think I am. My mother is thinking of moving to Mauritius, ten thousand miles away, so she doesn't have to cope with me; my sister Davina isn't speaking to me; I hardly know my sister Pamela, beyond Christmas cards from Scotland; and all of this is wrong for Patrick—my poor little son. One of us has to make a decent life for him and I can't do it alone. Marriage is not something you put on and take off. Right or wrong, I'm not going to leave him. All I really have is Charles."

"And the Stalewski."

"That's the dream. I don't mind finding a place to keep it here in England where I can occasionally see it. It doesn't belong in Royal Hospital Road. As long as it's mine, that's all I care about. It's the only thing that belongs to me."

"And someday it will belong to me. You'd better not die first!"

"Maybe I should. I know it will go where it's appreciated then. Charles wants me to sell it. The money would pay off his debts."

Chantal felt a sudden disgust with Charles. "Oh, he does, does he? And after all was paid off he would lose even more."

"Exactly, but I'm not going to give him a chance to throw the Stalewski away. That I will never let him do."

"You're not crazy, Amanda. What you said about people with money is true. They never understand people without it. You have to believe that I will give you any money you need, any time you need it. It can be a loan against the painting if you're too proud to let me give or lend it to you. A day might come when you need money, for Patrick. Promise me you will ask."

"Chantal, you're part of a dream to me. When things are rough, I think about John. And I think about the days in Paris with you. And then I think what a failure I am. If only I could have done what you told me to, I might have been able to change Charles. I was too in love with him, too weak to help him."

"What a fool I was to preach to you. Nothing could change Charles. His course was set, with Gavers's help, long ago. My father couldn't stand the sight of Gavers and when I wanted to marry him, it caused the greatest rift there has ever been between us."

"And yet your father loved John. Also a gambler."

"John gambled with life; Gavers gambles with other people's money. He preys on their weaknesses; John built their strengths. John gave; Gavers takes."

"He's trying, Chantal, I'm sure, as we all are. Is it strange for you to be criticizing him?" Hadn't Chantal loved him, didn't she still love him? She was still sleeping with him.

"Defense mechanism. I see him for what he is now."

It was Amanda's turn to laugh.

"We're birds of a feather. I love, you love, I think you're too good for Gavers, and you think I'm too good for Charles. We're both idiots."

"I'll get you back to Paris. You wait and see. I must go now. *À tout à l'heure.*"

Chantal's confidence in Amanda had revived after her visit to London.

"After she stayed with us," she said to her father and to François on her return to Paris, "I lost respect for her. That has now all changed."

"You're leading up to something," Philippe de Bdand said. "Or at least I hope you are, as I remember Amanda only slightly. She surprised me in her conversation, the things she was interested in. The family, the history of our family—she was sincerely interested in the family. Although she didn't seem to have her eyes on you, François."

"I had mine on her," François said. "She had allure about her, very un-English. I found her enchanting."

"She is still. However, she has some serious problems. A complex personality, with breakdowns, even a suicide attempt, and a miserable life with Charles Warrington. He does nothing but gamble. With all that, she remains exquisite."

"Charles Warrington is worthless," Philippe said. "An irresponsible aristocrat, the worst of the postwar generation. Totally selfish and basically crude."

"Crude?" Chantal queried, interested as always in the workings of her father's mind. Crudeness was a quality she had never associated with Charles.

"He has the nature of the brute disguised by the trappings of the aristocrat. I watched him when they were here."

"*Mon Dieu,*" Chantal said. "I had no idea you had even noticed him." She was half-teasing him.

"I study the bad seeds of families. Good men do not require close observation. It's the others one learns from. They can bring us all down."

"You've gotten me off the track with your usual brilliance." Charles Warrington was bringing Amanda down, not the opposite, according to her father.

"You were going to say something about Amanda."

"I found the Stalewski."

"Chantal, as always you astonish me. Where did you find it, and what does that have to do with Amanda?"

"John left it to her."

Both her father and brother were staring at her. Then Philippe threw back his head and roared with laughter. François grinned.

"Was he having an affair with her?" Philippe asked.

"I do not know," Chantal replied. "I had talked about the Stalewski at dinner the night before, as I wanted to find it and buy it for you. The next day at lunch Amanda told me. Charles knew its worth and wanted her to sell it to pay off his gambling debts. But Amanda stood her ground and said John had been her valued friend and the painting was hers and that she would never let it go."

"She's right. If she ever decides to sell it, she can live off it the rest of her life. It will quadruple in value, at least, in the next few years."

"She won't sell it. She has left it to me."

Philippe and François were once more brought to attention.

"Left it to you?"

"Yes. So I can give it to you, so it will come back to the family."

"I think you should ask her to visit us again. My interest in her increases by the moment." Now Philippe was teasing.

"I shall. She is an interesting girl and she needs help—she needs friends. There's a *tristesse* about her, a delicacy. A few more years with Charles and her life will be over. I'd hate to see that happen."

"I doubt if it will. Good blood, somewhere in her background. Unlike her husband's."

G avers called Chantal. He was going to India. Would she like to go, or would she prefer dinner in Paris on his way?

"Dinner. I can't leave."

"I wish you'd go. We don't see each other as we used to."

She put him off. "Perhaps I'll come to London when you get back. How is Robin? I want those drawings, and he'll forget to send them. Will you remind him? And how are Charles and Amanda?"

"He's fine. She's a mess."

"Gavers! You sound so hateful. Don't you have any sympathy for her?"

"No, I haven't any sympathy for her. She's a bore, and out of her league. Poor Charles."

"Poor Amanda."

"Poor me. You should go with me. Don't forget, we're dining tomorrow night."

★ ★ ★

Late August 1973

Charles and Amanda were invited to Lea Place for a summer week-end, as Charles was playing in a golf tournament. Amanda did not want to go and she knew Davina would have preferred not to have her, but she went.

What started as no more than a little tiff between them suddenly blew up out of all proportion, defining their true feelings for each other and crystallizing their future relationship.

It was a hot summer day and they were by the pool at Lea Place with the twins, Amy and Ariel, and Patrick. The weather had been unbearably hot for days and the children were irritable. Patrick was teasing the girls, kicking water in their faces, torturing them as best he could.

"Patrick, stop that!" Davina said sharply, giving him a whack on his legs. The slap on his wet skin hurt. His face puckered up.

"For heaven's sake, Davina, leave him alone," Amanda said. "It's just hot. He'll stop if you leave him alone." Patrick looked defiantly at Davina, then scooped up handfuls of water and threw it at the twins. Davina whacked him soundly again on the behind, harder this time. He let out a howl.

"Just a minute," Amanda said, rising from where she had been sunning on the other side of the pool. She went after Patrick. "I'll do the whacking if I consider it necessary. He's my child."

"Then perhaps you should have a little more to do with disciplining him," Davina retorted acidly.

"Oh, really?" Amanda replied in an equally nasty tone. "It wouldn't seem to be easy around here. Between you and that Nazi nanny you've got, the children are drilled rather than disciplined. Why can't you leave them alone to fight it out on their own!" She took Patrick firmly by the hand. "You're being naughty. You have to learn to be a gentleman. I'm taking you in now. We can go for a walk later."

Patrick started to scream. He pulled away from her and ran over to Davina, throwing his arms around her neck, blubbering. "I'm sorry. I won't do it again."

"That's all right, darling, Auntie Davina knows you didn't mean it. Now go back and play nicely with the girls." She kissed him on the cheek, tossing a mean, triumphant little look at Amanda.

Amanda was stung by Patrick's rejection. Her own child, running away from her.

"You think you own everything and everyone around here, don't you?"

"Actually, I do seem to. If you're going to bring Patrick here or leave him here, as you have, the rules are mine. You use my home as if it belonged to you. If you don't like what I do, you know what you can do about it."

Amanda heard venom in Davina's tone. She had become increasingly more authoritative, bossier, and more smug about herself lately.

"Yes, I know what I can do about it. I can remove Charles from your presence. You never have gotten over his preferring me to you, have you? And you only caught Richard because I didn't want him. You fawn all over Charles every chance you get. It's really revolting."

"Someone should fawn over him a little, and Patrick as well. They get no attention, either of them. With you, it's all bad nannies or migraine or both. You must be great fun to live with."

They were in full cry. All the underlying rivalries had surfaced.

"I'm sick of your looking down on me, treating me like your inferior sister," Amanda spat out. "You're a boring country harridan and you dress like an old woman. You aren't having my child or my husband any longer. I'm the only one you want to get rid of."

"You're right about that. In fact I have spoken to Charles and we agree that it would be better all 'round if Patrick started school out here. He needs a more stable home atmosphere. You are not exactly capable of taking care of him."

"What are you talking about, 'stable atmosphere'? He's perfectly happy at home."

"Then why is he still wetting the bed? He's torn between you and Charles, and half the time you go off with a migraine or nerves, confusing him more. Amanda, you are not a responsible person. The time has come to do what's best for Patrick."

Amanda fought back. "What would be best for Patrick would be if his father had a job, and we had our own country place. But you provide tea and sympathy, and free drinks and motherly love we can't resist. You'll not take him away from me, let me assure you of that. This is our last visit to Lea Place." She was shaking all over.

"You're right about that. This will be your last visit here." There was something in her tone that warned Amanda to control herself. "We're moving into Ransome House. Elizabeth's estate has been settled and I've persuaded Richard that we really should live in the big house." Elizabeth Marston's death several months before had saddened all of them. Now Davina would be the lady of the manor. Amanda's reaction was swift and unexpected.

"Davina," she said, her eyes alight, "when you move there, why can't Charles and I rent Lea Place from you? Could you ask Richard? How wonderful it would be if we could have Lea Place!"

"Oh, no, I don't think that would be possible at all," Davina said. "Richard and I talked about it, but he's decided to let one of the tenant farmers caretake it."

Amanda was suddenly enraged again. Selfish bitch that Davina was, she'd do anything to lord it over her, she thought, and now she was going to live in that magnificent house and a tenant farmer would be in Lea Place.

"You really are such a caring sister. You're the most totally selfish person I've ever known." To Amanda's supreme annoyance, she started to cry.

Davina realized she had gone too far. If she was ever going to get Patrick, she could not fight openly with Amanda. She had to be subtler than that. She reversed her tactics.

"You know Richard makes all the decisions—it's not me being selfish. It's his house and he can do with it as he wants. Don't blame me for everything. I'm sorry, Mandy." She called her that only when they had fought and made up as little girls. Even then Davina had been jealous of her, it was true. She and Pamela were the "easy" children and Amanda the pain, but it was Amanda who'd gotten all the attention.

"All right," Amanda said, brushing away the tears. She was still angry, but she knew she was helpless.

"Let's go in and get something cool to drink," Davina said. "The Nazi will look after the children." She gave a little laugh. It would be much better for Patrick to be here with her, especially now that they were moving into Ransome House. Amanda was quite impossible.

CHAPTER 15

London, August 1973

Gavers was not given to philosophizing, but on his fortieth birthday, in uncustomary fashion, he found himself taking stock. That morning he had received an offer to sell the Club at a price far beyond his wildest dreams. He had never before thought about selling. Why would he? It was his entire life, or at least it had been up until now. The offer came from an American syndicate, not the sort that Gavers knew socially as members of the Wyndham, but a solid group with an impeccable financial background and the capacity to own and operate such a club. The offer was too large for Gavers to dismiss.

He sat in his office, looking at the Stubbs tiger and the photographs that now covered practically every inch of wall space. He flipped idly through a few of the large red-leather scrapbooks filled with souvenirs, invitations, and press clippings, all the bits and pieces collected over the years. It was more than ten years now. One thing began to stand out clearly as Gavers inspected the memorabilia of the club he had created. His interests had changed. The more recent photographs were not of Gavers with some of his chums at the races or bobsledding or with beautiful girls; they were no longer of Gavers with Chantal. They were a record of the painstaking restoration of Melbridge, including aerial shots showing the intricate arrangements he had made to give the animals freedom. Only a knowing eye could detect the barriers that kept the wild creatures separated from human beings. Or vice versa, Gavers thought. The beasts deserved the best of that bargain.

Selling the Club would open the doors to an entirely new life, and with the sort of money he'd been offered, he could run Melbridge the way he wanted to. Like a lord.

His reverie was interrupted by Lillian's voice on the intercom.

"Mr. Driscoll?" she said. "Have you forgotten that you are lunching with Lord and Lady Warrington? He's just asked about you, and they have been waiting close to an hour."

"Good God, Lillian, tell them I'll be right there." He had indeed lost track of time. Amanda had called to say she would be at the Club with Charles for lunch. "You know it's a rare occasion when I come for lunch," she told him. "There is something I'd like to talk to you about. Do you think you could stay for a few minutes after Charles goes off to the backgammon table?"

As Charles left the table, Amanda came right to the point. There was no subtlety to her, apart from her looks.

"Charles is with the moneylenders now, Gavers, and they are charging him almost fifty percent interest. I never dare answer the front door anymore. Two nights ago when I thought my neighbor was ringing the bell, it was one of those men. I wouldn't let him in. I told him Charles was out of the country. He told me they'd be around for the furniture. Gavers, can't you stop him? Can't you do something? He's destroying himself."

"Amanda," he said, "Charles is a figure like myself, born out of his time. He should have lived in the late nineteenth century, in that sheltered, leisured time when men had their clubs and lived in a world of men. Gambling didn't exist in London as it does now. The atmosphere was safer, fortunes were more secure, and a gentleman had a better sense of self-esteem. It was a more elegant mode of life—one didn't have to do anything besides live like a gentleman. Women were a dazzling part of existence, but intelligent ladies knew their place and they knew how to use men. They combined sex with patience and charm. You don't use your head about Charles. You badger him. You nag him. And now you come to me, telling me things that should be kept in confidence. I can't help Charles, Amanda, don't you understand that? You can't help him either. Only Charles can help Charles. Leave him alone."

Gavers didn't give a damn about Amanda's hand-wringing, her constant complaints. He particularly did not give a damn about Amanda Warrington's troubles.

Amanda's response was furious. He couldn't blame her for that.

"Oh, do come off it, Gavers. I come to you for once in my life, to ask you to help Charles, and you give me that dream-of-a-century-past speech. It's your way of denying any responsibility for your contribution to Charles's destruction." She picked up her water glass and took a drink out of it. Putting it down, she knocked it over, the glass shattering on the marble floor beneath them.

Gavers struck back.

"Go on, dear Amanda, with your shrike's tongue. I take it you have more to say in regard to my criminal destruction of your husband?"

"You're nothing more than an envious son of a minor diplomat. Charles is a peer. You've always been jealous of him and I think you take pleasure in watching him lose everything. You have destroyed Charles, easily, along with some other big and little fish, because you're cleverer than they are. You prey on their weaknesses. And you *do* enjoy it, I've seen it, reducing a man like Charles to dependence on your strength, your money, your ability to keep him on your hook. You're no better than a drug merchant and money is the drug you push. Don't give me that blather about being born in the wrong century. Charles was, perhaps, but you? Never. You'd be a destroyer in any century."

Gavers watched Amanda's face as she poured out her venom. She was in a fury. His own anger vanished. He realized that she was desperate.

"Amanda, listen to me. Get hold of yourself. What do you think a gambler is anyhow? A man who stands around playing games and winning or losing money? That's not what a real gambler is. A real gambler is a man who goes to sleep when he's winning. Winning is nothing to him. It's losing that brings him alive and that's what a real gambler wants. They dote on it. I learned a long time ago to win because I want to win. I had no fortune to spill in the streets or at the tables or at the races, and I set out to make a business of it because it excited me then. I understand your hatred, anyone's hatred of me for it, but I am not the first nor will I be the last to provide the setting for men like Charles to send their fortunes down the chute. Why haven't you ever learned to cope? Charles told you before you were married that he had no intention of changing, that gambling was his work, and he gave you the chance to refuse him. If he didn't come to me, there are four hundred other gaming clubs in London at this moment. Then there's Deauville, Trouville, Monte Carlo, Beaulieu, Paris, and Cannes—many of them with an atmosphere more appealing than mine. When Tutankhamen's tomb was opened, the first thing found were dice. If Charles had discovered it, the first thing he would have done would have been to have a toss of those dice!"

Amanda listened intently but with no sign of understanding.

Gavers went on. "I am forty years old today, and I am no longer a gambler. I am just a man in the gambling business—which, incidentally, I have no intention of staying in. Charles has been very much on my mind lately, and although you may not know it, I have tried to stop him, many a time. It's like pissing against the tide. I can't help him. Believe me, I would." He reached over and took her hand, looking into her still-furious face. She pulled it away as if she had put it into a fire.

"You're rotten to the core. If I had known what to do with Charles when I married him, the first thing I would have done would be to remove him from your influence. He's not the brightest, but he should be better off than he is now, thanks to you. He's drunk all the time, a bad gambler, and a miserable human being who doesn't know where to turn. It must really please you to have an Earl as your indentured servant, bonded to you by debt. I loathe you." She stood up, shaking all over. Her voice had risen to a pitch that was being heard in the next room.

Gavers stood up with her. There was no controlling her; it was just a question of getting her out of the Club now.

"Amanda, stop it. I am telling you once more that no one, not you or anyone else, can help Charles."

He looked around for Robert to help him get her to the door. She strode ahead of him, head held high, fury still in her face. Suddenly, she turned back to Gavers.

"Call my husband," she said. "I want my husband to take me home. I'll find a way to get him away from your evil influence if it's the last thing I do."

Gavers saw the crazed look in her eyes. She is mad, he thought. She is truly mad. They had reached the hall. Gavers took her arm and forced her out through the front door with him, almost dragging her with his superior strength. He signaled to the doorman for his car.

"Shut up, Amanda," he said. "My car will take you home."

The scene with Gavers sent Amanda into a state of hopelessness. She had lost control of herself again. Each time it was worse. Was there no help anywhere? Where would it all end?

When Nanny brought Patrick home from the park a few hours later, she found Amanda on the floor of the bedroom, unconscious.

She looked first for a pill bottle, but there wasn't one. In panic, she put Patrick to work with his crayons in the nursery and called the doctor who had come before, and then the Wyndham Club.

"Are you sure she hasn't taken anything?" the doctor asked.

"I'm not sure of anything," the nanny said. "I came back and found her this way."

Amanda was admitted to Chelsea Hospital, and a brain specialist was called into consultation. Her vital signs were all fine; she was simply not conscious. She was anemic, but that was the only physical disorder the doctors could find. She remained comatose for six days.

On the evening of the sixth day, she opened her eyes and asked where she was. When she was told, she sat up and tried to get out of bed.

"I've got to go home. Patrick has to have his supper and he likes for me to be there." She got out of bed and asked for her clothes. She was considerably annoyed when the nurse would not let her go. Calls were made to the doctor and to Charles, who arrived at the hospital at the same time. They found Amanda in a flood of tears.

"Charles, please take me home. Why am I here? What have I done? Did you put me in here?" She was not hysterical, just miserable and pleading with him.

"Of course not," Charles said, holding her. "Don't you remember? Nanny found you unconscious on the bedroom floor, but there seems to be nothing wrong with you. You've just been asleep for a few days."

"A few days! There must be something seriously wrong with me. What are you keeping from me?"

"I am going to take some more tests now that you're conscious," the doctor said. "If everything comes up all right, I'll let you go home. Now you must calm down for tonight."

"I'm perfectly calm," Amanda said. She was.

Charles went to the Club to dine with Robin and Gavers.

"I think she's really gone off the deep end," he said. "She's a hellcat one minute, a little girl the next, and swallowing sleeping pills the next. It isn't good for Patrick."

Robin said nothing. He had bouts with manic-depression that he had never discussed with his friends, including Charles. He had succeeded in keeping his problems to himself. He felt sorry for Amanda, or rather he felt as if he was a kindred spirit.

"She probably needs Hatfield again," Gavers said, thinking about the scene at the Club. "As I see it, she seems to be getting worse. There was a time when she was vague and remote and not really there, but now you don't know what she's going to do from one day to the next."

"She did just walk out of Hatfield," Charles said. "Vanished into thin air, and she wouldn't tell us how she had gotten away, until one evening I heard her tell Patrick how she had gotten back to him. It seems that she took a bus that she flagged down, then a train, then the tube, and then she walked. It took her six hours, and when I came in, she greeted me as if she'd been there when I left in the morning."

"Amazing how someone can just vanish like that, isn't it?" Gavers said. "Suppose she hadn't headed for home when she left Hatfield?"

"Patrick was home," Charles said. "He's the magnet. But this sort of life isn't good for him. I don't know what I'm going to do about it, but something."

"Keep your pecker up, old boy," Gavers said. "Maybe one day she'll disappear for good."

"Wouldn't that be nice?" Charles said. "I wish it were as simple as that."

Gavers sold the Club. In the contract he agreed to stay on for one year as if he were still the owner, to guide the Americans on the finer points of running an English club. He took close to three quarters of a million pounds free and clear on the sale. Neil was to stay on with him. At the end of the year he could decide if he wanted to keep on with the new owners or not. By then Gavers might have something else for him to do.

Gavers handed Charles a large white envelope on the last evening before the sale was official. In it Charles found ten thousand pounds in returned checks that had been made good by Gavers.

"A gift, Winner, for you," he said. "The party's really over now. They won't give you any credit. They want you as a member, as a player, as their token Earl, but no credit. Never mind. It was fun while it lasted."

September 1973

In September, Charles left Amanda. The straw that broke the camel's back was Amanda's arrival at dawn in the mews house. Charles had been sleeping there for two weeks.

He had gotten home about three, and was sleeping as peacefully as he ever slept these days, when her screams sliced through his sleep, bringing him awake, groaning. Opening his eyes, he saw her standing at the foot of the bed, arms folded defensively across her chest, hair streaming wildly about her face. There was a mad glossiness in her eyes.

She was haranguing him about money. The milkman, the greengrocer, the London Electricity Board were all after her, the nanny had not been paid for three weeks, and Patrick's school bills had not been paid—they'd sent a note home with him the other day.

One more time, he thought, *and only this one more time, I am going to try to reason with her.* Ignoring her, he went to the washbasin and splashed some icy water on his face. A quick look in the mirror confirmed that he was puffy and bloated. Amanda was standing behind him, bullying him, her voice reaching the familiar pitch—but this time he heard the howl that had begun only recently, freezing his blood as it came from her.

He heard her take in her breath and suddenly she started sucking in desperate breaths, unable to get a word, a curse, or a scream out of her blocked throat. This was something new. He grabbed at her, trying to fend off her blows.

"Stop it," he said, slamming his body against her, backing her up to the wall. "Amanda, stop it! You're going to kill yourself this way. What good will that do any of us?" He locked his hands behind her back, holding her in a viselike grip, knowing that within moments she would go limp in his arms and the tears would come and it would take hours to calm her down, to soothe her to a point of rationality.

"Christ," he said, "what a terrible way to live. I'm leaving, and I'm not coming back."

He let go of her and she dropped softly to the floor, no more than a bag of pale bones surrounded by disheveled hair.

"You can't leave me," she said, her voice hoarse. "You're too much of a coward, too much of a loser to leave me. You don't have any place to go and you wouldn't have any one else to mistreat, to torture."

"I'd have a place to stay if you'd stay out of here. But as you won't, I will find a place of my own and you'll never get in the door—that I promise you."

"Oh, you'll be back," she said to herself. She often talked to herself lately. "You won't leave me." She got to her feet and looked out the window onto the mews. She heard the downstairs door close and she saw him take out the key to the Mercedes, get in it, and start off out of the mews.

Quickly, she flew down the stairs and through the garden to the other house. She let herself in through the hall door off Charles's study and stood in the downstairs hall, waiting as he parked out front. She heard his key in the door. When Charles saw her, he came toward her, looming over her, threatening her.

"I am not going to have another scene in front of Patrick. It's over, Amanda. It's over." He turned and left the house.

"Oh, he'll be back, he will," she said to herself again. "When he comes back, we'll patch this up." She felt quite chipper, almost gay this morning. Time for a bath and a giant fluff-up. *When he comes back, I'll turn that look on him. That's all it takes.* That's all she had ever needed to do. She'd get all cleaned up and wait for him. Humming, she went up the stairs.

★   ★   ★

When Charles left the house, he had no idea what he was going to do for the next hour and a half before Patrick went off to school. It was still too early to call an estate agency about a flat.

On a whim, Charles parked the car in Chester Square, planning to pick up the morning papers at Sloane Square. As he walked along the Square, the door to Number 18 opened and Therese Miller came out to pick up the newspapers. Seeing Charles, she gave him a cheery wave.

"Charles!" she said, in an even cheerier tone. "What on earth are you doing out at this hour? Come in and have a cup of coffee with Dan. He's waiting for his papers but I know he would enjoy seeing you."

Therese Miller was an American, a no-nonsense woman; Charles liked her, and her husband. Dan Miller was vice-president of an insurance firm that Charles had done some business with. They played golf together occasionally and the Millers' son went to the same school as Patrick. On impulse, he went in. They were an agreeable and obviously compatible couple. Charles envied them their peaceful existence.

Therese Miller was an intuitive woman. Charles had a bad headache from the recent scene. When Therese brought him the aspirin bottle without asking, he looked up at her and smiled. On impulse, he decided to ask her if she knew of a flat to rent.

Therese looked him straight in the eye.

"For you?" she asked.

"Yes," Charles said, returning her look. "For me."

"As a matter of fact, I do. This is a bit of a coincidence, but Prue Davis called me last night. She is going to New York to work for a year and she's had no luck so far renting her flat in Ormonde Gate. It's available the first of next week. There's a nice drawing room—fairly large, with masses of bookshelves and a fireplace—then a big bedroom and a smaller spare one in the back. It's on the ground floor with a pretty garden and there's a garage. She has some nice furniture in it."

"Any idea how much she wants for it?"

"I'm a veritable storehouse of information this morning, only because I talked to her last night. She wants eight hundred a month for it, without an agent, and there's a daily and a nice super there. If you would like me to, I can call Prue a little later on."

"I would indeed. Amanda and I are separating and I want to be as close to Patrick as possible." There, he had come out and said it. It was true, and would be known to everyone else soon enough.

Therese knew that it took a terrible effort for this strange, shy man to impart such personal information. He was stiff-backed and snobbish, but after all, he was a product of his environment. And the stories she had heard about Amanda Warrington were a little peculiar. With her vague smile and out-of-this-world aura, no one seemed to know her.

"I'll push off now," Charles said. "I do thank you for the coffee. Do you think I could see the flat later this morning?"

"I'm sure you can. I'll call Prue at ten-thirty. Why don't you come back here and I'll take you over? It's not far from here."

Charles rose to his feet.

"If it's not an imposition, I shall. Thank you, Therese." Robin could put him up for a few days. If the flat was acceptable, he'd be all set; if not, he would find another one.

Charles went back to Royal Hospital Road just after nine, dreading another confrontation. He had to get his clothes out of the house today.

Amanda was waiting for him, a strange smile of expectation on her face. *My obedient and respectful little wife,* Charles thought. She was wearing a pearl-gray cashmere sweater and a pair of darker-gray flannel slacks. Her Gucci loafers were perfectly polished and her hair was tied neatly back on the nape of her neck with a blue satin ribbon. She looked young and fresh and beautiful. Charles had been unnerved in the past by her chameleon changes of mood, and this morning was no exception.

"Charles!" she said brightly, greeting him as if he were an intriguing lover, as if nothing had happened. "Where have you been? Patrick's left already. He missed seeing you and wants you to pick him up from school this afternoon, if you can."

Without saying a word, he walked past her and climbed the stairs. He got his valises out and started to pack his belongings.

There was not a sound from below.

Charles took the flat on sight. It was just as Therese had described it. There was a large, high-ceilinged room that could actually be called a drawing room. One entire wall of bookcases surrounded a fireplace, and there was a huge refectory table on the other side with a handsome mirror above it. The room had a nice masculine feeling about it. There was a large bedroom, with a small one adjoining it where Patrick could spend the night. It was the ideal place, no more than a five-minute walk from the house.

He moved in the following Monday. He had sent Robin to the house several times to bring some of his books and his collection of opera recordings, including the Wagner. There was a good record player and Charles could turn the sound up as loud as he liked. Amanda cringed when he played his records at home, complaining so about the "depressing" music that he had stopped playing them. There were advantages to being a bachelor again.

The weather was filthy, an early English autumn, chilly and raining almost every day. For Patrick's sake, he made some changes in his regular schedule. He continued to sleep until noon and then made his rounds, having his martinis either at White's or St. James's before lunching at the Wyndham and playing a few rubbers of bridge. He picked Patrick up at school later on and brought him back to Ormonde Gate. They played games and Charles helped Patrick with his homework and saw to it that he was home in time for supper.

He had not seen Amanda since he had cleared out, but he had had one long conversation with her which was fortunately unemotional and helped clarify their situation. This was a temporary solution. Charles had taken the flat for one year but he was not going to see a solicitor about a permanent separation agreement yet.

To his astonishment there had been no trouble the day he left. Amanda stood in the doorway, watching him almost lovingly as he packed, setting his teeth on edge until she finally left the room.

As he had chosen to remain silent, she had done the same. When he finished packing and came downstairs to leave, he found her gone. There was a note for him on the hall table. "My darling," she had written, "perhaps this is for the best. I love you and I believe that we can make a new start." Charles could not believe his luck. Her mood swings were dramatic, but for the time being peace prevailed.

Money was a continuing problem. Charles went over the inventory of the things left in storage from Longholt; there was some Georgian silver of the most superb quality, but he did not want to part with it. However, there were two large Landseer paintings of animals that he cared nothing about, so he took them to Christie's and put them up for auction. They sold for almost double the reserve price and Charles paid off the most pressing bills.

Trouble arrived in October, when two disturbing phone calls came on the same day. His mother rang up as she always did, to his annoyance, at eight in the morning. He had discussed his separation from Amanda with her briefly. Penelope Warrington was devoted to her only grandchild, but Charles's parting from his unsuitable wife, if anything, pleased rather than disturbed the Dowager Countess.

"Charles, I read in the *Telegraph* this morning that two Landseers from Longholt were auctioned off for quite a good price. Did you put them up for sale?"

"Yes," Charles said, half-asleep and irritated at being wakened like this.

"Well, you are not to do any such thing again," she said crisply. "I gave you permission to take the things from Longholt for your personal use, not to sell. Amanda has everything in the house and we'll not see any of it again, you can be sure. How dare you sell anything without discussing it with me? Those pictures were your father's favorites and I wanted Patrick to have them. I have given instructions to the storage people that you no longer have access to any of it."

"I had some pressing debts to pay off," Charles said, "and I do not find it necessary to ask your permission to sell things that belong to me as much as they do to you."

"You have always had some pressing debts to pay off, most of which are incurred at the gaming tables. You have gone through every cent from your father and you are now supporting two households. I am simply informing you that Longholt possessions are no longer available for you to sell in order to support your questionable style of life."

She hung up when there was no response from him. If he had known this was going to happen, he would have sold the silver. He could have paid off everything he owed with what it would have brought. Damn the Dowager Countess of Warrington, stingy Labour lover that she was.

He had almost gotten back to sleep when the phone rang again.

"Hello!" he bellowed into it.

"Patrick tells me you plan to take him to Ransome House this weekend with Davina and Richard," Amanda's voice said. The shrillness in her tone always meant trouble.

"What's wrong with that? I've taken him to films and concerts that bore him the past two weekends I've had him."

"What's wrong? I'll tell you what's wrong! You are not taking my son to my sister's house. It's not on, Charles. It's just not on."

"All right," he said. "I'll take him down to Neil and Rosie's then."

"You'll not do that either. If you think you are going to take Patrick around people who hate me and say terrible things about me, the answer is no."

He sat up in bed.

"Amanda, we are separated and I have no intention of coming back. Davina is Patrick's aunt and he loves her. Richard is my best friend."

"You say we are separated," she hissed into the phone. "That's a temporary situation and you know it. I don't want a divorce. Do you?" Charles hung up the phone. He had to admit he was content with things as they were now. He had an old-fashioned principle against divorce, but he came and went as he chose now, with no battles, and he had his son with him every day. He would have to resolve the legal arrangements between them eventually, but not right now.

Charles felt a surge of parental pride when he saw the Keating looks, as marked in Patrick as they were in him: the same dark straight hair, the same dark-blue eyes, and the same aristocratic bone structure. There was no trace of Amanda in his looks—nor in his disposition, thank God.

A plan began to form in Charles's mind. He wanted Patrick to himself.

November 1973

On Guy Fawkes Day, Amanda took eight little boys to a Disney film and brought them back to the house for games and cake. When the doorbell rang at seven, thinking it was a parent arriving early to fetch a child, Amanda went to the door herself. Charles was standing in the doorway, holding a present for Patrick and an armful of yellow chrysanthemums for her. He'd forgotten that she hated yellow and that chrysanthemums were hardly her favorite flower. *Thank him,* she thought. *Don't complain. At least he's here.* She remembered John's flowers— lilies of the valley, tuberoses, white camellias, always in the most exquisite containers.

"May I come in?" Charles asked, handing her the flowers.

"Of course," Amanda said. "Patrick will be so glad you've come. This is your home, isn't it?" They had not spoken to each other since the row on the telephone about his taking Patrick to Davina and Richard's for the weekend. Perhaps he had thought things over. They had been apart for going on two months. Amanda didn't dare let the hope surface that the time for reconciliation had come.

Charles was in a fine mood and played games with the children until the party was over. When Patrick was sent up to bed, Charles seemed reluctant to leave.

"Mind if I have a drink?" he asked.

"Charles, this is your home. Of course I don't mind." She had thought it unusual that he hadn't had one during the party.

He opened the drinks cabinet in his study to find it as perfectly stocked as it had been when he'd left the house. He took one of his cut-crystal glasses and filled it with ice and Bombay gin. She had kept everything exactly as it was when he'd left. She must think he was coming back to her. He'd better get to the point right away.

"Amanda, you know that your mental problems, the erratic and unpredictable rages that you indulge yourself in, are the reason for our separation, don't you?" Both his tone and his expression were pompous.

"I don't know any such thing," she snapped back at him. "I thought your drinking and gambling and self-destructive way of life were the reasons for our being apart."

"Don't lose control of yourself. I want to suggest something to you."

Annoyed as she was by his one-sided attack, Amanda felt a tiny ray of hope. It was at times like this that she missed John the most. He had never attacked her. She had been protected, sheltered, loved. She had felt that she was getting well with him, that she could control herself. But he was gone forever and her only hope now was Charles. If only they could work it out. She couldn't help loving Charles. That was what was really wrong with her.

"What?" she asked, looking down at her hands.

"There's a doctor in Harley Street who I think might be able to help you."

Another doctor.

"Help me what? Help me live alone? Help me pay the bills? I'm now cutting down on light bulbs. And yet you have money enough to take me to Harley Street to one more doctor. Is this another attempt to have me committed?"

Charles put his head in his hands and Amanda was immediately sorry for what she had said.

"Amanda, I'm only trying to help us." Perhaps he was. Perhaps he really meant it this time.

"All right. I'll go see anyone you want me to."

"Fine. I've made an appointment with this man for tomorrow afternoon. I'll go with you."

"I wouldn't go without you."

"Let's try, Amanda. Let's try this one more time." His tone was gentle. Maybe there was something to hope for.

Through the month of November, Charles took Amanda to see not one but three different doctors. She spent a week with each of them, none of them anything like Dr. Stirling or Dr. Pennell. They were all psychiatrists and they all asked more or less the same questions.

None showed any personal interest in her, Amanda felt, but she knew well that psychiatric help took a long time. Charles explained that he hoped one of the three would be the right one for her, and they could stick with him. Amanda disagreed, feeling as if they were playing one against the other, unbeknownst to each of them, but she went. Charles would come with her to the first appointment, her concerned, supportive husband; after that she went alone.

Charles took to calling her every day or so as well, which baffled her. He had never been much for the telephone; now he was on it endlessly, discussing every detail of her life with her. He goaded her about the fact that she had not made up with Davina, her own sister, implying that she was to blame for the break between them. Amanda flew off the handle during more than one of these conversations and hung up on him. A fine way to try to get back together, she thought, needling her in every conversation. Charles would always call her back.

"I'm not trying to upset you. I just want to get all your troubles out on the table. That's the only way we are going to be able to work it out. Sometimes I'm afraid you'll do Patrick harm, the way you lose control of yourself."

Amanda exploded at that vilification, her language more alley cat than Chelsea.

"You fucking bastard, how dare you say anything like that to me? Patrick is perfect. He is a happy child who does well in school. The only problem Patrick has is a father practically in the bankruptcy dock who is drunk half the time. You're drunk now." She was hysterical.

"What's happened to the kitten I brought him? Nanny Roberts says she hasn't seen it. She thinks you may have killed it because I brought it to Patrick." His tone was vicious.

Amanda lost complete control of herself. Now this unsympathetic nanny was a traitor to her, too, just like the rest of them. Charles had probably gotten her confidence, as he had with the others, to turn them against her. "You have to watch Lady Warrington very carefully," she could hear him say. "She may try to kill her child."

"I told you what happened to that kitten," she screamed at him.

"You told me nothing." He'd gone daft. She *had* told him.

"Would you like me to dig it up for you right now? That kitten was sicker than any animal I've ever seen. It died, poor little thing, and I buried it in the back garden. I told Patrick it had run away. He hated the kitten—it shat all over his bed, and he prefers dogs to cats, as you well know." The injustice of it enraged her. What was Charles trying to do?

"That's not Nanny Roberts's version of it."

"Well, she can bloody well go, too. I'll not have her spying on me and reporting to you. She's a smelly old woman anyhow."

Nanny Roberts was gone when Charles came to take Amanda to the doctor. He shook his head when she told him she'd had her pack up and leave the day after the party.

"You shouldn't have done that, Amanda. Patrick needed her steady hand."

"Patrick is too old for a second-rate nanny, all you can afford to spy on me. He needs a governess and I need a housekeeper to help me keep up with this house. I don't know what you're doing or why, but I don't think it's so much that you love Patrick as it is that you hate me." She burst into tears, helpless in her self-righteous rage. By the time they got to the doctor's office, she was a mass of nerves, hysterical. She disliked this particular doctor, so she told him off and stormed out of the office and took a cab home. She clung to Patrick that night, crying and kissing him. She had brought him into her room to sleep with her until they got some new help in the house. She watched his beautiful Keating face, sleeping like an angel as she lay reading and trying to watch telly. He was all she would have of Charles, ever. She hated Charles now for what he was doing to her. What was he trying to do? She fell asleep with her arms around Patrick. As long as she had him, nothing else mattered.

The 29th of November was a lovely sunny day, a rare late-autumn reprieve. Patrick was playing in the park with the new girl Amanda had hired herself, with no interference from Charles. Her name was Alice, and she was "quite sweet," Patrick had told his mother the night before. He was surprised when his father appeared and scooped him up in his arms.

"Fly!" Patrick said with delight. When his father came to the park they had a wonderful time together. Today would be one of those times. There was a man with him, someone Patrick didn't know.

"Bufo," Charles said, picking him up in his arms. "Guess what? You're coming home to Ormonde Gate to stay with me. Your mother is sick and I've had to put her in the hospital."

Patrick's brow clouded as he looked at his father. "What's the matter with her? She wasn't sick when Alice and I came to the park." He squirmed and looked at Alice.

Suddenly Alice saw exactly what Lord Warrington planned to do and she sprang into action as swiftly as if she had been expecting this moment to come. Now she understood Lady Warrington's concern, her warning to her not to lallygag with other nannies, but to keep Patrick in her sight at all times. If Lord Warrington thought he was going to take her charge from her, he had another think coming.

She grabbed Patrick by the hand and started to run, screaming at the top of her lungs.

"Help! Help me!" she wailed, pulling Patrick along with her at a fast clip. "These men are trying to kidnap this child. Help me! Get the police! Help me!"

Charles looked stunned at her ferocity and at the speed with which she was running, Patrick running with her now. She covered the few hundred yards to Rotten Row still screaming out for help. With great good fortune, an empty cab was passing and she flagged it down and ordered the driver to take them to Royal Hospital Road as quickly as possible. She burst into tears, holding Patrick tightly until they arrived at the house, looking out the back window to see if Lord Warrington was following her. When she burst into the house she was hysterical and Patrick was sobbing. Amanda came running when she heard the commotion at the front door.

"He's tried to take him, Lady Warrington, and he had a man with him, too, but I ran and didn't let him get Patrick." She double-locked the door behind her.

Amanda was terrified. Her worst fears had come true. She tried to calm Alice and Patrick as best she could. Shaking, she went to the telephone and, in a mounting fury, dialed Charles's number. He answered on the first ring, bellowing into the phone.

"I have a court order for Patrick, Amanda."

"You must be mad, trying to kidnap him," she screamed. "You can't have him! I'll see you in hell first."

"I'll be at the house in the morning with my solicitor and a court order and we'll see about that. You're not a fit mother and I have depositions to prove it, from former nannies with more sense than this one. From doctors who have examined you, and from your violent hysterics on the telephone. I will have Patrick, and I'll have him tomorrow." His voice was hoarse. He was still fuming at Alice's quickness, as well as at his own stupidity for not getting Patrick away from her.

Suddenly Amanda realized that Charles must have been recording all of their telephone conversations, goading her into saying things she should never have said.

"You are a devil," she said. "You try to get him in the morning, just you try. I'll stop you." She hung up and looked at her watch. It was four-thirty. She knew the court was open until five. She put on her coat and admonished Alice not to open the door to anyone until she returned.

★ ★ ★

T rue to his word, Charles appeared in the morning. Amanda was ready for him.

"I reported to the court that you tried to kidnap Patrick yesterday. I have permission to keep him until a date is set for a custody hearing. Here's the paper."

Charles handed it to his solicitor without reading it. She was doing him in again.

"If you take him now, you'll be in contempt of court," she said.

Charles looked at his solicitor. "I'm afraid she's right, Charles. We cannot take him now. It will damage your case."

Charles shrugged and looked at Amanda's wan face.

"I'll have him," he said. "It's just a matter of time. Here's my deposition."

I t was hard for Amanda to believe what she read in Charles's petition. "Due to the dangerous mental condition of Lady Amanda Warrington, Lord Warrington has requested custody of Lord Patrick Keating. Lady Warrington has been diagnosed as manic-depressive with a long history of emotional disorders and she is of a potentially dangerous nature. Lord Warrington is concerned for the safety of his son."

Amanda noted the names of the two doctors who found her unstable and possibly violent. She was almost ill reading what the nannies had to say about her. One declared that she had refused to sleep with her husband, forcing him to stay in the mews house in order to oversee the safety of his only child. Nanny Roberts gave a deposition that she had actually seen Lady Warrington kill a kitten Lord Warrington had brought to his son, by choking it to death. There were tapes and transcripts of telephone conversations, all heavily edited, in which Amanda sounded like a maddened shrew.

With Patrick and Alice safely in bed, Amanda sat alone in Charles's study, looking at all the things that belonged to him. Aside from his clothes, he had taken some of his books and the opera records, but everything else was here. Perhaps that's why she felt that he would come back to her. Everything belonged to Charles. Even her jewelry was locked away in the bank in his name, except for the string of opals she always wore and a few small things he had given her. She had come with nothing and now he was trying to take away the one thing that was hers. Patrick. Was she really that ill, that mad? A manic-depressive? Did she frighten her own child?

I must be mad, she thought. *They are all right. I still love Charles Warrington, regardless of his drinking and gambling, and now trying to take Patrick. I'd take him back, do anything to get him back, even now. I must be mad. They are right, and I am wrong.*

Amanda went to the court and was given a solicitor to represent her. When she had finished telling him her side of the story, she looked at him anxiously while he studied the papers she had brought with her. When he had finished, he looked at her across his cluttered desk, a hint of sympathy on his face.

"I don't believe you have anything to worry about, Lady Warrington."

On December 17, Lord and Lady Warrington were called before the judge of the High Court in Albemarle Street to review the custody case involving their son. Amanda's lawyer presented depositions from Doctors Pennell and Stirling, and persons who had been employed by her, as to her character. A list of unpaid bills was presented. Amanda made a verbal statement that she had no objection to Patrick's becoming a ward of the court on a temporary basis if there was any question about her fitness to keep him.

The judge was succinct.

"When Lord Warrington approached the court to take custody of his son, he presented certain evidence as to the mental competence of his wife. In reviewing Lady Warrington's petition to the court and her request to keep custody of her son, I find the evidence against her superficial, at best, and prejudiced. The court has investigated certain allegations made by Lady Warrington. Since their separation, Lord Warrington has not paid the support agreed upon to his wife, nor any of the outstanding bills.

"He is indebted to at least four London banks. The tuition fees at Lord Patrick Keating's school are months in arrears. This evidence suggests to me that Lady Warrington's mental condition might have been aggravated by Lord Warrington's irresponsible mode of living. I see nothing that leads me to believe that the child would be in any danger with his mother. In fact, he would be better off in the custody of a mother with mental problems of an undangerous nature than with an irresponsible father who is in debt at every turn and whose registered profession and only occupation is that of gambler. It is his mode of living that is an improper atmosphere for the boy.

"Lord Patrick Keating is to remain in the custody of his mother. A court-appointed nanny will be in residence with Lady Warrington to oversee the boy. Lord Warrington will be responsible for paying the nanny's weekly salary."

T he rag newspapers were filled with the story.

"Amanda did her work well," Charles said bitterly to Robin. "That judge left no stone unturned to make me look like a bounder."

"It's the court costs against you I cannot believe," Robin said. "Thirty thousand pounds. That is unbelievable."

"The hell with the court costs. They are the least of my worries."

"How are you going to pay them? You'll never get Patrick until everything is paid and you have a proper job and can prove to that old bastard of a judge that you can support him. Patrick, I mean." Robin saw that Charles was very drunk. They were sitting over dinner at the Club. Gavers was in the South of France.

"Oh, shut up, Robin," Charles said, signaling the barman for another drink. "Nothing matters to me anymore but Patrick. So help me God, I'll find a way to get him back."

CHAPTER 16

Winter 1974

With Patrick in Amanda's secure custody, Charles's bitterness grew by leaps and bounds. The final words of the judge had enraged him. The child in question "would be better off in the custody of a mother with mental problems of an undangerous nature than with an irresponsible father who was in debt to every acquaintance and whose registered profession and only occupation was that of gambler." Irresponsible, was he? He would get Patrick back no matter what it took to do it. How dare an idiot judge excoriate him the way that vicious anti-aristocrat judge had? What sort of twisted person was he to have seen all the evidence and still return Patrick to the custody of his clearly demented mother?

It was a bitter January and all of Charles's friends were off somewhere on holiday in warmer climes, but there was no holiday money for Charles this year; in fact, there was no money at all. Thank God his mother had lent him several thousand pounds to defray at least a part of the court costs. Court costs! When Charles thought about them, more than twenty thousand still owing, a blood vessel began to pound in his neck. He had been lumbered with everything, including Amanda's enormous psychiatric bills and legal fees, plus his own. He had no idea where the money was coming from to pay them, and he had lost Patrick.

The pattern of Charles's life changed completely. Instead of enjoying the constant company of his friends, he now was alone most of the time. Gavers was gone most of the time, primarily at Melbridge. He had invited Charles to Spain for a week with him as his guest, but Charles couldn't afford to go, even with Gavers picking up every bill. More than that, though, he wanted to stay in London because of Patrick. He was also somewhat disenchanted with Gavers these days. He resented his having sold the Club more, rather than less, as the months passed.

The new owners had made an arrangement with Charles which he agreed to reluctantly, because it seemed he had no other choice. His position was no longer that of a privileged member and partner. He was now no more than a high-class greeter and shill. A declining Earl, he thought morosely. The new members were a cheeky lot. "You know the Earl of Warrington, don't you? Charles, come and join us." It gave them a thrill to be on a first-name basis with him and still be able to throw in his title.

Except for every other weekend with Patrick, Charles had nothing to do but while away his time at the Club. Every night he stood at the tables gambling, on the surface a sort of hail-fellow-well-met, a role that brought bile to his throat. There was no thrill to this fake gambling that his reduced circumstances had forced upon him; no concentration was necessary and none of it meant anything. He stood there to encourage the others to stand there and lose to the house. He was neither losing nor winning; he was simply going through the motions of gambling with house money in order to earn his free board and drinks. A titled shill.

He thought of nothing but how to get Patrick back. Unless Robin was around, he lunched or dined alone at the Club, usually taking both meals there, choosing not to sit at the communal table but at a small table by himself. He did not encourage the new lot to infringe on his privacy—that was not part of the deal. They could keep their distance until the time came to go upstairs. Charles could use all the time he could get to think.

Since he had packed up Patrick's things and taken them back to Amanda's, his hatred of her had grown every day.

Even his Mercedes was giving him trouble. It had recurring battery problems and was in and out of the garage.

The only real gambling Charles could do on his own was at the bridge table, and aside from the weekends with Patrick, it was his only pleasure. He played twice a week in someone's flat and another two evenings at the Club. He had become extremely aggressive in his play, and as luck would have it, the cards favored him for a change. He was winning a fair amount, pin money compared to what he normally lost at backgammon or chemmy, but it was a small victory, the only one, and his winnings paid for petrol and tips. All through the winter he avoided answering the door or the telephone in Ormonde Gate. The calls were always about money—bankers or friends who wanted some of what they had lent him back. He knew that any of the new members of the Club would be glad to accommodate him but he was reluctant to borrow from them. He had been warned obliquely not to, and he couldn't afford to lose his standing at the Club. He could hardly afford to eat and drink so well anywhere else. As the weeks passed, his inner turbulence increased. His life was at its lowest ebb, all because of that harridan Amanda. If only he could get rid of her, get her out of his life forever.

Charles was sure it would be only a matter of time before she would go into another decline. She would fire the nanny or have more of the crippling migraines or attempt suicide again. How could the judge have given Patrick back to her? Charles was prepared to use any evidence he could garner to build a case against her. He was obsessively afraid she would harm Patrick. He hated the thought of Patrick's being in a car with her, even crossing the street with her. She might snap at any moment. He had to get Patrick away from her. The thought buried deep in his mind began to work its way to the surface.

Charles had become an avid reader of detective and murder novels. He amused himself by placing Amanda in the role of the victim and he gloried in her being stabbed, hanged, drowned, shot, or bludgeoned to death. He laughed when she was shoved off a mountaintop. Nothing that happened to her was good enough. Or bad enough.

When Gavers came back, he and Charles dined together every night. One evening there was an unpleasant scene. A new member wanted to play above the limit and Gavers refused to allow it. The new owner came to him, furious.

"You no longer own this place," he said. "I do. And I'll thank you to arrange for Robinson to have as much credit as he wants and to play for whatever stakes he chooses to. Do you understand?"

Gavers looked at him, ice-blue steel in his eyes.

"Robinson can play the limit and no more. I have several months left here with you and if you want my presence, the rules are mine. I may no longer own the place but I run it. Do you understand that?" Gavers moved threateningly toward him, his body hostile.

"Sorry, Gavers. Of course you are right."

"I thought so," Gavers said, turning his back. He and Charles retired to a far corner of the bar by themselves and proceeded to get drunker than lords.

"Never should have sold the place," Charles muttered. "The buggers don't know anything about a place like this and they can't learn."

"All I want is the end of August," Gavers said. "Then I'll be out of here."

"Amanda will be dead by August, dead and gone. Let's drink to next
year—it will be a better one for all of us."

Gavers chose to ignore what Charles was saying.

"A perfect murder," Charles continued. "Not even murder. No one
will ever know. Just disappearance, much better, and I know how to do
it, have it all planned. What would you think if she was gone one day,
not around anymore?"

"I think *we* should disappear now and get some sleep. Come on,
Charles."

"Gavers, you don't believe me. Believe me." Gavers watched him
pick up his drink. He was looking straight into Gavers's eyes, his own
filmed over, his hand shaking so badly that the glass missed his mouth.
The gin spilled on his cheek and ran off his chin onto his suit jacket.
Gavers knew they were both very drunk. It was no more than the gin
talking. Let him get it out of his system, Gavers thought. Wishing
Amanda dead didn't mean he would do anything to make that wish
come true.

"All right, I believe you. How are you going to arrange for the lus-
cious Lady Warrington to vanish from our lives?"

The look on Charles's face changed to one of mistrust and suspicion.

"Never you mind," he said cunningly. "You'll know when the time
comes. I'm going to get rid of her for good, out of my bed, out of my
house, out of my life."

"Oh, for Christ's sake," Gavers said, tired and impatient. "Let's get
out of here."

Charles began to keep watch on the house. Amanda would look out
of the dining room window and see the car parked across the street with
him sitting in it, wearing dark glasses as if in disguise, reading the
newspaper. Or occasionally when she glanced up to the street level from
the basement kitchen, she saw his feet and legs, walking back and forth
in front of the house. She recognized his perfectly polished shoes and the
tip of his umbrella. It unsettled her to find him around like that. She
could never forget the day he had tried to take Patrick—steal him—
from the park. He might easily try something like that again.

Amanda had been as stunned as he at the court costs. How could it
possibly cost thirty thousand pounds to decide custody of a child? She
had no feeling of smugness about getting Patrick back. She knew how
horrible it had been for Charles to lose Patrick. Maybe all this would
bring him to his senses and lead the way to a reconciliation. In her heart
of hearts, she believed they might love each other again.

★ ★ ★

March 1974

Charles met Jeremy for lunch at the Club one day in early March.
"You're looking remarkably well," Jeremy said. "You've lost weight."
"Yes. Been working at it lately. I was in terrible shape—no exercise
for months."

Jeremy was relieved to find Charles in a light mood. He did look well;
he looked fit and younger.

Charles was asking a question.

"Jeremy, do you suppose you could lend me a car for a few weeks?
The Mercedes is giving me a lot of trouble, always in the shop. It needs a
new battery, which is simple, but it needs quite a bit of other work done
on it. Should have had it done long before this. They tell me it might
take a month or so."

"Of course I can, Charles. Why don't you take my Mercedes? It's the
wrong color for you—gray is not your favorite—but I'd be delighted to
let you have it."

"Jeremy, I couldn't possibly take your car. Don't you still have that
old banger, the blue Austin?"

"Yes, of course, but you wouldn't want it. Have mine—I hardly ever
use it."

Charles and his manners. He was too polite even to consider borrowing the good car.

"Wouldn't have it, Jeremy. The banger is just what I need. And only
for a short time."

"Very well, if you insist. I'll bring it 'round to you."

"No, not necessary. Why don't we lunch tomorrow, at Scott's? I'll
come to you and pick it up then. Thanks, Jeremy. It will save me leasing
one."

"Not at all. If you change your mind, the Mercedes is yours."

Charles had been exercising since mid-February. He had started
weight lifting in the Ormonde Gate flat and took up the regular exercise
program remembered from his long-ago tour of duty in Italy with the
Queen's Own Guards. He applied himself to getting in shape, having
discovered that he was huffing and puffing like an old man if he made

the slightest physical effort. He cut his smoking by half. Then, with Jeremy's old Austin banger, a more dependable car than his Mercedes had ever been, he started driving to Folkestone or Brighton two or three times a week to run on the deserted beach. As winter turned to spring, the air was bracing, and he dropped close to twenty pounds in a fairly short time. His flabby muscles began to take on some of their old tone.

The plan that had formed in his mind required timing, but a few minutes at one end or the other were not critical. He timed the trips to Folkestone and to Brighton carefully and found that either could be done in less than an hour and a half if there was no traffic. True, he was speeding most of the time, but he enjoyed fast driving and he was a skillful driver and much less of a target in the Austin than he would have been in the Mercedes. Still, he kept a wary eye out for the police.

He knew he had talked too much about what he planned to do several times during the winter, when he had been drinking heavily. He remembered conversations with Gavers and Neil when he'd said entirely too much. Neither of them seemed to have paid undue attention to him, so he let it go, determined to keep his mouth shut in the future.

Another nanny had come to work for Amanda in March. The new girl, Jenny, was young, fond of children, and Patrick liked her. Charles took stock of her when he picked Patrick up for their weekends together and found her perfectly adequate. She was off on the regular Thursdays plus the weekends when Patrick was with him, and she seemed to settle in well. She was cheerful, and that was nice for Patrick.

CHAPTER 17

9:00 P.M., April 11, 1974

Charles left his flat in Ormonde Gate and drove the blue Austin to Royal Hospital Road. He parked two doors down from the house on the same side of the street. He had no need for reassurance about parking. There were always spaces available.

He sat in the parked car and watched for any movement in the street. There was none. He closed his eyes and thought about what he was going to do. He was perfectly calm. He would enter this house in darkness wearing dark clothes, with a mask and a key in his pocket and a weapon in his hand, he thought, and he would come out of this house with a sail bag full of dead flesh, on his way to a new life.

He got out of the car and walked toward the front door. As he put his key in the lock, the music of *Tristan und Isolde* was ringing in his ears. The "Liebestod," the exquisite paean to pure erotic love, still filled his head. Its familiar theme of transfigured love appealed deeply to Charles. There was no perfect love, but the music of the opera was as good a substitute as he knew, and the story of a love that prefers night to day, that prefers death to life, had special meaning for Charles.

He turned his key in the lock quietly and opened the door, closing it softly behind him.

10:00 P.M., April 11, 1974

As Amanda started down the stairs, she wondered why it was so dark. Jenny would have turned the light on in the hall on the ground floor before she went down into the kitchen to make the eggnog. She should have, but it was not on. It was so dark at the bottom of the stairs that Amanda felt her way along the back hall to the door that led down into the kitchen.

"Jenny?" she called. "Jenny, why is it taking you so long?"

There was no answer. The kitchen door must be closed.

"Jenny," she called again. "What are you doing? Is something wrong?"

She felt a minor twinge of annoyance. It could hardly take this long to make her nighttime drink. Groping her way along the dark hall, she thought she heard a noise. Was there something wrong? A shiver of fear ran through her.

"Oh, my God," she said, involuntarily. There was someone there and the someone was not Jenny.

Suddenly there was a great swoosh of air and she felt a stunning blow land hard on her shoulder. As she hurtled forward in the dark, she screamed and immediately a second blow caught her on the scalp and knocked her off her feet. When she hit the floor, she rolled over quickly in a protective reaction, lights bursting in her head, temples pounding. She had been hit with something metal and if she was going to be hit again—which surely she was—the blow would come from the same direction and she'd best not be there. She heard her own voice, an odd voice, unrecognizable with the breath knocked out of her.

"Oh, Christ," she heard herself say. "What are you doing? Robbing my house? How did you get in here and where is Jenny? What have you done to her, you rotten bastard?"

She flailed out at her assailant, trying to find him in the dark, knowing the closer she got to him the more difficult it would be for him to hit her again. He needed space to swing that lethal piece of metal.

"Jenny, Jenny, answer me! Are you all right?" she heard her still strange voice call out. Why didn't Jenny answer her? "My God, what have you done to her! Have you killed her?"

Enraged by this evil, silent stranger in her house and terrified of what he might have done to Jenny, she found strength in her fury. She knew she was fighting for her own life. Anyone with a weapon like that meant to kill. She could feel blood flowing out of her head, her own warm blood. She had a mighty bright blaze of a red headache now, nothing like her silly migraines. She knew she had to defend herself against this voiceless thief she could not even see in the dark. She felt his body grappling with her, felt him reaching for her throat with his leather-gloved hands. Locked in mortal combat, they were rolling over and over on the floor. Amanda, gasping, suddenly knew she had a weapon of her own to make use of. She sank her teeth into his shoulder, biting him through his woolen sweater with all the strength she could muster. Her teeth found their mark. He let out a roar of pain.

"You fucking bitch, you fucking murderous bitch!" she heard him shout.

No, she thought. *Don't let it be. It can't be.*

The voice belonged to Charles. To no one else. She was battling for her life on the floor in the hall of her own house in the dark, and as the sound of his voice sank in, she would have traded decades of her life, past or future, for it to have been any other voice, any voice but his. Her spirit shattered. He would kill her now, just as he had probably already killed Jenny. It was Charles. It was Charles's voice.

"You," she said, reaching for the mask she had felt over his face as they rolled on the floor. "It's you. You came here to kill me. You've killed Jenny and you meant to kill me."

In a great haze of pain and blood and the awful realization that Charles had come intending to kill her, Amanda was torn between a desire to live and a stronger desire to die. She no longer wanted to know what had happened to Jenny—there was no hope for her, no hope for any of them. When Charles helped her up the stairs, all she could think was that if he had succeeded in killing her, at least the horror of their lives would be over. When she looked up at him from the bed and reached for his belt buckle, she wanted only to feel once more the love and desire they had shared in the beginning. A last goodbye.

Now, with Charles in the bathroom, her strength came back and with it a full desire to live. Charles was not going to kill her. She was going to have a life of her own, a world of her own that no one was going to take from her. That was what John had wanted to give her, and even without him, that was what she was going to have.

10:45 P.M.

Please God, Amanda thought as she ran, *don't let me faint now. I've got to get Patrick out of there before Charles kills him.* Now she was undone, frightened where she had been brave, shaking where she had been calm. Blood and perspiration mingled and ran down her forehead. She must be able to tell them to find Jenny and get to Patrick quickly. Jenny in that dark kitchen, alone, probably dead. Charles going into the bathroom to get a wet towel—*to wrap around my neck and strangle me finally to death.*

The amber light above the door at the Farrier's Forge had never looked so welcoming. Amanda pushed past the door to the inside warmth and cheer of the pub.

"Help me, please help me," she begged. "He's killed the nanny and tried to kill me. Call the police. My child is there with him. Help me, help me."

She dropped to her knees, seeing with crystal clarity the expression of horror on the faces of the regulars sitting at the bar and on the banquettes around her in the cozy room. Then she saw Ron, the barkeeper who knew Jenny, start around from behind the bar toward her, his brow knit, his face shocked. Ron would get the police—they were less than a block away. As he reached her, Amanda slumped to the floor unconscious, blood still streaming from her head, but she knew that she was alive and safe.

When Patrick got upstairs, as he had been told to, he went first to look for Jenny in her room, but she wasn't there. Maybe he should go back down and find her. He fidgeted for a minute. Her bedside light was on and her bed was all messed up but she wasn't there. She was probably still having her tea in the kitchen. Maybe he'd better go and get her—then she could read to him. He wasn't sleepy. No, he'd better wait. His father would come up soon now—maybe he would; he'd said he would —and he'd be angry if he had been disobeyed. He'd wait a little while and if she didn't come back up, he'd go and find her. Patrick went to his room and got into his own bed and listened for someone to come up and see about him. There was no noise. Was his mother all right? She'd looked awful with all that blood all over her, but she had told him she was fine. Maybe he'd better go and see if she was fine.

He fidgeted some more. He heard a noise below, some kind of a noise; he didn't know what it was, but it was a noise. Maybe his father was coming upstairs. He listened, waiting. Then he thought he heard the front door slam, but he wasn't sure and he hoped he was getting sleepy now.

He closed his eyes. There wasn't a sound. He opened his eyes. He hadn't turned his light out yet. Maybe he should go down now and find Jenny. His father must be gone. He could see if his mother was all right.

He got up and opened the door into the hallway and looked down the stairs. His mother's door was closed but there was a slice of light on the floor outside. He went down and tapped on her door but there was no answer. He didn't dare open the door, although he wanted to desperately. He started down to the floor below. It was dark; the hall light was out.

Halfway down the stairs, he became afraid. It was dark and there were still two flights down to the ground floor and one more to the kitchen. If he called, maybe someone would hear him.

He called out.

"Jenny, where are you? Are you all right?"

There was no answer.

He turned around and went back up to his bedroom and got in bed. He turned out his light. Then he started fidgeting again. He was lonesome. He got up again and went to Jenny's room and got into her bed. She'd be up soon.

Late evening, April 11, 1974

"**M**other."

"Charles, what is it?" Penelope Warrington looked at the clock on the mantelpiece. It was just after eleven.

Steady now, Charles thought. *What you say now is important. Steady.*

"Mother, something terrible has happened at the house. Jenny is badly hurt, badly, and so is Amanda. You must go to the house right now and fetch Patrick. Ring Richard immediately and ask him to help you."

"Charles, for heaven's sakes, what's happened? What about Patrick? Is he all right?" She knew from the sound of Charles's voice that whatever had happened was terrible.

"Patrick is safe but you must hurry over and take him home with you. I was walking by the house earlier and I saw a ruckus going on in the kitchen—a man was attacking Amanda and she was screaming. I ran in and a man ran out past me. There was blood all over the place. Mother, I cannot tell all of it to you now, but Amanda is going to find a way to blame me. Just go and get Patrick. I will call you later. Ring Richard right now."

The phone clicked off.

Penelope's hands were shaking. She dialed Richard's number. It rang and rang but there was no answer. Where in the world was he? She pulled on her coat, having decided to take her chances on finding a taxi in the street, rather than calling for one, which might eat up more time. The trip to the house couldn't be done in less than twenty minutes. Dear Lord, what had happened?

Fortunately, less than half a block later she saw and flagged down a taxi.

"Number Twenty-two Royal Hospital Road, driver," she said as she climbed into the cab. "And please, this is an emergency. As quickly as you can!" She would ring up Richard again when she got to the house.

Rosie heard Jimbo barking furiously at the front door. Someone had driven in. Friendly Irish wolfhounds were not necessarily fierce watchdogs but their barking was warning at least. Rosie, half-asleep, had been faintly aware of the sound of tires on the gravel of the circular driveway below. She looked at her little Asprey clock on the bedside table. Twelve-thirty. Was it Neil already? It was much too early for him, and besides, Rosie wasn't sure he was coming down until tomorrow night. Who else could it be at this hour? She went to the window and opened it, looking out to see who had arrived below. Jimbo, still barking excitedly, was jumping on a man in the driveway in delight, so it was someone he obviously knew.

"Rosie, it's Charles. Let me in."

Rosie could barely make out his familiar figure because of the dark clothes he wore but the voice was unmistakably Charles's. He disappeared under the overhang at the front door.

"Coming, Charles, at once," Rosie called, pulling her bathrobe on over her flannel nightgown. It was freezing cold out and the wind was blowing hard. What was Charles doing here at this time of night? She ran down the stairs, flicking on the hall lights as she went, and opened the front door.

"My God, what's happened?" she asked, seeing immediately the turmoil in his face. "Come in quickly. I'll fix you a drink." He was wild-eyed. They went back through the hall to the small study. Without asking, Rosie poured him a stiff brandy and handed it to him. She made herself a strong scotch and soda.

Charles sank into a chair and turned his face away from her before he spoke, as if he couldn't bear to look at her.

"Rosie, the most unbelievable series of ghastly coincidences . . . "

His hands were shaking and there were stains on them, peculiar streaks that looked like bloodstains. There were more on his trousers, dark stains that showed even on the dark color.

"Charles, look at me and tell me what's happened. Whose car is that? It's not yours. You haven't been in an accident, have you?" She had an odd feeling that she wished he *had* been in an accident.

"It's Jeremy's. I borrowed it a few weeks ago." He looked at her, desperation in his dark-blue eyes. "Rosie, Amanda will make this look as if it was all my fault. . . . " He was almost gulping as he spoke and Rosie was afraid he was going to cry—something else she had never seen in him. She went over to him and put her hands down hard on his shoulders.

"Charles, try to get hold of yourself. Tell me from the beginning."

"I was passing by the house earlier this evening, as you know I do to keep an eye on Patrick, and there was a terrible row going on in the kitchen. I saw a man attacking Amanda. I let myself in with my own key and started toward the stairs to the kitchen when the fellow ran out past me, right out the front door, almost knocking me down as he went. I slipped on something, but Amanda was putting up such a racket in the kitchen that I went to see about her and I slipped again. Rosie, it was blood—there was blood all over the floor.

"When I got to Amanda she started screaming that I had been there all along and that I had hired the man to kill her. She was quite out of her mind—you know how she is. I calmed her down and told her that I'd just happened to be passing the house and I got her upstairs to the bedroom. She was bleeding all over the place—the fellow had really bashed her head in. I went in the bathroom to get a wet towel to clean her up a bit and when I came back she was gone."

"Gone?" Rosie said. "Where? Why?"

"She'd torn out of the house—I guess to the King's Road Police Station to tell them I'd hired someone to kill her. And there I was, covered with blood. . . . Rosie, look at me. No one's going to believe me."

Two thoughts came instantaneously to Rosie. First, she knew the house on Royal Hospital Road well and it was highly improbable that anyone could see more than a foot into the kitchen from the street. Hard on that thought came the next. What was Charles doing here at this time of night, fifty miles from London? Why hadn't he simply called the police from the house? Amanda was the troublesome one, not Charles. In some vivid strike of clairvoyant lightning, Rosie knew what to do. She went to the telephone and dialed London.

"What are you doing? Who are you calling?"

"Neil," Rosie said. "He's got to get down here at once."

"Why, for God's sake? Don't tell him anything yet. Hang up, Rosie."

"Shut up, Charles. Pull yourself together. Pour yourself another brandy." She nodded her head toward the drinks table. "Neil, it's me. Charles is here. Something terrible's happened. You've got to come at once. Don't mention that he's here to anyone—just get here as quickly as you can." She rang off.

"Oh, Jesus, why did you do that?"

"Charles, you evidently think that whatever has happened did not happen, or you'd like to. Amanda has run out of the house, she's accused you of hiring someone to kill her, and you seem to have bloodstains on your clothes. Do you think I can do anything to help you alone? I need to know what else has happened. Come on, you must tell me."

"Jenny."

"Jenny?" Rosie said. "Who the hell is Jenny?"

"The nanny, the one who's been there a few weeks now. Nice girl."

"I'm sure," Rosie said succinctly. "What about her?" Amanda had nannies the way other people had houseguests. Rosie could not curb her hatred for Amanda.

"She's badly hurt. And I left. I should have stayed." There was a look on his face Rosie didn't like, something deceptive—devious even.

"My God, the plot thickens. Who hurt her?" There was a painful knot in her stomach suddenly.

"The man."

"The man who ran?" Rosie felt as if they were having a conversation in a madhouse.

"Yes. No. I think he did."

"You *think* he did? Who else would have? Amanda didn't wound whatever-her-name-is. Surely you don't think that, do you?" It was just one in the morning now. Neil would be here by two at the latest. Rosie couldn't decide whether to divert Charles and wait for Neil or whether to keep at him. She knew it was best to go at it while he was in this agitated and confused state, keep at him until he told her the truth.

"Charles, you have got to tell me everything you know, no matter what it is, no matter how dreadful. You're in a first-rate mess." She already knew there would be lies to be told after the truth came out. She sat down on the ottoman in front of his chair and held his hands, trying to comfort him. He was in such turmoil, poor darling. He had turned to her often when Amanda had exasperated all of them to a point of wanting to kill her. Trying to kill Amanda. Ah, yes, that brought Rosie back to the present point.

"Come on, talk to me."

Charles suddenly leaped to his feet and went to the phone on the desk. "I've got to ring my mother," he said, picking up the phone.

Rosie felt the madhouse doors closing on both of them. Ring his mother? At this hour of the morning? Was it her birthday or something?

"Mother?" she heard him say. "Is Patrick there with you? Is he safe? . . . Good. That's all I wanted to know. I can't talk to you right now but I'll ring back later tonight, I promise. . . . No, I can't speak to them either. Tell them I'll call in the morning." He hung up the phone.

"Who did you not want to speak to at your mother's?" Rosie asked. As if she didn't know.

"The police. They're there. I rang her earlier and told her to fetch Patrick, to take him home with her. I wanted to make sure he was all right."

Rosie said nothing. She had to make him tell her all of the story. Her eyes held his steadily. She waited.

Charles fidgeted and looked away, avoiding her eyes.

Then, despite how tough and resilient Rosie was, she began to listen for the sound of Neil's car.

Neil and Rosie did not have an outwardly devoted or affectionate marriage, but when it came to anything of real importance between them, they had a perfect understanding. Neil would not waste any time getting to her.

"Charles," Rosie said, "you've got to report this to the police—immediately."

"I'm not going to talk to the police at all," Charles said. "Rosie, I've got to write some notes. Have you got some notepaper?"

"Of course, right there in the desk drawer."

Charles sat down at the desk like a schoolboy at his homework. Rosie was grateful for his absorption; it gave her time to think before Neil arrived.

He scribbled hurriedly, and when he finished writing he licked the flaps, sealing the envelopes with the back of his hand. "Post these for me in the morning?" he said. Rosie nodded, and at that moment, with infinite relief she heard Neil's car in the driveway.

"It's Neil," she said, unnecessarily. "Charles, we can't just ramble on about this. Let me tell him what I know and you can correct me or add to it as we go. Do you understand? Time is of the essence. Neil will know what to do."

"Of course," Charles said. He looked numb.

Neil came in, giving Rosie the briefest of glances. He went immediately to Charles, his intensity filling the room.

"What's happened, Winner?"

"There's been a terrible accident at Royal Hospital Road. The nanny's hurt and Amanda has gone to . . . "

Rosie interrupted him. "Shut up now, Charles. Let me tell Neil."

With Neil's appearance, Charles had started to shake. Neil looked at him, at the look in his eyes and the empty glass in his hand. He fixed another drink for him, taking nothing for himself. Charles was a mess. He handed Charles the drink and sat down.

"Shoot," he said to Rosie.

She outlined exactly what she knew, with no interruption from Charles. When she finished, Neil said nothing for a few moments.

"You've got to get back up to London and to the police as soon as possible," Neil said finally. "You should never have left the scene. I'll go with you. Actually, we should call the police from here."

"*No!*" Charles said.

"Why not?" Neil asked, suspecting that Charles was not telling the whole story, but was keeping important details from them. "Don't you think the best thing for you to do would be to go to the police? No one knows what Amanda will say, has already said, but it's your word against hers, and this time yours should prevail. They know about her erratic behavior, not yours. You saw someone or you heard screams as you were passing the house and you went immediately to her aid. As you went in the house a man ran out past you. Then you found Amanda hurt and took her upstairs to tend to her wounds. When you came back from the bathroom, you found her gone. You panicked, knowing what she would do. That's all very human and very believable. Now that you've had time to think you have to tell them everything you know and hope to find the man who has injured the nanny and attacked your wife after breaking into your house. No matter what Amanda says, all you did was try to help her. Right?"

"In every confrontation we have had in our life together, she has always beat me at my own game. Why should it be different now?"

Rosie saw the weakness in him. She had never realized that he was afraid of Amanda.

"You have got to go back and face it," Neil said. "It's your word against the quite certifiably mad Amanda's—no one else's. You must go back. You have to go back."

"All right," Charles said. "But I can't lie—they'd smoke me out in a minute. If you think I am going to stand in the dock for attempted murder . . . " Tears came to his eyes. "Patrick's got an insane mother and now this from me."

"Charles," Rosie said. "What do you mean 'attempted murder'? Is the girl dead? Do you know she is dead?"

"I don't care if she's dead or alive," Charles said. "I wasn't thinking about her. I was thinking about Amanda."

Rosie's analytical mind took precedence again. He cared nothing about the innocent girl whose blood was on him. He felt no remorse about her; it was only his hatred of Amanda that meant anything, and it meant more than even his devotion to Patrick.

"I'm going with you," Neil said. "I can help you, and besides, you're in no condition to drive. Go clean up. I'll give you a fresh shirt and a pullover."

"No," Charles said. "I'm going alone. You're right, I never should have left. God knows what's happened. I'll go straight to King's Road, then home. I'll call you from there." Suddenly he was alert and looking better, more like his old self. Rosie heaved a sigh of relief, though still wishing that Neil was going with Charles.

"Good," Neil said, slightly thrown off by Charles's change of mind. They walked him to the front door and Neil saw him to the car. Rosie noticed a pained smile, more like a grimace toward her, as he swung out of the driveway. Neil came to stand beside her at the front door.

"He hasn't told us everything. You should have gone with him."

"I know," Neil said, "but don't blame me, Rosie, and don't blame yourself. He's on his own." He watched the car go down the long driveway and saw the taillights flash on as it reached the main road.

"Rosie," he said, "he's not going back!"

"What are you talking about?" Rosie almost screamed at him. "How do you know where he's going? Did he tell you something?"

"No," Neil said. "But he turned right just now. He's turned south instead of northwest to London."

As Charles took the road south toward Folkestone, he could think of only one thing. Brucie. His old nurse would take him in and listen to him and she would understand. Her little cottage was in a small cluster of houses about three miles outside of town. He knew the lights from the car would wake at least one of the neighbors at this time of night but he didn't care.

He got out of the car and tapped on her front door.

"Brucie," he called. "It's me, Charles. Let me in." There was no response, so he tapped a little louder. He heard her little terrier bark and was relieved when he heard her voice.

"Charlie! At this time of night? What's the matter—did you lose another bundle in France?" Charles often stopped by to see her en route back to London. A month or so ago he had returned from Deauville after a big loss and stopped in for comfort. She always comforted him.

"Worse than that," he said as she let him in. She lit one of the lamps and stirred up the embers in the fireplace.

"Nothing wrong with the boy?" Charles had never ceased to regret that Brucie's arthritis was too bad to allow her to have worked for him in London. Patrick would have been safe and well-off in her hands.

"No." He didn't know where to start now. She turned the kettle on. He could get the bottle of gin from the front seat. She would give him tea.

"Then it's Amanda?" He'd bitched to her for years about Amanda.

"Worse."

She sat down opposite him and looked at him.

"Charlie, what is it?"

He put his head in his hands and the words came tumbling out. She was the only one he could tell the truth.

"Brucie, Amanda's going to make all this look like it was my fault. . . ."

"Then whose fault is it, Charlie? From the look of you, it's pretty bad."

"I was passing by the house this evening. I try to keep an eye on Patrick, as you know, and there was this unbelievable row going on in the kitchen. I saw a man attacking Amanda. . . ." He gulped. It wouldn't do. It wasn't on—he couldn't lie to her. "Oh, Brucie, there was blood all over the place. And Amanda has gone, to the police no doubt."

"Why to the police?"

He looked her square in the eye, her strong face soothing him. "I've killed someone. I meant to kill Amanda but I botched it. Brucie, I've got to get to France."

"Who did you kill, Charlie?"

"The nanny. Jenny. I didn't know she had changed her night off. I thought she was Amanda, coming down for her nerve drink. It was dark. Then I heard Amanda's voice calling. 'Jenny, Jenny, what's taking you so long?' I heard her voice. I thought I'd gone mad and I went after her. . . ."

"Dear God," Brucie said.

"I didn't kill her but we had a horrible fight and I took her upstairs to the bedroom to take care of her. Patrick was there but I sent him up to bed. I went into the bathroom to get a towel to mop Amanda off and when I came back she was gone. I heard the front door slam. She's always been a door slammer and I knew she would go straight for the police. To discredit me." His face was flushed and a small blood vessel was pounding in his forehead.

"And Patrick now?"

"Mother's got him. He's all right."

"How did you kill the girl?"

"With a tire iron."

"Dear God, Charlie, what's come over you?" She got up to fix tea. He started toward the front door. He had to go get the gin. "Sit down, Charlie. You can get the bottle later. Now's not the time for drink."

He sat down as if he were still her obedient charge. What the hell did he expect Brucie to do? She couldn't get him out of this mess; she couldn't even punish him for it. He should call Neil and tell him he'd meet him in London in the morning. Neil and Rosie hadn't believed he was going back then, he knew, but he couldn't call them. There was no phone in Brucie's cottage.

"My poor darlin'," Brucie said, not a shred of sympathy in her voice but a world of understanding. "It finally got to be too much for you, didn't it? I told you the drink was going to get you in trouble. It's no good to go over that now—that's water over the dam, in a way of speaking."

"And you're going to tell me to go back to London to the police, too, aren't you?"

"Not necessarily," Brucie said. "I don't know what I'm going to tell you until you finish the story, right from the start, right from when you decided to kill Amanda. That's not like you, Charlie. You're not a killer. You've got to go all over it again. We'll figure something out. When did this start?"

"When she got to keep Patrick. In December. Since then I've wanted her dead every waking moment."

"Charlie, wanting her dead and killing her are two different things. I've got some trousers and a pullover of yours here from your last visit. Go in and clean up; then we'll figure out what to do. You're safe here for the while."

"But the car? The neighbors will notice it." There were no garages in the cluster of cottages, nor any cars.

"The Mercedes?"

"No, a car I've borrowed—not so grand."

"Never mind then. Off with you."

She gave him a towel and sent him to her small bathroom. Full of despair she sat down in front of the glowing fire. There was nothing she could do beyond keep him safe for a day or so. Well, that would be a start. She folded her hands and sighed, waiting.

Neil called Gavers.

"Gavers, listen to me carefully," Neil said. "I'm in the country, at Faversham, but leaving the minute I ring off. Winner has gotten himself into the most godawful cock-up. The nanny's been hurt, may even be dead, and Amanda isn't in much better shape. Winner swears he was passing the house and saw someone attacking Amanda and that he went in and the man knocked him down and ran out of the house. He's convinced Amanda is going to make it look as if he attacked her. He came fleeing down here to Rosie but he left, swearing he was going back to straighten things out. Neither Rosie nor I believe him, any more than we believe he's told us the whole story. He might call you or any of us. I'm on my way back."

"Meet me at the club," Gavers said. "The night watchman will let you in the back door."

Now Gavers was pacing the floor, prowling back and forth, back and forth. It was still dark out. Where the devil was Neil? He should be here by now. The nanny was dead; Gavers had heard it on the car radio, and Lord Warrington's whereabouts were unknown. Neil had probably not heard yet.

Gavers had called Richard Marston in the country, suggesting that he not tell Davina until they knew more; then he called Jeremy, who had heard it on the radio too. The police hadn't wasted any time. He called Robin next. Poor Robin. Awakened at the crack of dawn from a drunken sleep, he'd started to cry at what Gavers told him. Artist and *bon vivant*, Robin hated ugly things. This was an ugly thing. Where *was* Neil?

He sat down at his desk and stared at the phone, willing it to ring. *Winner, you bloody fool, what have you done? What has happened and where are you now?* Gavers's instincts told him that things were going to be worse rather than better as the story unfolded.

The chilling memory of a talk with Charles a few months before came back to him. No, he thought, no. He and Winner had not had that conversation. They had not had it. That was drink, far too much drink, talking that late night months ago.

Amanda's pinched, miserable little face came to him. Even before he called Richard, he'd called Chelsea Hospital. He had spoken to Mary Reilly, one of the nurses he had known there for years. Luckily, she happened to be on duty and told him everything she knew. Amanda had been brought in at about eleven last night. It had taken hours to get her cleaned up and to stitch up the wounds to her head.

"Whoever did it," Mary Reilly told him, "took a nice slice off her scalp—forty-three stitches needed—and left some heavy marks on her throat. She was a mess, and in shock about her son. Couldn't make any sense out of her. She might have a concussion and she was in such a state that the doctor sedated her heavily." The police were furious about that, Mary went on, because they had wanted to question her immedi-

ately, and now she was unconscious for no one knew how long. They'd
have a long wait before they could interrogate her. A superintendent
from King's Road and a Scotland Yard man were waiting, and the staff
had been given instructions that no one was to see her before they could
question her. No relative, no friend, no one.

Pathetic, Gavers thought. No one would try to see her. Amanda had
no friends. She and Davina had not spoken for years and her other sister
lived buried in the wilds of northern Scotland. Winner's mother would
no doubt call to find out about her but would never go to see her.

The door opened and Neil Riggs walked into the room.

"Thank God," Gavers said. "I was about to start smoking again. Five
more minutes."

Neil lit a cigarette. "Sorry," he said, sitting down opposite Gavers,
"I'll never give them up. And today they are imperative." As Neil took
a long drag from the cigarette, Gavers saw the fatigue and something
else he couldn't define on his face.

"The nanny's dead," Gavers said. "It came over the radio an hour
ago. I've told Richard and Jeremy and Robin. Did you know?"

"No," Neil said. "There isn't a lot we can do," he said, leaning across
the desk. "He's killed her just as sure as we are sitting here. He probably
made a mistake—he probably meant to kill Amanda. Did he ever tell
you that he was going to kill Amanda?"

The conversation Gavers had pushed away came back. Obviously,
Winner had told Neil the same thing.

"I wonder if he discussed it with anyone but you or me?" Gavers
asked. *Winner, you goddamned fool.*

"I doubt it. But he had a plan all right. I took the whole conversation
as too much drink. You?"

"So did I. Well, here we have it. One of our best friends, forty-one
years old, peer and gambler, has come to the end of his tether. In debt to
all of us, in debt to the courts . . . Christ, Neil, what about Patrick?"
Gavers had not given a thought to the boy.

"Not to worry," Neil said. "Winner called his mother. Two or three
times, once from my house. She went and collected Patrick from Royal
Hospital Road and has him with her now."

"Talked to her two or three times?" Gavers said. "Who else has he
talked to?" It was incomprehensible to Gavers that Winner would not
have called him first in this kind of trouble.

"I doubt anyone. Rosie and the Dowager are all I know of."

The telephone rang. Gavers and Neil exchanged a hopeful look. Winner. Gavers answered, but it was the Club operator who had just come

on duty. He listened and said, "Mollie, tell him I'm not here yet, but that you can get a message to me." He hung up.

"The police telephoning to talk to me. They aren't wasting any time. I've told Richard and Jeremy and Robin that they know nothing until after we get together in Carlyle Square at lunchtime."

Gavers made a swift decision. "We're leaving here before anyone shows up. I'll drop you at the flat. Come to Carlyle Square at one. Then we'll see what we can do. Do you think he came back up to London?"

"Jesus, I don't know," Neil said. "He turned right when he left my place, on the south road. That's not the way to London. Who knows where he is by now?"

G avers realized that the events of the night before spelled the end of the Club. In essence it would never be the same again, could never be the same. He understood the look on Neil's face. It was on his own face now.

They had been such a tightly knit group, the six of them, their lives intertwined. Charles Warrington, his schoolmate and friend through the years. Richard Marston, married to one of Amanda's sisters, a thoroughly decent man who would be drawn into this far more than he would have chosen, but he would stand by the decisions of the group. Neil Riggs—too serious always, but a tough and experienced gambler, deeply involved in everything Gavers did. Even Robin, Robin Bryce, who drank like an idiot instead of concentrating on his very real talent as a painter, with an irresistible charm and sweetness about him that lent spirit and gaiety to the atmosphere of the Club. Jeremy Morton. An outsider to some extent who had become one of them because, for more than any of them, the Club had been the entire nucleus of his life. As well it should be, Gavers thought; the Wyndham was a world of its own.

Gavers arrived in Carlyle Square and parked the car. If only he could drive down to Melbridge. All the camaraderie and pranks of the past, all the good times they had shared together were behind them now.

recent years he had thanked the gods that be for his having married
Davina, not Amanda, though it had been Amanda he'd been strongly
attracted to when he'd first met the Gordon girls.

It was incomprehensible to Richard that Charles had tried to kill
Amanda. That was far beyond rational behavior. What in God's name
had happened to him? There had to be an explanation, an accounting
for the brutal events of the night before that had now resulted in the
death of an innocent girl.

"Of course there's a possibility that he didn't do it," Gavers answered,
his patience at the snapping point. He was still the ringleader, and the
Wyndham was still a part of their lives, but the years of gambling had
changed Gavers. He had become more and more misanthropic.

"When Charles left Rosie he told her he was coming back up to
London to straighten it all out. He could be with the police now—how
would we know? We've ducked them for hours, hoping he'd show up.
But if we don't hear something soon . . ." His voice trailed off. "We'd
better all be sure to tell the same story."

"We don't have anything to lie about, Gavers," Robin said. "None of
us really knows a bloody thing."

"Which brings me to something that has to be done," Gavers said,
bloodshot eyes focusing on Robin. "Someone's got to talk to Amanda in
the hospital. You."

The claret bottle in front of Robin was empty. He reached for a full
one from the center of the table and filled his glass, queasy at the
thought of seeing Amanda lying in a hospital bed with forty-three
stitches in her head. Wasn't that what Gavers had told them earlier?

"Why me? You should go, or Richard, her own brother-in-law. Why
me?"

"For Christ's sake, Robin," Gavers said. "I'm the last person she
would talk to. Richard can hardly go. You know damned well the trouble between Amanda and Davina. She would never say a word to him,
nor to Neil or Jeremy. You're the only one of us she's ever liked at all.
You've got to get her version of what happened."

"Gavers is right," Neil said. "Robin, she would talk to you." Neil was
exhausted and it showed in the blue-black circles under his eyes.

"Like hell she would. She knows I'm Charles's friend first of all, and
she knows I've been with him more than any of you have since they've
been separated. Besides, the police are certainly there with her, asking a
few questions themselves. I'd never get anywhere near her."

Gavers's look at Robin was both hostile and contemptuous.

"One of us has to go, and that one is you. Let's go over it once more:
Charles has obviously gone off his head and is in a panic somewhere, not

CHAPTER 18

Late afternoon, April 12, 1974

The April sunlight shone weakly through the garden windows and fell on the polished surface of the dining room table. Dora, Gavers's cook, had put hot coffee on the sideboard and left several opened bottles of wine and port on the table for the men seated there. Then she and Mr. Rust, the gardener, left as they did every Friday after lunch, driving down to Melbridge to prepare for the inevitable weekend guests.

Gavers, Neil, Robin, Richard, and Jeremy were gathered around the luncheon table, still debating what to do, what could be done after what had happened. Each of them had become tenser and more concerned as the hours wore on with still no word from Charles. Gavers had only succeeded so far in fending off the police and Scotland Yard by having his secretary tell them that he was en route to Melbridge. He knew it was just a matter of time, shortening with each moment now, before he had to see them. They were all going to be questioned, and soon, but for the time being they were hoping against hope that Charles would call or appear.

"He could still turn up, any time now," Robin said, for the tenth time. "Here. At his mother's, where Patrick is. In the country, at your house, Neil, or at yours, Richard."

Richard Marston got up and went to the sideboard for more coffee. "Do you think, any of you, that there is a shred of a possibility that he didn't do it? Any chance of that?"

Richard Marston was a man whose life had been unmarred by tragedy or adversity. Born and brought up in a secure atmosphere, he was an attentive son and a devoted husband and father. More than once in recent years he had thanked the gods that be for his having married Davina, not Amanda, though it had been Amanda he'd been strongly attracted to when he'd first met the Gordon girls.

It was incomprehensible to Richard that Charles had tried to kill Amanda. That was far beyond rational behavior. What in God's name had happened to him? There had to be an explanation, an accounting for the brutal events of the night before that had now resulted in the death of an innocent girl.

"Of course there's a possibility that he didn't do it," Gavers answered, his patience at the snapping point. He was still the ringleader, and the Wyndham was still a part of their lives, but the years of gambling had changed Gavers. He had become more and more misanthropic.

"When Charles left Rosie he told her he was coming back up to London to straighten it all out. He could be with the police now—how would we know? We've ducked them for hours, hoping he'd show up. But if we don't hear something soon . . ." His voice trailed off. "We'd better all be sure to tell the same story."

"We don't have anything to lie about, Gavers," Robin said. "None of us really knows a bloody thing."

"Which brings me to something that has to be done," Gavers said, bloodshot eyes focusing on Robin. "Someone's got to talk to Amanda in the hospital. You."

The claret bottle in front of Robin was empty. He reached for a full one from the center of the table and filled his glass, queasy at the thought of seeing Amanda lying in a hospital bed with forty-three stitches in her head. Wasn't that what Gavers had told them earlier?

"Why me? You should go, or Richard, her own brother-in-law. Why me?"

"For Christ's sake, Robin," Gavers said. "I'm the last person she would talk to. Richard can hardly go. You know damned well the trouble between Amanda and Davina. She would never say a word to him, nor to Neil or Jeremy. You're the only one of us she's ever liked at all. You've got to get her version of what happened."

"Gavers is right," Neil said. "Robin, she would talk to you." Neil was exhausted and it showed in the blue-black circles under his eyes.

"Like hell she would. She knows I'm Charles's friend first of all, and she knows I've been with him more than any of you have since they've been separated. Besides, the police are certainly there with her, asking a few questions themselves. I'd never get anywhere near her."

Gavers's look at Robin was both hostile and contemptuous.

"One of us has to go, and that one is you. Let's go over it once more: Charles has obviously gone off his head and is in a panic somewhere, not

"Amanda, it's Robin." He started to cry. He wiped his eyes with a corner of the sheet.

"Robin?" Her voice was barely audible. "What are you doing here? Where is Charles?" Her mouth was swollen and there were ugly purple bruises around it. She looked frail and vulnerable. Where was the girl in the green dress at the Polish party so long ago, the girl who had turned every eye in Les Amis at that wonderful party? This pathetic waif couldn't be the same girl. The whole thing was going to be far worse than even he had expected. How could he ask this wounded creature any questions?

He felt her small hand pat his hair. "Poor Robin, did they send you to see me? You would be the only one to come, even if they didn't send you, wouldn't you?"

"No one sent me," he lied. "I'm so sorry about it, Amanda." That was the understatement of all time.

"Oh, God, where is Charles?" she said. Her voice was barely a whisper. "Robin, he couldn't have meant to do it. He couldn't have meant to kill me. Why would he want to kill me? Where is he? Don't you know where he is?"

"None of us knows where he is. He left Rosie's about one, said he was coming back to London to straighten it all out. No one's heard a word from him since then."

"Rosie's?" Amanda said. "He went to Rosie's? Why?"

"He told her he'd been passing the house and he saw someone attacking you in the kitchen. He said he went in and a man knocked him down in the hall and ran out of the house. Who was the man?"

"Why would he go to Rosie's?" Amanda tried to sit up, agitated. "There was no other man. Jenny went down to make my eggnog and she was gone so long that I went to see what had happened. Someone attacked me at the bottom of the stairway, hit me with something metal. At first I thought it was a burglar after the silver. Oh, Robin, there wasn't any other man but Charles. He had a mask on that covered his face, and I tore it off him when I heard his voice. It was Charles. We had a horrendous fight in the hall. He almost killed me but then he fell apart. I was so frightened when it was over that I think I told him I'd help him.

"Then he helped me upstairs. I was so dizzy and my throat hurt so— he'd tried to choke me. Patrick was there but Charles told him to go up to bed. I was bleeding all over the place and when Charles went into the bathroom—to get a towel he said, to clean my face—but I was sure he was going to come back and kill me. I don't know how I got out while he was gone but I did. There wasn't anyone but Charles, no one else. Poor Jenny, poor, poor Jenny. Is she really dead?"

Her voice was hoarse now and she fell back against the pillows. "Where is he, God? Where is Charles?" Her mouth was swollen and stiff from the bruises.

Robin got to his feet and held her, his heart breaking. She didn't know anything; she didn't even know that Jenny was dead for sure, but she did know there hadn't been anyone in the house but Charles. There had been no other man. Patrick had seen him. Patrick had seen his mother and father in the bedroom. Children don't lie. There had been no other man.

Mary Reilly came into the room.

"Now you must go," she said. It was an order.

"Robin," Amanda's lost voice said, "find my Charles. Find him. Bring him here. I love him and I know he didn't mean what he did. I've got to tell him I know that. Oh, Robin, help me. You must help me. He didn't mean it."

Robin kissed her bandaged head. "I'll try to find him, Amanda. Go to sleep. I'll try. I'll be here tomorrow to see you, I promise."

Robin rang Gavers from a call box and told him everything Amanda had said.

"She could be lying," Gavers said.

"She wasn't lying, Gavers. She's been difficult, but she's never been a liar. Her big problem has been always telling the truth as she saw it. I was the only liar in the room; I told her no one had sent me. She was telling the truth. I know she was."

"Don't be so sure, Robin." There was a superior tone in Gavers's voice.

"Fuck you, Gavers," Robin said, hanging up the phone.

CHAPTER 19

April 13, 1974

The discovery in Folkestone of the blue Austin that Jeremy Morton had lent Charles Warrington was the first tangible clue to his possible whereabouts. It was found thirty-six hours after the killing of Jenny Boyce, parked on a quiet terrace street, less than a ten-minute walk from where the ferries left for Calais. The car was found—in a routine check of vehicles that did not belong in the neighborhood—by a Folkestone policeman who, having been alerted to watch for the car, impounded it at once. Buster Manners was on the scene a few hours later, as was Scotland Yard. It seemed apparent that Lord Warrington had fled the continent for France on the regular ferry service. The finding of the car set off a huge manhunt. The police began a meticulous search of every boat and dwelling, every shop and office, and on the cliffs and beaches surrounding the small town. Calais was alerted as well, but it was not until a warrant for Lord Warrington's arrest could be issued that the French authorities were obliged to join the search.

Again in a routine manner, the police were able to establish the approximate time the car was left in Gerald Road by questioning the occupants in the terrace houses nearby. An old man, almost blind, who lived directly across the street from where the car had been parked, disclosed that his nocturnal habits included waking up and having a regular pee at exactly 4:00 A.M. His bathroom window looked down on a streetlight, which he used as a focusing point. He could still make out vague shapes, and at 4:00 A.M. on Friday morning, he noticed an empty space where his neighbor's car was usually parked. It passed his mind that his neighbor had probably left for a long weekend on Thursday evening. At exactly 8:00 A.M., when nature routinely brought the old man back to the toilet, he saw that a car was parked there. It proved to be Jeremy Morton's car, the one he had lent to Charles. "It wasn't there at four," the old man said, "but it sure as hell was at eight."

Excitement about finding the car reached a fever pitch with the press. They combed every inch of Folkestone as thoroughly as the police, but it all came to naught.

There was no trace of Charles Warrington.

Chelsea Hospital, April 12

Amanda was half-asleep when she thought she heard Chantal's voice in her ear.

"*Amie adorable?*" the soft voice was asking. "Can you hear me? Are you able to talk?"

"Oh, Chantal, I wish you were here," Amanda said out loud to herself, sure she was dreaming. Her bandaged head ached and her throat was painfully sore. When she felt the pressure of a hand squeezing hers, she opened her eyes. Seeing Chantal there, she let out a little cry and clutched her hand, speechless.

Amanda sat up and reached for her, tears in her eyes. Chantal put her arms around her.

"Don't try to talk," Chantal said.

"Don't talk! You're the only person in the world I want to talk to. I've spoken to every Scotland Yard man and every police officer in London—that's why I fell asleep. The doctor is letting me go home tomorrow. How did you know about what has happened?"

"I heard it on French radio this morning and went straight to the airport. Gavers didn't tell me."

"The only person who's come is Robin, and he was sent. Not my mother-in-law or my sister. No one but you."

"Can you bear to talk about it? Or shall we let it go for the time being? I wanted to see you for myself, see how you are."

Chantal would not have Amanda think that she might have been sent to question her. She was also angry and baffled that Gavers had not called her.

"Charles went off his head, Chantal. He absolutely lost his mind. He's had such terrible problems with money and losing Patrick. Here I was praying every day that we would be able to get back together. I know what they mean now when they say 'temporary insanity.' Can you imagine Charles trying to beat me to death with a piece of iron? With Patrick in the house?"

"I cannot." Chantal's brows drew together and she made a little fanning gesture in the air with her hands. *"Je ne peux pas"* was far stronger from Chantal in French than in English. She was so upset at the way Amanda looked that she spoke half in French, half in English.

"No one knows where he is, Chantal. Robin said he went down to the Riggses' that night. You know Neil and Rosie?"

"Only slightly."

"Charles told her he had seen a man attacking me in the kitchen and that he came to help me. Then he told her I ran out of the house to the police to try to make it look as if he'd killed Jenny and tried to kill me, because I hated him." She was sitting on the edge of the bed and she had started to rock back and forth, arms crossed, hands holding her elbows.

"Go on, darling," Chantal said. "Try to get it out."

"We'd had this horrendous fight downstairs when I still thought he was a burglar. Then I heard his voice and tore the mask off and he went after me, but all of a sudden he collapsed and told me he'd killed her. I couldn't believe what he'd done—I promised I'd help him and he took me upstairs to get some of all that blood off of me. Chantal, when he put me down on the bed and went in the bathroom for a towel . . . I had this feeling . . . I *knew* he was going to come back and kill me. I had to get away from him. Now I wonder if I wasn't wrong to leave. If I had just stayed there, he would be here. Where do you suppose he is? Where would he go? If he'd just come back, we could face it. I don't know how, because he told me he had killed Jenny—he did kill her."

Chantal believed what Amanda was saying, every word she was saying, but what she found hard to believe was Amanda's foolish faith in Charles. The full impact of the situation had obviously not struck her yet.

"Amanda, he almost killed you. What about that?"

"I don't know, I don't know. He didn't mean to—he was just crazy. I want to go home. I want Patrick. I want Charles." She started to rock again.

Chantal knew she must leave. Amanda needed sleep; she needed any respite from this horror story.

"Darling, do you have to go back to that house?" Chantal asked gently. She had no intention of voicing details she'd heard on the radio: the condition of the house, the kitchen sealed off after the body was found stuffed into a canvas sail bag. She had no idea how much Amanda actually knew. Did she know about the horrendous amount of blood they had found? Even with the body gone, the crime was still there. Chantal shivered.

"Oh, yes, I have to. Charles will come back there." Her mind shifted. "Chantal! I forgot to tell you that the Stalewski is stored safely in the country, with John's secretary."

"*Amie!* How can you talk of a painting at a time like this? I came straight over to tell you that *anything* I can do to help you, you must promise to ask. They are going to make me leave now but I will call tomorrow and every day, and you can come to us, stay with us—bringing Patrick with you. You know that, don't you?"

"Oh, yes, Chantal, but I can't leave. I have to wait for Charles. He's probably so ashamed. He didn't mean to do it."

The nurse appeared. Chantal pulled her coat on and kissed Amanda. "I hate to leave you." She blew another kiss from the door, undone by Amanda's ghostly, waiflike appearance.

Chantal's car was caught in late afternoon traffic on the Cromwell Road en route to the airport. The afternoon papers in the kiosks carried still more headlines about the Warrington case: VANISHED EARL STILL ON THE RUN. NO CLUES TO WHEREABOUTS OF MISSING PEER.

Chantal shuddered again at the thought of Amanda's going back to the house. She was frightened for her. Somehow Amanda actually believed Charles innocent. He might have murdered the girl, but he hadn't meant to. He might have tried to kill her, leaving her with a head full of catgut and scars, but it was not his fault—he hadn't meant to do it. Well, Amanda was right about Charles's taking leave of his senses, but he had taken leave of them long before the night of the murder. This was no crime of passion, Chantal thought. You don't just pick up a piece of iron at whim in the streets. It was a carefully structured plan that had backfired. She shook her head. Leave it to Charles. He couldn't even manage to kill the right person.

On the plane she wondered why Gavers hadn't called her about the whole thing. What possible excuse could he have? His usual selfish behavior? Possibly he felt that she might take Amanda's side. If so, then he had felt correctly.

April 15

A blaring headline in *The Daily Mail* four days after the murder signaled the first of many "sightings" of the missing Earl of Warrington.

The press were at white heat to find him, and, they hoped, before the police.

"*The Daily Mail* last night traced Lord Warrington to France, as police continued to search for him in London after the murder of his son's nanny," the story read. Still crowing, the *Mail* continued:

Immigration police in Calais have informed us that the 41-year-old earl landed off the last ferry from Folkestone at 11 P.M. Lord Warrington was alone and there was no doubt as to his identity, since they examined his passport. The French official informed *The Daily Mail* that they had no reason to hold him, as there was no request from the English police to watch for him.

Then, according to the *Mail*, the official they had spoken to expressed the opinion that it was "possible" that Lord Warrington had hired a car in Calais, as it would have been unlikely for him to have set off on foot. Highly unlikely. No, they did not know his whereabouts at this time. The *Mail* presented no proof of the passport's having been seen, nor any record of the rental of a car by Lord Warrington. The story ended abruptly. It was the beginning and the end of the first great scoop made by an English newspaper.

The *Mail* immediately found itself with egg on its face after a phone call from Chief Superintendent Manners of the King's Road Police Station. He informed *The Daily Mail* that he wondered about the accuracy of their story, since Lord Warrington's passport was in his possession—in case they would like to examine it. It had been left, as well as all other identification, in his lordship's flat in Ormonde Gate. The paper was invited to share any future scoops with him.

Buster Manners and Constable Briggs discussed the security measures to be taken when Lady Warrington and her son returned home. The house had been under surveillance since the murder, and the forensic people had been all over it for days. The kitchen area had been sealed off. Now, with Lady Warrington and the child coming back, new arrangements had to be made.

"Do you think Warrington might come back and go after her again?" Briggs asked. He was going to be responsible for her.

"I do not," Manners said. "Better safe than sorry, though. We're as much watching for him as we are watching over her. And if I read her right, if he should come back she'd be just as apt to lie for him as not. She talks about him day and night, night and day—have we heard from him? Is there any news of him? Looks to me as if they can't live with each other or without each other. Did you know a little lovemaking went on that night? From the timing, it was after he'd killed the nanny and after he'd gone after her. Strange scene?"

Briggs was intensely interested in Manners's flat statement. Had a little go at it, had they?

"Did she tell you that?"

Manners looked at him coolly.

"Hardly. Nor have we disclosed to her that we know it. It accounts for a bit of time that was left unaccounted for when we questioned her. The nurse who undressed her went over her clothes, everything she had on. Blood wasn't all they found, if you follow me."

Briggs was almost embarrassed. He changed the subject.

"You still have a packet of people to question, don't you?"

"Right on. I'm going down to the Riggs place this afternoon. The missus was the last one to see him that we know of. You will accompany Lady Warrington home from the hospital tomorrow. The child will be brought to her from the grandmother's. There's another nanny coming, a woman who worked for them after the custody case. The kid's a ward of the court, and the court asked the people who regularly employ this nanny to let her go for a few weeks so the child won't be too confused or upset. You are to stay with her ladyship in the daytime, no matter where she goes. When the household retires I want someone watching the house, and I want a man in the garden in the back too. It connects with the mews house they own. His lordship might be holed up somewhere— at least that's a logical assumption. He could come back to one of three places: Royal Hospital Road, the mews house, or Ormonde Gate, his own flat. We have his passport and keys, credit cards, all left in the Ormonde Gate flat, all at the station. A Cartier watch. 'God keep ye, Charlie,' it says on the back of it. God better be keeping him now."

"What are they going to use for a kitchen? It's still sealed off."

"There's a hot plate in the nursery that can be brought down to the bedroom. The best they can do is hot water for tea. For the rest they'll have to settle for take-out, or they have to go out. Can't touch that kitchen, not for some time, nor the downstairs hall. Anything else you need to know?"

"No. When will I see you?"

"Tomorrow morning at the station. Cheerio, then, I'm off down south."

★ ★ ★

April 18, 1974

A week after the murder of Jenny Boyce an arrest warrant was issued for the missing Earl of Warrington. This unprecedented scandal was of huge proportions. No one talked of anything else.

For the first time in history a warrant had been issued for the arrest of a peer of the realm. Lords were above the law, at least the common law. Peers had been entitled to be tried in the House of Lords by their fellow peers until the Criminal Justice Act of 1948. Peers simply did not go around killing people. Unaware of the unique nature of the case, the police had jumped the gun and issued an arrest warrant, convinced that Lord Warrington had left the country. They had more than enough reason to believe he had bolted when the car that he had borrowed was found on a quiet street in Folkestone, in close proximity to the ferry for Calais.

The day after the issuing of the arrest warrant, an inquest was opened in the Westminster Coroner's Court to investigate the circumstances of Jenny Boyce's death. The hearing was brief. The Home Office pathologist testified that Jenny Boyce had died of injuries to her head with a blunt instrument. Jenny Boyce's father had identified her body. Since there was nothing else to do in the absence of the man accused of murdering her, the inquest was adjourned until further notice. Where was Charles Warrington?

The police continued their work, questioning a number of Charles Warrington's friends. Along with his passport, his driver's license, and credit cards in his flat in Ormonde Gate, they had found his address books. There had been a hundred-pound note in the pocket of one of his suits. His key ring was in the flat, and held the keys to his Mercedes—which was parked outside on the street—and to the flat in Ormonde Gate, as well as several other keys, as yet unidentified. They discovered books and a collection of phonograph recordings of all the Wagnerian operas; the one left on the turntable was Kirsten Flagstad singing *Tristan und Isolde*.

On the desk were several pictures in silver frames, of Lord Patrick Keating with his father, and one picture of Lord Warrington at the helm of a swift sailboat, taken during the annual Cowes offshore race. A sheaf of bills and bank statements was found in a desk drawer; there were no personal letters.

Something had begun to happen: There was a very real resistance on the part of the vanished Earl's friends to give the police anything more than cursory information, and that in a patronizing and begrudging manner. Aristocratic backs were easily put up by the police's apparent assumption that Lord Warrington was guilty simply because he was missing. Lines were drawn; peers and police were at war with each other. The police were supposedly the servants of the aristocracy. How dare they take the attitude that he was guilty? How could they have any hope of understanding the insurmountable problems of Charles Warrington's recent life, bumbling idiots that they were? Chief Superintendent Manners and his men asked questions that were deliberately unanswered, and were generally treated as interlopers rather than protectors. Manners openly accused several people of withholding information— which they had. There was a deepening resentment on either side. Buster Manners, irritated and frustrated, dubbed the circle that surrounded Charles Warrington the "Harrow Mob," a name that stuck and delighted the press.

Nigel Rutherson, the Westminster coroner, could do nothing but wait, and wait he did. The police continued their painstaking homework, looked upon with impatient contempt by the group they were investigating. There were more than three hundred names in Warrington's battered blue leather address book, from a dozen countries and all walks of life. The investigation continued.

London, late April

Amanda, Patrick, and the nanny lived an uneasy existence in the house in Royal Hospital Road, watched over and protected by Constable Briggs. Amanda's main concern was for Patrick. He was at school during the week, and on weekends she took him to her mother's small house in the country, five miles and a million light-years from Richard and Davina at Ransome House.

Davina had called once after Amanda got home from the hospital, asking that Patrick come and stay with them. She and Amanda had a blazing row, which ended with Davina coldly telling Amanda she should "think about the child and not be so selfish." It was a rehash of their last fight.

"He's my child and I think of nothing but him," Amanda screamed at her. "His security is with me, not you, and he stays here."

"Very well, Amanda, have it your way," Davina said, and hung up.

Their mother was in a state, dwelling on the rift between her daughters, weeping softly when she was alone with Amanda. Patrick made the older woman nervous; she was not used to having a small child in her house. On top of it all, the publicity surrounding the murder had turned her into a miserable recluse and her circle of friends was horrified at what had happened. Her only confidant was the village parson. She envied her one untroublesome daughter, Pamela, living removed from all this. Mrs. Gordon was planning to move to Mauritius as soon as she could sell her house.

Amanda's primary problem in London was the press. For weeks they parked on her doorstep, and whenever she went out, Briggs had to intervene when they insisted on questioning her. She started slipping out through the back garden, letting herself out into the mews, but they found her there too. She was offered vast sums of money for interviews by every paper. She ignored them all, and, given no encouragement, they gradually left her alone, although the phone continued to ring occasionally with an offer for almost any amount of money if she would allow them to take pictures and interview her.

The forensic experts finally finished their work in the kitchen and the downstairs hall. They departed and the kitchen became part of the house again. Living without one had been a major hardship, so by the time it was returned to Amanda, painted and clean, Amanda was grateful to have it back. The new nanny fixed supper for them and brought it upstairs. Nanny had no feelings about the kitchen, no memories of what had happened there.

Time passed.

Where was Charles? Amanda started answering the phone when it rang. Where was he?

"Amanda?" the whispery voice inquired.

It was the shy voice of Pamela, and for some reason Amanda was so stunned by the sound of her voice that she started to cry. Poor darling Pamela, to have to know about all of this. She had always been painfully, agonizingly shy. Davina, her fraternal twin, was quiet but not shy at all. Amanda believed that the main reason Pamela had married at sixteen and buried herself in a great pile of Scottish brick with a monosyllabic husband was to avoid contact with her quarrelsome sisters.

"Oh, Pamela," Amanda cried softly. "I'm so sorry you even have to know about this awful accident."

"Do you want me to come?" Pamela asked. "My Richard says I must come if you need me." Davina and Pamela had both married Richards, Pamela's being an engineer in Edinburgh.

"I'd love to see you, but no, there is nothing you can do. Thank you, darling."

"What about Patrick? Is he all right?" Pamela had only one child, also a boy, whom neither Amanda nor Davina had ever seen. It was only in tragic circumstances like this that there was any communication between the sisters. Amanda had wished a thousand times lately that she and Pamela had been closer. Davina's behavior toward her was so bewildering and hateful that Amanda still couldn't quite believe it.

"Patrick is fine."

"And you?"

"I'll never be fine until Charles comes back."

"Why can't you and Patrick come here and get away from all that mess for a while?"

Darling Pamela. For a moment, Amanda longed to go and stay with her. Pamela lived a somewhat feudal life with a dominant husband who made her completely happy, but nothing like this had ever happened to any of them. And never would.

"I can't. I'm afraid to move, in case Charles should come home." It was true.

"Please stay in touch with me. I worry about you and Patrick now. If you need to send him to me, anytime, please do. Poor little tyke, I would love him as if he were my own."

"I know you would. I promise I'll call you at least every week or so now. You'll hear if anything happens about Charles—because the press hounds us every minute."

The shy voice was struggling to say something.

"Amanda, you know I'll help you if I can. I do love you." It was almost impossible for her to put the thought into words.

"I love you too," Amanda said, her voice breaking as they rang off. At least she had one sister who cared something for her.

London, May 1974

Chief Superintendent Manners was fed up with the swells, tired of tolerating their unrelenting superiority and their transparent lies. He had interviewed dozens of them now and found not one to his liking. What he would not admit to himself was that he had gotten nothing, not even a scrap to go on, from any of them. Manners knew that most of them were innocent, but several knew much more than they were telling. Why would the Earl's close friends continue to protect him? If he had returned, Buster could understand their closing ranks to help him— that was the real spirit of friendship, kinship. But gone as he was, and for as long as he had been, could any of them continue to believe that the man was innocent? Buster's thoughts were bitter as he made his way to one more interview. Getting away with murder, that's what the aristos wanted for their friend. So far, they had succeeded.

He sighed as he walked to his next appointment in the handsome building just off Trafalgar Square. A frigid receptionist informed him that Mr. Woods-Jones was still in conference. He would be called. Twenty minutes later, he was summoned into Mr. Woods-Jones's grandiose office and seated across the desk from him.

Buster Manners looked at the clown in the seat opposite him. *Careful now,* he thought. *Don't judge these people on your terms, as they do you. You're here because he might be able to tell you something.*

Woods-Jones was tall and thin, with watery blue eyes. His hair was wispy-gray and the veins in his perfectly manicured, slender hands were as watery a blue as his eyes. A poof, Manners thought, a poof he'd been chasing for weeks, one meeting after another canceled at the last minute. Never mind. The poof could know something.

"This is utterly ridiculous, Superintendent," he was being told. The man's voice was watery, too, and his tone insinuated a lack of respect for his interrogator. "Why you insist on questioning me, I cannot possibly fathom. I knew Warrington rather well once, but I haven't seen him for some time."

"How long?" Manners asked.

The watery blue eyes stared at him. "I should say six months to a year."

"Couldn't you pinpoint it a little closer than that? We need your help. Did you ever lend him any money?"

"Good God, no." He was lying. A check for three hundred pounds made out to Charles had come through in the accounts Manners was going over.

"We have a check of yours made out to Lord Warrington." Manners pulled out a copy of the check and handed it across the desk. It was dated February 10.

"My good man, I had forgotten about that. I bought a picture from Warrington last winter sometime, a small watercolor, nothing of any importance." He got up from his chair and came around the desk as if he were the guiding force of this interview. "Now let's get something straight. Warrington has quite obviously taken his own life. I don't know what would make anyone think he could still be alive. The man was a gentleman and he most certainly has fallen on his sword, honorably. It's quite obvious to me that after he parked his motorcar in Folkestone, he walked into the sea." Everything seemed quite obvious to Mr. Woods-Jones, including his capacity to ignore the question of the check.

"There was a force-eight gale blowing that night, from ten P.M. on and for forty-eight hours afterwards," Manners said. "Any man who walked into the sea would have been slammed right back on the beach, dead or alive."

Woods-Jones returned to his seat, a look of infinite patience on his face.

"As I've told you, I really know nothing. I would appreciate it if our conversation remains confidential. The press seem to write what they choose and I do not want my name involved in any way. I know nothing of the whereabouts of Lord Warrington." He rose to his feet, dismissing Manners.

And you're bucking for a title, too, aren't you? Manners thought, rising. Never mind. It was probably true that he'd bought a picture from Warrington in February. That's when money had been the tightest for him. He shook hands with Woods-Jones and left the office.

An odd lot, those aristos, Manners reflected as he retraced his steps across Trafalgar Square. It was depressing, how little information he had gotten out of any of them and this was a dead end. Woods-Jones knew nothing.

Étretat, France, June 1974

In June, another "finding" of Lord Warrington surfaced in the tabloids, this time from a small hotel in France. A Madame Lucienne Payot called Scotland Yard to inform them that she had seen the missing Earl in the Hôtel du Port in Étretat at least four times during the month of June alone. She would have reported his whereabouts sooner had she known they were looking for him, but she had just been shown his photograph, which was being circulated by Interpol. It was unquestionably the man she had seen. Scotland Yard informed the King's Road Police Station. When the authorities descended on the tiny town of Étretat, they were outnumbered by a flotilla of press, who had arrived hours before them and staked out every room in the hotel. No one knew how the press had gotten the information, but it seemed they had access to it before Scotland Yard.

Madame Payot was extremely helpful. At a press conference in the lounge of the hotel, she described Lord Warrington. *"Très agréable,"* she told them. He was *"un homme charmant."* He spoke perfect French but he was unmistakably *"un étranger."* No Frenchman she knew was so tall or had such good manners. The stranger, had he been Charles, would have had to learn the language swiftly. Charles Warrington had trouble pronouncing the word *oui.* He had no interest in or knowledge of any language other than English.

Even so, Warrington was known to have many friends in France, wealthy friends, titled friends, some of whom might well be sheltering him. But speaking perfect French? It soon became obvious that the man Madame Payot had seen four times in the month of June could not be Charles Warrington. Still, Madame Payot had drawn the press to her like a bear to honey, and the hotel, which was normally filled with seedy characters and a few ladies of questionable reputation, was alive with revelry paid for lavishly on unrestricted expense accounts. The *"étranger,"* the *"homme charmant,"* was nowhere to be found. Nevertheless, for a solid week the press fed stories to the waiting world datelined Étretat and specifically from the Hôtel du Port.

Then it was discovered that Madame Payot owned the Hôtel du Port. She was thrilled that the police and press had followed up her clue as to the lost lord's whereabouts and she was grateful for so much attention. Indeed, she would call them at once should he ever appear at the hotel again.

July 1974

Charles Warrington had become the target of the most massive worldwide search for one man in the history of British scandal.

The newspapers continued to report new sightings of Lord Warrington, blowing even the most fragmentary possibility into headlines. The stories came to nought. More than three months had passed without a tangible clue as to his whereabouts. The killer of Jenny Boyce and assailant of Lady Warrington was widely believed to be the missing Earl, since no one else seemed to be involved.

Scotland Yard and the British police painstakingly searched more than twenty houses in London, Kent, Sussex, and Hampshire belonging to friends of Charles Warrington. They continued to keep watch on several of them, including the country houses of Gavin Driscoll and Neil Riggs, where he had last been seen by Mrs. Neil Riggs. Melbridge was searched by the police—ransacked, to Gavers's way of thinking. He had left the country in a fury, disappearing to Africa for a month. His communication with animals and birds was beyond that of a normal man. He understood their needs and their dignity and gave both their due. Alone in the bush, Gavers thought about his friendship with Charles. They had become distanced from each other by Charles's failure to grow, but they were still old friends, still members of the same class. He cared for Charles, regardless of the man's intrinsic weakness, and felt helpless for the first time in his life. Where was Charles? What had happened to him?

Nigel Rutherson was as equally frustrated, although less involved than Gavin Driscoll. He waited and waited for new information. Surely something would happen; some clue would develop that would lead to the missing man. Charles Henry Edward Keating, Baron Keating of Longholt, 11th Earl of Warrington, had disappeared from the face of the earth or the sea. The trail was not only cold, there was no trail.

The sightings continued. Charles Warrington appeared, in some form or other, in eight countries, leading Scotland Yard and Interpol a not so merry chase. He was "seen" in Australia, in South Africa, the Bahamas, and Hong Kong. The madam of a French whorehouse, clued no doubt by Madame Payot, claimed that he had stayed at her house in Paris but that she had let him get away after some wonderful nights of love.

It was reported in the press by an authority that Warrington had undergone plastic surgery in the expert hands of a doctor who specialized in changing the appearance of Nazi war criminals. His shin bones had been shortened so that all six foot two of him had become all six foot of him. His head was shaved, he had gained forty pounds, his eyes were now dark-brown, thanks to contact lenses, and he had several sets of identity papers and spoke four languages fluently. He was known to be somewhere in South America, the "continent of fugitives," with at least a hundred thousand pounds at his disposal, provided by underground gambling figures. Everyone had a theory about him. Those who believed him alive fought ferociously with those who were convinced he was dead, that he had committed suicide before dawn on the morning after the killing of Jenny Boyce. If friends had helped him to his unknown grave, then they were true friends.

It was class warfare with friends, police, Scotland Yard, and the press all competing for new leads. Everyone talked and no one knew anything. Charles Warrington was gone. Not forgotten, he was simply gone.

20

August 1974

On a hot night in early August in his small house in Walton Street, Robin Bryce took a handful of Nembutal pills and a massive amount of straight scotch at the same time, meaning to kill himself, and succeeding. His body was found by his latest girlfriend when she arrived back from a holiday in Spain. When she opened the door with her key she knew immediately that something was very wrong. He had been dead for two days.

The headlines screamed: FRIEND OF VANISHED EARL FOUND DEAD. LORD WARRINGTON'S FRIEND DEAD OF OVERDOSE.

Robin left no note nor any letters, but there was no question in the mind of anyone who knew him about what had happened. He had betrayed his own class, giving or selling information about the private world of his friends to the newspapers. Regardless of the fact that he had done nothing of the kind, he was accused and found guilty by his own peers. The magic circle closed swiftly against one of their own.

His suicide stemmed from his own talent. He had been commissioned to do a painting of the so-called "Wyndham Group" for *The Sunday Observer*. It was a good bit of money, several hundred pounds—which he badly needed, as always. There had been no objection to the article being written by John Vexe, a well-known journalist and fringe friend of the troupe, who had suggested Robin as the artist. It was to be a set piece about London's exclusive gambling club. The Club had long since been sold, and one of its titled members was missing, but that made the article even more pertinent. Gavers had given an extensive interview to Vexe, explaining that his tangible interest now was in the rarity of his collection of birds and animals, rather than in dice. None of those in the painting raised any objection to posing for it—until the article, accompanied by the painting, appeared in June. John Vexe had revised his original position, or so it seemed, and the article depicted the members as privileged snobs who lived by their own rules and were basically an insensitive and arrogant group of not very attractive people. The about-face taken was partially the result of Vexe's having interviewed Amanda Warrington and having found her not as black as she had been painted. He saw her as a somewhat tragic figure, a reviled outsider in the tapestry woven by aristocratic mandates.

Vexe was impervious to the resulting criticism. Robin was not. He became the victim. The court jester, a buffoon with friends in high places, he had sold out on them. When he amused them he had been acceptable; when he did not, he was finished. Robin's hidden manic-depressive nature was of no concern to his fancy friends, and they did not hesitate to exorcise him quickly from their midst. The ranks closed. He was no longer invited and no longer welcome anywhere.

Robin was devastated, his life in shambles. Nothing had gone right for him since Winner's disappearance, and his visit to Amanda in the hospital had had a profound effect on him. Winner could never have bludgeoned her with a tire iron; he could never have planned to kill her. Every day since the disappearance, Robin battled his lack of knowledge and became obsessed with finding Winner. They had talked to each other every day, had shared their fortunes and their misfortunes, but Robin was a ship without a rudder without his best friend. His deepest fear was that Winner was dead. All the time he had worked on the painting of the Wyndham Group, he had felt the absence of Winner in it. He kept sketching his figure into it in one of the prominent positions. "I can't do it without him," he had said to Gavers. "He belongs in it. The Club is not the Club without him."

"Leave room for him. Put a palm tree in his place. You can add him when he's back," Gavers had said.

As the months passed with no word of Charles Warrington's whereabouts, Robin had become increasingly nervous and depressed. Pills and liquor replaced meals. Champagne was not strong enough. He had not gone to see Amanda again, although he had said he would come back. He was torn between his sympathy for her and the growing hatred of her by the Wyndham Group. He heard incredible and vicious stories about her from various people, things he knew to be exaggerated and untrue, and he would catch himself wondering what his friends said about him. But he did not call Amanda, or see her, and he felt uneasy about it.

His mother died in July. His mother, who had always denigrated his talent and had never understood his natural sophistication, thought so little of him that she left him nothing. What money there was, close to a hundred thousand pounds, went to a remote cousin.

Convinced that he was the one person Winner would communicate with, Robin had stayed in London through the spring. In June, when the article along with the reproduction of his painting appeared in *The Sunday Observer*, Robin saw that it was sympathetic toward Amanda and ironically critical of the Club members, but he really did not think of it as a blatant and unforgivable invasion of privileged privacy. Articles sniping at the upper classes appeared frequently, usually written by someone who was not quite one of them.

Now, however, Robin learned quickly that he had become the culprit, a traitor to his own class. His social life dried up. No invitations, no phone calls, no communications came from anyone. Worst of all, it happened behind his back. Jeremy was the only one who tried to stand by him to any extent, but then he went off to South Africa on business and Robin was left completely bereft.

On his last night, he was alone in the house, and in a deep depression, the worst ever, because he felt for the first time that Winner was dead. Four months had passed without a shred of evidence turning up about his whereabouts or what had happened. *Fuck it, Charles,* he thought. *If you weren't dead, you would have let me hear from you. If you're dead, I'm dead too.* There wasn't a girl he wanted to love, a meal he wanted to eat, or a drink he wanted to drink anymore. Straight scotch would do very nicely, thank you. There was no one he wanted to leave a note for, no one he wanted to call. There wasn't a song he wanted to sing.

He rummaged drunkenly around in the storage closet in the front hall where he kept his drawing folders and finally found the series of Amanda and Chantal on *Cattivo*, the ones he had promised to send to them and had never delivered. He'd forgotten that Winner and Gavers were in several of them; even John Latimer's hulking form was in some. When he saw the familiar lines of Winner's body, sitting at the backgammon table on the yacht with Gavers, he started to cry. He burned the pictures in the sitting room fireplace, every last one of them, crumpling them up and holding them one by one until they caught fire. Knocking back a handful of pills and refilling his glass with scotch, he had one last satisfactory thought. The bastards couldn't accuse him of selling those to the newspapers, and they'd have fetched a pretty price now. They'd blame him if they could, but this time they couldn't.

He looked down at the ashes of the drawings in the tiny fireplace.

Winner was gone, Amanda's half-mad, John was dead, and Gavers didn't return his phone calls anymore.

He raised his glass to himself in the mirror.

"Fuck them," he said. "They can't do it to me anymore."

On her way home from a doctor's appointment, Amanda saw the headlines about Robin splashed all over the evening papers. Briggs was with her; they had stopped in Boots Chemists in Knightsbridge to have a prescription filled.

He heard a little noise come from her, a sort of gasp, as if someone had struck her.

"You all right, Lady Warrington?" Briggs asked, looking quickly around at the people surrounding them in the street.

Her eyes were filled with tears. She fumbled for change in her purse to pay for the papers. Briggs saw what she was trying to do and paid for them quickly himself.

"Oh, no, Robin, not you," she sobbed.

"How's that, Lady Warrington?" Briggs asked.

"Nothing, Constable Briggs, nothing at all."

She wiped the tears from her eyes and folded the newspapers under her arm, in a daze. *Charles shouldn't treat us this way*, she thought. *Charles really shouldn't treat Robin and me this way. We're the only ones who truly loved him.*

When Chantal answered the phone, she knew from Amanda's tone that something had happened. Charles? Had they found him?

"What is it, *amie?*"

"Robin. He's killed himself." Chantal could hear Amanda blowing her nose.

There was a small silence and as Amanda listened she could almost see Chantal's face, almost feel her thinking exactly what she was. The drawings, Robin's drawings of the two of them on *Cattivo*. The sunny times.

"*Le pauvre,*" Chantal said, her voice full of sympathy.

"It wasn't all because of Charles," Amanda said, almost defensively. "It could have been, and the papers are screaming that, but it was not just Charles's fault."

"What else, then?" Chantal asked. "He was so sweet, and there was such talent there. He was lost without Charles, and then his friends all turned on him."

"He drank as much as Charles. He was as burned out as Charles. His mother died last month, registering her disapproval by leaving him nothing. He was probably as manic as I'm supposed to be; I saw his moodiness once or twice and I recognized it. No one really loved Robin, you know. They all used him as their personal pet, for their amusement. Then when Charles—who I think did love him—when Charles was gone, it was over for Robin too. The straw that broke his back. Charles. But a combination of things killed him."

"Whatever it was," Chantal said, "it doesn't matter now."

"At least we loved him a little," Amanda said.

"Not enough," Chantal said.

Amanda called Chantal again. "I went to the memorial service this afternoon," she said. "It was at Saint Peter's in Eaton Square. I knew I could go in by the altar door at the far end and sit where no one could see me. Scarf on my head, dark glasses—you know. But I wanted to go, to see about Robin, for Robin. And I wanted to hear what they would have to say. Chantal, the more I see of this bunch, the more I wonder who is really crazy."

"Tell."

"There weren't many people there. Poor Robin. Gavers of course, and Neil and Rosie and Jeremy. Several of Robin's girls, all rather sweet. There was a sister and, fortunately, a rather burly cousin-in-law."

"What happened?"

"The service was short and the priest didn't waste much time on him. Suicides are not a priest's favorite topic. Then Gavers got up to give the eulogy."

"Gavers?" Chantal said. "How could he?"

"I guess he didn't want to miss a chance to prove what a friend he had been to Robin. He raised his eyes to the heavens and said 'Robin, our dear Robin, why have you done this to us? How could you leave us when we loved you so?' And he went on in that vein. It was a star performance. It made me so angry I had to slip out before I lost control of myself, so I edged out the door and sat on one of the benches in the little park there, weeping with frustration. Then I saw them when they all came out and stood around looking at each other. I couldn't move, but the burly cousin didn't waste any time. He walked up to Gavers and said something about what a bastard he was, what a hypocrite he was. 'You're responsible for Robin's death and now you ask why he left you?' He was practically yelling. Then he knocked Gavers flat and stalked off toward the Connaught. I wanted to cheer for him."

"I don't believe you. He actually said that to Gavers?"

"Chantal, I swear he did."

"What did Gavers do when he hit him?"

"What he would do. He made a quip and got up, rubbing his jaw and laughing. A reporter asked him something I couldn't hear but I heard Gavers's answer. 'I'm used to animal behavior,' he said, still grinning his head off."

"They certainly make their own rules, don't they? They killed Robin as surely as if they plunged a knife in his heart and now they blabber their love for him. Poor Robin."

"Thank God for burly cousins-in-law," Amanda said.

The coroner finally set the date of the inquest for August 27, 1974, in Westminster Coroner's Court in Horseferry Road, London W1. Twenty-nine witnesses were to be called. The first would be Amanda Warrington.

Chantal wanted to come to the inquest but Amanda wouldn't hear of it.

"It's only going to put you in a difficult position with Gavers to be seen with me. Besides, I have to get through it alone. I don't want you having to take sides."

"I already have," Chantal said. "You know that."

"Even so. Stay where you are. I'll need you later, not now."

"As you like, *amie.*"

CHAPTER 21

August 1974

When Amanda eyed the space reserved for her in the first row of the Westminster Coroner's courtroom, she jerked to a stop, her escort, Private Briggs, bumping into her. Penelope, Davina, and Richard were sitting together in the second row. She would *not* have them stare down her neck throughout the proceedings. She spotted empty seats in the third row and indicated to Briggs that she was going to sit there.

"But they've kept a place in the first row for you, Lady Warrington," Briggs said. "You're supposed to sit right up front."

"I shall sit here," Amanda said, staring coldly at him.

Briggs shrugged. He got along very well with her—but only, he knew, because he had learned not to push her. They moved into the third row together.

Amanda was wearing a gray cloche and a charcoal-gray dress, buttoned primly to the throat. Her low-heeled, closed-toe pumps were soft black Italian leather. She looked wan and alarmingly thin. Wisps of pale hair almost covered the scar at the center of her forehead at the hairline. And the hair that showed was dun-colored and lifeless—nothing like the titian mass she had once possessed.

Seated, she found herself staring at the back of Davina's rather ostentatious turquoise and diamond drop earrings. So near and yet so far, she thought.

The coroner stood up and began to speak. The jury of five men and four women turned their attention to him, as did the rest of those assembled.

"The circumstances of this inquest are the most unusual of any I have held here in my seventeen years as coroner. An inquest is not a trial under normal circumstances, but the circumstances surrounding this case cannot be construed in any way as normal. This is an investigation into the death of Jenny Boyce, twenty-six, of Shepherd's Heath in southeast London. The cause of death was cerebral hemorrage from injuries to the head from blows probably administered with a blunt instrument. One week after her death on the evening of April eleventh, warrants were issued for the arrest of Charles Keating, Eleventh Earl of Warrington for the murder of Jenny Boyce and the attempted murder of his wife, Amanda, Countess of Warrington, who is present in this courtroom.

"You are aware that Lord Warrington was last seen at one-thirty A.M. on April twelfth. You also know that I have delayed this inquest for well over four months in the hope of additional evidence or the reappearance of Lord Warrington. You also know that Lord and Lady Warrington are separated and have been involved in a bitter custody battle for their son, Lord Patrick Keating. It is fairly clear from the two letters Lord Warrington left that there is a great deal of family animosity, and there are matters which, if aired here, can only be prejudicial and painful to all those concerned. I would allow that type of testimony only if it would help this inquiry. I am allowing hearsay evidence only as it is directly involved with the actual crime, as well as allowing into evidence two letters written by Lord Warrington, since they are presumably what he would say if he were here in this court to defend himself."

Lord Warrington's financial situation was obviously desperate, the coroner continued, and not eased by having to keep two establishments going because of the separation.

"I reiterate the unusual circumstances of this inquest. Again, under normal circumstances, in a case in which no one has been charged, the proper verdict would be murder by a person or persons unknown. A murder followed by a suicide would carry the appropriate verdict for those actions. But if a coroner's court finds that a person is responsible for a murder, the court still has the power to convict that person and commit that person to trial at the Crown Court. This court has been given evidence by twenty-nine persons both directly and indirectly involved, some of whom will be called again to testify during these proceedings.

"You are all aware of what I shall refer to as family tensions, and I want to make it clear that those tensions will not be allowed to enter into the proceedings in this courtroom. Considering the animosity felt by the family, it is only after a great deal of thought that I have decided to call Lady Warrington as the first witness. A wife testifying against her husband is prohibited from describing anything beyond a physical attack on her. All questions will be confined to the actual events of the night of April eleventh, when Lady Warrington was attacked and Jenny Boyce was murdered. There will be no questions allowed that deviate from that time frame. I call the Countess of Warrington as the first witness."

The Westminster Coroner's Court was in an ugly Victorian building, but the courtroom itself had the saving grace of a domed glass ceiling, which threw shafts of light into the paneled room. It was a perfect August day in London, not too hot, with a partially clouded sky.

When Amanda sat in the witness box she was so small that her head and shoulders just appeared over the railing. Those in the back of the courtroom could barely see or hear her. During the time that Amanda testified, light from the skylight above dappled her shoulders and struck her face, giving her the look of a tired but haloed angel. Those in the courtroom who spent the hours hanging on her every word, and watching her during the recesses called for court business and instruction, were struck by her eerie quality. All through her testimony, her voice was so low that she had to be reminded constantly to speak up.

In the last row, Jenny Boyce's father strained to hear her. Albert Boyce had come to the inquest alone; Jenny's mother had remained at home, her health broken by the shock of her daughter's murder. Jenny's estranged husband had been located and had given testimony in private earlier. He had proved that he had not seen or heard from his wife in over a year. A merchant seaman, he was cleared of any possible involvement because his ship had been no closer to England than the South China Sea.

Before the first question was put to her, Amanda saw Gavers and Jeremy Morton, seated in the first row. Neither of them acknowledged her existence—in the witness box or on the planet for that matter—even when her gaze fell on them.

After Amanda was put through the formalities of giving her name and place of residence, the coroner established that she and her husband had been separated in September of 1973. Then he asked "Did he never threaten you?"

"Never."

"How well did your husband know Jenny Boyce?"

"He saw her a few times when he came to pick up my son on the weekends, every other one, when he was allowed to see him or dropped him off after school."

The coroner asked her about Jenny's background. Amanda replied that she was a cheerful girl. She had boyfriends, including one of the bartenders who worked at the local pub.

"And her regular day off was Thursday?"

"Yes, and the weekends when my husband took Patrick with him."

Asked about Jenny's physical size, she answered that they were approximately the same height but that Jenny was not as thin as she.

The coroner then led up to the night of the murder.

"Why did she change her night out?"

"She had a terrible cold and wanted to change to Friday. She didn't ask until Thursday afternoon, but it didn't matter to me which night she took off."

The coroner asked Amanda to describe the evening of April 11, from teatime on. He interrupted her to ask about the locks on the front and back doors and on the windows of the house. At eight P.M., Patrick was doing his homework in her room and she was watching television. Jenny had gone to bed. Then, shortly before ten, Jenny had knocked on the door and said she was going downstairs to make tea.

Amanda's voice became softer and softer, and she seemed to be fading into a ghostlike figure. As she described the noise she heard as she went along the hall toward the kitchen, calling for Jenny, her voice faltered and she stopped.

After a moment the coroner prompted, "Can you tell us what happened then?"

She shook her shoulders slightly. "Before I was hit on the head I had this feeling that something awful was about to happen and I was afraid. I knew someone was there, not Jenny. It could only have been for a second. Then I felt the blow."

"How many times were you hit?"

"Five, six, I don't know. The first one sent me reeling. I wasn't exactly counting. The blows kept coming."

"Did your assailant speak to you at the time?"

"No. I thought I was going to be killed and I was so frightened I began to scream."

"After that, what happened?"

She looked beseechingly at the coroner. He made a gesture, almost nodding his head, directing her to continue.

"He got me by the throat then—he was trying to choke me. I bit him in the shoulder and I kept biting him. Then a voice said, 'You fucking bitch, you fucking murderous bitch.' " Her voice was barely audible.

"Did you recognize the voice?"

She inhaled and held her head up, her fingers touching the scar at her hairline.

"Yes," she replied.

"Can you tell me who it was?"

"My husband," she said, her voice clear now.

"What did you do then?"

"I pulled the mask off him. It was my husband. We kept fighting and then I felt my opals break and scatter all over the floor and I remember thinking what difference does it make, let him kill me. I gave up then. We were at the foot of the stairs. I could see his face and could tell he gave up then too. I said I would help him, no matter what had happened to Jenny. I thought I was going to be sick and then he helped me upstairs into the bedroom. He sent Patrick to bed and went into the bathroom for a cloth—to clean my face, he said, but I was terrified he was going to come back and kill me then. That's when I ran out of the house, down to the Farrier's Forge, our local pub."

"Is that everything you remember?"

She stared at him. He had instructed her in private session not to include Charles's admission that he had killed Jenny. That was considered hearsay. She could describe the attack and testify that it was Charles's voice she had recognized and that it was Charles who had tried to kill her. She had followed instructions and now she was being asked if that was all she remembered. She was suddenly very tired. It was torture for her, all of it. "It's difficult to remember every detail now," she said. "It was almost five months ago."

Amanda had given testimony to the police, to Scotland Yard, and to Dr. Rutherson, over and over, and it had been difficult enough then. Now, to have to describe the battle again, in detail, for strangers and members of the press, and knowing that none of the family believed one word she was saying, was agony. It proved to be nothing compared to the agony of cross-examination. Brian Watson questioned her on behalf of the police and then Sir Keith Graham, Q.C., Penelope's counsel, was given his chance.

"Is it not true," he began, "that you harbor a bitter hatred for your husband? Have you not expressed that hatred often?"

The coroner slammed down his gavel and admonished the Queen's Counsel. "I made it quite clear at the beginning of this inquest that we would have no such questions. If you continue this way, I shall ask you to take your seat."

Sir Keith was not to be herded.

"I withdraw the question, and I shall take my seat, but I would like to state for the record that I am doing so because there is very little point in my continuing. I have the inescapable and unpleasant duty of suggesting that Lady Warrington is not telling the truth, has not told the truth in the past, and will not tell the truth in the future. There will be no further questions to the Countess of Warrington from me." The supercilious emphasis on her title made Sir Keith's attitude toward Amanda Warrington quite clear.

The next evidence presented was of a statement from young Patrick Keating. It was read out by the policeman who had taken it during the week following the murder of Jenny Boyce. In it, Patrick had described the events of the evening of April 11.

I was watching television in my mother's room after finishing my homework and I fell asleep. I sort of woke up when Jenny knocked on the door and I heard her ask my mother if she would like her to make my mother's eggnog. My mother said at first she was going to do it but then she let Jenny do it. I was still sleepy and the next thing I heard was my mother telling me that she was going to go down and see about Jenny because it was taking her such a long time. I really woke up a little while later when I thought I heard my mother scream. The television was still on and I thought maybe I had heard the scream on the television. A few minutes after that, my mother and father came into the bedroom together.

Mummy had blood all over her and she was crying. My father helped her into the room and put her down on the bed. My mother told me to turn off the television and go upstairs. My father said he would come up and see me later, but he never did. I don't know how much blood was on Mummy but there was a lot on her face and in her hair. My father had dark clothes on so I didn't see if there was blood on him. I wondered what had happened but I didn't ask. My mother said she was all right when I asked her, and that my father would take care of her, so I went upstairs and got into bed and read my book. I didn't hear any noise from their room.

That was the last I saw of them that evening, but later my

grandmother came and woke me up and took me home to stay
with her. There was a police officer with us and I asked my grandmother what had happened. She told me Jenny had had an accident but she didn't say what it was.

I was surprised to see Daddy at our house on a Thursday evening. I spent the weekend before with him and my aunt Davina in
the country, but he and my mother were living apart, so he hadn't
been in the house, only to come to get me. It was different for him
to be there but I didn't ask why he was there. My mother said they
had had a fight but that he was coming back to live with us.

While the statement was being read, Briggs became aware that
Amanda was showing clear signs of distress. He felt sorry for her—she
was so frail and thin. In the four and a half months since he had been
assigned to protect her he had gotten to know her habits well and had
seen her have attacks of nerves like this. She was rocking back and forth,
back and forth, and he could feel the tension in her body. She was
strung up like wire. He knew the kid's statement was upsetting her.
Having to give her own testimony was more than enough for her in one
day, without having to hear the statement from her child. By and large,
she had been gentle and polite to him and she often seemed grateful for
his presence. He hoped she would look at him now for reassurance, but
her eyes remained on the policeman who was reading her son's statements. When it was finished, Amanda stared down into her lap, twisting
her hands. The rocking stopped.

The next witnesses called were Scotland Yard Murder Squad investigators and police officers. Ronald Manners, Chief Superintendent from
King's Road and in charge of the case for the police, was the last witness
of the day. He was asked to describe the scene in the Farrier's Forge
when Lady Warrington had burst in. He had arrived ten minutes later
and had questioned everyone about what had happened. He had sent
one of his men to the hospital in the ambulance with Lady Warrington
and proceeded directly to the Warrington residence with another. He
then described in detail the finding of Jenny's body in the sail bag.

He was asked about the absence of light. "Someone tampered with the
fuse box," he said. "The bulb was working in the light fixture when I
fixed up the fuse box." He described the condition of the downstairs hall
and the kitchen. Blood had been found thirty feet across the room where
Jenny Boyce's body was found. There was blood on the ceiling and
walls, as well as on the floor. Manners described it as looking as if the
blood had been sprayed on the walls with a hose.

On that grisly note the inquest was adjourned until the following morning.

Penelope, the Dowager Countess of Warrington, was the first witness called on the second day. Sir Keith Graham, representing her, was there to make sure there would be something in the court record favorable to her son and the Warrington name, anything that would show the unfairness of this lopsided inquest in which Charles Warrington, accused of murder and attempted murder, wasn't even there to defend himself.

Sir Keith had desisted in questioning Amanda Warrington, largely to put a dramatic twist on the point he wanted in the court record—namely, that she was lying. The Dowager felt—knew, rather—that public sympathy had begun to run high in favor of her daughter-in-law. It was that damned article in *The Observer* that had been so destructive to them all.

She would do the best she could under the circumstances. With the restrictions imposed by the coroner, Charles would be made the culprit from beginning to end. She chose to stand in the witness box as she testified that she had received a phone call from her son at around eleven o'clock on the evening of April 11.

"He sounded highly shocked," she told the coroner and the jury. "This was the first time I spoke to him. He told me he had been passing by the house and had interrupted a fight in the basement kitchen between his wife and a man he'd seen attacking her. The man rushed out past him when he went to her aid. He said that something terrible had happened there and that I should go to the house at once and make sure my grandson was safe and take him home with me. He told me to ring up Richard Marston if I needed help. I rang him, but as there was no answer, I went to Royal Hospital Road and found the police already there. The detective sergeant informed me that my grandson's nanny was dead and that my daughter-in-law was in the hospital. He then asked me if my son lived in the house and I replied that my son and his wife had separated some time before. I explained that she was a manic-depressive.

"I knew when my son called that something was terribly wrong at the house. The detective sergeant accompanied me back to my home with my grandson. It was after one in the morning when my son telephoned again. He asked about my grandson and after telling him he was safe and asleep, I asked him where he was. I got nowhere with that, but I then told him that the police were with me and I asked if he would care to speak to them. He said 'No, not now.' He said he would ring them in the morning and that he would ring me again then. That was the last time I have heard from him."

At the end of her testimony, Amanda watched her slide into her seat in the row directly in front of her. The Dowager did not deign to glance at her. She simply looked through her.

The detective sergeant from Scotland Yard testified next. In investigating Lord Warrington's personal finances, he had learned that a total of more than twenty-five thousand pounds was owed to several London banks, which he named, and gave the amounts owed to each. The Dowager Countess had advanced her son five thousand pounds a few months before his disappearance to help defray the costs of the custody battle, which her son had lost. The costs were approximately thirty thousand pounds for the custody hearing, and included counsel and costs for Lady Warrington, plus her outstanding medical bills. Several of Lord Warrington's friends had refused to disclose if they had lent him any money. The best estimate the detective sergeant could make of Lord Warrington's indebtedness was eighty thousand pounds.

Dr. Roger Leith, the court pathologist, was the next to testify.

"I conducted the postmortem on Jenny Boyce on April twelfth, the morning after the murder. There were five blows to her head, one over each of her eyes, one on her left cheek, and two to the left side of her head near the base of her neck. Her scalp had been split twice on the front left side of her head and there was another split above the ear, again on the left. She had multiple bruises on both her arms and her hands, which she probably used to defend herself. These bruises and additional ones on her neck were of a type compatible with having come from forceful hands, rather than a blunt object. After the second blow, her skull split, although a more descriptive word would be *exploded*. Blood had poured from both her nose and her mouth, and some had been taken into her lungs. Each of the five blows caused deep damage to her brain, and either the first or second blow caused her death. She was probably unconscious after the first blow, and certainly she was at the time of death."

Amanda began to rock slightly again. Briggs saw her turn and try to look behind her, and he knew she was looking for Jenny Boyce's father.

The court pathologist's horrific description of Jenny Boyce's death was a grisly memory brought back to life.

"The weapon used was an ordinary tire iron. One end had been bound with an Ace bandage. When Chief Superintendent Manners found it on the floor in the hall, the bandage was soaked with two types of blood. The forensic experts have identified them as Types A and B, those of Lady Warrington and of Jenny Boyce. The tire iron was certainly the murder weapon."

Dr. Leith continued: "No signs of sexual assault or intercourse were found in the autopsy."

The coroner asked a question. "Would it not be difficult for a man in the dark to manage to get an inert body into a canvas sail bag?" The "Harrow Mob" had been quoted as saying it would be impossible for one man to do such a thing. The coroner wanted that supposition set straight.

"Not necessarily," the pathologist said. "The girl weighed less than eight stone, about one hundred and five pounds. From the position of her body she looked as if she had been folded in two—in other words, her head was doubled up against her knees, with her arms and legs at the open end of the sack. It would not be impossible at all; it would only be awkward to do."

He produced photographs of Jenny's body and of Amanda, taken at Chelsea Hospital while she was unconscious, and X rays of both Jenny's and Amanda's heads. He was satisfied that the same weapon had been used on both of them.

The next witness was Richard Marston. He stated that he had known Lord Warrington for many years and had last seen him when he brought his son for the weekend, about ten days before his disappearance. He told of receiving a letter from Lord Warrington at his home in Hampshire on the Monday after the murder, a letter which he had turned over to the police at once. It was postmarked Faversham, the local post office nearest the Riggs house in Kent. He had written the letter from there and Mrs. Riggs had posted it the next day at Lord Warrington's request. The letter was read out by Marston.

"Dear Richard," it read. "Under the most bizarre and unbelievable circumstances tonight, which I did tell my mother about, I interrupted a fight in the kitchen in Royal Hospital Road. A man was attacking Amanda and when I let myself in he rushed out past me. Amanda hysterically accused me of hiring him. When I was able to calm her down and send Patrick to bed, I went to get a cloth to clean her up and when I returned she had fled the house. I know how strong her evidence will be against me so I will lie low for a bit. Take care of things for me and if possible, keep Patrick with you. Amanda hates me, as you know, and she will try to influence Patrick against me. I cannot stand in the dock for bankruptcy nor for attempted murder. Please explain to Patrick when he can understand, look after him, and tell him how much I loved him. Yours ever, Charles."

"Thank you, Mr. Marston."

Rosie Riggs was the next witness. Buster Manners wanted to hear what she had to say under oath more than he did any of the others. He had questioned the principals more than once, some of them repeatedly. But to his knowledge this little lady, making her way to the stand now, was the only one who had lied to him. She knew he knew it. Buster had done some exhaustive research and investigation of Rosie Riggs. He had also known her late father, a brilliant judge and a man Buster had respected.

Manners was convinced that the key to the disappearance of Charles Warrington lay with both Rosie and her husband, but more with her. Both knew more than they had told. Fair enough, Manners thought. One didn't get the right answers if he didn't ask the right questions, and he hadn't. He had been crippled by a lack of knowledge of the tribal rites and customs of the "Harrow Mob," but he knew a liar when he smelled one, and Rosie Riggs was a liar.

Manners wondered if the woman in front of him, this one in the green suit and the pink hat, was the true Rosie Riggs. As he watched her taking the stand, his thoughts went back to the first day at Faversham when he'd questioned her. She hadn't looked as trendy as she did today. She had been a wren in country garb of an old shetland twin set and woolen trousers. Her face had been scrubbed clean of even a trace of makeup. And she had an innocent demeanor, as well as a good mind. She was no dummy, Manners had realized at the moment he'd started questioning her.

Now the coroner was questioning her. He went right to the point.

"Lord Warrington arrived at your house at what time on April eleventh, Mrs. Riggs? It would please this court if you would tell us your version of the events from the time he arrived until he left. You may proceed."

"I was in my bedroom reading when I heard the dog barking. I went to the window where I have a view of the driveway. Lord Warrington was there, so I went down to let him in. He looked very upset and I took him to the study and fixed him a drink. He told me that in passing his house earlier he had interrupted a fight between his wife and a man who seemed to be attacking her in the basement kitchen. He had gone to her aid at once. The man rushed past him out the front door, and his wife hysterically accused him of having sent the man to kill her. He surmised that this man had killed the nanny. He told me that he had taken his wife up to the bedroom to reassure her and clean some of the blood off of her. He said that when he returned from the bathroom his wife had fled from the house. He knew that she would try to make it look as if he had done it—he repeated that she had accused him of hiring the man to kill her. I know this to be impossible. He could not hurt a fly and although he had been most unhappy, miserable, about losing custody of his son, he would never try to harm his wife.

"He had planned, he told me, to call a doctor after he'd gotten some blood off of her, but when she fled he knew things would look bad for him. He cleared out of there and came down to our house to try to figure out what he should do. He called his mother, who told him that Patrick was safe and that the police were there. He told her to tell them that he would ring them first thing in the morning, and that he would ring her then as well. He wrote two notes, to Richard Marston and to Jeremy Morton, and asked me if I would post them for him the next morning. I did not see the contents of the notes. I tried to calm him down and asked him to stay overnight with us. He said no, he had to get back up to London."

As she spoke, her voice got breathier and breathier, like a young girl trying to impress a first beau. Her eyes were wide and she was playing the same delicate innocent that Manners had seen in Faversham. *Go on,* Manners thought, *you're doing well. Let's hear what else.*

"I asked him if he'd like some coffee, since he was going to drive this late, and he said yes. After he drank only one cup, he rose to leave. It was then I forcefully advised him to talk to his solicitor before he spoke to the police. He said he would. I took him to the door, and—"

"Mrs. Riggs," the coroner interrupted, "was there blood on his clothing?"

"Not that I could see. He had a polo-neck shirt on and dark trousers, but if there was any blood, I certainly didn't notice it."

There she went, Manners thought scornfully. "Blood?" she had said to him. "What blood? There wasn't any blood." She was telling the same story, and Manners was annoyed and frustrated that the coroner wasn't asking questions that would bring more pertinent answers . . . or at least make it more difficult for her to lie.

"Did you see the car he left in?"

"Of course. There was a strong wind blowing, so I didn't go out, but I saw a small car, not his blue Mercedes." Truth, every word of it truth.

"What did you do when he left?"

"I went to bed."

"Have you heard anything from Lord Warrington since that time?"

"Nothing," Rosie said.

Her palms rested on the railing of the witness box. She, too, had stood during her testimony, and Manners noticed that she was in complete control of her hands. In Faversham he had observed her looking at them as if they could be witnesses against her, deliberately taming them in her lap. Now they lay untrembling on the railing. The wide-eyed innocent. Manners wished he could ask her a few questions.

"What about the letters? Did you post them?"

"No," she said. "I put them in the box at the gate when I went out the next day and the postman picked them up." Impeccably, the truth.

"Thank you, Mrs. Riggs. That is all I have to ask you."

Next, Sir Keith Graham questioned her, helping her to paint a word picture for the jury of a woman who felt that the description of the domestic scene of the night of April 11 had sounded no more serious than others in the past. She had not been unduly concerned. Rosie ventured the opinion that the marriage had never been a happy one, due to the emotional instability of Amanda Warrington. When her husband, Neil, had told her that the nanny was dead, she was sure Lord Warrington was innocent. He couldn't have killed the nanny or attacked his wife. He couldn't kill a fly. She doubted very much that he had attacked Lady Warrington—no matter what Lady Warrington had said in her sworn testimony. As far as Rosie was concerned, the police ought to be after the man who had been in the house that night. He was the murderer of the innocent girl. Why was he still at large? He was the one who should be searched out, apprehended, and tried, so that Charles Warrington's name would be cleared.

Again Manners addressed silent remarks to her: *A horrible surprise to you, wasn't it, Rosie Riggs, that anyone would think Lord Warrington had done the dirty deed? Wait until you hear what the forensic boys have to say. You've done good, Rosie girl, but not good enough.*

Rosie knew that Manners had been watching and listening to every word she said in the witness box, as if she herself were the murderer. She had reason to be afraid of him. She knew he would have told the coroner and Scotland Yard what he suspected, but what he suspected and what could be proven were two entirely different things. They had nothing to go on, nothing. She had been meticulous in her testimony; her intelligence warned her to tell the truth. She had not perjured herself in any of her answers—it was all a matter of interpretation. Had she seen the car he left in? Indeed she had. What did you do after Lord Warrington left? I went to bed. *I did for a while.* Have you heard from him? No, I have not, *but I am not the only one concerned.*

When she returned to her seat, Neil took her hand, holding it tightly. It was cold and shaking. He moved closer to her.

"Jeremy's turn now," he said. "You were excellent. It's almost over."

"I'm sure they will convict him in absentia. They believe Amanda," Rosie said quietly into his ear.

"We'll see," Neil said.

The only sign of outward annoyance that the coroner showed throughout the inquest was during his examination of Jeremy Morton.

"My name is Jeremy Morton. My residence is Number Seventy-two Lennox Gardens, London. Lord Warrington and I have been friends for over twenty years. We are both members of the Wyndham Club."

The coroner looked at him scathingly.

"Does the fact that you are both members of a gaming club put you in a special category, Mister Morton?" His emphasis on the word *Mister* was clear. The coroner had been antagonized by Jeremy Morton from the beginning, when he had been informed by Manners that the envelope to the letter Warrington had written to him was missing.

"What is your occupation, Mr. Morton? Do you work at the Wyndham Club?"

"I am a company director."

"Are you the one who lost the envelope to the letter written to you on the night of the murder by Lord Warrington?"

"I received a letter at my club, White's, on Monday. You have that letter now."

"Would you be so kind as to read it to us, sir?" The coroner handed a copy of the letter to Jeremy.

" 'My dear Jeremy,' " he read. " 'I have had a night of incredible happenings. However, I do not want to involve you with any of this, only to tell you that the car will eventually come back unharmed to you. Yours always, Charles.' "

"And where is the envelope to this letter?"

"I think I must have thrown it away. I don't recall the postmark."

"You *think* you threw it away? Knowing the importance of the letter, have you not searched your mind since the chief inspector questioned you as to what you actually did with the envelope? This cavalier attitude is damaging to Lord Warrington, I must tell you." The coroner's voice was brittle, and he had dropped his normal friendly-uncle demeanor, revealing the tough administrator he was in reality.

"I cannot recall what happened to the envelope. I believe I threw it in the wastebasket at the club."

"Interesting that Richard Marston, who received a letter from Lord Warrington on the same Monday, brought it immediately to the police. Interesting that the postmark on that letter was Faversham, near the Riggs home, where Lord Warrington was last seen. Interesting that there were smears on the envelope of the letter to Mr. Marston and that these smears turned out to be blood, as established by the forensic experts. Interesting that you have no recollection of what happened to this most valuable piece of evidence. It could be construed as your having withheld information from the police. Please proceed with your testimony in regard to the car you lent to Lord Warrington."

The coroner shifted his position so that his back was almost turned to Morton, and he let his gaze wander over the members of the jury. This parade of snobs with their upper-class manners and their patronizing air toward the police and Scotland Yard was exemplified by the behavior of Jeremy Morton. These people seemed actually to believe that they were superior to others and above the law.

Jeremy was asked to identify the blue Austin from photographs and was asked when and why he had lent it to Lord Warrington.

"He asked me to lend him a car some time in March. I don't recall the actual date. Lord Warrington had been having trouble with his Mercedes for some time. I offered to lend him mine but he was too well-mannered to take my better car, so he took the Austin. I was delighted to lend it to him."

He was shown photographs of the car, which he identified as his.

Jeremy was dismissed.

Dr. Richard Ferrara, the senior scientific officer with the Metropolitan Police and an expert on blood groupings, was called on the last morning of the inquest. The forensic evidence left little doubt about the identity of the person who had killed Jenny Boyce and attempted to kill Lady Warrington.

Dr. Ferrara had made a careful examination of the house in Royal Hospital Road. Lady Warrington's blood type was A; Jenny Boyce's was B. Splashes of blood found on the walls, ceiling, and floor in the kitchen were of Type B and belonged to Jenny Boyce. Those in the downstairs hall, on the stairway, and in the bedroom were a combination of Types A and B. Miss Boyce's blood, which had been on her murderer's clothes, had intermingled with Lady Warrington's during the battle in the hallway. Along with blood samples, particles of skin and hair of both types had been found in the house and in the car.

Extensive blood smearings had been identified on the front seat of the car Lord Warrington had borrowed from Mr. Morton which had been abandoned in Folkestone. There were additional smearings on the dashboard, the steering wheel, and the door on the driver's side. All of the smearings were of Type A, similar to Lady Warrington's, and Type B, similar to Jenny Boyce's.

Dr. Ferrara had examined the murder weapon. The coroner asked Dr. Ferrara if there was evidence that the blood found on the murder weapon was from both women.

"The bloodstains were from both groups."

"Would you say the murder weapon was used on both women?"

"It certainly seems so. The mingling of blood types makes that evident."

"And did you also examine the house of Mr. and Mrs. Riggs, the last known place where Lord Warrington was seen?"

"I did."

"When did you examine the house?"

"Not until one week after the murder."

"Were bloodstains found in the house?"

"No, none."

"Thank you, Dr. Ferrara."

Chief Superintendent Ronald Manners was the last witness called. He described an experiment carried out with one of his men to ascertain if the interior of the kitchen could be seen from the street. "I positioned my officer in the kitchen and I looked through the slats of the blinds on the windows. I could see nothing, not even his legs, from any position on the street."

"Have you been able to find any trace of another party being in the house that night?"

"None whatsoever."

"You saw the amount of blood on Lady Warrington in the Farrier's Forge. You were the first in the house, one of the first to see the car, and the first to question Mrs. Riggs after the murder. Were you aware of any bloodstains at the Riggs house?"

"There were none that we could see."

"Don't you think that unusual?"

"Most unusual," Buster Manners said, his eyes boring into those of Rosie Riggs.

"Thank you, Chief Superintendent."

Something bothered the coroner. Why was there no trace of blood at the Riggs house? The coroner was well aware that Manners believed the Riggs woman was lying. No sign of blood in her house, when the car, the Royal Hospital Road house, and Lady Warrington's clothing had all been covered with blood? Mrs. Riggs had been the last person known to have seen Lord Warrington. He had spent several hours with her. Why no blood?

The foreman of the jury requested permission to ask a question before the coroner summed up.

"During this hearing, we have heard almost nothing about the nanny who has been murdered. Yet we have a witness, the barman from the Farrier's Forge, who testified that Lady Warrington came into the pub screaming 'Help me, help me, he's murdered the nanny.' How did she know the nanny had been murdered?"

The coroner called the foreman to the bench and explained that hearsay evidence, given in private by Lady Warrington but forbidden in the courtroom, showed that Lord Warrington had told her that he had killed Jenny Boyce, and begged her to help him, which she had agreed to do in order to save her own life.

The inquest would resume with the coroner's summing up.

The coroner's summing up for the jury lasted ninety minutes.

Amanda sat watching impassively as the coroner spoke, looking neither to her right nor her left, but taking in the overall scene in the now familiar courtroom. For three days, except for her hours in the witness box, she had sat in the same seat, worn the same carefully chosen outfit, and been escorted by Briggs. And for three days she and Briggs had taken luncheon at the nearby Rose and Crown pub. Some of the spectators in the courtroom had chosen the same place, as had a few of the jurors. When several newspapermen had attempted to question Amanda on their first day there, Briggs had made them leave her alone.

The others—Richard and Davina, with Penelope, Neil and Rosie, Gavers, and Jeremy—joined forces for the lunch break in a fashionable

French bistro in Elverston Street. The press reaped more there, openly eavesdropping for tidbits of conversation from the family and close friends of the missing Earl, more than they would get from his wife in the Rose and Crown. Amanda could easily imagine the tenor of the conversation as the inner circle dissected the morning's testimony, voicing opinions in their authoritative voices, spouting forth the edicts of the privileged classes.

For three days Amanda's eyes had rested unavoidably on her sister's back and, at such close quarters, on whatever jewels Davina had decided to sport that day. Today, she was wearing a triple strand of pearls plus a large diamond ring. Was Davina's taste becoming just a little vulgar? Amanda wondered. Her mother-in-law, Penelope, displayed no such extravagance on her person and continued to wear the same plaid dress each day. Good solid Labour dressing. Rosie and Neil, in the same row as Amanda but on the far left side of the aisle, were not easy for her to observe. She had seen Rosie only when she testified. Her pink hat had been becoming, with the blue of her eyes, but she still had that dreadful heavy skin. Rosie had always looked like a prune to Amanda. Gavers and Jeremy sat together in the first row on the aisle, looking as if they were at an opening night. Gavers hadn't had to testify. He was mere decoration in this part of the affair.

The only person in the courtroom who was emotional about the proceedings, aside from Amanda herself, was Mr. Boyce, Jenny's father. Amanda had nodded courteously to him when she left for lunch the first day and he had nodded back. She had seen him once before, when he had come to the house unannounced for Jenny's clothes. She had cried when she found out who he was. Her heart went out to him now but there was no necessity for them to speak.

Jenny Boyce, the victim, seemed of no importance at the inquest, rather than the reason for its being. After Amanda's testimony and that of the forensic experts, her name had barely been mentioned. No, Amanda thought, this inquest was not about poor Jenny. It was about her. That's all anyone was interested in: Was she lying? Was she crazy? Or could the mad wife possibly be telling the truth?

Oh, there were those she missed today, those she loved and would never see again, she thought, barely hearing the coroner's voice as he continued his summation. Two of them gone forever, her father and John. Strange, she'd had only two years with either of them. Neither of them would ever have let this happen to her, would they? *John, dear friend, dear dead friend, dear lover.* If he had lived, this would never have happened. He would not have allowed it. They never closed ranks against John, because they knew his power, and oddly enough, Amanda thought, if she had left Charles and gone to John, she might have become one of them. Wasn't that odd? They hated her because they did not want her to have Charles. She had taken him from them, been loved by him, and they could not obliterate her. Had she been John's, they would have accepted her—they would not have dared not to. They knew his affectionate contempt for them. They knew he understood them and accepted them for what they couldn't help being. *John, I miss you today.*

And Charles, where was he? Why was he not there to defend himself? she thought. Was he alive? Alive to tell them that he never meant to kill that innocent girl, alive to tell them that he didn't mean to try to kill Amanda? It was a passing madness, madness that was only momentary. *We all have times like that and we must be forgiven.* John was right. She should have left Charles, but John knew that she loved Charles, that she couldn't help loving him. *Charles, I miss you today.*

And Patrick, her darling child, her only son. She missed him so. Little by little they were taking Patrick away from her. They were succeeding in turning him into one of them. After this, it would be even harder for her to keep him. Never mind. The magic wand of history might touch his shoulder one day. He would be a good Warrington. By the time he reached manhood, this terrible tragedy of his father's disappearance and his mother's instability would be over and done with. Something in the blood would enable him to bring goodness and victory back to the Warrington name. Poor baby, having to tell them what he saw that night. *Put it away from you, Patrick. It never really happened. Don't ever think about that night, those moments when you saw what you had seen before, but without the blood. Patrick, my darling, be one of them, but do not be like them.*

And Robin. Robin gone. *I was your friend,* she thought, *and in your way, you were mine.* Robin had come to her in the hospital, wept for her, for all of them, and she could still feel his tears on her arm. She would never forget the night he took her to John's Polish party, the night it began. And she would never forget or forgive Robin's death. They'd closed ranks against him, one of their own, with more brutality than they had ever been able to deal out to her. They'd killed him. They had no excuse. With all his wit and sweetness, with all his love of them, they'd turned on him, and someday they would all pay for it. *Robin, I miss you today.*

The coroner finished his summation and the jury was sent out.

In the warmth of the August day, the atmosphere in the courtroom was soporific. The coroner had excused those who wanted to leave the room while the jury was out. Practically no one had left. If the verdict was not returned by the end of the day's business, less than an hour from now, the jury would be sequestered. They could wait and see if the verdict would come in today.

Amanda yawned several times—which the press took note of. *And what will I have when all of this is over,* she wondered. *What will happen to me?* What would happen about the debts, the money Charles owed to everyone? For almost five months she had been living on money from Charles's solicitor: forty pounds a week for her; twenty-five for the nanny. What would happen now? It would be different; nothing would be the same after the jury's decision.

I am an ill woman, she thought. *I know I have an illness and sometimes I have it under control.* She had it under control now. She hoped it wouldn't come back, as she hoped the migraines would never come back. But the inquest wasn't helping much. And as ill as she was, she thought, she had not planned to kill her husband the way he had planned to kill her.

Thirty-seven minutes later, the jury returned to the courtroom. "Have you reached a verdict?" the coroner asked.

"We have, sir," the foreman replied.

The coroner read out the verdict.

"Charles Henry Edward Keating, Earl of Warrington, did on the night of April 11, 1974, in the City of Westminster, murder Jenny Boyce."

The pandemonium in the courtroom was subdued by his next statement.

"I will record that Jenny Boyce died from head injuries and that her murder was committed by the Earl of Warrington. In this case, there is no one I can commit to the Criminal Court for trial because we do not know the whereabouts of Lord Warrington. Should he return, he will be charged with the additional offense of attempted murder of his wife, Amanda Mary, Countess of Warrington. This case will remain open on the file. This inquest is adjourned. God save the Queen."

CHAPTER 22

On the street outside the courtroom, Rosie turned to Davina. They were standing at the curb, oblivious to the cameras trained on them, pretending not to hear questions shouted at them and not responding to anything asked of them.

"We've just got out in time," Rosie said.

"Yes, barely, but I think we'll make it. Where are Neil and Richard?" Davina was impatient.

"Looking for that idiot chauffeur. He was supposed to be right here when we came out. It's such a nuisance to have had this hearing run on till the day of the d'Avo wedding."

"Everything about this has been a nuisance, including that ridiculous verdict. Really, how can they convict a man like Charles? And a man who isn't here to defend himself?"

"If the boys don't show up with that damned car soon, we're going to miss the wedding. Chiquita d'Avo is going to be furious. These blasted photographers . . ."

"Here they come. Finally. It's too ridiculous, really. I hate this whole thing."

"Not as much as I. At least you didn't have to testify," Rosie said.

"I thought you were quite marvelous yesterday," Davina cooed.

The car drew up, with Richard in the front seat. Neil opened the door to the back for them and waved the girls in.

"Come on, come on. We're going to be late. It's an hour to Woodstock."

"Did you say goodbye to Penelope?" Rosie asked Davina, getting into the car. "She's right there. We really should speak to her."

Buster Manners was there. He had not spoken to her since giving his testimony the day before.

"Are you all right, Lady Warrington?" he asked. "Let me help you into the car. Take my arm."

Amanda looked at him vaguely, vacantly, as if she had never seen him before.

"I'm quite all right, thank you," she said in a stiff, small voice. "My husband has just been convicted of murder and attempted murder. My husband is not here presently but he is alive and he will come back to me some day. You wait and see."

She got into the car with Briggs. Manners leaned in and took the liberty of putting his hand on her arm. She was so thin.

"I hope so, Lady Warrington. I do hope so."

Gavers had invited Jeremy to Melbridge for the weekend, along with several others. The last summer weekend was an annual event at Melbridge and usually great fun. This year the mood was considerably dampened by the result of the inquest, even though most of those present had expected the verdict after Amanda's testimony.

Jeremy arrived on Friday in time to visit his favorites, the pair of clouded leopards. He changed for dinner and when he came down, the Riggses had arrived from Faversham, Rosie so vituperatively bitter about the jury's decision that Neil took her home soon after dinner. The papers were filled with nothing but the inquest, and conversation had been heated all through dinner about the unfairness of the trial. Jeremy could tell that Gavers was sick of it, as he was. The coroner had embarrassed him badly—deliberately, it seemed.

"Nightcap?" Gavers asked after the others had retired.

"Why not?" Jeremy said. "At least it's over."

"The inquest is over," Gavers said testily. "But that's all. The affair is going to go on forever and Amanda will no doubt sell her version to the press now. We can anticipate that."

They went into Gavers's study. Jeremy glanced around the room at the familiar objects and photographs, all of Gavers's distinct memorabilia, everything with a story. The Stubbs tiger hung on a wall near his desk.

"Hallo," he said when he saw it. "I didn't know you'd brought that here."

"It's been here since the Club was sold," Gavers said. "Where it belongs." He brought a brandy for each of them and they settled down on the big leather couch, feet up on the table in front of it.

Buster Manners was there. He had not spoken to her since giving his testimony the day before.

"Are you all right, Lady Warrington?" he asked. "Let me help you into the car. Take my arm."

Amanda looked at him vaguely, vacantly, as if she had never seen him before.

"I'm quite all right, thank you," she said in a stiff, small voice. "My husband has just been convicted of murder and attempted murder. My husband is not here presently but he is alive and he will come back to me some day. You wait and see."

She got into the car with Briggs. Manners leaned in and took the liberty of putting his hand on her arm. She was so thin.

"I hope so, Lady Warrington. I do hope so."

Gavers had invited Jeremy to Melbridge for the weekend, along with several others. The last summer weekend was an annual event at Melbridge and usually great fun. This year the mood was considerably dampened by the result of the inquest, even though most of those present had expected the verdict after Amanda's testimony.

Jeremy arrived on Friday in time to visit his favorites, the pair of clouded leopards. He changed for dinner and when he came down, the Riggses had arrived from Faversham, Rosie so vituperatively bitter about the jury's decision that Neil took her home soon after dinner. The papers were filled with nothing but the inquest, and conversation had been heated all through dinner about the unfairness of the trial. Jeremy could tell that Gavers was sick of it, as he was. The coroner had embarrassed him badly—deliberately, it seemed.

"Nightcap?" Gavers asked after the others had retired.

"Why not?" Jeremy said. "At least it's over."

"The inquest is over," Gavers said testily. "But that's all. The affair is going to go on forever and Amanda will no doubt sell her version to the press now. We can anticipate that."

They went into Gavers's study. Jeremy glanced around the room at the familiar objects and photographs, all of Gavers's distinct memorabilia, everything with a story. The Stubbs tiger hung on a wall near his desk.

"Hallo," he said when he saw it. "I didn't know you'd brought that here."

"It's been here since the Club was sold," Gavers said. "Where it belongs." He brought a brandy for each of them and they settled down on the big leather couch, feet up on the table in front of it.

"A man doesn't just disappear," Jeremy said. Charles was very much with them in this room tonight. They had been together here too many times over the years, uncountable times.

"One man seems to have," Gavers said. He looked washed out, fatigue and drink showing heavily on him. Jeremy was aware of something strange in his mood. They had no sooner sat down than Gavers was on his feet again, ranging the room. He took a gun from its place on the desk and examined it carefully, then put it back down.

"Jesus, Jeremy," he said suddenly from across the room. "I've got to get something off my chest. Sorry to be a bother but I have to talk to someone." He'd never been this outwardly agitated. It was more than fatigue.

"You've got me, whatever it is. Go ahead."

"The night of the killing I had the goddamnedest dream about Charles—more a nightmare than a dream. It's buggered me up ever since. I came down here alone that night after we lunched in Carlyle Square, hoping Charles would show up. Remember how off our heads we were about him?"

"I do. I thought if we could just find my car, we'd find him."

Gavers sat down on the couch again. "I fell asleep right here and that's when the dream started. I thought I heard a noise in the hall, so I took the gun and went to the door and flipped on the light. There stood Charles, disheveled, a wild look in his eyes. I told him it was a good thing for him the light was on or I might have shot him. 'Bad timing again,' he said. 'How's about a drink, old boy?' We came back in here and I fixed us a drink. Then I asked him about this post-midnight visit of his—what the hell he was up to. He was a mess, stains on his trousers, not the Charles we knew who was such a stickler about his clothes. 'I've killed someone,' he said, looking at me as if I were the truant officer. And, he went on, 'I didn't even kill the right person.' I saw what terrible shape he was in, like an animal at bay. Dangerous. This was a Charles I didn't know. I didn't want to tell him that all of London knew already, or at least assumed that he'd knocked off the nanny."

"What did you say?"

"I asked him about Amanda: 'Where is she?' I said. I wanted to lead him up to the nanny, to find out how much he knew about what he had done. 'Amanda,' he said, 'who gives a damn about Amanda? She's fled to the police to tell them a pack of lies by now. Patrick—what's going to become of Patrick?' He started to cry. Jeremy, I wanted to give him time to get hold of himself, so I sat down behind the desk as if I were a shrink and told him for Christ's sake to take it easy. 'Listen, Winner,' I said, 'we can take care of it. We'll have another drink and get some sleep and

go over it in the morning.' 'No,' he said, 'there isn't going to be a tomorrow, and I want you to do something for me now. You owe me one last favor. I want you to shoot me.' "

"Shoot him?" Jeremy said, as involved now in the dream as Gavers was in the telling of it.

" 'And bury me here, keep me hidden from all of them forever.' "

"Jesus," Jeremy said, recalling a report in the press that, among other houses, Melbridge had been searched some weeks after the murder by the police to see if Lord Warrington might be there. Gavers had been in such a fury about it he'd gone off to Africa for a month.

Gavers was speaking again. "I didn't know how to handle him, whether to get him sodden drunker and let him spew it out until he passed out or whether to knock him out myself. While I was deciding what to do, I tried to reason with him. It was a fatal mistake."

"Why?"

"He came over to me at the desk, weaving. He was beginning to babble. 'Come on,' he said. 'Shoot me. Put me out of my misery. Don't ever let them find me. Then Patrick will never know what happened to me, unless a time comes that you decide to tell him. That's the way I want it. Come on, Gavers, get me out of this mess with some dignity,' he said. I got up to fix us another drink. 'Come on, Charles,' I said, 'one more drink and we'll sort this out. You know I'm not going to shoot you.' "

Jeremy saw sweat glistening on Gavers's forehead. Gavers got up and went back to his desk. Jeremy knew he was acting it out, showing him exactly what had happened in the dream.

"What an ass I was. In a flash, he picked up the gun and put it to his head and blew his brains out in front of my eyes. All I could think of was what a goddamned fool I'd been not to have anticipated what he would do. How could I have let him get anywhere near that gun in the condition he was in, asking me to shoot him?"

"Jesus Christ," Jeremy said.

"Now I was in it," Gavers said. "He'd had his way. If I called the police, all hell would break loose. Don't think it didn't immediately cross my mind, that regardless of my innocence, the bad blood between us when I barred him from the Club would be brought up and I might be accused of murder too. You've seen the swill in the press since this happened—they say anything. I'd been a friend to Charles for as long as we could both remember, as much of a friend as I could be to any man. Now he was dead in my study, there on the floor, and he had out-smarted me and he was going to have his way. He knew I'd never shoot him, but he needed me to do away with him."

Hollow-eyed, looking at the place on the floor where Charles had fallen in the dream, Gavers sat back down on the couch beside Jeremy. Jeremy remained silent, waiting for him to go on.

"I didn't waste any time," Gavers said at last. "I slung him over my shoulder and carried him out to the incinerator. I dumped him in it. There was a lot of refuse there already. We'd been clearing the trees for days. It was almost like a funeral pyre. The scene was crystal-clear then and it is now. I'll never get it out of my mind. I fired it up—I can still see my hand on the valve. As soon as it was lit, I came back to the house and I laid myself down on this couch and blacked out. And that's when I woke up, bawling like a baby, thinking there was nothing I could do for him anymore. But at the least I hadn't let him be a common suicide. I'd done what he wanted, and no one would ever know."

He looked at Jeremy. "That's it. It haunts me, especially these past days of the inquest, mauling it all over again. I needed to tell you. I had to share it with someone." He put his head in his hands.

Gavers, Jeremy thought, not knowing what to say, forever the confident one, the controlled one, the cool one, always in charge. He had never before given anything away, beyond a tip on a horse, and now he'd shared something with Jeremy that he, too, would never forget. Jeremy couldn't think of anything to say. Right now he had nothing to say. He was still in the dream himself.

The windows were open to the night air. Gavers's head came up suddenly, as if he'd heard something.

"What is it?" Jeremy asked.

"Just one of the birds calling."

Jeremy was still thinking, still back in the dream. Suddenly he stirred himself.

"Gavers?"

"What?" Gavers answered impatiently.

"Don't fuck around with me, my friend."

Gavers turned to him. "What?"

"Was it a dream?" Jeremy asked, "or did it happen?"

September 1974

With the inquest over and no news of Lord Warrington, things quieted somewhat, at least on the surface. There were other murders, other scandals to take up the time of the reading public.

Five months had passed, and during that time hardly a day had gone by without a new Warrington story. Robin's suicide had infused new life into the headlines. Manners, as chief superintendent in charge of the case for King's Road, had been led on many a wild-goose chase and he had gone on all of them. Scotland Yard and Interpol remained on red alert in their search for the tall aristocrat.

There had been one very tangible result to John Vexe's somewhat contemptuous article. The Harrow Mob were tarnished, no longer the alluring figures they had seemed to be before the murder. They had been exposed as shallow and heartless, and, possibly for the first time, they were being maligned rather than envied.

Before the article had appeared, they had succeeded in dominating the attitude of the public. Obviously there had been someone else in the house who had murdered the girl, and even though Charles Warrington was missing, he was innocent. The Harrow Mob were the only experts; after all, Charles Warrington was one of their own.

Then, all that was changed. The mysterious screen of privacy thrown up around the privileged had been drawn aside, exposing an unattractive group of spoiled wastrels. The members of the ever-so-glamorous Wyndham Group turned out to be nothing more than heavy gamblers and racing touts who drank too much and lost money for a living. Few of them worked. Their tricks were cruel, their habits unattractive, and an innocent girl had been murdered. The reputation of the more visible aristocrats was tarnished beyond recall. And the inquest had put the seal on the matter.

But the mystery remained. Where was Charles Warrington? Was he dead or alive? It didn't matter what anyone thought he had or hadn't done. What mattered and continued to matter was: where was he?

November 1974

Buster Manners never let up for one minute on the case. He was fascinated—obsessed, rather—as time passed with no news, no clues, nothing solid to go on in the search for Charles Warrington. He was going to find him. Every instinct in his body told him that Charles Warrington was still alive. He had to find him.

"Why are you so convinced that he is alive?" Brian Billings asked him. "Just because you can't find a body? Hundreds of people a year vanish forevermore—why is it impossible for him to? I think he's deader than a doornail. It shows in those letters. 'Take care of my son.' 'Tell him how much I loved him.' Sounds like a dead man to me, a man who dumped himself where he planned to dump his wife, probably in the Solent."

"He's alive. Those letters make it look as if he's dead. He said himself that he would never stand in the dock for bankruptcy or murder, but that is not a blueprint for suicide. Gamblers don't kill themselves; they always think there's a win around the corner. Murderers don't either. And Charles Warrington was not as concerned, as obsessed with the safety and custody of his child as he was with the hatred of his wife. His plan for a perfect murder was so naïve that it's a wonder he didn't pull it off."

"What do you mean?"

"Look at it. He was playing Wagner—that seems to set them all off—*Tristan und Isolde,* the music of love and death, on his phonograph before he left the flat in Ormonde Gate. In his mind's eye he would fell and kill her with one massive blow. It would be painless; she would never know what hit her. Romantic death. He didn't count on his own savagery combined with his own bad luck to destroy him. He didn't know that a skull can crack like a melon, any more than he knew that blood rushes to the point of contact, rushes faster than the speed of light to surround, to protect the distress signals of a wound. I don't think it ever occurred to him that he had cracked himself, months before, just as Jenny's skull did. Maybe if he had hit her that one perfect blow . . . But no, he hit her and then he hit her four times more with a tire iron in the dark kitchen of his own house. It was the second blow that cracked her skull, and you saw yourself blood on the ceiling and thirty feet across the room."

"Never saw anything like it."

"There's one laugh in this, you know. If he had hit her one perfect blow, killed her dead with minimal blood, stuffed her in the sack, gone up to see if the coast was clear, found that it was and took her body in the sack and dumped it in the Solent, he would have carried out his perfect plan. Except for one thing: He wouldn't even know until the next day that he still hadn't killed his wife. She'd be alive and well and looking for her nanny. Think about it."

"You're getting a strange sense of humor." Billings was equally interested in the Warrington case. They never stopped talking about it.

"Nothing is as violent as domestic mayhem. Nothing can hold a candle to it. A man decides to kill his old mother, who he's always hated, for the insurance money. He slips a little arsenic into her tea over a period of weeks, and when the old lady croaks, he is the most surprised of the lot. Nice. A business partner discovers that his best friend has been stealing from him for thirty years, so he goes out and gets a gun and shoots him point-blank in the head. Simple. Things like that are always about money. The hatred between man and wife, woman and husband, makes all the rest of it look like baby shit.

"Charles Warrington could have done a dozen things that would have been more successful than trying to bludgeon his wife to death with a tire iron. What in the hell gets into them? Did he really think she would just drop softly to the ground, dead from one blow? Then he'd pack her up in the sack and lug her out to the car and dump her in the English Channel? He didn't think any such thing. He could have aided and abetted her in one of her suicide attempts. He could have persuaded her to take the pills. He could have shot her, stabbed her, poisoned her, shoved her in front of a truck, or taken her on a long trip up the Amazon. But no. Those were all too good for her. I think he was so obsessed with getting rid of her that he lied to himself: Just a little blow on the head and it will all be over, he said to himself, knowing he was lying. He hated her so that he wanted to kill her in the worst possible way, and bashing in her head is one of the worst possible ways."

Brian was intrigued with the thought of violent domestic mayhem. "Why? It might have worked. After all, one blow like that would fell her; she was a little thing—er, she *is* a little thing. Then would it matter if she was dead? She would be unconscious. He could stuff her in the sack and put her in the boot of the car and finish her off later. Wouldn't he enjoy that more?"

"Possibly. But—and this is a big *but*—he hit her five times. That is savagery. It was not necessary. He *wanted* to keep hitting her. All the anger came out in those blows, burst out of him in a torrent of hatred. That's what did the poor bugger in, when he lost all control of himself."

"It was the bloodiest mess I've ever seen."

"Jenny's skull cracked on the second blow and that's when the blood spurted thirty feet across that room, all over the ceiling and walls. Even in the dark, he had to know there was a lot of blood."

"Could he possibly have gotten away with it?"

"I doubt it. Let's say everything worked. His wife comes down on time, he hits her one walloper, he stuffs her in the sack, he dumps her, and he turns up at the Wyndham with his alibi intact, right on time. He would certainly be the prime suspect when she went missing, what with their domestic history. But with her problems, she could very well have been enough of a nutter to just walk off into the sunset. That's what he was counting on. No body, no accusation. But in that classically stupid mind of his he never planned for blood all over the place and murder most foul, any more than he planned to kill Jenny instead of his wife. He figured he had thought up the perfect murder. It would go just as he planned it and everyone would live happily ever after without little Amanda around to bother them. Classic stupidity."

"As long as we've been at this case, the one thing I can't put out of my mind is how he felt when he came up in the hall and heard that voice."

Manners stopped on the street and turned to Brian.

" 'Jenny, Jenny,' " he said in a feminine voice, imitating Amanda's. " 'Where are you? What's taking you so long? Are you all right?' "

He looked at Brian, his fingers holding a mythical teacup.

"Can you imagine what went through his head when he heard her voice? Talk about luck. I don't believe it to this day."

They crossed the street and strolled toward King's Road.

"Poor bugger. The only thing he ever succeeded in doing well in his entire life was vanishing. What a record."

"And you're convinced he's alive? To this day?"

"Two things. The car and the Riggs lies."

"Run through it for me. Make me believe."

"Let's start with the lies. When I first went to see her four days after the murder, I asked her if there had been any blood on him. 'Blood?' she said, all innocent-like. 'There was no blood.' Well, the forensic people and those of us who examined the car and the house knew there was a ton of blood. He was bracketed in it between the house and the car he left in Folkestone, with an intermediate stop to talk to her. There was never any evidence of another human being in the Warrington house that night. One man, bloodied, leaves the scene of the crime. He leaves his car, bloodied, in Folkestone, but on his intermediate stop to talk to his old friend, there was no trace of blood? The man who borrowed the car from Jeremy Morton is the man what done the dirty deed and that man is Charles Warrington. No burglar or professional killer ran out of that house and hopped in Morton's car. Okay?"

"Okay," Billings said. "Agreed. It was Warrington."

"While I was with Rosie Riggs, interviewing her, I asked her to show me where they had been while Warrington was there. She took me back to the study and showed me the chair that he sat in, she said. It was an upholstered wing chair. It was clean. She showed me the desk where he sat to write the notes to Marston and Morton. The only thing I noticed was not exactly riveting. There was a rug on the floor that looked too small—there was a lighter border of wood on the floorboards around it. You know, when a rug that was there for years is moved, it leaves a light place where it had covered the floor before. The forensics came down a few days later and they went over everything. It was clean too. They didn't find a fingerprint or any blood. Very odd. It got my hackles up.

He'd been there—bloody when he left the house and bloody when he left the car, but no sign of it in her house. They had cleaned it up before I got there. So I started nosing around in the neighborhood— you know, Faversham and Maidstone, even Canterbury. She uses a cleaner in Faversham but only for clothes. I fanned out to the places nearby, Margate and so forth."

"When did you do all this? Before the inquest?"

"Way before it. Finally one day I came across a wordy cleaner in Maidstone, and I went into his place on the High Street. 'Do you do any work for anyone called Riggs,' I ask. 'I have,' he says. 'They live over in Faversham.' 'Oh,' I say, 'do you work for them regularly?' 'No,' he said, 'no.' So I flash my badge and ask him what he's got. 'A rug and some slipcovers for two chairs,' he says. 'And can I see them?' I say, and he says, 'Sure, but they've been cleaned.' Well, it was her rug from that study and the slipcovers for the chairs. 'What was wrong with them?' I ask him. 'Blood,' he says. 'She told me the dog gave birth on one of the chairs and the rug. Luckily I got all the stains out—it was fresh. She doesn't want them back until the spring.' "

"And you couldn't do anything about it?"

"I took them into custody, told him not to tell her, and gave them to the forensics. If you ever need a good cleaner, this fellow was bloody marvelous. Not a sign of anything—just like new. Pretty frustrating."

"I'd say so. Now what about the car?"

"I know that car was used as a decoy. My theory is that the minute his lordship hit that house, they called her husband in London and down he came. They made a plan. Warrington drove his car to Folkestone and parked it, and Riggs drove his own car and brought him back to the house. Now, when the car is found, everyone is searching all over France. But the Riggses have cleaned him up, burned his bloody clothes, gotten rid of the rug and the chair covers, gotten him some clothes, and, through Riggs and Warrington's gambling connections, got him some false papers, a new identity, a beard, and a shaved head maybe. He was gotten out of the country. Flown by private aircraft to Switzerland or Spain. A fast powerboat to Calais, then Paris, then a flight to Rio. The police world is looking for Charles Henry Edward Keating, or Lord Warrington, and this man is someone else, and somewhere else. Far, far away, and out of the public eye. But he's alive."

"So you can't do anything about Riggs—her, that is?"

"Nothing. If I face her with the rug, she'll stick to the dog giving birth, and I have no proof of human blood on rug or chair cover."

"So what happens now?"

"I wait. Just like I have been doing. I wait and I think and I watch. Something will happen."

CHAPTER **23**

London, January 1975

A lone.
Alone in the house, but not for long.

It became more apparent to Amanda every day that she was going to have to sell the Royal Hospital Road house and move to smaller quarters. The lease still had forty-five years to run and it would probably sell for around thirty thousand pounds at this time. Charles had paid twenty thousand when he bought it, and since it was in the Chelsea area, it had increased in value substantially since then. Rent and maintenance and the heating bills were not enormous, but they were enormous if you didn't have the money to pay for them.

So she would move into the little house in the mews. Charles had bought it for Patrick, for his future. The future was now. Amanda no longer had need for a five-story house with a drawing room, a dining room, or a study. There was enough room in the mews house for them. Patrick could sleep in the spare room, or she could turn the large bedroom into a nursery for him with a nanny. How could she afford a nanny any longer? Besides, at almost ten, it was past time for a proper governess. In this house, that would have been possible, but no governess worth having could live in such cramped quarters. Still, she had to have someone; Patrick was a ward of the court and there had to be someone to oversee him. The court had not decreed how she was to pay for that someone. She was in a quandary.

Before she could think it through, she was summoned by the Official Receiver in the Bankruptcy Court. She saw that Charles's debts were insurmountable when the list was put in front of her, piled up like cordwood. She was responsible for them. Her only assets were the lease on the house, the mews house, the furniture, silver, and paintings, all of which would have to be sold to satisfy creditors. The banks had no intention of taking a beating, and four of them were owed a total of more than twenty thousand pounds. Amanda could sell her jewelry but it wouldn't bring enough to cover what was owed to the bank it was kept in. Inland Revenue wanted three thousand. The North Thames Gas Board was owed almost a thousand. Another fifteen hundred was owed for repairs and payments on the Mercedes and her Triumph. His personal debts to friends added up to fourteen thousand. Amanda had thought all of Charles's gambling was centered around the Wyndham Club, but there was a claim from Ladbroke's, another gambling club, for eleven thousand in dishonored checks. He had doubled up, trying his luck there to stay afloat at the Wyndham. Borrowing from Peter to pay Paul. Even the little things seemed enormous. Two hundred pounds for repairs to two shotguns valued at four thousand pounds. The military tailor was owed two hundred and fifty pounds for storage and repairs to the silver coronet and ermine-trimmed robes worn by his father at the coronation of the Queen in 1953. Harrods came in for some, and Cartier was owed nine pounds for a leather watchband.

And, when the lease on Royal Hospital Road was sold and she moved to the mews house, all profit realized would go toward the debt. The court was owed still for the custody case. The school bills were in arrears and she had no cash for food, clothing, or help.

There were other even more subtle pressures being put upon her. When she went to talk to the headmaster at Patrick's school, to assure him that he would be paid in due course, he suggested that Patrick might be better off at school in the country with his aunt for the coming term. He'd had a letter from Mrs. Marston, offering to pay up the tuition and suggesting that Patrick might be with them for the following year. *Over my dead body,* Amanda thought.

A letter came from the Dowager, demanding certain things from Longholt out of the house. She had lent Charles thousands of pounds for court costs. There was nothing friendly in her letter, although she did suggest that she would be willing to take Patrick should Amanda not feel capable of caring for him.

Amanda's reaction to the actions of her sister and her mother-in-law was at first fury and then fear. They meant to take Patrick away from her. She was helpless. Pamela would help but she, too, was helpless, living a frugal life with an ungenerous husband.

She was going to Hatfield every day to talk with Dr. Pennell. He had suggested that she let Patrick go to Davina or the Dowager until the house was sold and the move made into the mews.

"It would be better for the boy. The security of his grandmother's life or his aunt's would be steadying for him now. You could try to make peace with them by turning him over to one of them this year, while you were getting moved, then take him back. He misses his father and he is confused."

"What about missing his mother? Patrick and I are very close. I don't know if I could do without him, and his security is mine." She felt all the nervous anxiety with Dr. Pennell that she normally felt with Davina and Penelope. Was he against her too? Was he, too, a part of the plot to take Patrick from her?

Charles would come back. If she had to sell the house, he would understand and he would come to the mews house. If she moved anywhere else, how would he find her? He would come back.

In the back of her mind she knew that there was an answer. All she needed was money. If she had money, she could pay off the creditors and stay in Royal Hospital Road with Patrick and get a good governess and get on with her life. Money. The Stalewski. She could sell the Stalewski. Chantal would buy it. That would solve all the problems.

Before she could even consider selling, events were taken out of her hands. Patrick started wheezing and coughing, the first of some serious asthma attacks. Nothing like this had happened before; he had always been perfectly healthy, and now he was turning purple in front of her eyes and his breathing actually stopped twice. She was frantic. Nothing else mattered but Patrick's health.

"The boy must be gotten out of the city. He needs to be in country air," Amanda was told by her pediatrician. The sale of the Stalewski was not going to help Patrick breathe, and if she bought a house in the country, Charles would never find her again. When he came back, this was where he would come. It was the only home they had had together. Never mind what had happened in the hall and the kitchen; he would come back and find her waiting for him. Patrick should be in the country.

"What about Scotland?" Amanda asked.

"It would be fine for him, but what about his schooling? He's emotionally better-off in familiar territory. Besides, these attacks don't last forever," the pediatrician told her. "They are sometimes part of growing up. In a year's time, he could be rid of them."

* * *

"His cousins are there and he needs a stable atmosphere in familiar surroundings right now. While these attacks last, let your sister care for him," Dr. Pennell told her again on her next visit. "Move out of the big house and when you get settled, take him back."

Amanda called Davina. She could ask Pamela but it was so far away, Scotland—she'd never see him then.

"Will you keep him this year?" she asked.

"Of course I will," Davina said. Her voice was cool, impersonal. "I think it's very wise of you, Amanda."

"Can I come and see him?" It was a huge concession for her to request to see her own child, but if peace was better for all of them, then someone had to make peace overtures.

"Of course," Davina said. Her voice was still cool.

"All right," Amanda said. "You know we are in the bankruptcy courts now and I am going to have to move to the mews. Getting everything settled will take months. I don't know what I'll do without him, but I have to do what's best for him now."

"He will be better off here certainly. Richard will come for him." Her voice was still cool.

Amanda almost screamed through the phone: "Help me, help me! I'm your own sister—why do you hate me so?" But she didn't.

When she rang off, she wept. She couldn't bear the thought of giving him up.

Alone. Soon she would be even more so.

Alone. Alone. Alone.

April 1975

In the time it took for the Bankruptcy Court to get around to the settling up of Lord Warrington's debts, Amanda prepared herself for the inevitable. The mews house had a tiny sitting room with a fireplace, and a kitchen and large closet on the ground floor. There was a decent-sized bedroom and a tiny spare room and bath on the next. She brought a few pieces to save them from going under the auctioneer's hammer. A table, a few lamps, some chairs and rugs would make the place fairly livable. Patrick came in to see her and to go to the doctor on Fridays. He missed his mother, but he saw her every week. Amanda was totally excluded from Ransome House on one excuse or another. She was not surprised.

She set herself to making the move; then she could concentrate on getting Patrick back home. Surely the asthma attacks would be gone by then.

May 1975

Amanda called Chantal and told her the situation. She was fine, Patrick was better off where he was for the moment, and she was moving to the mews house soon.

"I've got the Stalewski," she told Chantal. "I talked to Sally and she will send it up from the country when I move in. God knows it's the only really decent thing in the house and it's much too grand for it, but it seems to be the only thing I have left."

"Will it be safe?" Chantal asked.

"Safer than it was," Amanda said. "Why don't you come and see it, and me?"

"*Amie*, you must come here. You don't have to worry about Patrick. I know you miss him dreadfully but he is growing up and it's only a matter of time before he'll be away at school forever. You have to make a new life for yourself."

Amanda hesitated.

"Chantal, I'm sure that Charles is alive and will come back. I can't leave. I hate to leave the house, even to shop for groceries or to go to the doctor. Sometimes I have a feeling he's watching me."

"Do you still have the police guard?"

"No, they went after the inquest."

"Our offer is always open. When you feel you can get away, come to us at any time."

"Why don't you come here?" Amanda asked.

It was Chantal's turn to hesitate.

"The climate," she said. "The English climate. It's filthy."

"It's exactly the same as Paris!" Amanda said.

"I mean around the Wyndham Club. The climate has changed there."

"Oh," Amanda said. She almost said *good,* but she refrained. Gavers had never so much as spoken . . . Oh, well, let the past be the past. She was glad Chantal wasn't seeing him anymore.

★   ★   ★

On the day of the sale, Amanda spent the morning wandering aimlessly around in Harrods. She walked past the house at lunchtime and stopped in the Farrier's Forge for a pub sandwich. Then she went back to Harrods. When she returned to the house at five, the auction was over.

The remaining years of the lease on the house had been sold to a *nouveau riche* wine merchant for nineteen thousand pounds. He had gotten a bargain. The Georgian silver from Longholt had been sold at Christie's and had brought twenty-four thousand, and two dozen George III serving plates had fetched another ten and a half thousand. The furnishings and porcelains and crystal brought nothing, compared to what they would have at Christie's. The two landscapes in the drawing room had gone to an antique dealer from the Pimlico Road. The ancestors from the dining room had gone back to storage at the request of the Dowager Countess. She had had to pay for them; even though they were her ancestors, they were in her son's possession, and his possessions were on the block. Amanda had hidden the Hochst parrot away in the mews house before inventory was taken. Charles loved it and he would have it when he came home. To hell with the auctioneers.

Amanda sat in the stripped house, in one room, then another, looking at the emptiness of what had been her home.

She had no material possessions to cling to now, not that she ever really had owned any of it. It had all belonged to Charles, but it was all gone. She had her few clothes, and her bed and some sticks of furniture in a cold mews house in the only truly ugly mews in London. Her car was gone and her jewelry gone, except for the opals. She didn't care about any of it. She took a last look around the house, then locked up and went out through the garden to the mews.

Her child was gone and her husband was gone.

They were all she wanted back.

The proceeds from the sale paid off Charles's debts. What little money was left over was to go toward Patrick's school tuition in the country and for Amanda to live on. It wasn't much, but it was something.

★　★　★

By the time Patrick went to stay at Ransome House on a more or less permanent basis, he was thoroughly confused and a miserable, sullen child. He'd stayed with his grandmother—he still did from time to time—and she was nice, but she kept her distance from him. He'd been with his mother in the big house when his father was gone from them, before she moved to the mews. No one seemed to know where his father was or if he was coming back ever, and if they did, no one explained much of anything to him. He knew his mother was sick a lot and that worried him. Sometimes she was around and sometimes she wasn't. He couldn't remember one nanny from another.

Ransome House was different. Richard and Davina were always there and the twins were his friends and he liked going to school in the country. He woke up a few times, choking and gasping for breath, but either the twins' nanny or Davina was always there to help him. He'd go up to London to see the doctor and spend the night with his mother every week, but then that stopped and he spent all the time at Ransome House. That was fine with him; he had his own room next to the girls' and pretty soon he stopped coughing so much.

There were things he didn't want to think about, things that worried him. He didn't have a father or a mother anymore and no one was telling him why. Once in a while he'd ask Davina, but then he stopped doing that too. He had a funny feeling that they didn't like his mother too much, but he didn't know why. He'd ask his mother someday. Meanwhile, he liked it at Ransome House. It was much nicer than London.

September 1975

Amanda began to retreat more and more into herself. Having nothing to do, she slept much of the time. She was used to having Patrick and a nanny to keep her company, and without them, with only Lily, the little cat she'd adopted for company, she felt abandoned and lonely. After a few months she realized that she was sleeping her life away, practically a recluse except for her weekly visits to Hatfield and Patrick's Friday visits to the doctor. She took him to the doctor herself, then kept him overnight and sent him back to the country by train on Saturday afternoon.

She started spending hours every afternoon in the Sloane Street library. There was nothing in particular that she wanted to read or research or learn, but it gave her something to do. Gradually she found herself taken up with studying France, a country that had always appealed to her. She gobbled up information about Paris. She pretended that she was Chantal—just for the fun of it—to see how she might behave as a Duchess. The library offered a free course in French, which she took, but as she had no one to converse with, all she learned was the structure of the language. She did dream of one day going back to Paris, and she knew Chantal's invitation was genuine. But her life now had nothing in common with Chantal's life of incredible wealth.

Her mood was benign. It kept the nightmares and migraines in abeyance. She tried not to think about the past. But underneath her sweetness-and-light façade, she was terrified. The demons were still lurking. Patrick's asthma attacks were less frequent, but even the occasional ones were violent. When he came in on Fridays he seemed quiet and well-adjusted but restless. There was nothing much he wanted to do in London.

Occasionally he clung to her.

"When can I come back?" he asked one day, to Amanda's utter surprise. Did he think she had sent him away? Didn't he know that he was in the country for his health? Of course she had explained it to him, but she went over it again with him.

"Aren't you happy there?" she asked, her heart rising.

"Oh, yes, I love it with Aunt Davina," he said. "But I miss my father. Don't you miss him? Will he ever come home?"

Amanda did not know exactly what Patrick understood of the murder. Dr. Pennell had advised her to answer his questions but not to tell him too much.

"Of course he will come back."

"When? Do you know where he is?"

"No, darling, I don't know where he is. We just have to wait for him." She knew schoolchildren talked, and *Warrington* was a household name in England now. She hoped Patrick hadn't been disturbed by it. She certainly had.

From time to time someone from the press either telephoned or appeared outside her front door, offering her vast sums of money if she would be interviewed. One day when she came out the front door with Lily, a photographer started snapping their picture.

"Stop that," Amanda commanded. "Why can't you leave me alone?"

"Is that your cat, Lady Warrington?" he asked, coming closer and closer to her and continuing to snap her. Her patience broke. She held Lily up to him defiantly as he continued taking his pictures.

"This is *not* the cat that I supposedly strangled. Get out of here and leave me alone."

The next day her picture was on the front page of the newspaper. "This is not the cat I strangled, Lady Warrington asserts," the caption read.

Amanda went back to Hatfield to spend a week. The first day she was there, she read in some column that she had been paid for the picture with the cat and that it was part of a plan of hers to discredit her missing husband.

What more could these people want? What more could they do to her? Would it never end?

24

November 1977

"**H**e's dead," Rosie said to Neil.

"Why do you say that?"

"I know him. He can't survive for long in any world other than the one he knows. He wouldn't want to."

Neil had learned through the years of his marriage to Rosie never to take anything she said too lightly. She had a first-rate mind and an instinct that never ceased to amaze him, often about the most unlikely things.

"Maybe you know him too well. Your normal predictions are usually involved with more impersonal subjects than this."

"No, that doesn't make any difference. When the trail dried up, at first I thought he might have been able to make it on his own. I don't think so now."

"It hasn't been cold that long."

"Long enough. We've lost track of him. None of us knows where he is now. He's taken himself away from us. He knows he can't come back. Even if we're able to have him declared dead after seven years, he can't wait that long. Sometimes I can feel how he thinks. He can't live with any other identity than his own. He's Charles Warrington and that's who he wants to be. To have to be someone else, just to avoid a trial—he would never do that."

"But we don't know anything." Neil saw that Rosie was upset. She had come to a conclusion about Charles, an emotional one, but a conclusion.

"Suicide, I imagine. He did talk about it that night. Remember?"

"Yes, but that was the desperation of the night. What's the difference now?"

"All the difference in the world. For Patrick. As long as Charles remains a mystery, as long as no one finds him, searches him out, there is a question as to his innocence. At the inquest he was convicted without being able to defend himself. We know more than most about that. He might be able to survive if he had any hope of being declared innocent. But the forensics alone seem to prove his guilt. He could go off a cliff into the sea, or be buried in the jungle. He'd know how to do it so his body would never be found. We used to talk about that story of Evelyn Waugh's, *A Handful of Dust.* Do you know that story?"

"No," Neil said. He was not much of a reader.

"It's about a man who had a bad marriage. A terrible, shallow wife whom he never should have married. She destroyed him. He loved his home, so she got him moved out of it. She did away with everyone surrounding him. She got him out of his natural environment and eventually, silly twit that she was, she was responsible for his death. It's known as the tyranny of the weak. That's what Amanda's done to Charles. She's responsible for his death, one way or another."

May 1978

The subject of Charles Warrington was not taboo in the Marston household, but his name was rarely mentioned. It was a policy agreed upon by Richard and Davina when Patrick came to stay with them. They all lived with his memory in a diffuse, somewhat shadowy, way. He had been a part of their lives for so long, but under the present circumstances he was gone and the less said about him the better. His presence surfaced from time to time in the natural course of events, inevitably on the anniversary of his April disappearance, which they all were well aware of, although they avoided bringing it up. They could hardly escape the memory of him then. The press made an annual field day of his absence, tossing the story about again as each year passed, speculating fruitlessly about his whereabouts or whether he was in fact dead. Richard and Davina had agreed that the best course to follow for Patrick's emotional well-being was never to leave the subject of his father closed but not to foster it. Richard had talked with Patrick to try to make him feel more secure.

"I can't help a lot. You know the situation and you know I'm here if you need to talk. You can always come to me."

Patrick fidgeted and hung his head. He was growing so quickly, getting quite tall and as yet unable to cope gracefully with his swiftly changing size. His emotions were buried in his new bulk. He was reluctant to talk to anyone.

"It's all right," he told Richard. "There isn't much to say, is there?"

There were times when he was moody for days and not able to shake off his feelings. Then he knew he wanted to ask someone, even a stranger, about his father—anyone, but who? He was uncomfortable for reasons he could neither think through nor define. Then his mood would pass and he would let it be. It was better left alone.

The one person he instinctively wanted to talk to was his mother, but the thought of her made him the most uncomfortable. He had bouts of guilt about her. He missed her affection but he avoided the thought of her, really not wanting to see her. He would allow himself to be tortured with guilt about her; then he would rebel in his thoughts and turn against her. She didn't care about him—she was in London and never came to Ransome House and he was safe here in the country and at school. Occasionally he would overhear a brittle remark about her from Davina in a passing conversation that he was not a part of, and that made him nervous and even more uncomfortable. Gradually, he wrapped himself in a defensive cocoon and put from his mind anything that he heard and most of what he felt.

Still, there were times when his subconscious feelings surfaced and he longed to know more about what had happened. Not in the bedroom at home: not the memory of his mother and father there, his mother covered with blood, telling him to go up to bed. Not that—he knew all about that. He had been there. But what happened afterward? In his memory, his grandmother had taken him home with her that night and then he'd been back with his mother and they never talked about it. Where had his father gone, and why had he gone, and what had happened to him? Where was he? Was he dead, gone forever? Had he killed himself? Why would he do that?

Then Patrick's thoughts would become too painful and he would obliterate them, in a fury against both his parents. He would think about school and Richard and Davina and the twins, and he knew he was better off putting all of it away, out of his mind. He didn't have to think about it. The cocoon became a hard shell.

September 1980

Philippe de Briand died. When Amanda read his obituary in *The Times*, she flew to the phone. She had not talked to Chantal in months and she felt like a false friend—which she told Chantal.

"No, darling, I don't think of you that way. He turned up with a swift and deadly cancer of the liver not two months ago. François and I were sworn to secrecy so he could get his affairs in order. I knew you would call. I should have told you myself."

"I'm so occupied with doing nothing I'm ashamed of myself. I don't know what to say. You've been so thoughtful always about me."

"Any news of Charles?"

"None," Amanda said. "None at all."

March 1981

"**L**ady Warrington," a remembered voice said, "this is Dr. Rutherson. I wonder if you could come by and see me at your convenience."

The unfamiliar sound of the telephone ringing had almost startled Amanda. She had transferred the old number over from the big house to the mews when she moved. She would have cut it off long ago except for the slender possibility of Charles's calling, trying to find her. It rang rarely.

"Of course I will, Dr. Rutherson. I can come any time. This afternoon? Tomorrow morning?" Amanda had not forgotten the coroner's courtesy to her during the inquest.

"The sooner the better. Let's fix it for three this afternoon then. I'll be in my office at the court in Horseferry Road. You remember where it is?"

"Oh, yes, Dr. Rutherson. I remember very well where it is."

Nigel Rutherson had never been one to beat about the bush. Once Amanda was seated in his office he went straight to the point.

"Your sister has been here. She has petitioned to have your husband declared dead. It's coming up to seven years since his disappearance, and it is perfectly legal for her to do so. I thought you should be informed as to what she has done." He sat back in his chair, observing the quick angry reaction on Amanda's face.

"On what basis can my sister apply to have my husband declared dead, Dr. Rutherson? She's my sister, not my husband's sister. Therefore she is no blood relative of his. The Dowager Countess is dead. I have no intention of having my husband declared dead and I thought that I would be the only one who could do so. Can my sister meddle in this against my wishes?"

"I'm afraid she can, Lady Warrington. I informed your sister that I was going to call you. The circumstances surrounding this case have always been unusual, and this is no exception. Your sister has custody of your son. She and her husband are bringing him up. He has lived with them for the past number of years and they have seen to his support and education. He is still a ward of the court, and your sister has reported to the court faithfully as to his welfare. She states in her petition that you are removed from any responsibility toward your son. She presented medical records showing that you have been diagnosed as manic-depressive and that you have a history of continuing treatment at Hatfield. As your sister, she is a blood relative of the boy. She wants to clear the title for your son now so that the press won't drag the case up all over again when he comes of age. She feels it is the best thing for Lord Patrick Keating. He does live with them, does he not?" Rutherson knew that he had given Amanda the full load, but he remembered her patient, almost stoic quality during the trial and he felt that she would prefer a direct approach in learning of this new attack on her.

"Yes, he does," Amanda said, "but because of an asthma condition that makes it necessary for him to live in the country, away from London. I have had to deal for several years now with the settling of my husband's affairs in the bankruptcy courts. My house was sold out from under me and I felt it best for Patrick to be in a family environment with my sister, until his asthma condition improved and I got settled. He's at Harrow now."

Amanda felt trapped. It did look as if she had relinquished any claim to her only child. He was almost sixteen now. She had managed to go to see him when he was first at school, away from the lack of welcome that she felt at Davina's, but it had been a depressing experience for both of them. Patrick was wrapped up in sports and his classmates. Amanda had no money for trips or luxuries and they had very little in common at this time. His home life with Davina was the best thing for him under the circumstances, but did that mean that Davina could move to have Charles declared dead? Without so much as discussing it, as if *she* were the head of the Warrington household? What else could they take away from her?

How could she fight this? She looked at Dr. Rutherson.

"So it can be done, regardless of any objection on my part?"

"Indeed it can, and it has been. But that does not mean it will go through. There are my objections." He had given her the bad part; now she deserved some of the good.

"Yours, Dr. Rutherson?" A ray of hope?

"Mine. Lady Warrington, I have no proof, not a shred of evidence that shows me that your husband is dead. Men have been known to disappear for decades, sometimes generations, and just as suddenly to reappear. Usually, when a family declares a member dead it is for the common good. Money that is tied up, the sale of properties, a dozen reasons why it is better for the family as a whole. None of that is of any relevance in this case. Simply wanting to clear title for Lord Patrick Keating can wait until he is of age, and then he can do it himself if he chooses to. Meanwhile it can wait. And it is going to."

Amanda laughed out loud. An ally, an unexpected ally! *Our motivations may be entirely different but our desires are the same,* she thought. She had done what she felt was best for Patrick, what Charles would have thought best for Patrick. Dr. Rutherson believed that Charles was still alive. He'd had no proof to the contrary and he wasn't going to let anyone try to slip anything over on him. There was no proof of any kind that Charles was dead.

"So," she said in a lighthearted tone. "They can do it regardless of me but not regardless of you?"

"Exactly." The look in his eyes was warm, but she saw the determination on his face. "That's about it, Lady Warrington. I am refusing the request and a copy of my letter will be sent to you. In the future, I should see as much of the boy as possible if I were you."

Amanda knew that he was admonishing her, but wisely. He hadn't had to call her, but he had. She couldn't have stopped them, but he could and he had. Now she had to find a way to get Patrick back.

What Rutherson had not said to Amanda was that he had good reason for not allowing Charles Warrington to be declared dead.

"Over my dead body," he said to Buster Manners later on in the evening. "The old Harrow Mob are up to something, I think, and I believe this request through the sister was masterminded by Driscoll and Riggs, the ringleaders of the Warrington fan club. You're retired now and off the case, and your successor doesn't give that much of a damn about an old murder and an old disappearance, but he doesn't need to be made a fool of either. If this bunch knows the whereabouts of Charles Warrington and are manipulating to make it safe to bring him back with a new identity, they should be watched now for a while. I've informed Scotland Yard and King's Road about the petition, and of my refusal. I'll not sign a death warrant on him and in the ultimate, I am the only one who can. If Lady Warrington petitioned on a hardship basis, I'd listen to her, but she won't and I'm not listening to her sister. Lady Warrington may be half daft, but she will never have him declared dead. I'd like to see it stay that way."

"Bastards," Buster Manners said softly, his good nature showing on his face. "The words *obstruction of justice* still sting in my mind every time I think of them, all of them. I don't care as much as I used to, but I care. Whatever's going on, you've got it stopped for the time being."

After her meeting with Dr. Rutherson, Amanda sat alone in the mews house, thinking. If it weren't for the coroner, she would not have come face to face with the fact that she could be looked on as a mother who cared little about her child. She had seen herself through someone else's eyes in her meeting with Dr. Rutherson, and the time had come for her to do something about Patrick. Asthma or no asthma, she had to find a way to bring their lives back together.

She was living on the pittance sent by the solicitors who had handled the bankruptcy proceedings for Charles. With all debts paid off, the little that was left went to Amanda to pay the costs of the mews house and her food, nothing more. She had spent hours in the library but she found herself needing human companionship. Someone to talk to. Finally, she had taken a secretarial course in order to get some sort of job. She had gotten a series of scrubber jobs for scrubber wages, none of which lasted for more than a few weeks. Her head ached and the letters and figures danced before her eyes in the long hours of typing required for a beggar's wage.

Occasionally, a bout of depression would send her flying back to the haven of Hatfield to stay for a few days or weeks. Dr. Pennell was the only dependable influence in her life.

"Don't be too hard on yourself," he advised her. "Two dreadful events in your life wounded you deeply: the loss of your father when you were no more than a baby and the killing of your nanny by your husband." Dr. Pennell chose his words carefully. "You are not emotionally strong and you are a sensitive, perhaps oversensitive person. You have survived. Life is not all bad and eventually you may come into some peaceful waters. When you need help, you know you can always come here."

Amanda wanted to correct him. There had been three terrible events. The third was John's death, which Dr. Pennell knew nothing about. She had begun dreaming of John, a recurring dream in which she would ask him for something but would never quite be able to reach him, touch him. She could hear his voice, the deep tones, saying to her: "Of course, little Countess. Whatever you want I will arrange for you." But as he was saying it, his voice would fade until she could hardly hear him, and his image would be gone. She would come awake weeping. John was dead. He would never come back. She had nothing but blind belief and instinct to go on, but she never lost her faith in Charles's being alive. She would know if he was dead.

Dr. Rutherson was correct in his assessment of her relationship with Patrick. She had to bring them back together. She needed money; she had to have it. The time had come to sell the Stalewski.

She pulled it out from its hiding place behind the couch, where she'd kept it since Sally had returned it to her. She lit a fire in the grate and sat down to feast once more on the glorious simplicity of the white blossoms blowing across the green land.

It would probably bring two hundred thousand pounds. For that she could buy a house near Harrow and arrange a decent life for herself and Patrick.

Amanda wanted to discuss her plan with Patrick. It would be impossible to see him at Ransome House, so she went to Harrow. To her delight she caught him between classes, with a good hour to spare. His face lit up when he saw her, but when she explained her plan to him, she saw that he was immediately uncomfortable.

"A little house nearby where we can live together again as a family. What do you think?"

She could hardly bear to look at him. The Keating looks were so pronounced since he had matured that he was like a clone, a twin of Charles.

"Mother," he said, "I don't want you to spend the money to buy a house near here. You come and see me and I will come into town more often. My real home is with Aunt Davina and Uncle Richard and I love them and I don't want to leave Ransome House. I love the twins and I have my horse and my friends all around. . . ." He looked down, upset. He was so honest.

Amanda started to cry, furthering his discomfort. She took his hands across the rough wooden table in the ancient little tearoom.

"I'm sorry, darling. Of course I can't split your life. We'll be together sooner or later. I just want you to know that I love you, care about you. Davina and Richard are not your only family."

He kissed her goodbye and Amanda knew he would be relieved to have her gone, but she also knew that he did still love her. Being alone together as they had been, even for a short time, made that clear to her.

On the way home she finally admitted to herself that she felt the same sort of relief that Patrick had on seeing her leave. She could never provide the social background he already had with Davina, but that wasn't really it. She didn't want to sell the Stalewski. She would have, for Patrick's sake, but now she didn't have to.

★ ★ ★

November 1981

Dr. Rutherson's prophecy came true. It was over his dead body that the Marstons succeeded in having Charles Warrington declared dead.

Nigel Rutherson died of a massive heart attack six months after he had refused Davina's petition to have the Earl of Warrington declared dead. The new coroner, Dr. James Milner-Keyes, had known the Marston family for years and was a devoted friend of Richard's mother. He was also a close friend of Gavin Driscoll's, having spent several years in the Far East on the same post with Gavers's father.

In due time, Davina and Richard called upon Dr. Milner-Keyes and discussed their desire to have Charles Warrington declared dead.

"I believe that we have my nephew's best interests at heart," Davina told him. "The boy has had a traumatic past, what with the loss of his father and the condition of his mother. My sister has recently tried to intervene in his life again, even though she has had little communication with him in the past and we have brought him up. My feeling is that the sooner we can make the inheritance of the title clear, the better it will be for Patrick. It is a tragic story, you know—his mother is quite mad. If we wait until he comes of age, the press will have the same sort of field day at his expense that they had during the trial."

"You say she has no real parental relationship with him and she is still in the care of doctors for her mental condition?" Dr. Milner-Keyes asked.

Richard Marston answered. "We have tried to discourage any hold on him. Her behavior is erratic at best. We have always insisted that his father is innocent, did not have a fair trial, and that if he were still alive he would have come forward in order to clear his name long before this. Davina and I believe—even with no proof, but knowing Charles as we did—that he is dead. Patrick is a young man with a future to be considered. We both care deeply for him, as he does for us."

The new coroner had been invited often to the Marston house and he knew the stability of their lives. He was not unaware of the Marston lifestyle and the advantages of their nephew's life with them. Certainly better for the boy there than with a deranged mother.

A few weeks later, Charles Warrington was declared legally dead. For inexplicable reasons, the press took no notice of the petition made by

Davina Marston, nor of the death warrant signed by Dr. James Milner-Keyes, Coroner of Westminster.

Amanda was informed several weeks later by an official letter from the coroner's office. It was over and done with. They had put one more thing over on her.

She was now officially a widow. Lord Patrick Keating had become the twelfth Earl of Warrington.

December 1981

Amanda called and asked to speak to Patrick.

"I'm afraid he's not here now, Amanda," Richard Marston said. "He's gone away for the weekend. I'll ask him to call you when he returns."

"No, you won't," Amanda said. "I've called him dozens of times and you have stopped me from seeing him or speaking to him. You went behind my back and got Charles declared dead against my wishes. You've made me a no one, you've taken my husband's life from me, and you have my son. I have nothing left."

"You still have the one thing that means the most to you, Amanda," Richard said, impatient with her accusations.

"And what is that?" she asked.

"The title, Amanda, the title. You're the Dowager Countess now. That should be enough for you."

There were bitter lines around her mouth as she looked at herself in the mirror. She had slept badly again, and ever since the letter from the coroner's office she had been eaten alive with frustration and despair. What else could they do to her? What else could they take?

She now lived in fear that something would happen to the Stalewski painting. They had taken everything else, and they did know about it, how valuable it was.

They wouldn't stop when there was one more valuable thing they could take away from her. And if they didn't get it, suppose someone broke into the house and stole it? Suppose there was a fire? She knew she was being irrational but it was the last talisman of her former life. It would vanish like everything else. Charles. John. Patrick.

She picked up the telephone and rang Chantal. She was always running to Chantal; she might as well run to her once more. The voice on the other end of the telephone informed her that the Duchesse was at the Château Quatre Mai. Would she like to telephone her there, or should the Duchesse return her call?

"Ask her please to ring me when she can," Amanda said. Chantal was probably tired of hearing about her ill-fortune. She could call or not, as she liked.

Chantal's call came a few hours later.

"You sound strange, *amie adorable*," Chantal said. "Are you well?"

"I'm well enough. I'm just angry."

"Good," Chantal said. "It's about time."

"Can I come to you? Tomorrow?"

"Of course you can. But you must come straight to Quatre Mai. We are in residence, François and I, cataloguing and inventorying everything. My father was precise in his instructions in his will. It's going to take us years."

"Include the Stalewski," Amanda said. "That's why I am coming—I need to bring it to you. I am so sorry your father had to die before he knew that it was his."

"We'll talk about that when you arrive. Call and tell Roland which flight you're on. He will bring you directly here. I can't wait to hear about your anger."

"I can't wait to see you. I look pinch-faced again, but this is the last time. I will miss your father being there."

CHAPTER 25

December 1981

The great château of Quatre Mai was two hours drive from Paris, in the château country of the Loire but not on the river. Its name was derived from the original land deed, a faded document framed and hung in a place of honor in the towering entrance hall. Four centuries before, on the fourth of May, the first of the De Briands had been granted land holdings that comprised several thousand acres of property. Thanks to the acumen of the original De Briand, a feudal fortress embellished with towers and ramparts and moats was built. Small tributary rivers flowed through the rich land on their way to the Loire. The hunting forests of Orleans were nearby—hardly necessary, as the hunting at Quatre Mai was excellent.

Eventually, as life became peaceful, richer and more civilized, the old fortress of Quatre Mai was torn down and a new château built in the turreted fashion of the century. By the end of the eighteenth century it had become an architectural wonder. There were paneled drawing rooms and dining rooms and reception halls and libraries and thirty bedrooms. No more the harsh architecture, the stone battlements of the original dwelling. Now, the rooms were confections of lavish grace. Priceless tapestries were woven with De Briand history as their theme. Savonneries and Aubussons covered the floors. One of the Chantals of the past added formal gardens bordering the lake that lapped at the east walls of the present château. Amanda had spent a weekend at Quatre Mai when she had first visited Chantal all those years ago; she wondered if her head had been attached then, since she had no recollection whatsoever of its incredible beauty.

Roland and Amanda arrived just as dark was falling, but it was still light enough for her to see a herd of fallow deer making their graceful way toward their nighttime forest habitat. She stopped the little *femme de chambre* from closing the curtains in her rooms when she caught a glimpse of a full moon rising. She hung out of the window like a child, leaning on the ledge, mesmerized by the soft beauty of the night and the silver shimmer of moonlight on the frost-spangled gardens.

She bathed and changed and, as instructed by Chantal, put on a simple long woolen skirt and a silk blouse. The Warrington opals were all she had left in the way of jewels and a passing thought reminded her that they at least were still in her possession. Her clothes were old but they were classic, and looked right in country France.

Before leaving London, Amanda had taken the Stalewski out of its gilded frame. She carried it, rolled up in newspapers and tied with string, onto the airplane with her. It pleased her that it was coming back to France the way John had first brought it in, rolled up and under her raincoat. John would have liked that touch. No one in customs questioned her about it, but once she saw Roland waiting for her on the other side of the glass customs booth, she knew that he had eased her way. The Stalewski was safe now.

Joining Chantal and François for drinks in the library before dinner, she was grateful that only the three of them were staying at Quatre Mai. She was in a dilemma about the Stalewski. She wasn't being noble—she wanted Chantal and François to have it, but still, she didn't want to lose it completely. She had left it to Chantal, and now she needed Chantal and François to keep it safe for her. She knew they were more than willing to buy it but she could not sell it. Even so, money was a part of her thinking. She no longer needed a house in the country but the centering theme of her life now was Patrick and she would certainly need money in order to establish a new life with him. She was sick of the confusion she felt. She wanted the painting and she wanted money. She could not have both. She wanted the painting more. The best thing to do would be to throw the problem out to Chantal and François and see if they could come up with a plan. All that really mattered was that the painting was safe.

A simple, delicious dinner was served in a tiny dining room next to the huge formal one. The tasseled silk and satin curtains on the wide windows had been left open so they could see across the moonlit lake. The moon was so bright that the turrets of Quatre Mai were reflected in the water.

"It's magic tonight," Amanda said. "Do you remember those nights on *Cattivo* with the moon on the water?" They had returned to the library and Amanda was sipping her third demitasse of the strong French coffee she loved.

"Of course," Chantal answered. "How many times I have wished that we could relive that summer, do it all again. I loved Gavers so, and you still had Charles, and none of this ugliness had happened. François, I wish you had been with us."

"The best summer for you was the worst for me. That was the year I lost Ghislaine," François said, his face expressionless. "Then Amanda came to stay with us in Paris, making me more miserable—although it was no fault of hers."

"*I* made you miserable? Why?" Amanda asked, surprised at the openness of what he had just said. François had never said two words about himself before.

"You looked like an English version of the girl I loved," he said.

"What happened to her?" Amanda asked, afraid she shouldn't have.

"My father found her unsuitable. You remember the moon on the water off the yacht, and I learned that young love is rarely terminal." His clear eyes danced a little. "You still remind me of her. You are looking extremely well."

François sounded like Chantal, full of verve and style. His compliment to her was genuine. He had said what he wanted to say and she found his candor delightful.

"All the De Briands find wonderful things to say to me," she said. "I am sorry about your father. You must both miss him terribly." She saw a quick brother-sister glance exchanged, enough to let her know that Philippe de Briand was not a subject for discussion right now.

"Little *amie*," Chantal said, changing the subject, "why did you so suddenly make up your mind that you had to bring the Stalewski to us, now, right this very moment?"

Amanda answered in a tumble of words.

"They have managed to have Charles declared dead. That's what sent me rushing to the plane with an invaluable painting tied up in newspapers under my arm. Fleeing to get it safely to you here in France." With each sentence, Amanda knew that the bitterness and fury she had accumulated was not something she would passively continue to live with. That was over. They had everything, those dreadful shallow people who had stripped her. What did they matter to her? She could say exactly what she felt to both Chantal and François.

"They have managed to have him *declared dead*?" Chantal's words came rushing. "How *could* they? *You* could, the Dowager could have before she died, but no one else has the legal right to do it. *How* did they do it?"

"My beloved sister went to the coroner with depositions that showed me a mental incompetent, and my son a ward of the court, in her custody since Charles has been gone. They neglected to mention that his support came from money given to them by the solicitors after the bankruptcy sale. They have taken him away from me, inch by inch, month by month, and year by year. They've done it, had my husband declared dead over my objections. I used to heel to whatever happened, but no longer. Gavers must have masterminded it all. He had the influence needed to have a new coroner appointed and approved, a man who just happened to be friendly with that exalted group. I am nothing. I am not a widow, not a wife, and not even a mother. I do not exist beyond— as Richard pointed out—being the Dowager Countess."

She stopped. François handed her a glass of cognac.

"But there is something that does bother me, something I have not a shred of knowledge about, no proof of, and no reason to suspect that it might be true." She was almost stuttering.

"That Charles is alive and they know where he is?" It was François's voice, flat and clear.

"François, how did you know that?"

"It was the way John thought," François said. "You know, we were quite young when he was here with us during the war, and as a young boy I adored him. He was so huge. He would tell me the most fabulous stories—it was like having a private giant in the house, all adventure and intrigue. He taught me to always suspect the least likely thing. Charles being alive is unlikely. To be able to sustain a life out of his own element for any length of time . . . I think he did away with himself the way he planned to do away with you, probably with the help of his friends. You have always wanted to believe that he is alive—I assume so he could somehow pay his debt to society and clear his name. That's why you refused to have him declared dead. They have no reason whatsoever to arrange a death warrant unless they know he's alive. If he were they would know where he is, and feel the time has come to bring him back. That's how John would think."

"Is it just instinct on your part, Amanda? You know nothing of substance?" Chantal asked.

"I can't help but suspect them. That's why I've stayed where he could find me. When Davina first tried to pull this off, I started having dreams about Charles. I could see him living in a cottage, hidden away at Richard's. Dr. Rutherson, the coroner who died but who tried to help me, felt that they knew what had happened to Charles, did know that he was alive somewhere." *Oh, God, I miss John's strength so,* she thought. François's mention of his name brought back her longing for him.

"Unless Charles is alive and they can keep him from you," Chantal said, "there is nothing more they can take from you."

Amanda was calmer now. It was a relief to be able to say terrible things about terrible people and not be judged insane.

"I've brought the Stalewski to you. It belongs to you, and I don't have to die for you to have it," Amanda said, her mood lighter.

"It's safe here and it belongs to the three of us," Chantal said. "You don't have to go back to London for weeks. We'll have plenty of time to think more about all of this."

"I'm ashamed of myself," Amanda said. "Pouring my complaints all over you, not even telling you that I'm sorry about your father, but I never would have come out with all this had he been here with us."

The same look was exchanged between François and Chantal again.

"What is it?" Amanda asked. "Have I said something wrong?"

"Of course not," Chantal said. "This is an evening of confidences, isn't it? It's good to have someone to listen to, to clear the air occasionally. François, let's have a whiskey. I cannot drink any more cognac."

"I think we should get roaring drunk," François said. He went to the bar and fixed tall scotch-and-sodas. "The moon full. Amanda in a rage because she has been manipulated one more time. You and I here at Quatre Mai, resenting the position our father left us in."

"Resenting? What do you mean? I thought you inherited everything."

"We did, and with it all the knowledge that we would be inept, incapable of taking proper care of it. Our revered father saw to it that our confidence rested in his dominance. He did all he could to destroy us in his way. He succeeded, until now."

Amanda was nonplussed.

"Your father? That strong, wonderful man who thought you both hung the moon—or at least I felt that about him. Destroyed you? How?" Chantal and François had always had everything. What had he done to them?

"François and I have lived as prisoners of my father, as his chattels, all our lives. We could have anything, except our own lives. He was right about one thing only and he never let me forget it. Gavers. When I first loved him, I revolted against Father's control but I obeyed him. His word was absolute and we did as we were told, without exception. When François mentioned Ghislaine earlier . . . what he did to Ghislaine . . . I still can't believe that he left everything to us with no strings. I was sure we would have directives from the grave, belong to him even more after death."

"Chantal, don't," François said. "Amanda doesn't need to hear all that."

"Drink up, François. Tonight's a good night to pull it all out. Then we can put it all away. Let me tell about Ghislaine."

"As you like."

Chantal turned to Amanda. "He ruled us in his way, exactly the way you have been controlled. We have spent our lives in his shadow, as obedient children. We were never allowed to come to Quatre Mai when my mother was alive. His opinion was that she was mad, even though he knew we didn't believe it for one minute. How does that make you feel? I thought you were weak because you were unable to handle Charles, but I never thought you were mad.

"But Ghislaine was something else; it was unforgivable, what he did out of sheer selfishness. François was madly in love with her. She was the loveliest girl in France, from one of the best families, and they were a perfect match. But because my father held an old grudge against hers, he refused to even hear of François's marrying her. François was forbidden to see her, as if he were still a child. Of course they ran away together, but Father found out and, with his own hooligans, stopped their marriage at the altar. It was done in a very rough way and it broke Ghislaine's spirit. My father justified it to François by saying that she was inferior to him, and he didn't hesitate to rub it in when she broke down."

"Stop, Chantal," François said. "Leave it alone now."

"Sorry, darling. You're right. It was the same with Gavers, except that I defied him. I saw Gavers when and where I chose; we lived together. That was allowed, as long as Father knew I wouldn't marry him. Then the time came when I no longer wanted him." She sighed.

"You know he's never loved anyone but you," Amanda said. "You could marry him now."

"No. Father was right and now it's too late. In his way, he was an extraordinary man."

"And now you can do as you like." Amanda wished she had some of what they had. She was used to having nothing.

"Yes," François said. "Now that the fires are banked." As he said it, he got up and went to stir the logs on the fire. Chantal and Amanda burst out laughing.

"You are funny, and I adore you," Chantal said. "Stir it up well. You might burst into flame again some day."

"I intend to," François said. "Now that I can do as I please."

They talked for hours, about everything and nothing. When Amanda got into bed, exhausted from the emotional content of the evening, she felt for once that she was not alone. *I always think everyone*

else has everything, she thought. *Everyone has troubles.* The knowledge
comforted her.

Amanda stayed on at Quatre Mai. The days stretched into weeks
and she found herself helping Chantal and François complete the inventory of Quatre Mai's treasures. No inventory had been taken for more
than twenty years before Philippe's death. There had been many new
acquisitions, and the catalogue had to be updated now that every thing
belonged to them. The work was painstaking, listings and descriptions,
but Amanda loved doing it. All the beautiful possessions that one could
have and care for . . . She only wished she could have seen Longholt
in its glory. When she got back to London, she would see if she could
get some sort of job at the Victoria and Albert or the British Museum
doing the same sort of thing.

The Stalewski had been hung in the small library where they sat every
evening after dinner, and if the door was open it could be seen from fifty
feet away down the long hall. Amanda was not reconciled to going
home without it, even though it had rested ignominiously behind a
couch for several years. She, Chantal, and François had discussed every
aspect of it and agreed it should remain safely at Quatre Mai on a
friendly sort of lend-lease agreement. When her life improved and Patrick came back to live with her, then she could take it back. If she
needed money, François and Chantal would advance it to her. After the
weeks at Quatre Mai she was feeling altogether more secure. Her fears
subsided. There was nothing further Davina and Gavers and the whole
lot of them could do to her, not now.

Most afternoons, unless it was pouring rain, she and François walked
along the river and through the many small farms on the De Briand
property. Chantal didn't go with them. François relished talking to his
farmers, pausing to smoke a cigarette or two with them, always at ease,
unrushed, enjoying their conversations. Amanda understood everything
said and gradually slipped into speaking French herself, glad she had
taken the lessons in London.

She loved the walks. They talked about everything from pig hus-
bandry to philosophy. Philippe de Briand's name came up often. François consistently referred to "my father this" and "my father that."

"He was a natural tyrant," he said amiably one afternoon. "He was
used to being obeyed and being right about everything. The *droit de
seigneur.* As a result, I learned patience. It has crossed my mind that he
might have made it impossible for either of us to marry because his own
marriage was such a battleground. I think my mother detested him, and

I know she feigned madness so she didn't have to live with him. She stayed here at Quatre Mai, completely happy to have him in Paris. She was crazy like a fox—she'd gotten it fixed so she didn't have to live with him and jump at his every command. We hardly saw her, as he would not risk letting us be exposed to her sort of defiance, her independence. He never mentioned her name and he knew she had it the way she wanted it, and I'm sure that's why he was so demanding of us."

"Have you forgiven him for Ghislaine?"

"I suppose so," François said, kicking at twigs on the path beneath his feet. "It's all so long ago now, and we were so young. I miss what Ghislaine was and how we might have been, but I no longer want to change it. No more."

"Where is she?"

"In a clinic in Switzerland, near Montreux. I went to Gstaad a few winters ago and stopped to see her for the first time in a long while. She was the same. She didn't recognize me—she thought I was some unknown member of her family. She has the mentality of an eight-year-old and she's going on forty. She will remain in that childlike state for as long as she lives, after that horrendous scene of our marriage when she broke. . . ." His voice trailed off and he stopped, lighting one of the Disque Bleu cigarettes he was never without.

"Things we hate to remember," Amanda said. "No one else in your life?"

"Mistresses," François said, a sardonic half-smile on his face. "Mistresses, most of whom long to be duchesses. I change them frequently, although that is not to my liking."

Amanda could hear John's voice. "Mistresses . . ." he, too, had said. She looked at François.

"You can't go on forever with them," she said. "One of you—both of you have to marry and provide an heir. You should have someone, and at least that someone can now be of your own choosing."

"And you? Are you going to spend the rest of your life with Charles?"

"With Charles?" Amanda was baffled.

"You're still back there with him, more than seven years back," François said. "You went to sleep the night he tried to kill you and you've refused to wake since then. You closed your eyes, blaming it all on the others, knowing he couldn't have killed the girl or tried to kill you. You stopped there. You still seem to have a blind belief in his innocence, no matter what your heart and mind tell you. Perhaps you should allow him the dignity of his mistake, Amanda. Hope that he is dead. Convince yourself that he is—there's honor in that for him. And let him go. If he is dead, he can't come back to you. If he's alive, perhaps he doesn't want to."

Amanda flinched. François went on.

"Are you going to stay alone in the mews house, a slumbering beauty whose life ebbs away day by day, year by year, waiting for a man like Charles?" His voice was gentle. He wasn't looking at her; he kept his face straight ahead, and there was no anger in what he said. Amanda couldn't take offense.

"It's for Patrick."

"Why for Patrick?"

"Growing up with a mother who's supposedly mad and a father who supposedly tried to kill her. I want Patrick to know that I never felt that his father was guilty, to understand that his father was driven temporarily out of his mind because of debt and bad luck."

"Then let his father die," François said. "It would be much better for him, I would think, growing up with it settled in his mind. My father's death gave me a new lease on life. I have been as much asleep as you, Amanda. My father had a long and rewarding life and I intend to do the same. I hope you can. Those people who have surrounded you have done you a great favor, having Charles declared dead. They've set you free."

"I never thought about it that way before," she said. She took a deep breath and turned and faced François, eyes shining. "But I'll tell you what I really do think."

"Tell me."

"I've never been able to talk to anyone the way I can to you and Chantal. What you said about dignity—allow Charles the dignity of his mistake—helps me. I have been lying to myself for years, pretending, not facing the truth. It started as far back as five or six months before the murder, when I was trying to get Charles back, to do something constructive. My mental condition was erratic, to say the least, after John's death. All the time I was with him before he died, I was all right."

She had never told anyone about John. Now she had made it clear to François that there had been something between them. She went on.

"When John died, I hit the lowest ebb in my life. When I began to come out of it, I knew that I had to control myself; I had to get well. I had to be the backbone for Charles as well as Patrick. Dr. Pennell at Hatfield said I could, that it was possible. 'Manic-depressive tendencies do not a manic-depressive make,' he said, and that line's always stuck in my mind. It's not much fun to be told you're crazy, or think that you really are."

"It was, for my mother," François said, grinning. They both burst out laughing.

"Chantal's right—you are funny."

"Never mind. Come on, how you really feel."

"At a certain time, Charles snapped. I can pinpoint it exactly: It was when he couldn't get custody of Patrick. At the very same time, although I didn't know it until long after, I had snapped in the other direction, gotten control of myself. And he had started planning to kill me." Her voice was low.

"Did he know about John?"

"Nothing, ever. He suspected it when Chantal came looking for the Stalewski for your father. I knew that our future depended on my being able to convince him that John had been no more than a friend. I did."

"That did take away the motive he might have had for trying to kill you. Are you sure?"

"I've thought about it a million times. I know he never knew—he couldn't have kept it to himself. I wish he'd had that for a motive; it would have made it forgivable, understandable. But he didn't."

She took a deep breath. "Charles came into our house that night with a quest in his head and a tire iron in his hand, and he wanted to kill me more than he had ever wanted to do anything in his entire life. It wasn't his love for Patrick, and it wasn't the troubles—debts piled up everywhere, money owed to every friend. It wasn't standing around in the Club that had been his life, the Club that he'd made by his presence, as no more than a come-on, a shill. It wasn't any or all of those things. It was his hatred of me, which was really his hatred of himself for all the failure. He would get rid of me, he would get his son back, he would move back into his house, and all his debts would vanish, just as I would have. 'The mad Lady Warrington just disappeared, never found a trace of her. Probably the best thing—she was a trial,' they'd say.

"He had snapped all right. He'd become a psychopath. All he had to do was kill me, and, idiot that he was, he even botched that—or rather Jenny did by catching a cold. But the biggest idiot was me. I let those awful people, including my sister, get away with using me as their whipping girl. Lady Masochist, they should have called me. I spent my life trying to believe he was wonderful, believing he would change, trying to love him. I was lying to myself all along and I've paid for it, almost with my life, and with my wasted time since then. I married him because he was an Earl and I wanted to be a Countess. I believe I've buried him now, dead or alive."

She took another deep breath. She'd begun to stumble over her words.

"If he ever came back, I'd like to see the look on his face if he had to face me. He wouldn't have an ally in me ever again, unless I was truly mad. At the inquest, when the coroner was summing up, he said, 'If Lord Warrington was trying to help his wife when she was under attack from a stranger, and obviously trying to help her afterward when they had gone to the bedroom, why then did she flee from the house screaming murder?' I'll tell you why: I knew he was going to come back into that room and kill me.

"I'll never say these things again—once is certainly enough. But the great mystery of Charles is his only protection. If we ever found out what's happened to him, it would destroy his myth. Is he dead? Is he alive? Did he kill the girl? Did he try to kill his wife? Was he declared dead so he could come back with a new name and never come to trial? Where is the missing Earl? As long as those questions remain unanswered, he has an innocence. Poor darling. I hope he's dead, for his sake."

She shivered. The light was fading fast, and with it the meager warmth of the December day. François put his arms around her shoulders, pulling his coat over her.

"No wonder John loved you," he said.

Amanda remained at Quatre Mai. Every time she suggested leaving, Chantal and François found something else they needed her to help them with. They urged her to stay with them for Christmas. Patrick was spending the holidays with school friends in the Caribbean, and her Christmas would be a lonely one in London.

She dreaded going back to England. The companionship with Chantal and François warmed her soul. She realized how desperately lonely she had been. She would stay for Christmas, and on until the inventory was complete; then she'd face up to going back to London.

January 1982

"May I come in?" Her door had already been partially opened, and she could see François silhouetted against the light in the hall.

Amanda sat up in bed. Had she been waiting for him?

"Of course you can come in."

He closed the door behind him. The moonlit path between her bed and the window gave off more than enough light for her to see his robe drop to the floor as he came toward her, naked. Before she felt him upon

her, she saw the rapier body of a man in perfect condition, not camouflaged by the quiet clothes, no longer concealed by quiet demeanor. This
was a hunter whose intent was clear. He climbed into the bed, folding
his arms around her, burying his face in her hair, and with no hesitation
began making love to her as if for the thousandth time. She knew she
had been waiting for him.

They lay in each other's arms afterward, hours afterward, tumbled
together against the pillows, the moonlit air from the open window
cooling them. She could feel that he wanted a cigarette, so she lit one for
him from the box on her bedside table and then another for herself. She
sank back against him, head on his shoulder.

"Were you afraid?" he asked.

"No. Yes," she said.

"Which first?"

"The no."

"Why the yes?"

"Because it's been so long. Too long."

"No more."

"No?" she said.

"Not if you'll have me. You shouldn't be afraid. I knew how you
would be."

"I didn't. You didn't give me much time for fear. But I thought I'd
forgotten what it was like to make love. I stopped thinking about it long
ago."

"You haven't forgotten. How long ago?"

"When Charles was gone." She took what was left of his cigarette and
stubbed it out, along with hers, moving back against the rock-hard muscles of his shoulder, warm against him. His body amazed her. How
could she not have noticed it, never thought about the physical being
beneath the façade of French gentility? "You're asking me a lot of questions for a man who has invaded my room in the dead of night."

"I answer questions as well," he said, his tone light, moving her closer
to him, fitting her into his arms.

"Then, you of the mistresses, how long has it been for you, since you
last made love?" She felt the lightness between them, the security in
their banter.

"A long time, too," he said. "Last night."

"Last night!" she said, astonished. She sat up. "Who?"

"The maids."

"The *maids*?" She reached for a pillow, slugging him with it. He was
laughing. "*All* of them?"

"All of them. There are eleven of them here and I am fortunate enough to be the one who hires them. Younger every year."

"I'll never ask you a question again. And here I thought you had such manners, that your father had brought you up to be a gentleman." Her arms wound around him and she felt a sense of delight in being with him.

"He did indeed, and they were one of my few privileges. Until you."

"They are pretty, the maids. All of the staff are handsome. Impeccable. That footman at dinner, the one with the rosy cheeks. Did you hire him too?"

The pillow came crashing on her, muffling her laughter. "I may have to let him go tomorrow."

"Double standard again," she said, then added in a mock tone: "Send Marie and Helene to me at midnight, Pierre, but I'm afraid I'm going to have to let you go. You do understand, don't you?"

François reached for her. "You do understand, don't you, that I am never going to let you go?"

Ransome House, February 1982

Davina had a puzzled look on her face. She reread the brief paragraph in the Court Circular column of *The Daily Telegraph.* There was some mistake. She read it again.

"Richard," she said, handing the newspaper across the breakfast table to him. "Read this." Her mind was racing.

Richard read the paragraph aloud.

" 'Announcement is made of the marriage of Amanda, Dowager Countess of Warrington, to François, Duc de Briand, at the Hôtel du Vallieres in Paris on February 15. Prince Philip attended the wedding, accompanied by Sir Ralph Orr-Martin.' "

He put the paper down and looked at Davina's astonished face. He let out a long, low whistle.

"Our little Amanda," he said.

Davina picked up the phone and dialed Gavers at Melbridge. When he came on the line she handed the phone to Richard.

"Who the hell is the Duc de Briand?" Richard asked.

"Chantal's father," Gavers said. "He's dead."

"No," Richard said. "François, Duc de Briand."

"Chantal's brother."

"He's married Amanda," Richard said.

There was a silence. Richard and Davina could see Gavers, seated in his study, feet on the desk, looking out the window into the branches of the huge two-hundred-year-old oak tree.

"Fucking hell," Gavers said. "Our Countess is now the First Duchess of France."

CHAPTER 26

Paris, March 1982

François helped Amanda with her letter to Patrick about their marriage.

"Short and sweet. Since you haven't been able to reach him by phone, you must see him as soon as possible. Invite him here. He will come, Amanda. He will."

"Not if Davina can help it. I'm afraid I've lost him. It's my fault. I'm the one who let him live with them, without any me there, for all those years. It's nobody's fault but mine."

"Never mind. You and Patrick love each other. That love has lain fallow but it is there. He will come to us. If there's any snob in him— and he's been brought up in a classic English-snob style—he won't be able to resist." From anyone but François, it would have sounded shallow, but he was so aware of his role, so aware of social structure and human nature, that it was simply the truth. Amanda wanted her son. Now there was a chance to get him. The shoe was on the other foot.

Her letter was brief. She would be living in France. The sooner he could come for a visit, the better. The mews house was being taken care of for him. There was a small threat in the letter. If he couldn't come to France very soon, she would come to England to see him. She sent the letter to Ransome House rather than Harrow, knowing Davina would read it first. She ended by saying that she loved him very much.

There was no answer.

François took her to England.

"We're going to settle this now. They will not treat me the way they have treated you. That's why my subtle presence is desirable."

They went to Harrow, where François left Amanda in the headmaster's office. He was going on to Windsor. He kissed her.

"It's important for you to be alone with Patrick. I'll send the car right back, to bring you to join me, but take your time."

What he did not say, Amanda knew: He was having tea at Windsor Castle with the Queen and Prince Philip. She would be received when she arrived. Ordinarily she would have been nervous about meeting the Queen. Now she was only nervous about seeing her son.

Patrick, having no idea that she was there, came into the headmaster's office wondering if he had done something wrong. Amanda was once again undone by the uncanny resemblance of son to father. He would be seventeen in a few weeks. He was as tall as Charles, his eyes were the exact blue, and his voice had the same deep tone. His physical beauty brought tears to her eyes.

They spent an uncomfortable few minutes together until the headmaster suggested that they have a walk through the grounds. Patrick led her through the garden, and suddenly he threw his arms around her and kissed her, a little boy again. Amanda wept. They sat on one of the wooden garden benches. What was this boy-man like? What were his feelings for her? She was proud of what he seemed to be, but she knew her emotions were clouding her perception of her son's basic character. He was so beautiful.

"Why didn't you answer my letter, or call me?" she asked, holding his hand.

"I was going to. I couldn't think of anything to say. There's too much to say. You look . . . lovely."

"Do you remember the last time I was here, when I wanted to get a house for us? I didn't have one then. I have one now—in fact, several of them. When you can, will you come?"

Patrick put his head down in his hands.

"I don't know. I hate all this, everything that was in the papers when you married—they dug up everything about my father all over again. Aunt Davina is . . . Well, she goes on a lot about your getting married without telling us. She thinks you're not grateful to her for all she's done for me. I love her. She has been like my mother and you've been a shadow. Why can't you make it up with her?"

Amanda saw his obstinacy. Davina, no doubt, had rehearsed him for this moment. Still, she was relieved that he would talk to her at all, not close himself off from her, as Charles always had.

"I can't make it up with Davina now, even for your sake. I'm not sure it can ever be made up. I don't want to criticize her ever to you, but I love you and I expect you to come to France. You are my son. When can you come?"

"Some time. End of the summer?"

"Sooner. That's months from now. I'll arrange it."

He walked her back to the car. It was a start. Only time would change things. She had time.

April 1982

Patrick did not come to Paris or to Quatre Mai. He had another series of asthma attacks and missed classes, then had to be tutored for exams. The headmaster wrote, telling her he was having a tough time getting through and it would be best for him not to take even a few days off at this time. She suspected Davina's hand, and told François.

"They're at it again. He'll never come."

"Let it be," François said. "Wait. He will come."

"You learned patience. I didn't."

"Now's your chance," François said.

Ransome House, May 1982

"Sometimes I think she is doing this on purpose," Davina said, a surly expression on her face.

"Doing what?" Richard responded, knowing exactly who and exactly what. He was beginning to tire of these conversations. Damn Amanda.

"Look at this," Davina said, passing him over the latest copy of British *Vogue.* "Keep looking. It's eleven pages. It makes me so cross. She invited Patrick and not us—how dare she? I still have that elaborate invitation she sent to him."

Richard looked at Amanda's face staring serenely out into the audience of British *Vogue* readers. She was sitting in the library of the De Briand château, Quatre Mai, stretched across a blue satin *fauteuil,* wearing a blue-gray dress with some formidable pearls and sapphires. Her beauty was almost indescribable. There was something about her face, a compelling tranquility in her expression. Behind her hung the Stalewski. Richard remembered having seen it once in the house in Royal Hospital Road. It had been too large there, out of place in the confines of the house. At Quatre Mai, it was resplendent. So was she.

He turned the pages slowly, looking at the photographs taken at the great ball Amanda and François had given at Quatre Mai to celebrate their marriage. The wedding had created an international social furor that had not died down yet. It was almost as riveting as the scandal that erupted when the King abdicated to marry his Mrs. Simpson. The beautiful, still young Dowager Countess of Warrington, widow of the vanished Earl of Warrington, who had been missing for almost a decade now, had married the first Duke of France. Years before, at the inquest investigating the murder of the Warrington nanny, Lord Warrington had been convicted of slaying the unfortunate girl. He had been convicted as a result of his wife's testimony and forensic evidence. There were still many in England who believed Lord Warrington innocent, but his disappearance was inexplicable and nothing more had come to light as to his whereabouts. The story had been forgotten to some extent until Amanda Warrington married François de Briand. None of this was reported in the pages of British *Vogue*. They chose only to give details of what was known now as the "ball of the century."

"Looks like a lovely party, doesn't it?" Richard asked, baiting Davina. This constant carping about Amanda and her new life in France, her ingratitude for all Davina had done for her, had to cease. Richard was at the point of becoming defensive about Amanda. No one in their crowd had ever given her much of a chance; she had been made to feel like an outsider from the beginning. Now they were all jealous of her.

Davina exploded.

"Yes, it looks like a lovely party. How could she possibly have invited one sister and not the other? I've brought up her son. How dare she invite him, and Pamela?"

"And not us? Tit for tat, my dear. We closed our doors to Amanda years ago. She could hardly be expected to invite us anywhere. If you want to heal the breach with the first Duchess, you'd better start thinking up ways to make it up with her if you can. She'll never come to you again."

Gavers had been in high temper about not having been invited to the party either. He'd called Chantal. He hated being on the defensive, but he wanted to be invited to the ball of the century. They'd discussed the surprise of Amanda's marriage, but no invitation had been forthcoming. Finally he'd asked if he could come. Chantal had been more than cordial, explaining that it was François's and Amanda's party, and why didn't he call Amanda? "God damn it, I want to be your escort. That's why I'm calling," he'd spluttered.

"Gavers, I'm afraid I can't. The list is theirs. I wouldn't presume to suggest anyone to either of them."

"I know that ploy as well as you do," Gavers had said. "We seem to have lost touch with each other." He'd tried a new tactic. "We've been through it all together, and I'm the one who put us together in the first place. Come on, Chantal, I have nothing against Amanda. You know that. This would be a way to smooth things over."

Chantal had been direct.

"I'm not sure Amanda has nothing against you, Gavers. There seems to be a slight misunderstanding about your role in having Charles declared dead. Why don't you call her yourself?"

Gavers had given up.

"You win, Chantal," he'd said.

"Not I," Chantal said. "Amanda."

Paris, May 1982

"**D**avina, this is Amanda."

Davina was unnerved by the sound of her sister's voice on the telephone. Amanda didn't wait for her to respond.

"As you know, I went to Harrow a few months back to see Patrick. I had written to him but had no answer. Now I have again heard nothing from him." Amanda's voice was unrecognizable to Davina. She'd never sounded like this before. Her words were cool and impersonal, her tone sweet, and there was a new authority to what she was saying.

"Yes," Davina said, feeling featherheaded.

"I would like you to arrange for Patrick to come to us in France before the spring term ends—say ten days from now? I'm sure you agree that Patrick should meet François. He is old enough now to begin to take his place in France with me, as well as in England with you. Will you let me know which flight he's on?"

Davina recovered her breath. She found herself in a helpless fury.

"Suppose he doesn't want to come?" she queried, in her most supercilious tone.

"I don't think you will have any trouble persuading him. I'll leave it up to you. Let me hear from you when his flight is set. Until then."

"Goodbye," Davina said frigidly.

"Goodbye, Davina," Amanda said affably. She hung up.

"You were perfect," François said.

"We'll see," Amanda said.

"You were perfect. He will come. Patrick's beloved Auntie is going to arrange it for him."

"You are clever," Amanda said, putting her arms around him.

"No," François said. "He may be as shallow as the rest of them. We have to find out."

Ransome House, June 1982

Davina and Richard sat down with Patrick on Sunday morning for a family discussion.

"Patrick, your mother called. She wants you to come to France for a weekend before the end of term."

"That would have to be next weekend."

"Yes," Richard said.

"Well, what about it. Do I have to go?"

"It's up to you," Davina said. "If you want . . ."

Patrick looked at them. This was a bit of new stuff. Until now, when Amanda's name came up, they all did away with it quickly. Now he was being invited to make his own decision about going to France. Something had happened.

"Can I think about it?" He would take Richard aside and find out what was going on. He knew Davina didn't want him to go; she only wanted him to tell his mother that he would never go to France, that he never wanted to see her again. Richard was fairer.

"You have to decide before you go back to school."

"I think I'll go, then." He saw the look of quick shock on Davina's face and a faint look of approval on Richard's. "I'm not saying I want to. I'm saying I think I should. If it's not now, it will be later, so why not get it over with?"

"Damn her," Davina said. "We've kept you all these years. Now you run off to her houses, her château, her life."

"Stop it, Davina," Richard said. "You let him make his own decision. He's assessed it properly. Let him go."

Davina was not to be stopped. "I never thought you would do this, Patrick."

"Look," Patrick said. "I'm not running off to her houses or her château any more than I ran off to the mews house with her. She wrote to me and I didn't answer. She invited me to her party and I didn't go. She's not going to let up. I am going to go. I'll be back."

★ ★ ★

Patrick called Amanda.

"Sorry I haven't answered you before this. I'll be there on Friday. Air France 0411—it arrives at Orly at five." His tone was flat.

"Good. I'm so glad you're coming. Our driver, Roland, will meet you and bring you to the country. It takes about two hours. I can't wait to see you."

Patrick rang off. *Bloody hell,* he thought. *I'll be there, but just to get it over with.*

Quatre Mai, June 1982

François was the patron saint of dinner conversation on Friday evening after Patrick arrived at Quatre Mai. There were only the three of them. Although Amanda didn't show it on the surface, François knew she was nervous, and Patrick was equally jumpy. He talked about Harrow and about sports and anything else he could think of. François told him some of the history of Quatre Mai. It was a beauty.

François is not bad at all, Patrick thought. *Quite civilized actually. She has her life with him, and I'm doing what she wants me to do. I'm here. I don't have to come again. If she thinks she can just crook her finger and get me back now that she's the biggest Duchess in France, she cannot. After leaving me for all those years, now she wants me back just to make it tough on Davina. Why can't they make it up?*

François was asking him something.

"When do you have to be back at school, at what time?"

"Tuesday afternoon," Patrick replied. That was more than three days from now. He was miserable.

"Good," François said. "We're going to the yacht on Sunday morning. We can get you on the early morning flight from Nice on Tuesday—you'll be back in plenty of time."

"I didn't know you had a yacht," Patrick said.

"It was my wedding present to your mother," François said. "We are having a small dinner dance here tomorrow evening. My sister is coming, bringing some friends, some of whom are your age. Then we'll get off on Sunday morning early. The captain tells me the weather is beautiful in the South."

"Would you mind if I went to bed now?" Patrick asked. "I'm awfully tired."

"Of course not, go ahead," Amanda said. She stood up and kissed him lightly on the cheek. Nothing personal. Her perfume was wonderful.

"We'll see you in the morning." François walked with him to the foot of the stairway.

Patrick fell asleep in a tortured state, filled with conflicting emotions. He didn't want to think about his father; he never wanted to have to think about Davina, how hurt she was that he had come here to see his mother, how angry she had been with him. Most of all, he didn't want to think about his mother.

He hadn't realized how beautiful she was; the last few times he had seen her she had looked awful. She weighed much less than Davina, her figure was like a girl's, and her skin was nice. She'd certainly done all right, he thought, wrestling around in his bed. Yachts and a château and a great house in Paris. Resentfully he thought, *I am her son, the Earl of Warrington now, and I can use some of what they've got, and them.* But if his mother thought she was going to fight over him with the woman who had loved him and brought him up, she could think again.

Patrick fell asleep angry and confused.

"He's not going to give me a chance," Amanda said, as they undressed. "You are marvelous with him and I'm a tongue-tied dummy. Davina has done her work well. He resents me so."

"Patience, my love," François said. "He is assaulted by all our possessions. He's come so he can put us out of the way, but he may not feel that way when he leaves. He's bound to be curious about you and your side of the story. Give it time."

"He makes me feel the exact same way *they* always made me feel. He's cut from the same cloth."

"Not necessarily. He's only seventeen and he doesn't know you. He's been filled up with distortions. Don't say anything; wait until he asks you. He is your son. He will ask."

"He's so much like his father. I could never talk to his father either."

"You don't seem to have that trouble with me."

Caught again by François's gentle sense of humor, Amanda found herself laughing.

"Just you wait," she said. "I've only started to tell you my troubles."

★ ★ ★

Chantal arrived in the morning, bringing her friends. The younger ones François had told Patrick about were his age, and they quickly discovered friends in common, English friends of Patrick's who were at school in Switzerland. He started having a very good time. There were no pressures put on him. Amanda was there but she wasn't all over him.

On Sunday morning they flew to Nice from Quatre Mai's private airstrip, on the De Briand jet. It was a beauty. They boarded the *Amanda* at eleven and set off at once for the Isles of Cannes, where they swam and had a marvelous lunch on the top deck in the hot sunshine. The yacht was a beauty too.

Chantal, whom Patrick liked, and his new friends, who had to be back in Paris, left on Monday, and once again the three of them were alone. At least Patrick was more at ease with Amanda now. He had taken a long swim with her in the early morning and it had been fine. She loved to swim, as he did. There was some talk with Chantal about the yacht's being sent out to the Far East for the summer months. They would pick her up in Bangkok in July. They might ask him to go, Patrick thought. Perhaps he could. There were plenty of cabins. Maybe they would let him bring the twins. He knew better than to think that. Davina would never let them go. Never.

The three of them sat on the afterdeck in the dark when they had finished dinner, having coffee and watching the long line of lights on the shore. The *Amanda* would put back into the harbor in Cannes later. Tomorrow he'd be home in England.

François finished his coffee and rose to his feet.

"I think I'll turn in," he said.

"You're not going to turn in at all," Amanda said, laughing up at him. "You're going to watch that film again." They had showed *The African Queen* the night before, François's favorite film.

"I know every line of it. I've seen it ten times but I never tire of it. Once more won't hurt. Patrick, what about you?"

"Thanks, no. I think I'll stay here and talk to Amanda." The word *mother* still came hard for him. Amanda had suggested that he call her by her proper name if he'd like to. This was the first time he had used it.

"Fine," François said, smiling when he left them. Patrick had been given the chance to leave and he had elected to stay where he was.

Amanda remained quiet. She couldn't see Patrick in the soft darkness of the night, but she could feel him there, feel his unfamiliar largeness taking up space beside her. She could feel his tension, just as she felt her own. He obviously had something to say to her. Should she try to help him? No, she would wait for him to speak.

They sat for a few minutes, feeling the calm swing of the yacht, watching the lights along the shore. Finally he gathered his courage.

"May I ask you something?" he said.

"Of course."

"Do you think my father is still alive?"

It was the last thing she had expected. Her heart went out to him. She had been thinking about the conflict between Davina and herself. All Patrick wanted to know about was his father. She remembered François's words.

"I would never have married François if I thought there was any hope of your father's being alive," she said.

"I was told that you had my father declared dead so you could marry François."

"You were told *what*?" she said, sitting up. "You don't believe that, do you?"

"Why wouldn't I believe it? All I know is one day Richard told me that I was now the Twelfth Earl of Warrington and you had married a Frenchman. And that you had fixed it, had him declared dead so you could marry again."

Amanda stood up. She couldn't believe what she had just heard her son say. She sat down on the edge of his chair, peering into his face. Could he be telling the truth? Of course he was telling the truth. She was in a white-hot rage but in perfect control of herself.

"No wonder they didn't want you to come to me," she said. "Patrick, Richard and Davina must have known we would have something to say to each other."

"No, they didn't. I told them I would come, since you insisted, and get it behind us once and for all. Davina said you had forced her hand, threatened to cut me off if they didn't let me come to see you. I said I would be polite, say nothing, and the next time you asked me to visit I could say I'd rather not. But you haven't said anything to me against them and I started thinking about it. You seem to have a lot of money and things. Why would you cut me off? And you haven't even mentioned them."

"Cut you off?" she said. "From what? Patrick, there isn't any money; there never has been any money—only debts, which were paid off in the bankruptcy court. Don't you know that?"

"She said all the money went for your medical bills. And that by declaring him dead, you'd get money from the trusts as his widow and they might have to sue you to get it for me."

"Jesus Christ," Amanda said. "They thought they could get away with it. Not this time. Come on, Patrick, we're going to talk to François. I know how to straighten this out, once and for all. What could they possibly gain from this? Nothing but to keep us apart." She dragged him up from his chair.

"Mother," he said, taking her by the shoulders and looking down into her eyes. "Do you think he's still alive?" The look on his face was tragic.

"Patrick, I don't know. I pretended, prayed, tried to believe that he was, for so long. I refused to have him declared dead so he could come back, if he ever could, and pay the price for what happened and hold his head up again. So many friends loved him. They all knew the trouble he'd gotten into, and he . . ." She stopped. Patrick's mind had been poisoned against her for half his lifetime, since he was nine years old. Would he believe her now?

She half-dragged him along with her, down to the salon. Katharine Hepburn was steering *The African Queen*, looking suspiciously at Humphrey Bogart. François was asleep on one of the long couches. She snapped on the lights and he opened his eyes.

"Wake up, darling. We have some new dialogue for you."

He sat up sleepily, Amanda wild to tell him but giving him time to come awake. He saw from her face that whatever had been said had been dramatic, to say the least.

"Patrick has been told that I had Charles declared dead so I could marry you. Patrick has been told that I have taken his inheritance away from him. Patrick has got to go home to England tomorrow and face the aunt he loves, who has brought him up, and his uncle, whom he admires and loves, too, who have told him all these lies. What are we going to do?"

François got up from the couch and brought a bottle of champagne from the bar, and three glasses. He put the glasses on the table in front of them and opened the bottle, filling a glass for each of them.

"I had a feeling something like this had happened," he said. "Sit down, Patrick. It's going to be a long night."

★ ★ ★

Ransome House, June 1982

The first step toward smoothing the path in the reconciliation between Patrick and Amanda was taken by François. He flew to London with Patrick the next morning, and drove with him to Harrow, then continued on to Ransome House for a meeting he had arranged with Richard Marston.

The night before, François had listened to Patrick tell everything he could remember being told about his mother. It was not a pretty story. For years, Davina had woven a subtle web of lies and Amanda had been helpless against her. When Amanda became a threat to her own security, an outcast with everyone, Davina had not hesitated to desert her. The obviously half-mad Amanda should be hospitalized and Patrick should be brought up the way Charles would want it. Davina would remain secure.

Mercilessly, and with the subtlety of a sledgehammer, Davina removed Amanda from her life and took her son. She chose to justify herself. Amanda was the reason for Charles's misfortune.

The day of reckoning came with Amanda's marriage to François. It was too much for Davina. First, Amanda had been a Countess in a miserable, moneyless marriage, and now she had become the first Duchess of France, with the world at her feet. And now François was sitting here in her own drawing room having a serious discussion with Richard, and she had been specifically excluded from the conversation.

François knew that Patrick would not, could not turn his back on Richard and Davina, any more than he could turn off his love for them. But now that he knew how they had treated his mother, as an adult human being he was bound to have strong feelings. Patrick should certainly never be made to choose among them, but they had to come to terms.

François suggested a reasonable plan to Richard Marston. There were some misconceptions in Patrick's mind that should be cleared up. He had not been the 12th Earl of Warrington for a year yet. It was the proper time for the boy to be informed of his future responsibilities and inheritances. Was there not some money from his grandmother's estate due him? Were the trusts arranged to be paid when he was eighteen, or not until he was twenty-one—if there was any money at all? Richard

Marston was sure these matters could be sorted out in future meetings. Patrick's interests had to be looked after in detail, now that his father had been declared dead and his mother had remarried.

They parted on amicable terms. François had one thing more to suggest.

"By the way," he said to Richard. "We are taking the yacht out to the Far East. Patrick is coming along. He thinks your twins might like to come also. Do you think that could be arranged?"

Richard looked at him almost affectionately. The man was a civilized human being, truly civilized, and his message was clear.

"For the time being, I doubt it," he said. Over Davina's dead body would be the only way the girls would be allowed to go. "At this point, our plans are inconclusive. May I let you know?"

"Of course," François said, "I quite understand." And he did. Parental tyranny was not unknown to him. "As we will be meeting next week in my office in London, I can give you our exact dates. Amanda is delighted that Patrick will be with us."

"I'm sure she is," Richard said.

She would be indeed, he thought. Amanda was a winner.

London, October 1982

Patrick took over the mews house, somewhat reluctantly because of the memories there, but he needed a place of his own. He wanted some space, away from Davina and Richard, from Amanda, from the lot of them.

"Of course you can have it," Amanda said when he called and asked her about it. "What am I saying: 'you can have it'? Your father bought it for you. It's not the lap of luxury, but it's yours."

"Ransome House is home still, but I need to be on my own more. I'm having trouble studying and there's always too much interruption in the country. Or I'm so lazy I welcome anything that takes me away from the books."

Patrick was somewhat of a loner, as uncommunicative in his way as Charles had been. He enjoyed keeping to himself. He had become a voracious reader. He was reading English history, and while his marks had improved, he just barely got through. Again like his father. Amanda turned to the practicalities.

"There's no heat except for floor heaters and I'm sure they're no good anymore. There never was enough hot water and you'll have some fixing up to do. The phone is there and you can probably have the same number hooked up again. LEB will turn the lights on for you."

She had blotted out the years she'd spent there alone. It was the unhappiest time of her life, when Davina had been busy taking Patrick from her. Never mind, the house belonged to Patrick now.

"I can handle it," Patrick said. "It will be fine, especially now that I have a car."

François had given Patrick the car, not as a birthday or Christmas present, just as a present. François was the only person really close to Patrick. Amanda understood why his heart went out to him. It was either a feast or a famine, wasn't it? François had been totally dominated by his father, and Patrick had had no father at all.

"We're much closer now," Amanda reminded François. "Thanks to you. But you're the only one he communicates with on an emotional level."

"That's because we never say a word. He knows I sympathize with him without putting words on it. Have you ever been able to talk to him about it, how he felt when it happened?"

"Never. I can't, nor can he. I've tried, but maybe we're both too close to it, forever. Maybe when I'm very old, or if I got sick and knew I was going to die."

"What would you tell him then?"

Amanda thought, trying to work out a far future. She linked her arm through François's; she needed his warmth. There were still times of panic. Now it was fear of something happening to François. John came into her mind. What would she have told him if she'd known he was going to die? She wouldn't have told him anything; she would have packed her bags and gone to him.

"I would tell him that his father loved him, that he probably loved only him, no one else."

"Darling, tell him that about yourself. That's all he needs to know."

She put her arms around him. "You tell me you and Patrick get along because you never put anything into words. Now you're telling me I should put it into words?"

"Of course. He doesn't want to believe that Davina was as deliberate as she was. He wants to believe that she simply helped take care of him in a bad situation. He'd have to break with her, choose between you. None of us wants that. But you have to find a way to tell him that *you* love him, not that Charles did or Davina does. Just that *you* do, and that you always have. He deserves that. There's no great hurry. But when you can."

"What would I do without you?"

"You couldn't. We both know that. Think about it the other way."

"There you go again."

"What would I do without you?"

CHAPTER 27

Early 1986

Buster Manners never ceased to enjoy expounding on the Warrington case. He deserved to enjoy something about it. It had taken up four frustrating years in his life and had taught him, involuntarily, how to grind his teeth. To Buster Manners, now retired and owner of one of the most charming pubs established in the Kentish countryside a century before, it was the best hobby a man could possibly have.

"Half the press of the world still comes down here to see me," he said cheerily, potbelly hanging well over his lowered belt line, hazel eyes alight with mischievous glee. "Just like you have."

"Buster, you can hardly lump me in with the press. I'm your brother and I haven't seen you since long before any of this happened. Of course I'm interested in your role in the case but it was a long time ago."

"And Australia's a long way away. You must have heard about it down there when they picked up someone who looked just like him. Don't you remember that?"

"Vaguely. Why do they still come to you? You've been off the case for years. Is anyone still that interested?"

"You'd be surprised. It's mostly still the press. Been coming for years . . ." His eyes were dancing. The fire crackled and the old beams seemed darker against the white wall as the afternoon faded. Brass trappings glowed in the firelight and the faint smell of bitter, the true pub smell, lingered.

"So he or she walks in and sits down with me and I offer them a drink and then I get into my rote with them. I start my story and I tell it. And I tell it. I have my story to tell and they're going to listen till I'm finished

—that's the price they pay. First, I describe the murder—every word of what I tell them the truth. Most of them are from some rag they haven't mentioned, looking for a new angle to the Warrington story, and most of them either know nothing about it or have some preconceived theory that nothing I say is ever going to change. I love them. One or two a month, still coming after all these years."

Shifting in his chair, he looked apologetic about what he had just said. "Ah," he went on, "I don't mean to be so hard on them. They've got to make a living like the rest of us. What I mind is that not any of them care about what really happened—they're just looking to make a little money. Do you know that the bloody bugger's worth two million now? Warrington, I mean. Two million pounds to the press, the bloody press.

"The Harrow Mob," he said. "Dumb sods that they were, sticking together to protect the likes of him. The only one of them I ever felt sorry for, and she wasn't like them, is Lady Warrington. I spent a lot of time with her, and my men did, protecting her. At first, the feeling was that he might come back and try to kill her again, so we kept four men watching over her for months. I never felt that; I knew he was long gone, but it was the best thing to do at the time. My boys were very protective of her. She was pathetic then. And then you know what happened to her. The family got him declared dead. They went around her, getting a new coroner appointed when good old Rutherson died, and they managed to have their way. They didn't know they were giving her the best present ever. It freed her to marry that Prince or Count or Duke. . . ."

"Duke. The first Duke of France. I read about that, even in Australia."

"Well, whatever he is. I was only interested for her sake. She topped them all. I hope she's happy. There's no paradise, you know, and she was a poor sick little thing for a long time."

"And you? How do you feel about it all now?"

The light came back into Buster's eyes.

"You'll think I'm daft. You know anything about fantasy? I could never afford one until I retired, not in my profession. But I can now, and I've got a fantasy about him. It's probably just as good as any of the other theories." His eyes were dancing again.

"Come on, come on, tell me. You cops are all like lawyers, waiting for someone to ask. You're all actors."

"I'm savoring it," Buster said. "It makes me happy every time I think about it. You know, I never laid eyes on Warrington, and he never saw or heard of me. But I know him—I know him better than I know myself. He could gain one hundred pounds, he could shave his head, he could grow a beard, he can do anything, but I'd know him. I know the tone of his voice—there was a tape of him we took out of Ormonde Gate, talking drunk, going on about Hitler. I'd know him, I tell you, and I'm not going looking for him. I'm waiting for him to come to me."

His look was almost triumphant. He took himself back to the bar for two more beers, almost swaggering.

"Come to *you*?"

"Remember, it's fantasy."

"Go on."

"He comes back. It's the boy. His son will be of age this year and he did love the boy. Now back zooms his lordship, and he's been declared dead, so with new papers and a new identity, he feels safe. A dead man can't be tried. They can't get him anymore. He's a dead man. His chums have seen to that. How come they're not so keen to know about him when he once more joins their midst? I'll tell you why. Because I've got his teeth." His eyes were dancing up a storm.

"You've got his teeth? What the hell are you talking about?"

"Well, among other odd things on this case, his dental records disappeared from the Queen's Own Guards. The only dental records on him and one day, whoosh, they were gone. Isn't that odd? I asked a lot of questions about that and got bollocked around as usual. It took me a few years, and a few more after I was off the case. I got them."

"How?"

"I don't just give everything away, you know. I bought them. I found a way to purchase the vanished Earl's teeth, in the form of his dental records from the Guards."

"And?"

"In my way, I let the Harrow Mob know. Now a new identity does him no good. If he ever comes back, with the record of those teeth, we can convict him. And that digs it all up for them. He can only wreak havoc in their lives. The Marstons can't wait to get rid of him. He's a thing of the past, and Davina Marston is sucking up to her sister now that she's a Duchess. The Riggses will shoot themselves if he doesn't go back where he came from. Little Rosie could go to the clink. Gavin Driscoll is a little different—he's okay about it. He's the philosopher, living in his nature world now. 'Charles,' he'd say to him, 'it's over. You're an embarrassment to us now.' "

He stopped and shook his head. "You know what's the worst?"

"What?"

"Her. The Duchess. She's probably the only one who would care, and that only for the sake of the boy."

He paused deliberately, for dramatic effect.

"Imagine this," he said. "He drives south again, takes the same road he took that night, the same one he came right back up after he and Neil Riggs planted the car as a decoy in Folkestone to throw us off. Now, he's decided that this time he will take that ferry from Folkestone to Calais, the one he didn't take that night. He has all his identity papers for whoever he is now and he thinks he might as well spend some time in France, then get back to his safe little home on the continent of fugitives. On the way down the road, he's thirsty. Maybe a little gin would taste good. He looks for a pub and he finds mine. I know it's him the minute I lay eyes on him. He doesn't even look at me and if he did I wouldn't mean anything to him—he's never seen me or heard my name. 'A drink, my good man,' he says, waving at me the way you wave up a lackey. 'Right away, sir,' I say. I come over behind my bar and I fix his drink without asking him what he wants. That lot always assume you know what they want. Now I have here the only thing I ever stole in my life."

Buster Manners held a heavy cut-crystal double old-fashioned glass in his hand. He was looking at it fondly.

"I nicked it from her, Lady W., when I spent a lot of time in the house with her after the murder. I don't know why I nicked it, because I'd never dreamed this fantasy then. I only knew I wanted one of these glasses badly. A souvenir." He held it up to the light, fondly.

"You are driving me right off my rocker."

"Hold on. I fill the glass with that especially cold ice that he likes and I pour a more than generous dollop of Bombay gin over it. Then I hand it across the bar to him. 'Chin chin, Lord Warrington,' I say. 'Drink up and you're under arrest.' "

Buster took an imaginary swig out of the glass and looked at his brother, beaming.

"Pretty good stuff, eh?" he said again.

"Pretty good. Then what happens?"

"I make a citizen's arrest and that's all. It's all over for him and for me. How do you like it?"

"I think it's pretty good stuff."

"Aaw," he said, "it's just a fantasy. I don't think about him much anymore."

London, March 31, 1986

Patrick heard the phone ringing as he let himself into the mews house. It was close to midnight and it had taken him half an hour longer, thanks to traffic, to get back from the weekend at Ransome House. Tomorrow was his birthday and Davina had insisted on his staying for supper, ending with a birthday cake. He had hoped to get up to London earlier, but he'd stayed to please her.

He thought of not answering the phone, just letting it ring. It was probably Davina, in her cups now, calling to make sure he had gotten back safely. She always did that, he thought, annoyed. Better to answer. Otherwise she'd ring again and wake him up.

He picked up the receiver. There was a tinny noise at the other end, the echoing sound of long distance. Not Davina, thank God.

"Patrick Warrington," he said firmly. Who would be calling at this time of night?

"Bufo?" he heard the voice at the other end say. He couldn't have heard correctly. He must have misunderstood. It must be a wrong number. No one used that name to him—no one knew that name. Only one person had ever called him that.

"Hello?" he said, straining to hear. The connection was filled with static. He sank down into the chair by the telephone table. He was sweating. It was only a voice, he thought; it was not his voice. *It's a voice I hardly remember, using a name I could never forget.* The voice couldn't have said "Bufo." Not that childish name anymore. *I'm grown up now. It's too late for that.*

There was a rock in his stomach.

"Father?" he said. "Fly, is that you?" He was full of conflicting emotions, confusion and fear predominating.

The line went dead. Patrick jiggled the receiver, clicking it over and over, but there was no sound. He put the phone down, his hands shaking, and waited in dread for it to ring again. There was only cold silence in the room.

If the phone rang again, he wasn't going to answer it. It might possibly have been a chum on the line playing a trick on him. Some friends had told him that people played tricks, using his father's name. They got someone to call some poor sod, pretending to be Charles Warrington, asking for help. The voice would say he was nearby in a phone booth, could he come over or meet them some place, maybe the local pub? Then, of course, no one would show, although the tricksters would, ridiculing the hapless friend for falling for the trick. It was a pretty cruel thing to do.

Still the silence held. Time for bed. As a matter of fact, he thought, maybe it was time to get out of there, out of the mews house, for good. Just a few weeks before, an estate agent had made him a surprisingly large offer. But he wasn't interested at the time. Now, he realized, might be the best time to sell. So what if this place was the last link with his father, a known place and a telephone number in case he ever came back?

Ever came back? *The hell with that. We've all lived with that thought for too long.* If he did reappear, if he happened by any remote chance to be still alive, let his father fend for himself. Let *him* find *them*. No more, Patrick thought, no more. He'd call the agent up the first thing in the morning.

The phone rang again. He jumped, but it was an involuntary reaction. He knew now exactly who it was. He picked up the receiver and almost shouted into it.

"Davina, I'm home and safe and I was almost asleep. Now get some yourself, and remember you don't have to keep checking on me. I'm not a child anymore. Good night."

He hardly heard her mumbled response as he put down the receiver. He turned off the lights and went upstairs to bed.